# POINT OF NO RETURN

# The Promise Me Series, Book 7

# By

# Tara Fox Hall

Published by
Melange Books, LLC
White Bear Lake, MN 55110
www.melange-books.com

Cover Art by Caroline Andrus

# Point of No Return
## Tara Fox Hall

When Sarelle discovers Theo's love for Tasha is not all it seems, she breaks the love spell, even as she fears the consequences. Dreaming with Theo again awakens old feelings, even as Devlin's possessiveness increases when Sar is discovered to be pregnant. Influenced by her blood bond to Devlin and Danial, and her magical bond with Theo, Sar is determined to make the relationship with her lovers work. But can Sar trust her heart fully, much less her own desires?

*To my beloved mom, the Wind Beneath My Wings, who said it was about time she was mentioned in another dedication.*
*And to Eric; my anchor, my oak, and my rock. I love you.*

# Chapter One

An hour after Theo left, I washed my face, pulled myself together, and called my lawyer. He said he would draw up separation papers, and that Theo and I would need to be legally separated at least a year unless one of us was willing to admit we'd broken our marriage vows. Technically, we both had, but I wasn't about to have my sins written on a piece of paper. If Theo was in a hurry to marry that wench, he could admit his own infidelity. After instructing my lawyer to fax the separation papers to Danial's office, I went back to bed and cried some more.

I cried for Theo and me, for the years we had lost and now would never regain, for the marriage we might have had, if he hadn't been taken from me that year and a half. For what might have happened, if I hadn't made the choices I had, like loving the vampire Danial and turning to him to help me raise Theo's daughter Elle, when I found myself alone. Or giving into my desire for Danial's brother Devlin, on the more than several occasions he had saved my life.

When there were no more tears, and my nose was so stuffed I couldn't breathe, I got up. "It's time I was about my day," I told the dogs bitterly. "Crying and second guessing myself isn't solving anything. Want to eat?"

After feeding them, I showered, put on fresh clothes, strapped on my snowshoes, and took them for a long, long walk.

The day was clear and cold. Everything was sparkling in the sunlight. Angrily, I told God it was unfair that everything could look so good and new when I felt so bad. Oddly enough, right after, light snow began to fall. By the time we got home, the snow coming down wasn't light anymore.

After brushing off our extra coats of cold white powder, I gave the dogs some Cheweez, and went to check the wood situation. Seeing it was more than adequate, I settled down with a good book near the wood stove, my black cats Cavity and Jess on my lap. Before long, I was so comfortable that I put the

1

book down just for a moment to rest my eyes.

Sometime later, I awoke. The power had gone off. Then two red eyes appeared, looking at me from across the darkening room.

I let out a surprised yell, the cats bolted in fear, and I howled again, rubbing the fresh painful claw scratches on my legs.

"Sorry, Sar."

"Terian, what are you doing here?" I asked irritably.

"Danial sent me to check on you. It's already known around the compound that Theo came and got his stuff today, not to mention the storm. The highways are closed for the entire county." He paused. "And I wanted to apologize for how I acted."

"Apology accepted."

"Do you love him?" Terian asked grudgingly. "Devlin?"

"Yes," I said, glad it was dark so I couldn't see his expression.

"Do you feel for him like you feel for Danial? Do you want his child?"

"Why are you asking me these questions?" I said harshly. "I never asked you how you felt about Sundown, compared to Erin or those other women you knew."

"It matters to me you're happy. If he's what makes you happy, then I'll be content."

Using that word was odd, but I let it slide. "It has to be this way, Tears. You know that as well as I do. And yes, in time, I think I'll be happy. Right now I'm still in shock."

"I liked Erin," Terian said, after a moment. "But the demon side of me scared her, and she tried to hide it—acted like it didn't matter. I finally realized that she was behaving as if she had to work herself up to being intimate with me, and I never trusted her after that."

I said nothing, knowing he didn't want my pity.

"Sundown I loved, pure and simple. I really thought she cared about me, wanted me for me. But she didn't."

All these years later, he still hurt. "I'm sorry," I said softly in the darkness.

"So am I," he whispered. "I still miss her very much."

The lights came back on with a click. Terian and I blinked at one another for a moment, letting our eyes adjust. Relieved, I got up, and started resetting the clocks. "You want some dinner?" I called to him. "I'm going to make pasta now the stove's on again."

"Not that nasty whole wheat stuff," Terian said distastefully from the other room.

"I'll make you regular if you want," I promised. "Pour us some wine."

2

\* \* \* \*

Two hours later, we'd had dinner, discussed the Vampire Gathering in detail, and had moved on to his newfound mother and father with the help of the better part of two bottles of wine.

"I can't understand why she did it, Sar," Terian said for the fourth time.

"Leri loved your father, Titus," I repeated. "That didn't make what she did right, but—"

"No, why did she make sure I was taken care of?" He paused. "Keriam protected me his whole life. He gave up so much for me. He was smart and he really wanted to be a doctor, but he had to work to support me. By the time I was old enough to help him, he was stuck in a dead end job, pushing paper in an office, his dreams of medical school dead." He downed his wine again.

I had serious thoughts about downing mine, too, listening to this tragedy. But that would put me in squarely into drunk territory. Instead, I set my wineglass down on the table. "What happened to him wasn't your fault. You loved him like a brother, and he loved you. None of that was fake. It was real." I put my hand on his shoulder. "You can't know that his life would've been any better without knowing you."

"I feel so guilty, though," Terian said emotionally. "I want to do something, but I don't know what to do. Keriam wasn't even his real name."

"There is something you can do," I said, an idea forming.

"What? He's gone. I can't tell him I'm sorry."

"No, but you can find out who he really was. Maybe give him a marker near his parents with his real name on it. With Danial's help, and his contacts out west, you should be able to find his family, if any are still living."

Terian hugged me hard. "You're right," he said, teary. "How is it you always know what to say?"

"I don't," I replied quickly. "Most of the time, I wing it. It's when I plan what to say that everything usually comes out wrong."

He looked down into my eyes. "You've never done wrong by me," he said, still emotional. "You're a good woman, Sar."

I felt uncomfortable for a moment, then he laughed, and the moment passed.

"But no more wine. I've got to drive the Expedition back to Danial tonight."

It took my alcohol-muddled mind a moment to understand that Theo had taken his truck back to Danial's house with his stuff, but had driven one of Danial's vehicles here. "Not tonight in this storm. Teleport instead."

"Most of it is over by now," he said, looking out the window. "There's maybe five inches out there, but that's it. I don't know why the power went off; it's not bad at all." He turned back to me. "Keriam told me we lived in Dallas right after I was born. I'll start there."

"I wish my problems could be solved that easily," I said ruefully.

He nodded. "It's good Christmas and the other holidays are over."

I nodded. "Thank God."

Terian winced.

"Sorry," I said awkwardly, kicking myself for reminding him with my religious faith of his demonic nature. "Danial mentioned Theo would likely leave soon. Has anything been said to you? I'm asking because I just arranged for separation papers to be sent to Danial's house. If Theo is leaving, I want him to sign them before he leaves."

"No one's mentioned anything to me," Terian answered. "Theo hasn't talked to any of us about anything personal. He's all business."

"I'd rather he left," I admitted. "But the truth is we need him now more than ever. Perseus and Samuel may have relented, but they would still like Danial and Devlin dead. Then I'd be fair game." I put my hand on his arm. "Please don't leave in the spring."

Terian looked uncomfortable, but didn't reply.

"I'm sorry about what I said, back at the hotel yesterday—"

"You were right about all of it." He paused. "I've tried my best to subvert the demon part of me. But the more I draw on its strength, the more I feel the desire for violence. Sometimes I feel like I can't control it at all." He looked up, his glowing reddish eyes meeting mine. "I went into the Gathering hoping someone would attack us."

I was repulsed by his eager tone, but didn't drop my eyes. "Are you going to leave Danial's employ?"

"I'm going to look for Keriam's family to do what you suggested, but it'll be for only a week or so. I won't leave this spring, if at all."

"Thank you," I said, discreetly wiping a relieved tear away.

"You're welcome," he replied, giving me a small smile. "Is there any dessert?"

"No," I said, taking his plate and mine to the kitchen. "I wasn't expecting company, and Aran cleaned out all the leftover cookies."

Terian followed me to the kitchen, aghast. "Nothing? No pie? No cake?"

"If you want to wait, I'll make you some brownies," I offered.

"Brownies would be good," Terian said, mollified.

Stifling a comment about men's appetites that would have come out all wrong, I mixed up the brownies. I was pouring batter into the pan when the phone rang.

4

"I'll bet I know who that is," Terian sang out. "Danial."

"You answer. I've got my hands full."

Terian picked up the phone. "Sar's right here. She's baking, but she'll be on in a minute."

I put the brownies in the oven to bake, set the timer, and took the phone from him. "Hello?"

"The power must have come back," Danial mused. "When Terian reported in, it was off."

"Yes, we're all fine here now," I said jokingly. "How are you?"

"You are a far cry from Harrison Ford," Danial chuckled, recognizing my quotation. "Remember, you need to lock up after Terian leaves."

"I always do. Don't worry so much, Danial. I can teleport."

"There are other dangers in the world besides vampires—"

"Yes, there are," I interrupted gently. "But I'm fine."

"When Theo was there with you I didn't worry so much. Please consider coming back—"

"No," I said as firmly as I could. "I'm not moving back in, much as I want to."

"Why not?" Danial said, incredulous. "If you are going to be living with Dev half the week, it's only fair to live here for the rest."

"He said that, not me. I need my own space. By the way, I can't believe you're proposing me moving back in guised in the form of equal time-sharing."

"It's apparent now that this might have been what I should have done from the beginning," Danial said sarcastically, the old arrogance and possessiveness in his tone. "All of my compassion and understanding has gotten me nowhere. It was Devlin's refusal to take no for an answer that made you finally accept him."

"No, you have it wrong, Danial," I said coldly. "It wasn't force; it was him asking me what I wanted that let him into my heart. I never needed him to take charge of me, like some bimbo that needs a man to make up her mind for her!"

"Sar—" Danial placated.

It had been a day from hell and I'd had enough. "Goodnight, Danial." I hung up on him, and turned to face Terian, who was staring at me openmouthed.

"Devlin and you…when he rescued you last fall?"

"Yes," I said curtly, downing my wine. Grabbing the bottle, I poured the rest of it in my glass. "Don't ask me anything more. I don't want to talk about it."

"All I need to know is you're okay," Terian said, coming closer. He put his hands on my shoulders. "Are you?"

"I don't know," I replied honestly. "But I think I will be, in a little while." I swallowed hard. "I shouldn't have drunk that wine so fast. I'm all emotional now."

"Come sit down." Terian led me back to the couch, and sat facing me. "Will you give me permission to look through your memories?"

My better instincts were advising against it, but I'd drowned their influence in alcohol. "Why?"

"Because nothing makes sense to me," he said worriedly. "Theo's behavior, Devlin's sudden love for you, even Danial's sudden return to arrogance is all odd. Nothing adds up, which means I'm missing too many pieces." He touched my face gently. "I think you might hold a few pieces that could solve this mystery."

"There's no mystery," I replied, relieved my words weren't slurred. "Devlin's after a baby, because he loved a woman once with blood like mine. They tried to have one and she died. Danial's just being Danial; he's always been jealous of Devlin. As for Theo, he's an asshole."

"Please?" Terian pleaded. "It won't hurt. I'm not after anything but the truth."

I almost said no, that everything else he'd ever done for me magically had caused problems. But I was buzzed enough that the danger seemed small, and instead I closed my eyes. "Go ahead."

Terian put his hands on either side of my face. "Think back to when you and Theo were together, before he was taken."

"Okay. Stay out of my intimate memories."

At once, I began reliving the past three years. Most of the memories flashed quickly past. Terian slowed certain ones of Theo and Devlin, and again I listened to them pour out their hearts, declaring their love and devotion, telling of their pasts and all they'd endured. As Devlin was telling me farewell before the Gathering, the stove buzzer went off, startling Terian and I.

I shook my head to clear it of memories, and got up. "These are ready. You want two or three?"

"Keep them," Terian said hastily, buttoning his coat. "I've got to go."

Disgruntled, I turned to him. "What's the rush?"

"Please drive the Expedition back for me to Danial's when you can," Terian said. Then he disappeared.

"God damn it!" I shouted in frustration. The dogs leapt to their feet, growling.

"Sorry," I consoled them, petting each one. "I'm just on edge. I don't know what that was all about—"

The phone rang.

# Chapter Two

I cleaned up the dishes and let it ring, not wanting to talk to anyone. It rang ten times and then stopped.

A minute later, it began ringing again. I ignored it, covering the brownies. This time, after ten rings, it stayed quiet. "Let's go to bed," I told the dogs.

Just as I was drifting off to sleep, the phone rang shrilly. Wide awake and angry, I lurched out of bed, and grabbed the phone. "What?" I screamed into the receiver.

"Sar," Devlin said curiously. "I've called three times. What's the matter?"

"Sorry," I said more quietly. "I'm on edge."

"What's the matter?" he asked.

"Nothing," I said, pushing my hair back from my face. "I was sleeping."

"Oh," he said. "I forgot you don't yet keep my hours."

It was the "yet" part that made me most angry. "Why did you call?"

"I wanted to hear your voice," he said, concerned. "The easiest way was to call you. Now, what is wrong? I don't have to be Danial to know you're upset."

Instantly, my anger dissolved into despair. "Theo came and got his stuff today," I said hollowly. "It's been a long day—"

There was a prompt click.

"Hello?" *Had he hung up on me?*

"Sar?" Devlin said from the kitchen. "Where are you?" Sudden blackness hit me, making my skin crawl.

That had to be Titus. "I'm in here."

Devlin stood in the doorway, looking stunning. He gazed at me for a moment, then crossed to my bedside, hugging me tightly. Blinking back tears, I hugged him back.

"Come back for me in a few hours," he said to Titus. The black feeling vanished as Devlin got me back into bed, then lay down beside me, covering us both with a blanket. He held me for a long time, stroking my hair, not speaking.

"Thank you for coming," I said finally, then blushed, sure he would say something sexual about my remark.

"How could I not?" he said tenderly, tightening his arms about me. "You needed someone, and I said I'd be here for you. It is never easy to lose a lover, even if all they are to you is sex. It's a hundred times worse when it is someone you actually love."

I burrowed my head into his chest. "I don't know why I care after all he did."

"If love was an easy thing to rationalize, there wouldn't be so many poems about it," he said kindly. "As much as I'm happy Theo's out of the picture, I don't want you to be unhappy." He tilted my head up to look at him. "Do you want me to remove Tasha?"

I gaped at him. "You can't just—"

Devlin's gold eyes were serious. "I can, Sar. Lash could take care of it easily," he kissed my forehead. "Just say the word, and it's done."

I drew back from him, horrified at his casual offer. "You would kill her just because I asked?"

"It's in my power to do," he said simply, as if we were discussing buying new sheets. "Besides, she doesn't have to die; she just needs to disappear for a while. I could have Titus teleport her back to Russia, to her father. If she married another—"

"No," I said forcefully. "I don't want to get him by default, to know I killed someone he loved. I could never live with it."

"I had to offer," Devlin said quietly. "I'm impressed as always with your fortitude, Love. Many a deserted lover would have taken what I offered and never looked back."

"I'm not them," I said tiredly. "I don't love that way."

Blackness caressed me again with icy fingertips.

"Your demon's back."

"I have to go," Devlin said reluctantly, getting up from the bed. "Alas, I have a lot more to do before dawn."

I got up, too. "Why didn't you come to me before using him as transport, instead of on the Harley? You would have been warmer."

Devlin shrugged. "Titus says he can't teleport somewhere he has never been. And he had never been here before, Sar."

Made sense. I certainly had enough trouble teleporting to places I had been. "Oh."

"I'll be back to you soon, perhaps in a few days. Get some sleep," Devlin said. He kissed me almost chastely, then left, closing the door behind him. The blackness receded, then vanished.

\* \* \* \*

When I awoke, it was about eight in the morning. I opened my eyes, looked out the window to a clear and bright winter's day, and smiled. Then I remembered everything that had happened, and tears flooded my eyes.

I wiped them angrily away. They weren't going to get me Theo back. I was stupid to want him back, anyway.

Once I tended to my pets, I called Danial and left him a halting message on his cell voicemail.

"Danial, it's Sar. I know you closed the business for January. I'll come in once a week, as there's bound to be a few clients to handle stuff for, at least on e-mail. If you need me more than that, call me back, and let me know. But I'm going to need some time…um, by myself. I won't be coming to your home for a while. I'm not saying that you can't have what it's within your right to take—" *God, could I sound stupider?*

I cleared my throat, then quickly finished. "If you want to come to me here, just call me and tell me you're coming and I'll…um…get ready. Bye."

That embarrassment out of the way, I took down the few Christmas decorations I had put up, and thought about what kind of life I was going to have now.

Devlin had been understanding last night, but he'd summon me as soon as he had a free night. There would be fireworks if I didn't come when he called. While I couldn't wait to be back in his arms again, I didn't like him ordering me around. The same went for Danial.

My first priority was to see Elle, both to tell her what had happened and to find out how best to arrange time with her while avoiding Theo. There was still the matter of him signing the papers, but maybe Danial could assist with that. I also wanted to see Theoron, but that would be easy, as Theo never went near him.

Thinking that annoyed me. Theo had never liked Theoron, not really. He'd acted like he did at first, but after he'd always made some excuse…

Stop thinking about him. There's no point.

Terian, well, who knew what the hell he was doing, or where. Some bodyguard…

Ghost came up and pawed me.

"Yes, its time for the daily walk," I said with a reluctant smile. "Come on, Darkness, let's get the snowshoes."

\* \* \* \*

As I was dozing that night sandwiched between sleeping dogs and cats,

Danial called.

"Greetings, Oathed One," I said. "You're lucky I put the cordless phone within reach. I'm buried in animals."

"I'm glad you're feeling better," he said neutrally. "Take off all of January if you want to. You don't have to come in once a week. Consider it a paid vacation, Sarelle."

He was calling me by my full name. Something was wrong. "Danial, I'm sorry I yelled last night—"

"You are right, you need time alone. Take it."

"I want you to know—"

"Sar, I know. I love you, too. Good-bye for now." Click.

I listened to the dial tone and debated calling him back, then hung up instead.

Later that night, as I was falling asleep, the phone rang. I fumbled for the cordless phone on my nightstand. "Hi, Dev," I said, groggily.

"Hello, Lover," Devlin purred. "Are you ready for me?"

"Now?" I replied, rapidly trying to awaken. "Tonight? I'm not—"

"No," Devlin laughed. "I was just teasing. I want to see you this weekend, Sar. How about Saturday?"

"What time?" I stalled, thinking hard on how best to respond.

"Is there someone else you were planning to see?" Devlin said sarcastically.

"No, Danial's told me to take some time off," I replied. "But you need to understand that seeing Elle has to come first. I need to talk to her about Theo leaving me, and make sure she understands I'm not going anywhere. She was upset before we left for the Gathering about everything that was happening, and she's probably more upset now. I don't want to see Theo, so I'll have to see her when he's not around. That may interfere with your proposal."

"Ah," Devlin said, mollified. "I'll call Danial, and ask him to arrange Theo to be somewhere else for most of Saturday morning and afternoon, so you can visit her. I'll send someone to pick you up at Danial's about five. Is that enough time?"

"It should be. Thanks, Dev. Danial's acting oddly."

"He's likely preoccupied with his business, Love. He had a tough case he said was requiring all his attention. Don't concern yourself. If you need to talk to me, just call."

"Um," I said, my face coloring. "I don't have it."

"Call my cell. It will be in your phone's incoming call log under D. Dalcon. I called you last night from Hayden, and that number will be under my full name, same area code. Whomever answers, just tell them your name, and they'll put you through."

I should have thought of that. "Do you sleep all day? Should I call only at night?"

"You can call anytime," he purred. "Especially if you're missing me."

I was simultaneously aroused and unnerved. "You said you had a lot to do in Canada. Unless it's an emergency, I won't interrupt you."

There was a brief pause. "Pack for a day, Sarelle. Oh, and don't worry about your pets. I'll arrange for Serena to come and see to them."

"Who is Serena?" I asked, curious.

"She is the woman I employ to see to the sexual needs of my guards," Devlin said bluntly. "She's trustworthy and kind, also."

I floundered for words and found none.

Devlin took my lack of reply for doubt in her abilities. "She is good with animals, Sar, really. I trust her with my cat when I am away. Besides, she will enjoy a night off, so to speak." He chuckled.

*Say something.* "Is she a werebear?"

"A werecoyote/werefox half-breed," Devlin said. "She keeps to herself, but she does her job well."

*How would he know?* I colored, wondering if she'd been one of the fifty women he'd mentioned having sex with after me.

"Sar? Are you still there?"

"Were you and she ever together?" I whispered.

"I don't bed my employees," Devlin said, half amused, half irritated. "Though I understand why you ask, after Danial and Monica's little tryst."

"Then that's fine," I said, relieved. "How long has she worked for you?"

"I found her in Rio last fall. Having her around does ease a lot of the tension. I don't have any female guards, as Danial does."

"Do you not trust women enough?"

"I trust them equally. They just aren't as physically strong as males, and guards have to be strong. In any case, Lash is the one who has final say in hiring. Why do you ask? Would you prefer a female guard?"

"It doesn't matter," I assured him. "But my pets don't like strangers, and they'll probably accept a female in their house more easily than a male."

"Take care, Sweetheart," Devlin sang to me. "I'll see you on Saturday."

After hanging up, I lay there a while trying to talk myself into being happy. I had Devlin, who was quite possibly the world's best lover, and his brother, too. It went without saying that I'd not be alone ever again at night unless I wanted to be, waiting for someone to come home. This wasn't a fling. They both had essentially married me. So what if my third husband had left me for another woman. It wasn't that bad, right?

11

My eyes went to the carvings on my dresser of the cougar and myself, and my eyes flooded with tears. Hell, yes, it was bad, it was awful, and I wanted Theo back if I had to give my soul to do it. I cried myself to sleep.

\* \* \* \*

The next morning, after showering off some of my despair, I called Danial's house looking for Elle. She was in lessons, and called me back at lunchtime.

"Hi," she said softly. "Are you coming to work anytime soon? Dad said you might not come here for a while. He told me you were okay, but you needed some time by yourself."

"That's true, but I'd like to see you, if you want to see me."

"Yes," Elle said tearfully. "Please."

*Damn you Theo, what did you tell her now?* "What is it, Sweetheart? You're upset."

"Theo is living with Tasha in the place the guards stay," Elle said angrily. "He has her come along on all of our walks together now."

"Do the best you can to be nice," I said, trying to be calm about it. "But if you want some time with him just by yourself, tell him that. He loves you."

"You're alone there," Elle said softly. "I don't understand why you won't come back and be with Dad—"

I couldn't deal with this, not now. "Elle," I said sharply. "We aren't going to—"

"You went right from living with Dad to living with Theo," Elle interrupted. "Why was that okay and this wouldn't be?"

Shit, I was always going to be paying for that. Well, I'd done it, and I guess I did owe the coin. "Elle, there is a lot you don't know, but I'll do my best to explain on Saturday. Okay?"

"Okay," she said sullenly. "See you then."

\* \* \* \*

I spent the rest of the week reading, exercising, and deciding what to tell Elle and what not to. I did my best not to wonder about how my life might change, though the constant tension gnawed at me, getting worse each day. I grew so antsy that I finally called both Kat and my mother, and set up lunch dates with them. Then instead of talking over my worry with either, I pretended that everything was fine.

\* \* \* \*

Friday night, Devlin called from Mexico to say that he would be a little late getting home. "Things are different here, and often meetings take much longer that they do in the States. Mexicans, as well as most Latin Americans, value family and friends over business."

"It must be important," I said, curious. "Will you be back tonight?"

"No, early tomorrow morning."

"What about dawn?"

"I have Titus to protect me, Sar. Don't worry."

"I'm just worried," I said hesitantly. "When I burned you, I saw how much it hurt. I'm sorry for that."

"I healed, with your help," Devlin assured. "It was not a bad burn, as they can sometimes be."

"Danial told me how much being burned hurt. I remember your screams. I just wanted you to know I was sorry."

"I hurt you much worse before," Dev replied sadly. "Let it go. We can't make a new start if we hold past grudges." He paused. "Sleep well, Love. I'll be kissing you tomorrow."

"You're right. Take care, Dev. Goodnight."

* * * *

Saturday dawned clear and snowy. I picked up Elle at nine, and we drove into Alan's Creek for breakfast.

The little town was growing slowly, a few chain restaurants having opened in the last year. More houses were on the surrounding hills than were there two years ago. While I was happy the town was prospering, I couldn't help but be a little nostalgic for the town I'd first come to know. I was also saddened and scared, wondering how much more it and the other things I loved would change in my lifetime.

After a movie, and a sumptuous lunch of fried food, I brought out Devlin's choker from under my turtleneck. "Do you see my choker?"

She looked up and froze. "That's not Dad's symbol!" she squeaked angrily. "Whose is it?"

"It is Devlin's. He interceded at the gathering. Three powerful vampires stood against Danial. They wanted me to leave him and go with them. Devlin got them to back down, but to do it he had to lay claim to me."

"Why didn't Dad make them back down?" Elle said tearfully. "He said he would protect you, Mom."

This was the question I dreaded answering most. I took a breath, and let it out slowly. "He did his best, Elle. But they didn't fear him enough to make them go away."

"Yet they were afraid of Devlin."

13

"Yes."

"I'm afraid of him sometimes," Elle whispered.

I did a double take, worried and alarmed. "Elle, has he ever done anything that would make you think he would hurt you?" I demanded.

"Nothing," she answered, meeting my eyes. "He's always polite to me when I see him, and he always calls me Little Lioness. But sometimes the things he says, or the tone in his voice…I know that he's faking. I can almost see another person under his smile. That person, he's…he's…"

"He's what, Elle?" I said, reaching out and touching her hand. "You can tell me. I won't tell him or anyone if you don't want me to."

Elle shivered. "He doesn't have any rules. He does what he wants when he wants. That's the best I can say it, Mom."

I hugged her tightly. "You don't need to worry," I told her gently. "He isn't going to hurt me. And he's not going to hurt you either."

"Are you sure, Mom?" she said, staring searchingly.

"Yes." *So long as I did what he asked of me, anyway.* "Now come on," I said, mustering a smile. "We have a little while yet before I take you home. Let's go to the art store and get you some new supplies." I got up, and began clearing the remains of lunch.

"Mom, can we go somewhere else?" Elle said suddenly.

Her request was so uncharacteristic that I turned to look at her. "Where do you want to go?"

"I want to get lipstick."

"Why?" I asked, before I could stop myself.

"I want to wear makeup," she said stubbornly.

I gave her ten-year appearance a thorough looking-over. "You're too young for makeup, Elle."

"No, I'm not," she said arrogantly, folding her arms over her chest. "Tasha said she got to wear lipstick when she was my age. She let me try some on, in fact."

My eyes went to slits, my rage building instantaneously. "Did she?" I purred.

My voice had the same tone that Devlin's did. Elle backed up a step. "Yes."

"And what else, pray tell, did Ms. Tasha have to say about you and makeup?"

"She said she got to wear lipstick when she was ten, but she had to wait for the rest until she was fourteen."

I wanted to make a crack about how Tasha wasn't too much older than that now, but worried Elle might ask me how old I was. I looked at Elle, standing so resolutely, and debated how to handle this new development.

Tasha would most likely be her stepmother sooner or later. Could I make her into a bitch? It would be easy: Elle already disliked her, she was just using this as an excuse, knowing how I would feel. Part of me wanted to. It said Theo was getting everything he wanted way too easily, and I was the one fighting to hold onto what was left of my life. But the person who'd fare the worst wouldn't be Tasha, or Theo, or even me. It would be Elle.

"Come on," I said, giving her a smile. "I'll take you to a department store and we'll get you some high-end lipstick."

She gave me her most winning smile.

"But," I said, grabbing hold of her. "You are not going to get a dark shade, Elle. Makeup is supposed to accentuate your appearance."

"What does accentuate mean?" she said, grabbing my hand.

"It means that makeup is supposed to make you look nice, but people aren't supposed to think you are wearing it. Come on."

* * * *

After buying Elle a light shade of dusty pink lipstick, we headed out of the mall towards the exit. As we neared the outside doors, I noticed some beautiful light gray chenille sweaters almost silver in color. I was instantly reminded of the sheets Devlin had brought to my home. Better yet, when I touched a sleeve, it was soft as a cat's fur.

"Isn't this pretty?"

"Mom, I've never seen you wear that color before," Elle said.

"Does it look good on me?" I asked, holding the sweater up in front of me.

"Yes," she said. "It makes your hair look more golden."

"Sounds like a sale," I said, grabbing one. "Hurry. We've got to go back to the registers and find a short line."

* * * *

We got to Danial's around five thirty. He met us at the door.

"You're late, my dears." He looked down at Elle, then blanched. "Is that lipstick you're wearing?"

"Yes," she said proudly. "It's called Lusty Kiss."

Danial looked at me, appalled. "You are letting our nine-year old daughter wear a lipstick called Lusty Kiss?" he choked out.

"I didn't know it was called that," I said lamely, flushing. "I had her pick a light shade."

"Go take that off," Danial said, glowering at Elle. "You are too young for lipstick."

15

"I am not!" Elle said, and flounced away.

He grabbed her before she went three feet. "You are my daughter, and you will do what I said," Danial said, his eyes red. "Now take it off!"

I expected she would cry, or maybe say she wasn't really his daughter. Instead Elle got a tissue, wiped off the lipstick, and tossed the tissue away. "I'm going to see Cia," she said sullenly. "I said I'd watch Aran Jr. for her tonight. Brian is getting a movie, and Demi said we'd make popcorn."

"Go," I said gently. "Have a good time."

Elle ran back and hugged me. "Thanks for today, Mom."

I looked at Danial over her shoulder meaningfully. He stared back, then threw up his hands.

"Elle, keep the lipstick," I said. "But wear it only when we go out, not here."

"You mean it?" she said excitedly.

"Yes. But that is all you are wearing, Elle, until…until another two years pass, no matter how old you look by then. Understand?"

"Yes," she said, then turned to look at Danial questioningly.

"That's okay," he said, nodding. "Go see Cia. Your mother and I have things to discuss."

Elle gave him a brilliant smile, then bounded out the door.

"She is growing up too fast," Danial said worriedly.

"It's Tasha's fault," I said nastily. "She is the one who put wanting lipstick into Elle's head."

"If it hadn't been her, it would've been someone else," Danial said soothingly. "Elle has seen you in makeup, Sar. Tasha does wear some, but not much more than you do."

I was irked, and didn't reply.

"What did you buy?" he asked.

"Just a sweater. Can I use your bathroom to change?"

"You can use my bedroom," he said, trailing kisses down my neck. "And perhaps you can delay putting your new sweater on for a few hours." He pulled his body tightly against mine, his hands caressing me gently. On my neck there came the slight brush of fangs.

My knees went weak instantly. "Stop," I said breathily. "I can't stay with you tonight."

"Why not?" Danial said, in between kisses. "I can send over someone to watch your home and pets. Elle will be gone for the evening with the weres. We'll be alone."

"Devlin asked me to come to him tonight," I said quickly. "One of his men is coming for me shortly."

16

Danial abruptly stopped in mid-kiss. He didn't speak, but it was obvious he was pissed off. "How long until he's here?" he growled finally.

"He could be here anytime now."

Danial gave me a slow smile. "Then he'll have to wait a few moments."

"A few minutes? You know that's not enough time," I said, exasperated. "Get real."

Danial flipped open his cell phone then and dialed. "Brian? Drive out to the middle of the driveway, and knock over a few poplar trees onto the driveway, blocking it. Make sure they're big enough a Hummer can't cross them. Never mind why, just do it. There's a bonus in it for you if they're over a foot in diameter."

Danial hung up the phone, then grabbed my hand. "We have enough time now," he said eagerly, pulling me into his bedroom.

\* \* \* \*

I lay in Danial's arms after, my heart still racing. His was slow and steady. I nuzzled close, listening happily to the regular beats.

Danial pushed my hair back from my face, and kissed me softly. "Much as I'd like to lay here with you, Sar, you should dress," Danial said languidly. "Even several trees won't delay Devlin's bears for long, not for much longer than it took Brian to knock them over."

"You're right," I said reluctantly, getting up. "I'd better go."

Danial sat up, handing me my underwear from the side of the bed. "Come back to me next weekend. We'll stay in like we did back in the fall, maybe ride, if the weather's good. I'll get you a pizza."

"You know just what I can't resist," I said, laughing, slipping into my new sweater.

Danial gave me a knowing smile. "He'll like it. That's his favorite color."

"Should I get one in red for you?" I teased.

Danial lovingly kissed my hand, then gently gestured toward the door. "Go, Sweetheart, before I change my mind and keep you here."

I blew him a kiss, then went into the great room, closing the door behind me.

A few minutes passed. I checked my watch. Maybe I should call Devlin and make sure something hadn't come up in Canada...

A knock came from the front door. I quickly grabbed my purse and keys from the table. As I walked into the mudroom, Theo opened the front door.

# Chapter Three

Lash stood there waiting in the doorway, his eyes as flat as ever, his forked tongue flicking angrily. He was dressed warmly all in black, save for a blood red scarf at his neck.

"What do you want?" Theo said gruffly.

"Sarelle," Lash hissed angrily, drawing out my name in a long sinuous sound. "Devlin wants her at Hayden."

"I'm here," I said, trying to slide past Theo. "I'm ready."

Theo blocked me, eyeing me frostily. "No one said anything to me about it," he said stonily.

"No one need tell you anything, Cat," Lash hissed. "You have no say."

"I have a say in Danial's property," Theo growled. "I need to check with Danial before I let her leave."

"Then go check," Lash said, baring his fangs. "I'll wait inside."

"You'll wait outside," Theo said, and slammed the door in his face.

"Theo, he's right—"

Theo grabbed a hold of my arm and hauled me to Danial's bedroom door. "Danial," Theo said, pounding on the door loudly. "Lash is here. He said he's here for Sar."

Danial came to the door, dressed. "Theo, it's okay," he said calmly. "It was good of you to check, but I knew Sar was headed to Hayden tonight. Let her leave."

"You're just going to let her go to him?" Theo said, his tone dagger-filled. "I can smell that you were just together."

Danial gave him a slow smile of gratification. "Devlin has rights to Sar now, just as I do, whether you like it or not. She'll often leave one of us to go to the other, something that doesn't invoke my jealousy, as it's a given under our Oath. Reconcile yourself to this situation, or leave my employ."

"As soon as the ranking's settled, I probably will," Theo replied curtly.

"And I'll be taking Elle with me."

Danial's eyes flashed red. "We've been over this. If you want to leave with your woman, you're free to go. But Elle is staying here."

"Then stop the digs," Theo shot back. "None of us planned how this all worked out. If you want Elle to stay here, then we need to work together." He glanced over at me, then back to Danial. "I don't want to see anyone hurt."

"He isn't going to hurt her," Danial said patiently. "He loves her."

"He loves nothing but himself, and you know it," Theo growled.

Danial gave me a gentle kiss. "Have a good time. Call tomorrow from Dev's, and tell me when I can expect you to return. If it's a few days or more, that's no problem; I'm neck deep in cases."

"I will," I said uneasily.

Danial nodded, then went back into his bedroom.

"You must have worn him out," Theo said sarcastically. "He's right about his work—"

I tried to push past him. He blocked me.

"Let me past, Theo."

"Sar, don't do this," Theo said, grabbing my arm. "He'll hurt you without Danial there to mediate—"

"I've been alone with him before," I said meaningfully. "He didn't do anything to me I didn't want."

"Didn't he?" Theo said just as meaningfully. "Give him time. He will."

"It's really not your business anymore, is it?" I said mockingly. "Why does it matter to you, anyway?"

The door suddenly banged open. Lash glared at the both of us with his flat eyes as he walked in.

"You broke the lock," Theo bitched.

Lash threw some money on the floor. "We are late already, Sarelle," he hissed. "Get moving. Now."

Everything happened at once. I went to move past Theo, he put out his hand to stop me, and something slid through the air with a sharp crack. Theo went rigid, grabbing at his neck, choking, his eyes bulging, the end of Lash's whip tight around his throat.

Lash held the handle of his whip in one hand, and pulled it back toward him with the other. Theo went to his knees, struggling frantically to get his hands under the whip, his face purple. Lash looked up at me, smiled coldly, then gave the whip a yank. Theo swayed, still clawing at his throat.

"Stop, please," I said wearily, moving between Lash and Theo. "You're right; we're late. Let's go."

Lash nodded, pushed me out of the way, then flicked his wrist, uncurling

19

the whip from Theo. Theo gasped, going down on all fours on the mudroom floor, breaths tearing out of him. Assuring myself he'd be okay, I went past Lash out the door. Lash closed it behind us.

"Let me get my bag, it's in my truck—"

"We will take your truck," Lash hissed sharply. "I'll drive. Get in."

I gave him a wary look.

"Devlin said it was closer for you to drive home from Hayden than all the way back to Danial's to get your vehicle," Lash hissed. "My orders are to drive you there in your vehicle. Hopefully you can drive yourself back and forth in time."

I bit back my sharp retort, shrugged, and handed him the keys.

As we headed down the driveway, a black Hummer fell in behind us. It had been waiting near the poplar trees Brian had felled. Even lying on the ground, all were more than a foot in diameter, and had been at least fifty feet tall. They would have soundly blocked the driveway, requiring hours of work for normal humans to remove. They had been pushed aside, without any cutting, into the forest.

"Nice trick with the trees," Lash hissed sarcastically. "It's good Devlin insisted I bring the bears with me, or I'd have frozen stiff in this cold." He stared over at me. "Maybe you'd have liked that."

His suggestive tone repulsed and angered me. "You were the last, um…person I expected to show up here—"

"You don't have to put yourself out and call me a person," Lash said witheringly. "But I warn you, I don't answer to Snake."

"I'm sorry you got cold," I said frostily. "Don't worry about me calling you anything other than your name."

Lash didn't answer.

We drove through Alan's Creek, I turned to him. "Do you mind if I stop and order some Chinese food?" I said hopefully. "It's close to dinner time."

"I'm to take you to Dev immediately," Lash said, his eyes on the road. "So, no."

"If I clear it with Dev, can—?"

"Call him if you want," he said, giving me a cold smile, "But he'll tell you no, too. He's never gone this long without someone in his bed. He's going to want more than a little of you."

"I'm already late," I answered, dialing. "He won't care if I'm a few moments later."

Devlin answered. "Sar, are you on your way?"

"Yes, but I'm hungry, Do you mind if I stop—"

"Forget it," he said curtly. "You can eat here, later."

"Dev—"

"You are already late, due to Danial's games. Need I remind you of your promise to me, Sar?" he said angrily. "You want me to tell Perseus he's welcome to take you? You know how fast he would be at your door?"

"I'll be there soon," I said tonelessly, and hung up.

"See?" Lash hissed, grinning so his fangs showed. "I told you—"

"Shut up and drive," I said, slumping in the seat.

Lash gave me a cold look, but didn't speak for the rest of the trip. Within an hour, we were driving up a long, long driveway, bare trees lining either side. I thought they might be oak, but it was too dark to tell.

A large, forbidding stone house stood on top of the rise, most of the windows ablaze with light. As we drove past it into the attached four-car garage, some tumbled and broken stones were visible near the foundation. The intermittent raised gardens nearby looked like a mess of tangled dead weeds and snow banks.

Lash pulled my vehicle into the first open spot inside, then closed the garage door behind us using a remote opener. With one hand he slid the clip of the garage door opener onto my truck's visor, and with the other, he turned off the engine. Outside came the sounds of truck doors closing, and men talking.

Lash got out, and gestured for me to follow him. He led me through a small kitchen. It was empty of all normal appliances except a large elaborate wine rack on the counter, a supersize refrigerator, a dishwasher, and a microwave. Adjoining it was a dining room, a living room with a big screen flat screen TV on one wall, and finally a hallway, with a stairway leading up into darkness.

"She's here!" Lash called out with glee.

Devlin came to the top of the stairs. He wore a gray robe, dark as steel, gleaming in the dim light. "Thank you, Lash," Devlin said roughly. "Now leave us."

Lash grinned at me. "Have a nice time, Doll." With a flick of his tongue, he turned and made his exit, heading back through the door to my left.

"That's the door I came in with him," I said in surprise. "Right?"

Devlin came down the stairs and scooped me up in his arms. "Miss me?" he asked. Then, before I could answer, he kissed me hungrily, his tongue sliding into my mouth, his stubble scratching my face. He carried me upstairs into the nearest room, and shut the door behind us.

He set me down in front of him. "Tell me, do you like it?"

This must be his bedroom. It looked like a high-end bachelor pad. Near the fieldstone fireplace, there was an overstuffed love seat made of gold silk with carved wood arms. The only other piece of furniture, a heavily carved king-

21

sized oak bed, dominated the room. The bed linens and numerous pillows, all of silver gray luxury cotton, shone softly in the gloom. If there were any pictures on the walls, or bookcases, it was too dim to tell. A faint crackling came from the fireplace.

"You like it?" Dev said, his arms sliding around me to pull me tight against him.

It was a bit hot in here, but very pleasing. "Very much," I said, and gave him a kiss.

He groaned and pressed himself into me, grinding hard. "Come. Now." He crossed the room, pulling me with him, tossing his robe aside. "I need you."

The moment we reached his bed, he was tugging off my clothes, almost frantic. When I tried to help him, he knocked my hands away in frustration. Scared of his desperateness, I lay still, sweating, and let him strip me.

As he spread my legs, tilting my hips up to receive him as he got into position, it suddenly registered that his skin was warm.

"No!" I yelled, scrambling out from under him. I shrank back against the headboard, drawing my knees to my chest.

"Get over here," Devlin snarled, reaching for me, his words rough with lust and anxiousness. "I've wanted you for days and I'm through waiting."

"No. You're warm," I said fearfully. "You've only been on the potion a week at most. That's not anywhere long enough, Dev. I'll miscarry for sure. I can't go through that again. I won't!"

"Ah," he said, pausing in his reach for me. "My apologies, Love. In my desire, I forgot to give you this." He leaned over, turned on a bedside lamp, and handed me a piece of paper from his nightstand.

I read it quickly, blinking in the sudden light. "This is in Dr. Camlyn's writing. It says he verified you're fertile. But that can't be possible."

"Yes, it can," Devlin assured me. "Titus made me a potion with his blood, Sar. It's a variation on the spell Terian used for you and Danial with one huge benefit: it works much faster. Something about the full demon blood being a lot more potent. In only hours, I am ready to give you our child."

"Is this what you were doing in Mexico?"

"Yes," he murmured, his eyes shining from the firelight. "Titus needed a few ingredients that were rare, and I needed to call in a few favors to get them on such short notice." He stroked the top of my foot. "Stephen tested me today at dusk. After he confirmed the results twice, I had him write out that paper, so you would know that you wouldn't be at risk."

Hearing that, I was much more afraid than I had been. I curled myself tighter in a ball, looked at him as if he were the Devil, and didn't answer.

"Shh, Sar," Devlin said, slowly working closer, then drawing me to him.

He was shaking slightly. "Danial said you would be nervous when I told you that I was ready. Don't be afraid. My decision to take this potion was not only to lessen risk to you, but also to waste less time." He kissed me softly. "I won't hurt you," he said softly, laying me down beneath him. "I promise. Now relax, so I may enter, Love."

He was right: this was safer all around. I'd been worried with trying too soon with Danial, and then been frustrated when it took so long. We should begin trying now, in case it took six months, or a year.

"Relax, Love," he murmured gently, kissing up my neck, even as his hips thrust lightly against mine, his erection straining. "Please. I want to be inside you so much…"

I made my muscles relax. The moment the tension left me, Devlin began pushing, shuddering slightly. Within a short time, he worked himself inside. I let out a groan of contentment, the familiar feeling of being filled by him utterly satisfying.

Devlin began thrusting deeply, groaning, his arms supporting his weight while he kissed my neck. There was some pain at the deep penetration, but I was expecting it. I tried to move with him, willing my body to relax. As his fangs pricked my neck, I suddenly surrendered with a moan, his excitement stoking my own.

Devlin quickened his pace. I slid almost easily into orgasm. As it hit me, he bit down, sinking his fangs into my neck. I jerked beneath him, awash in pleasure, my ecstatic moans loud in my ears. Devlin swallowed in long pulls, his muffled groans of pleasure echoing mine. Abruptly, he drove harder, then let out a loud cry of release, shuddering as he spent himself.

He moved off me, and pulled me into his arms. "It seems forever since I was with you last," Devlin panted. "Much too long."

"It was just a week, Dev," I said, my breaths also coming fast.

"Never again," he murmured, biting me gently. "You'll come to me every few days, Sar." He licked my neck, sighing gently. "I had wanted to do this again," he said contentedly. "And now you are well enough to do it with me."

A small part of me had been worried that Dev wouldn't be as interested in me now that I was his and no longer forbidden. Instead, he acted more excited now than he had been before. Relieved, I reached up to caress his face, running my fingers into his hair.

"I love the way you touch me," he whispered softly. "So casually, but with such emotion."

I didn't reply, just continued to stroke him gently.

"You like my touch as well, Sar," he whispered. He sucked gently at my neck.

"Ouch!" I said, jerking back from him. "Why must you do that?"

"I like to do it," he said, giving me a satisfied smile, and then did it again.

"Stop," I said grumpily. "Bite and drink, or just lick me, but stop doing that. It hurts."

Devlin blinked his eyes at me curiously. "Does it really hurt, or is it that it feels unsettling?"

"It makes my nerves jangle, like a pinch does," I said with a rueful smile. "Is it some kind of vampire foreplay, that you enjoy it so much?"

"It's my kind of foreplay," he whispered, baring his fangs in a wide smile.

Blood still stained his teeth. My blood. I shivered.

That seemed to excite him. "Tell me you'll scream for me later, Sar. Tell me that you've fantasized about tonight, here with me. About the things you know I'll do to you." I didn't respond immediately, and he leaned closer. "Tell me," he said harshly. "Now."

"What do you want me to say?" I stammered.

"You didn't think of me?" he hissed, his eyes reddening. "You didn't long for me?"

*God, he was odd.* "I did think of you," I replied carefully, caressing him again in hopes of soothing his temper. "But I wasn't thinking about sex. I was thinking about seeing you again, and wondering what your home would be like, and looking forward to being with you. This week has been a week from hell, Dev. My life's turned upside down. Two weeks ago if you told me I'd be here in your bed Oathed to you and Danial and trying for another baby, I'd have told you that you were insane. So much has changed."

He hugged me to him. "I hope they are all not unwelcome changes."

"No," I said tenderly. "But like I told Danial, it's going to take me some time to adjust. I wake up and think I'm still married some mornings."

"That will pass," Devlin said quickly. "How is Elle?"

"She was upset to see I had on your choker. But I explained to her how things were and are now. I think she accepts it."

"She is tough," Devlin said, murmuring into my hair. "She'll bounce back from this in time. Children are resilient."

I nodded.

"Are you hungry?" he said next. "I had planned to take you out, but I couldn't wait to be with you, Sar. I had to have you like this, at least once before anything else—"

"I'm not protesting," I said wickedly. "I love that you wanted me so badly, that you couldn't wait to have me. I worried I might not still make you feel that way—"

Devlin cut me off with a hard kiss, and pulled me on top of him, so I was straddling him. With a wicked grin, he clamped onto my hips with his hands, and simultaneously thrust up with his hips, impaling me. I let out a scream of shock, then braced myself, my hands splayed on his chest, his heart beating wildly beneath my fingers. We had never done this position, and it was too much. I felt every inch of him as he slid in and out of me as fast as he could, slamming himself into me hard. I let out a cry every time he shoved himself home, both from sensation and also the pain as he hit my cervix. He was hissing, crying out himself with every thrust, writhing beneath me as tremors rocked his body. All at once, he screamed, pumping into me, his back arching.

Devlin gave a large satisfied groan, lowering my torso to hold my body against his tightly, his member still inside me. "Ah, Sar," he said contentedly into my hair, his breaths ragged. "I have wanted to do that since the moment I first laid eyes on you. To see you above me, riding me, and to get into you as far as I could, as fast as I could. To hear you scream as I entered you, and to hear your cries as I had you." A tremor went through him, and he gave a long delicious sigh. "It was just as good as I imagined it would be," he said, giving me a kiss. "Thank you."

"You're welcome," I said, drawing back to look at him. "But why didn't you do this with me before now, if you wanted it that badly? You could have told me your fantasy."

"Because the fantasy was a selfish one," he said tenderly. "I was afraid of hurting you that day in the hotel. You were so nervous, even after you gave in."

"What about last week?"

"When I came to you then, you needed more from me than what I just did to you. Both times you needed gentleness and love. Rough sex had to wait, at least until now."

"You didn't hurt me," I said, fingering his golden hair fanning over the pillow

"In a way I did," he said ruefully, stroking the small of my back. "I came and you didn't." He sighed contentedly, and closed his eyes. "I'm sorry for that, Love," he whispered. "I'll make it up to you later."

Strange that not giving a woman climax was a crime, yet forced sex wasn't. Still, he had grown up in another time, when women were property, and any man of power could have any woman he wanted below his station, whether she returned his affections or not. In view of that, what he had done to me that day in the hotel was likely the norm back then for men of his class. Given that fact, I got how he might think it wasn't wrong, or hurtful to me. Briefly, I wondered why he cared if I came or not, knowing how different women were perceived to be than men four hundred years ago, and how little rights they had. I finally chalked it up to pride, that he relished knowing after an encounter was over that the woman would be counting the moments until the next time he made love with her.

"Penny for your thoughts, Love."

"I was happy to give you that fantasy, Dev. I don't have to come each and every time, so long as you make love to me again later on, and give me an orgasm or two then."

He gazed up at me, considering. "I'll be slower with you later," he said with an easy smile. "You'll have at least two orgasms, Love. I promise. But first," he said, rolling me off him carefully, "we have to get you something to eat. I'll dress."

He went to his closet, and rolled back the mirrored door, revealing more clothes than I had in my closet at home. Some were casual, jeans, denim shirts, T-shirts and heavy cotton shirts. Yet over half were suits, leather pants, silk shirts, with some at the far right being so ornate as to be almost costumes.

Devlin was a clotheshorse. That was something I hadn't seen coming.

He slipped into some jeans, and a heavy heather gray cotton shirt, putting a white T-shirt on under it. Then he noticed my staring. "What?"

"I'm surprised you have so many clothes," I said, getting up to look for my own garments.

"You are comparing me to Danial," he said, rolling his eyes. "He would wear denim all the time if he could. When you are a king, Sar, you have to dress like one. People expect it. And I get invited to a lot of parties, some requiring costume, like Danial's."

"I understand that," I said, slipping on my sweater and thinking I really didn't. *Why not put costumes worn once a year, if that, in the attic, or a spare room?* "Can I use your bathroom?"

"Go ahead," he said gesturing with his hand to a door by the right side of his bed. "It's through there. It's stocked. I'll wait out here."

Wondering what 'stocked' meant, I grabbed my overnight bag and went in. His bathroom was a surprise. I'd expected grey or just white, but it was done in black and white. Black tile, black towels, and white walls with mirrors everywhere, accented with silver fixtures and silver throw rugs. There was an oversize shower like Danial's with two showerheads and also a full size Jacuzzi, the clear water steaming.

Casting a longing look at the inviting water, I closed the door and put on a fresh pad. I'd had a lot of sex, so that was the wisest thing to do. Then I washed my face, and put on a touch of makeup. When I went looking for a towel in the nearby closet, I saw what Devlin had meant by stocked.

He had everything a woman could conceivably need stocked there on shelves: pads, tampons, nail care items, foot care items, bottles of hairspray, several types of high-end shampoo and conditioner, body lotion, massage oil, hairbrushes and pins, aspirin, cold medicine, thermometers, toothbrushes, mouthwash, toothpaste, several packages of pantyhose and even several lipsticks, all in shades of a deep rose pink.

Everything was in the packages it came in, and seemed to be trial sizes, the kind bought when going on a trip. Or the size a man would have on hand if he expected a lot of different women to need something they forgot, and wanted to have something handy to slip in their purse before or after bedding them. That was who all this was for. Danial had said Devlin was a lover of women. Lash had been telling the truth.

I had never met a man I considered a Don Juan before, but Devlin clearly was. How many women had stood where I was now standing, or been on their back in his bed? He'd had over fifty in a little under four months or so he had said. Taking that as average made him bedding close to a hundred and fifty women a year. Doing the math with his four hundred years made the sum total something like forty thousand. It was sickening. I was disgusted with him for being like that and with myself for caring for someone like him, no matter what he had done for me.

There was a knock at the door. "Sar, are you done? We should leave soon, unless you want to eat in."

I didn't want to look at him, or talk to him. I wanted to leave, and never come back. But that wasn't an option.

"Sar?" he said a little louder, agitated. "Answer me."

"Almost," I said softly, then washed the makeup off my face. I got out the toothbrush and paste I had brought with me, brushed my teeth, then rinsed out with one of the single use mouthwash bottles. After smoothing some of the skin lotion I had brought into my face, I took a deep breath and opened the door.

I tried not to look at Devlin, but he was standing right there and I couldn't avoid it. He took one look at me and his eyes narrowed. "I see distaste in your eyes, Sar," he hissed dangerously. "Is it for me?"

"It's for me," I said tonelessly, leaning against the doorframe. "For being with someone to whom a woman isn't a person, just an experience, something to wile away the hours with and forget in a few days, if you remember their faces or names at all, that is."

"I like being with women," he hissed harshly. "And they like being with me. I am not going to apologize to you for it, Sar."

"I'm not asking you to," I said, moving past him towards the door. "But you should let me go then, Dev. I'm not going to be content as a face in your adoring crowd. And you clearly need that, a crowd of women to sate you. You have one-stop shopping in there."

"What really bothers you, Sar?" Devlin said, cutting and sarcastic. "Is it really that I've had many lovers, or that you think that you might not be enough of a woman to hold on to my love? That I might compare you to one of them and find you lacking?"

Bastard. I let all of my disgust show on my face. "It's neither," I stated flatly. "It's that the women in your bed were all one night stands, Devlin. You didn't care anything about any one of them past the night you spent with them, did you? How can you be so shallow? And how can I trust that you really care about me after seeing that?"

"I didn't care about any of them, it's true," Devlin said seriously. "But I care about you. Anything you don't want in my bathroom, feel free to toss out. You'll be the only woman using it now. I promised you that, and I keep my promises. I already tossed out all the lipsticks that would not complement your skin tone—"

His eyes met mine, and saw I didn't believe a word. His eyes slowly bled to red gold and he snarled at me, baring his fangs.

"You pretended so well with me, I believed you," I said bitterly. "God, I've been an idiot—"

Devlin crossed the room to me, cutting off my words with a rough kiss, his tongue almost choking me. Scared, I jerked back and moved my hand to slap him. He grabbed my wrists, both of them. I tried to back away from him, but my back was already against the wall and there was nowhere to go. He put both wrists in one hand, holding them over my head, still kissing me.

I broke free of his lips. "Stop, please!" I pleaded shrilly.

"No." He tossed me onto the bed, holding me down with one hand and using the other to yank off my jeans. "This is what I want, right now. I've waited a long time for it, sweet Sar. And like I said, I'm done waiting!" He pulled down my underwear.

"Stop!" I yelled, and then cried out as he slipped his fingers inside me.

"I've barely touched you, Sar, and you are oh so ready for me," Devlin purred, stroking me. "Because you know what all those other women knew; how good I can make you feel."

"No," I denied. "Your behavior repulses me."

"Tell me you don't want me then," he whispered back, kissing my neck as he massaged me. "Tell me you don't love me, Sar. Let us both hear you lie."

I blinked back tears and didn't speak.

He grinned, and pulled me to my feet. Then he stripped my sweater and bra off, pushing me against the nearest wall. I pushed off it, trying to turn and he grabbed the back of my neck, holding me with an iron grip, my cheek pressed flat to the wall.

"Don't move," he purred in a warning tone dripping with ominousness.

Afraid, I went absolutely still.

Devlin's hand stroked the bear at my hip. He sighed, his face pressed into my hair, then unzipped his jeans, shoving them down. He bent his legs, and pressed to me, his stiff organ sliding against my bare cheeks, flexing gently. "Feel that, Sar?" he whispered, tilting my hips to put the head of his cock against my moist glans. "Only you excite me this way."

He pushed up and into me suddenly, again tearing a scream from my lips. Devlin moaned, the sound all encompassing, primal, and utterly possessing. I scrambled to get away from him, scrabbling at the wall with my hands as he pounded into me. Devlin tightened his hand at the back of my neck, and clamped down on my hip with the other, holding me fast. With a snarl, he bit down again into my shoulder, and began drinking.

I let out a cry of surprise, then pleasure flooded me, and I sagged in his arms. Devlin swallowed me down, still moving fast, then withdrew, his breath hot at my throat.

"You're mine," he hissed in a sinister tone. "Do you hear me, Love? You are mine."

"I'm yours," I moaned loudly, climax flooding me. "I'm yours, Dev. Yours!"

Devlin went rigid at my words, then shouted my name in a scream, his body jerking as he let loose inside me for the third time. "SAR! Aahhhh! Aaahhhh! Aaaaaahhhhhhh!"

He loosened his grip on me as he finished moving, then separated from me. Gently he turned me to face him, shaking slightly and breathing hard. "I'm sorry if I was too rough," he said. "Did I hurt you, Love?"

"I don't think so. Do I have bruises?" I said hesitantly, looking down at my body.

"Yes," he said haltingly. "From my hands, where I held you to the wall. They should fade in a day, but I'll heal them for you if they hurt."

"I'll be okay," I said wearily, then staggered.

Dev steadied me. "I'm sorry," he said gently. "I should've waited to do that until later." He guided me to the bed, sat me down, then handed me my jeans and underwear. "Let me dress and I'll help you."

Disconcerted, I watched him dress, wondering what other fantasies he planned to enact tonight. I was already bruised, and I'd only been here an hour. I slipped back into my jeans gingerly, careful of my tender flesh.

Devlin regarded me. "Do you want me to carry you downstairs?"

"I think I can walk," I said, giving him a look.

"You can walk when we reach the food," he said firmly. "I want to carry you, and you're clearly worn out." He reached down, I put my arms around his neck, and he picked me up. Grabbing my purse with his free hand, he handed it to me, then repositioned my weight in his arms. Leaving his door wide open, he walked downstairs with me in his arms.

I expected his security to be like Danial's was, for someone, maybe Lash, to meet us in front of the house with one of the Hummers. Instead, Devlin carried me into the living room where at least ten people were watching TV. Blood splattered on the big screen, as some young virgin died a messy death. Lash was sprawled on the couch by himself, no one nearby, the others scattered here and there, some on the floor, others on chairs, a few standing against the walls.

As Devlin came to stand in the doorway with me in his arms, everyone looked up. Lash paused the movie, his blatant stare knowing. I flushed crimson, realizing they'd all heard our screams of climax from upstairs.

"We're heading to Davy's," Devlin purred. "We need an escort of three, at least. Drinks are on me. Who wants to come?"

I was appalled he let them drink on duty, but didn't speak.

"I'll come," Lash said quickly, uncoiling himself from the couch. "I was bored anyway."

Two other men came forward. One said, "Vince and I'll go too, Boss."

"Good," Devlin said, gesturing with his head for them to go out in front of us.

Devlin helped me into a Hummer parked past my truck, then got in beside me. One guard drove, the other sat behind us, and Lash rode shotgun. We drove out just missing the garage door.

"This is Vince, and that's Kev, Sar," Devlin said, gesturing. "You already know Lash."

"Good to meet you," I said politely.

They were all silent. I gave Dev a questioning look.

"They remember you, Sar," Devlin said ominously. "They were the only survivors from that night I came for you at Danial's house."

I shrank back from him, opening my mouth to tell him to take me back to the house. Devlin grasped my hand. "Don't worry. They, like all my men, now have orders to protect you with their lives, Sar. They are not going to hurt you, even though they might wish to."

"Comforting," I said under my breath, and leaned into Devlin's shoulder, my eyes locked on the floor.

# Chapter Four

The journey to Davy's didn't take long, maybe ten minutes. I wasn't sure what I expected, but the place itself was pleasing. It was a large room, the walls unsanded wood, the floors stained. A large jukebox played some AC/DC near a long bar that ran along the back wall. There were clearly some unsavory people here, besides my present company, though no one was being loud or rowdy. As we entered, a couple people I guessed were weres of some kind saw us, then quickly paid their bills and left.

We sat down at an empty table. At once, a barmaid came over. As soon as I saw her eyes shift to snake, as cold and flat as Lash's, I understood his reason for coming out on a cold night. "What can I get you, Girl and Boys?" she said, looking squarely at Lash.

"The usual for me, Cin," Devlin purred "A pitcher of beer for each of my men here, and a bottle of your finest Shiraz. Also, I need a menu for my lady."

Cin raised her eyebrows at that, but only nodded. "And for you, Darlin'?" she asked Lash, her tone a low and sultry hissing.

"Bring me what you're bringing Dev, and when you come back over here, be prepared to go on break," Lash said, his hiss raspy with lust. "Because that's as long as I'm waiting for it."

"You got it, Darlin'," Cin said, winking, and she sashayed back towards the bar.

I stared at her swaying form, then quickly looked down.

"We're going to play pool," Kev said to Dev. "Yell if you need us."

Devlin nodded. Kev and Vince got up and went through a door to the side of the bar, where I assumed the referenced pool table was.

Cin was soon back, setting down the wine, an opener, two wineglasses, and two regular mugs that were steaming in the air. Dev and Lash picked up their mugs, then slammed them together, blood sloshing over the sides.

"To good times and women," Dev said, grinning.

31

"To good times with women," Lash amended, grinning back at him.

They drank the mugs dry, then slammed them back down on the table, as I stared. Cin removed the mugs, carried them quickly to the bar, then came darting back. Lash was already on his feet, waiting. He grabbed hold of Cin's hand, then led her through the door Kev and Vince had used.

Had they really gone to play pool, or was there a brothel in back? I turned questioning eyes to Dev, who was opening the bottle of wine. "Not that it's my business, but why aren't they going outside to use the backseat of the Hummer?"

"Too cold," Devlin said, popping the cork. "There's another pool table back there. Lash will use that, he's done it before."

I was so appalled I didn't know what to say.

Devlin saw my face and laughed. "Sar, Cin is an exhibitionist, she likes that. She could easily come to Lash at Hayden or somewhere else and be with him in private, but she likes him to come to her just like this. If he doesn't care, why should you?"

*Had Kev and Vince gone back to get front row seats at the show? Ugh.* "I don't care, so long as you're not going to make me watch."

"Only if you want to," Devlin teased, then noticed a huge man towering over him. "Hi Gary. How's business? It looks light tonight, for a Saturday."

"It's early yet," Gary replied with a smile. "The rough crowd won't come in until midnight, which makes me surprised you're here so early." He looked me over with kind eyes, his mean features softening. "Nice babe."

Gary was a huge man, with burly arms, a bald head and a big bristling salt and pepper beard, but that didn't mean I was going to take his shit tonight on top of everything else. "I'm not a babe, Gary. My name is Sarelle."

"Whoa," Gary said, putting his hands up. "I didn't mean anything."

Devlin put down the bottle of wine very deliberately. "She isn't one of my babes, Gary. This is Sar, my lady. I expect you to give her the same respect that you give me, and address her as such." His tone was exacting. "You will see her with me from now on."

Gary nodded, his eyes on my choker. "My mistake. I apologize, Lady."

"Good to meet you," I said, mollified.

"What would you like, Lady?" he said.

I handed him the menu. "A grilled cheese sandwich, some fries, and your Death by Chocolate after, please."

"About fifteen minutes," he said. "I hope the both of you enjoy your evening. Let me know if you need anything." He went into the kitchen.

"Why isn't his name Davy, if he owns the place?" I asked Devlin as he poured the wine.

"His father was Davy," Devlin said, handing me my full glass. "He was a good friend for many years, till his death about seven years ago. His son Gary is a good man, too. I frequently used to come here with Lash and some of my men, when I lived at Hayden. I hadn't had a chance to come by since my return, until now." He paused. "Do you like this atmosphere?"

"I'm comfortable," I said hesitantly. "But I'm surprised you do. This seems more like Lash's idea of a good spot than yours. Danial wouldn't be caught dead in a place like this."

"I'm among friends here," Devlin said, sipping his wine. "That tends to matter more than pretentious surroundings, the older I get. And my men tell me the food is very good. But I asked what you thought."

I gave him a real smile. "I like it," I said, putting my hand on his. "And I thank you for saying what you said."

"It's only proper, Sar. We're Oathed. I expect you to be given respect, and not treated as a plaything of mine."

"You always put things so nicely," I said, rolling my eyes.

Devlin raised his glass. "To us. To our first night together with everyone knowing what we feel for each other. And to you, Sar, who have taken my heart, long after I thought I could ever give it to anyone again."

"To us," I said softly.

We clinked glasses and drank. "This is great," I said appreciatively afterwards, eyeing my glass. "What is it?"

"Castillero del Diablo," Devlin said, turning the bottle label so I could read it. "A favorite of mine."

"Cellar of the Devil," I said, grinning. "How appropriate."

About the time my food arrived, Lash returned, his attitude almost friendly. As I ate, he talked to Devlin about Ebediah's affairs.

"You know we've got some of his guards still alive and under contract. We don't need them in Canada, not with Ebediah's home almost completely destroyed. Those polars and wolves pledged their allegiance to you, Devlin, but that means nothing."

"And if I cut them loose, they'll band together and attack me, just like Garret's vulturemen did to Danial after Danial killed him. That always happens if you negate the guard contracts after taking power. You know how these things go, Lash," Devlin said, his tone dark, sipping his wine. "We've got to find a way to put them to work, but not where they'll cause trouble."

"Just bring over the polar bears," Lash said, hissing a little. "Leave the wolves. They will just be trouble anyway. Wolves always are, they are as bad as lions—"

Racist, I thought but didn't say.

"Maybe you're right," Devlin said, reluctantly. "I'll have to decide next week. Maybe I can divide them up and sell most of the contracts to some vampires up there."

"We're going to stay at Hayden, right?" Lash said, his eyes seeking out Cin as she waited tables. "I don't want to have to stay in Canada for more than a night, no matter if that's your territory now or not. This is home, here."

"How are you going to arrange it?" I asked hesitantly. "Can you Rule a territory you don't live in?"

"Yes," Devlin said, stroking my hair. "It might not be possible, save Canada is close by and is very stable, at least the hierarchy I've seen thus far. Most of my travels will be via demon, per usual After I check on Ebediah's former holdings—mine now by law. It should amount to only a few nights a week, Lash, if that."

"Good," Lash said, moving his eyes from Cin back to Devlin. "I need a woman I can coil with near me to be happy, and Cin is my favorite."

"Lash, why don't you tell her to come to Hayden, live with you?" Devlin said lightly, smirking. "You can have some little snakelings or whatever—"

"Shut up!" Lash hissed, smiling out of the corner of his mouth. "I'm too old for children. Frankly, I don't know what you think you are going to do with a child yourself, Dev. You aren't the type."

"Maybe you just haven't seen that side of me," Devlin said, giving me a tender look.

"I haven't seen it because it's not there!" Lash said loudly, laughing. "You have always been what you are, Dev, all the decades I've known you. You can't be anyone else!"

Devlin didn't reply, though his irritation showed.

"How long have you known each other?" I said quickly, trying to diffuse the situation. "Lash, you can't be that old. I'm bad with guessing ages, but you can't be older than forty, right?"

"I'm a hundred and seven," Lash hissed proudly, grabbing a used wineglass off a nearby table and filling it full. He knocked it back, then poured another, emptying our bottle. "I take a potion that slows my aging tremendously, but it can't stop it altogether, Sar."

"What's in it?" I asked, amazed.

"Never you mind," Lash said coldly, fixing me with his flat eyes. He drank his second glass down, then put it down on the table with a sharp clack.

I looked away. "Sorry I asked."

"Back to what you said about me, Lash," Dev interrupted. "You didn't know me, back when I was with Annabelle. I loved her like I love Sar. I would have given anything for her. I want this chance very much. Don't think this isn't serious for me, because it is."

Lash looked over at Devlin, and his expression didn't soften so much as it became a little less cold. "You are different with her," Lash agreed with a shrug. "We all see it, Dev. Don't take offense over what I said before. I was just teasing." He turned to the bar. "More wine," he said.

Cin brought us my cake, and another bottle, which Lash quickly opened. He filled our glasses.

"To friendship," Lash hissed softly. "And second chances."

The three of us clinked glasses. Lash downed his in one long swallow, placed it on the table with a clack, and eyed his snakewoman waiting. "I think it's time for another break, Cin."

Cin held her hand out to him wordlessly. Lash took it, and she led him back into the other room.

"What is it with you two?" I asked Devlin. "He's your friend, but he works for you?"

"Yes," Devlin said. "I pay him well, but he could work for anyone, Sar. He's the best there is, the highest ranked. He could make a bigger salary if he worked for Perseus, or Samuel, or even for a less powerful vampire. There are some now in other countries richer than I. But he likes working for me. We've been together a long time."

"Much like Danial and—" I stopped myself, saddened.

Devlin touched my arm gently. "Yes, like them, though Lash and I have been together for some sixty odd years, Sar, not ten." He paused. "To us." I raised my glass, as he raised his. "To having you in my bed, where you belong," he said, his eyes full of desire.

Angry at my remembering Theo, I added wickedly, "To you having me everywhere in your bedroom, and to you being where we both think you belong."

Devlin gaped a moment, then his eyes changed from slightly molten gold to hot burning pools of pure wanting. He cast his eyes around, then began to get up purposely.

Whether he had been going to take me right over our table in front of everyone or lead me to the back room, I never knew. For at that moment, a man walked out from the back room with a bunch of his buddies rubbing his jaw, furious.

"God damn him! He interrupted our game an hour ago, too!"

"Come on," one of his friends said cunningly. "Let's get the guns from the truck. We'll wait until he's busy with that whore, and then blast him to Hell."

"Yeah," another laughed. "A bullet or two in his ass is going to cramp his style."

The five of them walked outside.

Devlin glowered, then got to his feet. "Sar, stay here. If you hear gunfire, duck under the table. I need to get the bears, and head those men off before they get back—"

"If Lash is the best, can't he defend himself?" I asked. "Can't you just warn him?"

"He'll kill them; he's been in a foul mood for days. As for warning him, I'd have to interrupt him and get close enough he'd hear me over the music. If I startle him or her as they're mating, either might strike."

"You don't have to worry, I'll wait in the car," I said, getting to my feet.

Devlin sat me back down forcibly. "That's exactly where I don't want you. Stay here, where you're safe."

I nodded grumpily.

Devlin headed outside a moment later with Vince and Kev. There were no shots, but a minute later, the three of them came back in. Vince had a spray of blood across his face, but otherwise they seemed unmarked. Kev and he left, and Devlin came back to the table.

"Lash should be done shortly," Devlin said, sitting back down. He stuck the cork in the bottle, then handed it to me. "I want to get you home. We have unfinished business, Love."

The last thing I wanted at the moment was more sex. I nodded anyway, playing along.

Lash came strolling back, grinning hugely, until he saw us. "What's the problem, Dev? Kev and Vince left before finishing their game."

"It's time to go," Devlin replied. "You ready?"

Lash cast a longing glance backward. "I suppose," he hissed. "She is on the clock. Let's go."

The ride home back to Hayden was uneventful. As soon as we'd parked, Vince and Kev left without a word. Lash followed Devlin and I inside, then upstairs. I watched him with alarm, until he went into the room beside Devlin's.

"He lives here with you?" I said, as Devlin led me back to his bedroom, then shut the door.

"Yes," Dev said, stripping off his shirt, and tossing it aside. "It's safer for everyone. He can hear if I'm in danger. Serena's is the room next to his. Titus and Leri used to share the one beyond that, at the end of the hall. There are more rooms beyond the kitchen, where the rest of the guards sleep."

"I don't feel him. Titus, I mean."

Devlin led me to the fireplace. "Sit, Love." He began to build a fire. "As for Titus, he put a buffer on his room. Think of it as 'blackness-proofing'. I'm used to the feel of a demon nearby, but I'd never be able to have anyone living here with me if he hadn't. Lash and the other weres are uncomfortable around demons, as a rule, so that was easiest." He blew on the flames. "Titus is most likely not there tonight, anyway. He's probably in his basement workshop, concocting something. Hand me that bottle, please."

I gave it to him, then lounged back on the loveseat, my mood more relaxed. "You do have a talent for romance."

He poured the last of the bottle of wine into two ornate wineglasses that had been on the mantel, and handed me one. "Yes, I do. Now repeat that toast of yours for me," Devlin purred.

I flushed. "To you having me everywhere in your bedroom, and to you being where we both think you belong." We clinked glasses, and sipped.

Devlin took the glasses back, and set them on the shelf. He came toward me slowly, light from the fire flickering over him as he moved. "Let's see if we can make your toast come true, Love," he said, reaching for me.

* * * *

Devlin made my toast come true, literally, sating and exhausting us in the process. It was near dawn when we finally slept. Only a few minutes later, someone began pounding on the door.

"Go the fuck away," Devlin shouted venomously, sitting up.

I opened my eyes. "What time is it?"

Dev reached down and brushed my hair back from my face in a gentle motion. "Way too early, Love."

"Call for Sar, Dev," Lash hissed through the door. "Danial demands to speak with her immediately."

"Tell him to fuck himself," Devlin called, almost gleefully. "We're sleeping."

"I have to talk to him," I said. "There may be some emergency with one of the kids."

Devlin nodded permissively. "Lash, bring the cordless phone in, please."

Lash came in, handed me the phone, and then left, shutting the door behind him.

"Danial, are the kids okay?" I asked worriedly. Devlin leaned close, listening.

"They're fine," Danial said, relieved. "I'm glad to hear you're fine, too."

"Of course I'm fine," I said exasperatedly. "Why wouldn't I be? You worried me, demanding to talk to me."

"I wanted to calm down Theo," Danial said tiredly. "He went after you last night, and Terian had to forcibly stop him. He was wild, almost crazed. Terian barred him from the house, as I didn't want Elle to see him this way. Instead,

Theo left and started trouble at the fox compound. He fought with both Hans and Aran. Brian broke it up, but there was blood—"

"Why is he acting like this?" I said angrily. "He's the one who left me!"

"He was sure Devlin would hurt you. He said I was a fool to trust him with you, that he couldn't stand the thought of the two of you together. He seemed so sure I began to worry."

"He needs to deal with his issues, Danial," I shouted. "I'm dealing with mine!"

"He still loves you, Sar."

"He has a funny way of showing it," I said sarcastically.

"I'll tell him you're fine when he wakes up," Danial said, yawning. "Go back to sleep, I'm sure you were up all night. By the way, please tell Dev that you're seeing me next Saturday night, and he can go fuck himself."

"I heard that!" Devlin growled good-naturedly.

"I knew you would," Danial laughed. "But I mean it about Saturday, Dev."

"Fine," Devlin said agreeably, pulling me closer to him. "But Friday's mine. Now go away and let us sleep."

"I love you, Sar," Danial said. "Get some sleep. Remember, you don't have to come in next week unless you want to. But I have those papers for you, from your lawyer. According to his cover page, you and Theo need to sign them as soon as possible."

"I'll be in tomorrow or the next day," I replied wearily. "I want the separation started."

"I'll see you then. Theo will be here both days. We can make plans for Saturday, too."

"Danial—"

"Be here by five, or I'll come looking for you," Danial growled, then hung up.

I turned the phone off, then dropped it over the edge of the bed. "What is wrong with him?"

"Dealing with Theo, probably," Devlin said, hugging me. "Or thinking about you here with me, having too much fun to call. It might just be work, though. The life of a Ruler is a demanding one."

His resentful tone made me turn to look at him. "How are things with you really, Dev? Are you in danger?"

"I'm usually in danger," he joked. "But why do you ask?"

"I'm asking because I care," I said, stroking his arm gently. "I want to listen, if you want to talk. You said there was a lot you had to deal with. As you told me, there is more to being a lover than making love."

"I don't want to talk," he said, after a few moments. "I'd like you to hold me, as you did months ago, that day in the hotel, the day I first came to guard you. Do you remember, Sar?"

"Of course," I said, putting a few more pillows behind my shoulders. "You saved me. If you hadn't been in my arms then, I'd have died."

"A portent of things to come," he said softly. Easing down on me, he nestled his head on my left breast, his arms around me loosely. I held him, stroking his hair soothingly, my other hand on his well-muscled back.

"I can hear your heart," he said softly. "It seems so fast."

"That's because you're near," I said, kissing his forehead. "You always make my heart beat fast."

He sighed. "I could stay here like this for days with you," he said contentedly. "I love you completely."

"I love you, too."

"But I scare you still," he added. "Don't I, Love? Last night, those first times?"

I didn't reply, tense with worry that he'd provoke another argument.

"I have not gotten anything I have from being cautious," Devlin said. "Everything I've achieved has been from taking chances, from daring to do what no one else will. What I've done since assuming power... it has done something to me."

"What do you mean?" I ventured.

"I hoped being with you would make me...lighter, I guess would be the word. I feel heavy sometimes, both with grief and with the weight of all my years and deeds, both evil and good. But Lash is right, I can't be anyone but who I am."

"It's never too late to be happy," I said softly.

Devlin seemed not to hear me. "I think I knew it even then, but I was reaching for anything I could to make my existence worthwhile. I looked for many years for a miracle. Being with you showed me what I'd lacked. It wasn't power, respect, or lovers. I needed to love someone again." He paused, then sighed. "I needed to love you."

I didn't speak.

He held me tighter. "You make me happy, being with you, seeing you smile, hearing you laugh, and seeing your eyes at that last moment before you reach oblivion." He paused again. "Your heart is racing now, Love."

"Because of you," I said gently, kissing him again on the forehead. "From the words you say and the feelings they stir in me." *Plus worry over your mercurial moods.*

"I meant what I said, about the bathroom. Change whatever you want. It is going to be just me and you."

"Sleep, Dev. Don't think any more on that now."

"You sleep," he teased. "You need to rest after last night. I'll have Lash drive you home later today."

*Was he kicking me out?* I masked my surprise. "I can drive home, really—"

"No," Devlin stated. "I want you safe, Sar, and you are going to be tired today, no matter how much you sleep. Lash will not mind."

# Chapter Five

As Lash drove me home that evening, my mind retraced the events of my stay with Devlin.

His cat, Phantom, had awoken us in late afternoon, yowling and scratching at the bedroom door. Devlin hadn't said anything; he just got up and left the bedroom naked. I had grabbed his silver and gray velvet robe, put it on, and followed him. He was in the kitchen, petting a large tiger cat that was wolfing down food.

"This is Phantom. I usually have Serena feed him, and he was reminding me he hadn't been fed, that he was hungry."

Phantom finished his food, then began winding about Devlin's ankles, purring. Devlin picked him up, and handed him to me. As I took him, I noticed his scarred face.

"What happened?"

"He was hit by a car, right before my eyes," Devlin said, patting Phantom on his head. "He was dying. I healed him with a little of my blood. It left a nasty scar, but he can do everything a cat normally does." Devlin touched my shoulder. "Do you want something to eat? I could order you something, and have one of the men go and get it."

"Just some water," I said, yawning. "I'd rather go back to sleep. Maybe later."

"Do you mind if he comes with us?" Devlin asked. "He usually sleeps in my room with me during the day."

"Not at all," I said, handing the cat back. "Lead the way."

Upstairs, Phantom curled up at the bottom of Devlin's bed, and was soon asleep.

Devlin lay down again in my arms. "It's been a long time since I slept next to a woman, since I woke up in one's arms. You are the first since Annabelle, Sar."

I wanted to believe him, but remembered the bathroom and doubted his words.

He caught my expression before I could mask it. "I never trusted any of the women I was with over the years enough to sleep myself, though they sometimes slept. Usually after the sex was over, I sent them home, or to one of my guest bedrooms."

"Why?" I asked. "Lash was right next door, and you had to be much stronger than they were."

"Too many people want me dead, Sar. I'm a heavy sleeper, and therefore, vulnerable. I found that out the hard way: I was attacked right after I became Ruler in the States. A woman stabbed me with a poisoned dagger as I lay beside her, still shaking from climax. She was overeager. If she had waited for me to fall sleep, I'd be dead."

I squeezed him in my arms to comfort him. "I know some poisons can hurt vampires. What happened?"

"I had enough strength in me to scream, and my guards broke down the door. They brought me to Ravel, the sorcerer I employed at that time. Ravel knew what the poison was, and gave me an antidote before I succumbed. There was a good deal of pain involved. It was a hard lesson, one I never forgot."

"What happened to the woman?"

"I had my men find out who had sent her, and made a harsh example of him. Then I had her killed, for daring to do that to me."

Devlin looked up at me, his eyes filled with raw, deep emotion. "Do you understand now what you mean to me, to Danial? He trusted you from the first, Sar, because you saved him. Vampires rarely sleep with their lovers, even those they love, because it is so dangerous for us. In a way, being intimate like this with you is just as important to me as bedding you." He paused. "Maybe more important."

I was moved by his heartfelt words. "Sleep, Love," I said tenderly, kissing his forehead again. "You are loved and safe."

Devlin gave a contented sigh, relaxing in my arms.

It was much later when we were saying goodbye that Devlin mentioned he was leaving that night for Canada. "I'll be gone a few days."

"You know where I am, when you come back," I said with a smile.

"You're sure you don't want a bit more healing on that one remaining bruise?"

Devlin had healed my bruises by rubbing a tiny bit of his blood into my skin. I'd thanked him, not voicing my worry that his healing me would be a regular thing. "No, I'm fine."

"I saw you cleaned out the bathroom. If you'd like to bring anything, or you want something here for your use, just email me a list."

Most everything I'd left as it was, though there were a few brands I didn't use, so I'd tossed them. In my cleaning, I had also discovered a few personal care items of unsettling nature, and put them back. I had an open mind, at least for now. "Thanks, but let me use up what's there, before I stock it with my own things."

Devlin hugged me, then gave me a chaste kiss. "If there comes a time you want to stay, you have only to tell me. Please keep in mind the invite's there, though I won't push."

Relieved I hadn't been kicked out after all, I hugged him again. "Be safe."

Devlin returned to bed, propping himself up on one arm. "Come here, if you want a last kiss, Love."

I sat on the bed and kissed him again. "You drive a hard bargain."

"Tell me you'll miss me," he whispered. "Tell me you love me."

I beheld him lying there on his side, his hair shining on the pillow, his golden eyes open and watching me. A rush of feeling enveloped me, and I longed to throw myself into his arms, and tell him I'd never leave. Instead, I got up on uneasy feet and walked to the door. "I love you, and I'll miss you," I said hoarsely, then shut the door quickly.

I'd only barely been able to leave. His hold over me was that strong. It had to be the blood he'd given me. If he'd healed that last bruise…

"You getting out or not?" Lash hissed loudly, breaking my thoughts.

We were in my driveway. How long we'd been there, I didn't know. I got out with my bag and purse and shut the door. Lash nodded once, parked my truck in my garage, then walked off down the driveway. Halfway down it, Titus appeared, and then they both vanished.

There was no one in the house waiting, but it was clean, the pets even brushed, a fire warmly burning.

"Serena, I'll have to bring you a present," I said aloud. "You went over and above just watching over things." I beckoned to Ghost and Darkness. "Let's go, daylight's ending."

* * * *

That night, instead of dreaming of Dev or Danial, I had the same dream of Theo dying in my arms. I woke screaming for him, tears on my face, then lay there panting.

Was this some kind of premonition? Was Theo in danger? Or was this just me needing closure?

I needed to give him the papers. I needed to get him out of my life. Maybe then I'd get rid of the nightmares.

43

\* \* \* \*

The next morning, Monday, I drove the Expedition back to Danial's house. I brought with me a bag of belongings Theo had left behind. Maybe it would convince him to sign the papers without a fuss. "You'd think he'd want to," I bitched aloud. "God, he's a jerk."

Theo had parked the vehicle of Danial's he'd driven to my house in his spot in my garage. Whether he had done that to make a point or to protect it from snow, I wasn't sure. He'd left my garage door opener resting on the hood, next to a haphazard pile of my CDs that had been in his truck. I'd swiped them angrily, laying them beside me on the seat. "Who should I offer the remote to, Danial or Devlin?" I'd said aloud. "Or should I just put it in a drawer, because no one needs it now? I'm the one that's going to be travelling all the time—"

My phone let out a beep. When I stopped at a light, I viewed a text from Cia, that said Terian had returned, but nothing else.

Odd he hadn't called me. Maybe he'd been unable to locate Keriam's family. Depressed, I decided to take a few minutes and pick up lunch.

After a fattening meal of Chinese takeout in Danial's kitchen, I went looking for the faxed separation papers. Danial had left them on his desk for me in a pile. I signed them, and marked where Theo had to put his name with yellow "sign here" stickers, the kind we used for clients. I put that on Theo's desk, beside the padded envelope that had come for him over Christmas and the DVD he'd forgotten of "King Arthur". I remembered watching that last one with him, chiefly his comment during the sex scene that if it had been him there with Guinevere instead of Arthur, he wouldn't have needed so much help from her to get into the moment. Instead of smashing the DVD like I wanted, I put it down gently, and got to work. Since Theo wasn't here yet, it made sense to get some work done while I waited.

There were a few emails from prospective clients. I handled them, and then came to one from Devlin from early this morning. He'd responded to the poem I'd sent him before he had claimed me as his own, before Theo had moved out, before my life had changed so much.

*Sar, I loved your poem. As always, you are full of surprises. This past weekend was beyond my expectations. I hope to be with you again soon. I leave you with this thought by Charles Jefferys:*
> *Let us hope the future*
> *As the past has been will be*
> *I will share with thee my sorrows*
> *And thou thy joys with me.*

*Love, Dev*

I printed the email out to take home and hang on my fridge. I'd paid well for the privilege, so I might as well enjoy it.

After turning off the computer, I wandered downstairs, debating whether to knock on Danial's door or not. If I did, he might want more from me than I could give him right now. But if I didn't, he was going to think I was still angry about what he had said yesterday.

Like so many other things lately, I had no choice. I knocked gently. "Danial?"

"Come in, Sar."

I opened the door. "I figured you heard me."

"Yes. Come to me," he said, patting the bed beside him.

I sat down on the bed.

"I'm sorry about what I said on the phone. Forgive me?"

"I know you didn't mean it. It's okay."

Danial switched gears. "Something is wrong with Terian. He left a voice mail for me last Monday, telling me he would be gone for a few days. He was gone all week, Sar. He came back briefly this weekend, to deal with Theo's outburst, then he was gone again in a few minutes. Do you know what he's up to?"

"I'm not sure," I said, shrugging. "He accessed some of my memories of Theo and Devlin before he left. Afterwards, he was agitated."

"Which memories?" Danial said, curious. "To what purpose? It had to be something critical, for him to leave Theoron unguarded here."

"If I knew that, I'd understand why he left," I said good-naturedly.

Danial bit my neck gently, running his fangs over me, then drew back. "Sar, you smell faintly of Devlin."

"I just got home last night," I said apologetically. "I showered at Hayden."

Danial didn't reply, which annoyed me. I got up and faced him. "Do you want me to go?"

"No," Danial said quickly. "I'm sorry, Sar. I have no right to give you grief. It is old jealousy; one that has no place in what you, he, and I share now. Do not think on it again, or worry about coming to me with his scent on your skin." He paused. "Do you want to lie here with me for a while? Nothing needs to happen between us beyond that, if you're not in the mood. I just want very much for you to stay."

"Yes," I said, sinking back gratefully. "I need to wait for Theo to report in to you tonight. I need him to sign those papers, and also give him a few things that he left behind at my house." I paused. "And there's more. Devlin started trying with me, Danial."

"Do you feel rushed?" he said. "It may take a while to make you pregnant."

"It's not that, it's his mood swings," I confided. "I think everything's wonderful, and then he suddenly angry, or melancholy. He said he feels heavy with all of his past on him. I don't know what to say to him when he's like that."

"Devlin is often like that," Danial said. "When he is in his moods, just let him be. He'll take comfort from your nearness and your love." He snuggled close. "I do."

I hugged him, not replying. Minutes later, I fell asleep.

* * * *

"Sar, it's afternoon," Danial whispered. "Wake up."

Groggily, I looked over at the clock. It was close to four. I stretched, and my hand brushed his naked hip.

I froze. Danial began to kiss me gently down the back of my neck, his hands easing beneath my clothes to cup my breasts. I turned to him and kissed him deeply, running my hands over his cool skin.

Danial pulled back from me. "Are you sure?" he said seriously, looking into my eyes. "I want you, but only if you want me."

"I want you, Danial. I'm your Oathed One, aren't I?"

"Yes," he said, full of contentment and love as he pulled me close to him to kiss me. "Yes, My Love, you are."

* * * *

After, I lay in his arms as he kissed me contentedly. "Are you happy?" I asked.

"Completely," he said, giving me one of his rare wide smiles. "I have everything I ever wanted, Sar. I only wish you were as happy as I am."

"There will come a day when I will be," I said with a faint smile. "Just be patient."

"It is easy to be patient now," he said confidently. "I will have you with me for many years, not just a few. For the first time I see the future stretching before me and am not somnolent." He nibbled my neck, his fangs pricking lightly. "My happiness aside, you should shower, Love. Theo will cooperate best if you don't have anyone's scent but your own on your skin."

"Why?" I said recklessly. "He knows I'm with you and Devlin. He'll expect me to smell like one or both of you. Even if he's bothered by it, why should I care? We aren't together anymore."

"Because you still love him," Danial said wisely. "Your jealously is talking, and you want to hurt him. Don't do it. You'll just regret it. There is Elle to consider."

"You're right," I said, chagrined. "As usual."

"I wish I was right more of the time," Danial said wishfully. "But you're just being generous with me."

There was a knock. "Danial, phone call," Brian said from outside the door.

"Just a minute." Danial got up and put on his robe. "Sar, if you'll start the shower, I'll join you shortly." He left.

When I used Danial's shower, my toiletries were still where I'd left them months ago. Happy they hadn't been tossed out, I used them, then began conditioning my hair.

Danial finally came in. He embraced me immediately, almost in desperation.

"What is it?" I said, worried. "What's happened? Is Dev okay?"

"Another death threat," he said wearily. "This one for both Theo and I."

"Tell me everything."

"You remember Peterson?"

"Yes," I said bitterly. Peterson was the man who'd tried to kill us in Europe. His plan to use Theo and Danial for experimental subjects for his new explosive bullets gun had resulted in Theo's abduction and our time apart, not to mention his meeting up with Tasha.

"Well, he has a brother, Maury, who has taken over the company. He knows Theo and I were behind the death of his brother, and the carnage of that night. He knows where we live. He knows Theo lived with you, Sar. Most likely he thinks he still does."

"Who told you all this? Dev?"

"Samuel."

"Why would he care? He hates Theo and he fought with you over me—"

"He would never have warned us, except that he wants you safe, and he's worried you may be injured or killed by accident when Maury attacks Theo. He has information Maury plans to send a bomb by mail—"

My eyes went wide. "The package!" I screeched.

"What package?" Danial said sharply. "When did it arrive? Where is it?"

"Right after Christmas, a small package came to the house for Theo. I brought it with me today. It's up on Theo's desk."

"Who was it from?" Danial said, dialing his phone.

"There was no return address."

"Theo?" Danial said. "Get over here. I don't care what you were doing, get over here now! We've got a bomb or something worse here."

Danial hung up, and turned to me. "Sar, go upstairs and carry it out of the house."

I gaped at him. "Are you crazy?"

"If you could set it off, you'd already be dead. I'll wager any were who touches it will get a nasty surprise. I might even be enough to set it off."

"You can withstand an explosion better than I can," I shot back. "I might be pregnant, Danial."

"Sar, you have been carrying that package around all day. It won't do anything to you. You are the only human here to do it. Please, go now. Elle may come in at any moment. If it was engineered to be activated by a werecougar, she will surely set it off!"

I hurried upstairs, carefully picked up the package, then carried it down the stairs and out of the house. I walked down to the driveway and set the package on the ground, backing away a few paces. *Should I leave it here? It was getting dark. What if someone coming in the driveway ran over it?*

"Mom!" Elle shouted. I turned as she started running toward me, leaving Brian standing near the house.

"Stay back!" I yelled but she either didn't hear me or didn't listen. She reached me before I'd gone two steps. I grabbed her and pulled her close, and kept backing away from the package. "Move slowly!"

"What is it?" Elle said, scared. "What's wrong?"

"There's a bomb or something bad in there. But don't worry, your father's coming."

Theo pulled up in his truck. He slammed the door and got out, swearing loudly, his clothes askew.

As he went to go inside, he saw us and stopped still. Then he came running at full speed for us. Grabbing our arms, he dragged us backward as fast as he could by our clothes.

Danial came outside, still buttoning his shirt. "Elle! Elle!"

Elle ran into his arms with a sob. "Dad!"

"What's in there?" Theo said curtly, looking from Danial to me and back again. "That's not a bomb, unless it's a fake one."

"Samuel warned me a bomb meant for you was sent by Andrew Peterson's brother, Maury. He's out for blood, Theo, yours and mine. That package came for you over Christmas to Sar's house."

Theo swore yet again. "When did it arrive?" he asked. "Why didn't you give it to me before now?"

"It came while you were gone," I said icily.

He looked away from me. "Was there anything you can remember about it? Weight? Was the contents heavy? Soft?"

"I remember it was light," I said, thinking back. "It was too light to be a book, or anything metal, even a bullet. There was no return address, and the postmark wasn't airmail, it was domestic. It felt like the package was empty, actually."

"The postmark doesn't mean anything," Danial said. "It could have been sent here to the States from abroad, and then resent again though a mailing company."

"We need Terian," Theo said finally. "I'm betting it's a poison, probably in dust form. We need to incinerate it. Where is he?"

"Off checking something for me," Danial lied smoothly. "I can't reach him."

"Titus," I said suddenly. "He can do it."

Both of them looked at me. "How do you know Titus?" Theo said, his eyes narrowing.

"Good thinking," Danial said, nodding to me. "I'll call him now." He headed inside, bringing Elle with him.

Theo followed me into the great room. "I asked you a question, Sarelle," Theo said angrily.

Elle let go of Danial's hand and snarled at Theo. "Go away!"

"Elle, go into your room. Stay there until I come and tell you that everything's okay," Danial commanded. Elle cast a last angry look at Theo, and then left.

I faced Theo. "He helped Devlin mark me, not that that's any of your business. But I'm glad you're here, because I've got something for you." I walked upstairs, then returned with the papers and DVD. "Here."

He took the DVD, and lay it on the table, his eyes scanning the papers. Then he handed them back. "I won't sign these, Sarelle."

"Why not?" I said nastily. "Don't you want this over so you can ride off into the sunset?"

"I don't want to wait a year to get divorced. I want our marriage annulled for the farce it was."

I gaped at him. "What? You can't do that."

"I talked to a lawyer, and it's the fastest way," he continued. "I committed adultery. I'll admit it as the cause. I'll pay for it, even." He took some folded papers from his back pocket. "Sign these, and you'll be done with me."

My fury at his lack of caring boiled over. I ripped his papers up and threw them at him. "That may be what you want, but it's not what I want! You don't sign these papers, fine. I won't make you. But I'm not signing any paper to have our marriage annulled. So you either sign mine, or you'll never be free to marry Tasha."

He snarled at me, his eyes yellow. I faced him resolutely, my eyes flashing.

Theo took the papers and signed them, almost tearing the paper in his rage. He threw them down on the table, where they separated, some falling off. "You won't bring me back to you, doing this," he growled. "You're just making things harder on everyone, including yourself."

He turned abruptly and left, slamming out of the house. I gathered up the papers slowly, tears falling on them and wetting the pages, glad no one had witnessed our fight. Leaving the papers on the table, I went into Danial's bathroom to wash my face.

I fingered the bear pendant. Maybe it was better to give in, to get free of Theo. Our love had been so powerful it devoured everything. When he was out of my life, I could concentrate on making a new life with Danial and Devlin.

Danial burst in. "Titus can't come, at least not right away," he said quickly. "But I finally got Terian. He insists on speaking to you privately before anything else."

I put out my hand for the phone.

Danial shook his head. "He said to meet him at his lab."

"What about the package?"

"Brian is guarding the package in bear form from a safe distance," Danial said. "It's not a bomb, but until its ashes, I'm going to be uneasy. Finish as fast as you can with Terian, and then bring him back."

I nodded and vanished, teleporting to Terian's lab. He was waiting for me, pacing the floor.

"We need your blue fire," I said hurriedly. "Now what's so urgent it can't wait?"

"There's no easy way to say this, Sarelle." He paused, searching for the right words. "You wanted to know what was going on, why Theo didn't wait for you as you had for him. Why he loved someone else."

"And?" I prompted.

"He didn't have a choice. Theo's under a love spell."

# Chapter Six

"Love spell?" I said. "That can't be right, Terian. He loved not only Tasha but Aspen, too—"

"Tasha is similar enough in feature to be Aspen's twin, Sar. They look closer than sisters. He probably fell for Aspen for that reason alone. She resembled the person of his forced affection so closely he couldn't help himself."

"No, someone would have noticed—"

"No one could have," he countered. "You avoided Tasha and none of us had ever seen Aspen. If I had, I would have suspected at once, as I did when I saw her in your memories."

"But he left Aspen easily for me," I said, confused.

"Aspen didn't do this to him. She has no hold over him except her appearance, and when you renewed the dream with him, you lessened that. But if you had left him with her, he would have come to love her as an aftereffect of the spell."

"All this about renewing the dream," I said bitterly. "If our bond was as special as you make it out to be, how did Tasha get Theo back with just a letter?"

"Most likely there was a little of the spell on the paper," Terian growled. "Theo was the one who opened it. That together with his character was enough to make him run to her rescue. Once he was with her again, it was likely easy to enfold him under the spell completely."

Theo had said that he'd planned to come back to me after helping her, but that everything had changed in the space of a day. Just as it had changed the first time he fell in love with her. She'd used him to escape her father and her bored, rich life not once but twice. I was so angry I could barely talk. "You can break it, right?"

"No," Terian admitted. "This spell was specially designed to hold Theo.

It's complicated and powerful. It had to be, to subvert what you and Theo share. Most love spells wouldn't work on either of you. Everlasting Love is the most powerful spell of its kind. I don't know how to break it. Even if I did, I don't have enough magical power."

I screamed in utter frustration, and dialed Devlin. Whatever Titus was doing, this was more important.

"Sar?" Devlin answered, purring. "Are you missing me?"

I bit back my scream. I had no time for games, but with his moods, I had to play this cautiously. "Devlin, send Titus to me," I said with forced calm. "Immediately."

"Sar, as I told Danial, he's busy working," Devlin drawled. "Now about this weekend—"

I lost it. "Dev, if you ever loved me at all, ever, send him to me! Terian needs his help desperately! Stop screwing around, God damn it!"

Terian let out a gasp. "No, wait—!"

"What in hell is going on there, Sar?" Devlin said, agitated. "Are you under attack?"

"Come and see for yourself!" I yelled. "Do whatever you have to, but get here! We're in the werecompound, in Terian's lab."

"I'm coming now, Sar," Devlin assured. "Stay there and don't move." He hung up.

"I'm not ready to see him," Terian grumbled.

"Titus can help," I shot back. "Besides, he's your father and it's about time you faced him and stopped dicking around."

There was a knock at the door, then Titus strode in, followed by Devlin. Devlin came to my side immediately, as Titus approached Terian.

Seeing father and son together, the faint resemblance in their build and the shape of their jaw was noticeable.

"Terian, this is your father, Titus," I said.

Terian held out his hand. Titus took it, then slowly pulled Terian into his arms for a hug. Terian didn't resist. Soon he was holding his father as tightly as Titus was holding him.

"I'm sorry, Terian," Titus rumbled softly. "If I'd known of you, even had an inkling, I'd have moved Hell and earth to find you."

Terian swallowed hard.

"I always wanted a son," Titus rumbled. "But Alerian didn't want children. I never even knew she was pregnant."

Terian began to tremble.

"Forgive me?" Titus rumbled, his low timbre breaking. "I'd like the chance to be your father."

Terian pulled back slowly, tears in his eyes. "I'd like that."

Titus hugged him again.

"Not that I wasn't touched by that," Devlin said, looking from Terian to me. "But you led me to believe there was some emergency here."

"Theo is under a love spell," Terian said gratingly. "The most powerful one there is."

"What?" Devlin said, shocked. "Since when?"

"Which love spell?" Titus growled, his ferocious expression similar to the earth cracking open, a jagged maw of jagged sharp edges. "Who put it on him, and why?"

"Tasha, the woman he left Sar for. She bespelled him with Everlasting Love," Terian said quickly. "I can't break it, but maybe you can."

"That makes sense," Devlin said slowly. "That would explain how he could give Sar up so easily, despite the dream they shared together."

"How do you know of that?" I said sharply to Dev.

Titus laughed, but it was a cold laugh, devoid of real humor. "You have much to learn. Brian reports regularly on everything that affects you, Sarelle. Before him, Lander sometimes gave us information."

"And others, as well," Devlin added.

"When you said you knew everything about me you needed to, Dev, I didn't realize how much that entailed," I said slowly.

"I know of the dream, how it happened the first time, and how it affected you both the second time," Titus said. He looked at Devlin. "Whomever did this spell intended to entrap Theo, and keep him from Sarelle. This spell, if it is indeed the one Terian says it is, was both costly and complicated." He looked at Devlin with red eyes. "I can break it, if that is really your will, Master."

"You're implying I put this spell on Theo," Devlin said icily. "I didn't. If I wanted Theo out of the way, I'd have had Lash kill him, like he's wanted to for years. I wouldn't have bothered with a spell."

"Lash mentioned he was in Russia, that night he came to see you at my home," I countered. "When was he there, Devlin?"

"He was in Moscow a few years ago," Devlin said to me smoothly. "A werelion had been killed there, and he went to make sure it wasn't Theo. When he verified it was not, he came home."

"Why send your best man?" Terian asked.

Devlin rounded on him, snarling. "Because the person who killed the werelion was Samuel, Terian. He killed him at his estate. Lash was the only one who was good enough to get in and out without being detected."

"If Devlin did this to Theo, he did it without my help," Titus rumbled. "Leri is not skilled enough in love magic to have done this spell. Logically, he is innocent. That leaves the next most likely suspect: Samuel himself."

I sank down to the floor, sitting in a heap. "All this time, it was Samuel."

Devlin crouched down, and helped me back to my feet, settling me in a chair. "Why do you say that?"

"Samuel hated Theo, thought he'd interfered with me as Danial's Oathed One. He promised Danial he'd look for him, and wouldn't kill him. I thought that meant he was helping us. Instead, he found a way to keep us apart without breaking his word to Danial."

"Even if Theo found his way back to America and met Danial and you again, that spell ensured Theo would move on," Devlin mused. "Ingenious."

"Perseus knew already that you were splitting up before any of us did," Terian added. "It makes sense now that Samuel told him."

"I'm not pleased to have ridden to your rescue, Sar, only to be accused—" Devlin said, glaring at me.

"Ease off her!" Terian said, blackness flowing out of him. "She loves you, and she wants to trust you, but she's afraid to. She remembers what you did to her, all of it, not just that day you made love to her, if you can call the first time she was with you by that moniker."

Devlin stared at Terian. "Who are you to tell me what she feels?"

"I saw her memories, looking for signs of the love spell I suspected was on Theo. I saw a lot of you in them, Devlin, and felt her emotions through every encounter."

I flushed. Devlin gazed at Terian, a small amount of respect in his eyes. "Forget what you saw and felt," he said finally. "Sar and I will build our own relationship without any help from you or magical means."

"I'm sorry for suspecting you," I said awkwardly. "It made sense at the time."

"You were being logical," Devlin said with a wave of his hand. "Now that we determined what's going on and who is behind it, what do we need to break this spell?"

"I can break the spell, Devlin," Titus said, his warning tone that of stone grating on stone. "But you should make sure you want me to."

"Explain," Devlin commanded.

"This isn't a simple spell he's under," Titus continued. "To make matters worse, he's got two layers now, with her addition of another on top of the previous one that was waning."

"Why did it wane?" Terian said. "Everlasting Love is supposed to be, well, everlasting."

"Distance," Titus explained. "That was the only thing that saved him. That and his character, I suppose. A lesser man would have been unable to leave her at all."

"Why did she do it?" I asked. "Why force someone to love you?"

"As long as there has been magic, there have been love spells," Titus growled. "Everyone craves it, and few feel safe in it, even when they have it."

"Why caution me?" Devlin said to Titus.

"Because once it's broken, Theo is going to come looking for Sar. He is not going to be able to stay away from her, not for anything. No matter where you take her, Devlin, he'll follow you."

"Why is that a problem?" Devlin replied. "I said I'd share her with him."

"He will not want to share her with you," Titus stated. "That is also the nature of the dream they share. He must possess her utterly, and she will not want to give herself to anyone else, not you, not Danial. Her bond with Theo has been lessened by the spell. When it's dissolved, it will spring back in full force, enveloping them both."

I wanted no part of what he was describing. "Fuck, can't anything ever be simple?" I cried.

"Not this," Titus said, his red eyes on mine. "Make a decision, Devlin."

"Tell me what you need to do," Devlin said. "And what will happen, if you know."

"I can break the spell. I have a mixture with me that will do it. But it is going to prompt Theo and Sar to dream of each other one last time. When they wake up after, what is between them will be stronger than ever. As before, they will seek each other out."

"Terian told me long ago that we renewed the dream, by dreaming a second time together," I interrupted. "We didn't know what that meant."

"What you shared that first time made you reveal your feelings. When you acted on your feelings, dreaming of each other, the magic deepened your love for one another, made it all it could be. When you dreamed a second time together, you made the love you share much stronger than normal love is, much more powerful. The third time, you may make the bond between you unbreakable."

"What are you saying?" I asked, scared.

"I mean if Theo should die, you may die as well, Sar."

"I'll not risk that," Devlin said stridently. "I want Sar safe. Do not break the spell, Titus."

"It is your decision," Terian said curtly. "But is also Sar's as well."

"The question isn't can we do this, but should we do this," I said wearily. "I think we should leave well enough alone."

"You want to leave him under her spell?" Terian said, aghast. "How can you say that when I know how much you love him, how much you are dying inside from him leaving you?"

"It is because I love him that I'm suggesting this," I said angrily. "He's happy, really happy with her. As he said to me so eloquently, he doesn't have to share her with anyone. If we break the spell, not only is he going to cause trouble with the new Oathing arrangement, but my personality—who I am—is also going to change. I don't want that."

"Don't ask me to do it, because you know I won't," Devlin said, his tone hard as stone.

"I know you won't release me from my Oath to you," I retorted. "I don't want you to. I'm saying this bond sounds not too much different than the spell he's under with Tasha. Theo never asked to be bound to me, not the first time or the second time. I don't want to enslave him against his will."

"You would be binding yourself as well as Theo," Titus added in. "But it isn't false love, like he knows now with Tasha. Your love is real, and the depth of it is rare, Sarelle. Your wills, your wanting of each other, your love for one another is the strength of the spell. It cannot be against either of your wishes, by the very nature of what you share. In short, you cannot bind him against his will."

"You want me to do this," I said in surprise, looking at him. "Why?"

"I was under a love spell before, many, many years ago," Titus said, remembered pain in each word. "I hurt someone I cared for badly, and stayed with someone I hated. By the time my brother broke me free, the woman I loved was lost to me. I still regret it."

"Do it," Devlin said, sighing. "I'll never hear the end of it from you or her if I don't agree." He turned to me. "But you, Sar, are going to make me a promise here and now with them as witnesses."

"What promise?"

"Even if your feelings for me change, even if you don't love me anymore, I expect you to honor your vow to me, to work with me to have my child. Even after it's born, I expect you to come to me when I ask you to, and to come willingly."

Devlin's eyes were cold and cruel, but it was a cruelty born of his fear of losing me, not malice. I kissed him. "I swear it," I said. "I'm not going to break my promise, either to you or Danial." I turned to Titus. "Are you sure there isn't another way?"

"No," Titus said. "Everlasting Love was meant to be forever. Most often death is the only sure way to break it. Even then, when one of the lovers dies, the other usually commits suicide out of despair."

"Do it now, Titus," Devlin said. "Where is Theo, Sar?"

The package! How in God's name had I forgotten it? "We have to get to the driveway!" I shouted frantically. "There is a package that needs to be incinerated! Theo is most likely there!"

In a second, the four of us appeared on the driveway, bumping into Danial and Theo.

"Danial," Devlin said with a winning smile. "How good to see you again."

"What are you doing here?" Danial said, his eyes narrowing, looking from Dev to me.

Theo growled, looking at Devlin with murder in his eyes. "What do you—?"

"Where is it?" Titus said, ignoring everyone but me.

"There," I said, pointing to the package lying on the driveway.

Titus walked up to the package noncommittally and picked it up. We all watched, riveted. Titus vanished, then reappeared by us in a few seconds, sans package.

"What did you do with it?" Danial said. "What was it?"

"It was poison, all right," Titus said cheerfully. "A high grade, made for werelions. No point wasting it."

"I'm sure you'll put it to good use," Theo said sarcastically.

Titus bared his teeth at Theo in a half smile, half snarl. "Stay on Dev's good side, or I will." He turned to Devlin, Terian, and I. "Let's go inside," he said urgently. "Terian has discovered something on his travels this past week. He needs to share it with all of us."

We went inside, Terian following. Just as we entered, Terian disappeared.

"Where is Terian?" Theo said angrily, folding his arms across his chest the moment we were inside the great room. "I need to get back to work."

"He's coming," Titus said, moving to Theo's side. "He needed to bring in one more to hear what he has to say."

Terian blinked back into view abruptly, holding a woman. She was struggling frantically. When her eyes saw Theo, she let out a scream. "Theo, help!"

"Tasha!" Theo shouted, lunging for her.

"Hold him!" Titus yelled.

Devlin and Danial moved as one, grabbing Theo fast. He snarled, and tried to bite them, but they held him.

I gaped at Tasha. God, she was Aspen's twin. If I didn't know better, I would think she was Aspen.

"Theo!" Tasha cried, her Russian accent slight. "Help me!" She suddenly saw me and froze.

Rage filled me at her guilty face. "Tell him what you did to him," I said, moving toward her. "Tell him what you did to us!"

"I did nothing!" she said defiantly. "Now let me go!"

I decked her as hard as I could. She went down on her side hard with a grunt. She looked up at me in fear, blood from a split lip trickling from her mouth. I moved closer. She cringed back.

"Stop it, Sar! Don't hurt her!" Theo screamed, flailing.

"Do it, Titus!" Devlin shouted. "We can't hold him much longer!"

Titus hauled Tasha to her feet, and stood her in front of Theo, his hands on her arms. Theo was screaming, his cougar fangs snapping in the air, his yellow eyes furious. Danial and Devlin held him, bleeding from scratches inflicted by his clawed hands.

Titus threw some wet sparkling stuff over Theo. He swayed, and stopped struggling.

"Release him from your spell," Titus rumbled to Tasha. "Or I'll break every bone in your body, little girl."

"No!" Tasha said stubbornly. "I need him! I need him to love me, to protect me! I'm all alone here! We're in love!"

Titus opened his mouth and growled at her, revealing his many rows of teeth. Tasha screamed, her eyes wide. That woke Theo from his stupor and he lunged for her again, roaring.

I grabbed a hold of Tasha's hair, and yanked it back. "Do it, you fool! Or I'll kill you here and give your soul to that demon!"

"Never!" she screamed. "I love him!"

"Do it," Devlin snarled. "Or I'll kill your lover before your eyes. And you'll kill yourself from despair because of your Everlasting Love." He yanked an explosive bullets gun from his back, and pressed it to Theo's neck. "You know I mean it, even if they don't. Release him!"

"I release him!" Tasha screamed frantically. "Don't hurt him!"

Theo went to his knees suddenly, then to all fours, his body racked with tremors, pulling Danial down with him. Devlin released Theo as he fell, and grabbed Tasha.

Tasha struggled in Devlin's grip, her eyes on the gun. "No, please don't kill me—!"

Devlin tossed away the gun, then gave her a wide grin, showing her his fangs.

"Vampire," she breathed, her eyes wide.

Devlin sank his fangs into her throat to the hilt. Tasha screeched, writhing, but he held her, swallowing her down even as she fought him.

"Don't kill her, Dev," Danial said.

Devlin made no sound, gave no sign he heard, still swallowing her down just as fast as he could. As she went slack in his arms, he stopped, letting her fall to the floor with a thud.

Terian went to her side and put pressure on her spurting neck wounds, giving Devlin a nasty look.

"What?" Devlin said, licking his lips. "I don't want that one coming back a vampire. I don't dare heal her, but you can, if you choose."

"Devlin, Danial, get ready!" Titus rumbled. "He's coming out of it!"

Theo had stopped shaking, and was pushing himself up off the floor.

"What will he remember?" I said quickly. "Anything?"

"Everything," Titus answered. "But all he will want is you, having you, however he can get you. He hasn't felt the full effects of what you share for years now. It's going to hit him like a sledgehammer—"

Theo's head snapped up at that moment and his eyes darted, and then they focused on me. "Sar," he said softly. In that one word was all the love and tenderness I'd thought never to hear again. Wanting and desperate need enveloped me, squeezing my heart like a vise. I staggered, then lunged for him.

"Hold her!" Titus warned.

Danial grabbed hold of me. I tried in vain to shake him off. "Let me go!"

Theo exploded in movement. Devlin and Danial together almost couldn't hold him back. "Sar!" he screamed. "Sar!"

I had to get to him, had to be with him. "Let me go!" I shouted, breaking free of Danial.

"Sar!" Theo screamed again.

Terian grabbed me, his skin hot. "No, don't go to him!"

"Let me go!" I shouted

"A little help, Danial!" Devlin yelled, grappling hard and fast with Theo.

Just as Danial grabbed Theo's arm, Titus passed his hand over Theo in a delicate movement. Theo slumped to the ground, unconscious. Danial and Devlin both fell with him.

"You could've warned us," Devlin said nastily, getting to his feet. He and Danial lifted Theo's prone form up and put him on the couch.

I went to Theo's side, clasping his hand. "Is he okay?"

"He'll stay like this until you fall asleep, Sarelle," Titus said. "Then the dream will start for you two, as it has before."

"Why is it always the same night?" I asked. "Is there a reason?"

"It doesn't have to be, Sarelle. It can be any place you want it to be," Titus replied.

"You mean it's a blank slate?" I said in wonder. "Anything?"

"Yes," he said, giving me a small smile. "Use it wisely. I don't expect you'll ever have this opportunity again."

"Thank you," I said giving him a hug. "I owe you for this."

"No, you don't," he replied, hugging me. "If you had not been with Terian when Leri attacked him, he'd be dead. I know also how you saved him from being killed at Theo's hands. It's I who owe you still."

"He's my friend," I answered uncomfortably, roasting from his heat.

"Thank you for that, too," he replied, then let me go.

"What should we do with her?" Devlin said, eyeing Tasha's prone form. "Lash would really like her—"

"Send her home," I said, grimacing at that unsavory fate. "Her father can punish her worse than we could. Maybe he'll marry her off."

"You don't want vengeance?" Danial said, astonished. "After all she did?"

"This was Samuel's doing, not hers. She could never have done it by herself." I turned to him. "All I care about is that Theo is free."

Danial looked at me, then quickly looked away.

"Bring her to me," Titus grated out.

Devlin picked Tasha up, and brought her over. Titus held his hand over her heart, and said something. His hand glowed, and she writhed as if in pain. Then the glow sank into her skin, and she stopped moving. "She'll never again do any magic, or even be able to handle a spell of any kind," Titus said, still angry. "She deserves worse, but this will do."

"Someone want to clue me in here?" Danial said. "I have no idea what just happened."

"Theo was under a love spell," Terian supplied. "I wasn't strong enough to break it, so Sar called Titus. Devlin came with him. Titus broke it."

Danial's eyes narrowed. "I know you," Danial said, rounding on Devlin, who was licking his lips. "What did Sar have to promise you this time, Dev? It had to be a lot, to get your help with Theo, knowing how you feel about him."

"Nothing she hadn't already promised me before," Devlin said arrogantly.

Danial moved to speak again, but Titus interrupted. "I would have done this in any case, Danial. I was once under a love spell myself. Devlin speaks the truth."

"Thank you, then," Danial said, clasping Titus's hand. "Can I repay you?"

"The poison you let me take is good enough," Titus grinned. "Easily worth tonight's trouble."

Danial looked uncomfortable, but just nodded, and let go of Titus's hand.

"What now?" I said, gazing at Theo lovingly.

"My son and I will teleport you and Theo home," Titus rumbled. "It's almost dawn. You'll sleep at least eight hours once you fall asleep. You and Theo will wake at the same time, as before."

I went to sit beside Theo's prone form. "Where is he now?" I said, glancing at Titus. "Waiting in the dream?"

"No. He's sleeping deeply, a sleep he can't wake from unless you join him in the dream."

"Why?" I asked slowly. "Is that a side effect of being released from the love spell?"

Titus shook his head. "No. That I did to give you time."

"Time for what?"

"Time for me," Devlin said, encircling me in his arms. "Titus, you need to return me to Hayden before you take Theo and Sar. I need every bit of night that is left. Afterwards, I need you to get back to Canada and finish up what you were doing."

"Very well," Titus said, turning to Devlin. "We should go now, then."

Devlin cupped my face in his hands. "Tell me you love me, Sar."

The touch of his cool hands on my face startled me. I blinked, then leaned into them contentedly. "You first," I teased.

"I love you," he said simply, his golden eyes searching mine.

I hugged him tight. "I do love you," I said softly. "And I thank you for this."

"Remember your promise," he said, his eyes tinged red. "For I will remember it."

I pulled back from him and nodded.

Dev kissed me again with everything he had. When he felt me melt into his embrace, he pulled back and sank his fangs into the side of my neck. I let out a gasp, trying to pull back from him. There was pain now, though pleasure was still there faintly.

I forced myself to be calm, to relax as he sucked persistently. Abruptly Dev stopped, withdrawing his fangs from me, his eyes melting fire. He kissed my neck gently, then kissed my cheek. "Remember you are mine, Sar. I'll come to you soon."

I nodded uneasily. Devlin went to Titus, and they disappeared together.

"I'll teleport Tasha to the werecompound for now, and make sure she stays sleeping," Terian said, picking up her limp form. "I can contact her father in the morning by reading her memories, then we'll get her back home."

"Go, please," Danial said, coming over to me. "I need a moment with Sar."

Terian disappeared.

"Sar, what he did hurt, didn't it?"

"Yes, a little. It's healed, isn't it?"

"For the most part," Danial said, putting his lips to mine. "Hold still."

I kissed him gently, then drew back and guided his head down on my neck. Unexpectedly, instead of healing me, he sank his own fangs in. I let out another gasp of surprise, shifting uneasily. Danial drank a few long pulls, then withdrew, healing me.

"Why did you bite, when you know it hurts?" I said warily, stepping away from him.

"If your pain is returning, this may be the last time I can casually," Danial said, grabbing my arm. He embraced me again. "I wanted to take advantage. I'm worried that once you dream of Theo, you'll decide to leave again."

He'd done it because Devlin had, no matter what he said. "I promised not to," I replied. "I didn't want to do this."

"You seemed besotted enough just now," Danial said, his tone despondent.

*I had been, until Devlin touched me.* "Titus said there wasn't another way."

"Maybe not," Danial sighed. "In any case, it's done. Please, whatever happens, do not cease your weekly visits to me. I don't want to lose you again, even if the price is separate beds. Let us remain Oathed, even if it's only in name."

I stared at him. "I took a vow. I'm not breaking it."

Danial looked back, unflinching. "Even if Theo asks you to?"

I clung to him, wanting to assuage his despair. "I don't want that, either. I was and am happy being Oathed. What I really want is to stay here and not leave," I admitted, looking over at Theo's sleeping form. "This was starting to work with you, me, and Dev."

"It still can," Danial said stubbornly. "If everyone is respectful of everyone else. When you wake, talk it over with Theo, and try to convince him of that." He kissed my forehead. "For both our sakes."

"I will," I said, hugging him. "But I'm afraid. You're right about me being affected. I felt like a different person, those few moments in the great room."

"Remember who you are, Oathed One, and be strong: the fearless woman I fell in love with. Remember that I love you—"

Titus and Terian reappeared. "It's time, Sar," Titus rumbled.

I hugged Danial again. "Can you please explain what's happened with Theo to Elle? She'll accept it easiest coming from you."

Danial nodded. "Of course. Go, Love. Call me when you can."

Titus picked up Theo's prone form, and Terian grabbed my hand. In an instant, we were inside my house. Ghost and Darkness went crazy yelping, snapping and snarling at Titus. I grabbed both of them, and hauled them by their collars out into the backyard.

"Where do you want him?" Titus said from the door.

I came back inside, as the dogs began to howl. "In the bedroom, quickly."

Terian squeezed my hand, then disappeared. Leaving the dogs outside, I followed after Titus into the bedroom.

Leaving Theo sprawled on the bed, Titus turned to me. "Good Luck."

"Will he be safe, when we wake up tomorrow? Could this happen again to him or to me, that a love spell might ensnare us?"

"No, not to either of you," Titus said seriously. "What I told everyone was true. You are going to be bound to each other. Whatever you feel for Danial or Devlin is going to be weakened and not by a little."

"Then why are you doing this?" I asked him. "This goes beyond you freeing him from a love spell, Titus. As far as I know, you and Theo aren't friends and from his tone, you two don't get along at all. You barely know me. Isn't Devlin your master? Shouldn't you be looking out for his interests?"

"I owe you for my son," he rumbled, his red eyes on mine. "You helped him, were a friend to him when no one else was. You helped him become what he is." He hugged me again, his heat almost suffocating. "You have his blood in you, Sarelle. My blood. We are kin now, according to demon custom. I am looking out for your interests, but I suggest you keep that to yourself."

Titus let me go. I stepped back, sweating. "Go," he rumbled gently. "Theo is waiting for you." Then he was gone, the blackness ebbing as if it had never been.

I took a deep breath, brought the dogs in, and then walked out onto the deck with them. It was dawn now, the edge of the sun peeking out from the horizon.

I watched the sunrise, my belly rumbling. When had I eaten last? Davy's? No, that couldn't be right. What day was it? Monday? No, it was Tuesday now.

My last meal had been the Chinese food yesterday at lunch. That had been less than twenty-four hours ago. God, it felt like weeks…

Ghost barked insistently, pawing at me.

"Yes," I said fondly. "Let's go have breakfast. Then we'll decide what to do."

* * * *

After breakfast, and building up the fire, I took another shower. I had blood, demon residue and dirt on me, and getting in a clean bed like that wasn't good. Afterwards, I dried off, conditioned my hair, and slipped into my blue velvet robe. Fastening my hair up with a clip, I went into the bedroom. Theo lay there, still dead to the world.

I didn't want to do this. The danger sense I'd always had was telling me not to, that dreaming again with him was just going to bring me more grief. There had to be another choice besides leaving Theo sleeping forever while I wiled away the hours with Devlin and Danial, or forgetting everything I'd promised them in favor of my "true love." I had to find a way to dream with

63

Theo and remember who I was, no matter how the spell affected me. I pondered the problem for a while, then reluctantly took the only precaution I could.

Taking some paper and a pen, I wrote out five sheets of paper, detailing the day's events, my fears of forgetting my Oath, my blissful (and fearful) memories of Devlin this past weekend, and Danial's devotion and despair at possibly losing me again. I tucked them into my magical box with Devlin's poetry, and replaced it in my drawer, putting Danial's choker inside, also. It quickly winked out of sight.

Resigned, I went into the bedroom, and lay down near Theo. Sleep didn't come even though I was exhausted. Near ten, I finally took a sleeping pill, praying it would ward off any dreams.

# Chapter Seven

I expected the same scene from my previous dream of our encounter on New Year's Eve long ago. Instead, I dreamed again of Theo being hit by a car, of screaming as he died in my arms. But this time I awoke within the dream, Theo holding me. Our eyes met, and then he was kissing me, tears running freely from his eyes. "I'm here," he said, his voice breaking. "I'm here, Sar. I'm so sorry for everything—"

I cried out wordlessly, and pulled him down on top of me. He was kissing me, we were both crying, and I was trying to get his clothes off. He was trying to help me, but we were both too upset, and it took much longer than it should've. Finally, he was naked, his body against mine, and I cried out in pleasure just feeling him touch me.

"Sar," he said raggedly, yearning. "Sar, please, Sar, please let me—"

I spread my legs and he thrust inside eagerly, both of us letting out a cry. There was nothing but him, being with him in this moment, a moment I'd thought would never come again. We came together, screaming out utter release of finally being together once more.

He pulled back from me. "Forgive me, please," he asked, tears in his eyes. "The things I said to you, the things I did, the way I acted—"

"I forgive you it all," I said, kissing his cheeks, his eyes. "You were under Tasha's spell. You had no choice—"

"I couldn't stop myself," he said bitterly. "I never loved her, never, Sar. After we slept together that first night, she told me she loved me. Told me I was her first, though by then I'd guessed that. I told her I was sorry, that I hadn't meant to hurt her, but I couldn't stay with her, that I had to get back to Elle and you. She cried for a long time, and I felt terrible, even as I made preparations to leave the next evening."

"Tasha came to me that afternoon, told me she wanted one last time before I left. I should've known something was off. Women never switch from tears to horniness that fast—"

"Hey," I said, irritated. "Sometimes a woman has to take what she can get when she can get it."

My words didn't stop the onslaught of his confession. "That afternoon we drank a bottle of wine together. By the next morning, I was head over heels for her. God, I was so fucking stupid—!"

"What about Aspen?"

"When she showed up that night at my door, I thought she was Tasha. I couldn't stay away from her, not that I tried." He took my hand. "You were right about what you said all those times: I used her for sex. I'm ashamed of how I treated her, and you."

"There wasn't anything you could've done," I said, hugging him. "But I appreciate the apology."

"Did you really Oath to Devlin?" Theo asked. "You're still wearing his choker. It was a farce somehow, wasn't it?"

"No," I said regretfully. "It wasn't. Devlin included you, Theo."

"Not what I expected," Theo said after a moment. "He's never liked me."

"He still doesn't. He just didn't want the Oath broken under any circumstances. He still wants his child, no matter what."

Theo gaped at me, floored. "Are you pregnant?"

"I don't know," I said, shrugging. "I could be. He's on the potion."

"I thought he felt warm when he was holding me," Theo sighed, rubbing his eyes. "I'd hoped I'd imagined it." He looked over at me. "How did you and he get together, anyway? I thought you were scared of him. Was it when you were in the hotel together, after he saved you from Al?"

I nodded. "He was the man I described to Carol. He saved me for himself, Theo. I was afraid to tell you, and have you kill him."

He said nothing for some moments. "Tell me everything, Sar," he said finally. "Start from when you were abducted. Don't leave anything out."

I told him everything, starting with what had really happened that day in the hotel to when Devlin had left me last night, after making me repeat my promise. The longer I went on, the angrier Theo became. When I finished, Theo pulled me into his arms, and hugged me.

"I'm going to kill that fucking bastard if it's the last thing I do."

I swallowed hard. "I'm sorry, Theo."

"It wasn't your fault, none of it," Theo growled softly, his arms tight around me. "Just because you find someone sexy and fantasize doesn't make it okay for them to take away your choices. He came to you under the guise of a friend, then betrayed you. Then he used the Vampire Gathering to put him in a position to get what he's wanted all along."

I eased out of his arms, irked. "Without his help a few days ago, I wouldn't be with you now. I'd be somewhere with Perseus or perhaps Samuel, waiting to be their... um, brood mare. And you'd be dead. That could still happen, if Dev broke our Oathing."

Theo swore and closed his eyes. "There has to be a way out. We just have to find it."

"There isn't."

"Tell me something," he said hoarsely. "Did you go to him again, after that day in the hotel? Did you continue seeing him during the Fall?"

"He was in Rio—"

"And Titus can teleport him anywhere in a second. Answer me."

"No," I admitted. "I told him that I loved you, that he should forget me."

"But he didn't give up," Theo said hatefully. "The bastard."

"He'll never give up," I said tiredly. "I'm his."

"You aren't, you're mine."

"I've got his marks on my throat, his choker on my neck, and his symbol under my skin—"

"Where?" Theo roared, throwing back the covers.

I cringed back, tears escaping my eyes.

"I'm sorry," he said quickly. "But I didn't see any tattoos. Is it on your back?"

"No." I rolled over, and showed him the bear on my hip.

He looked at it, then shut his eyes as if in pain.

I sat up and took his hand. "I'm sorry."

Theo hugged me. "I'm not angry at you, I'm pissed at him. You just did what you had to, Sar. God, I am going to beat Devlin into a pulp at the first opportunity."

"You'll do nothing of the kind," I said sharply. "He's looking for an excuse to kill you. He wanted to kill you last night. So does Lash."

"What do you expect me to do?" Theo said, exasperated. "I'm a man. I'm angry, and I've got to hit something. I'd prefer it was Devlin."

I didn't reply, my thoughts centered on my emotions. I'd expected to dream with Theo, and wake up entranced with love. Instead, I felt like my normal self, my desire for Devlin emerging the instant I heard his name spoken. How could that be?

"They can take your blood, and give you theirs, when you need it," Theo said grudgingly. "But that's all of you I'm sharing with them, Sar."

Try to be calm and rational. "I made a vow, Theo. I have to honor it."

"Your vow was to me," Theo said flatly. "You're my wife."

"We're separated," I shot back. "I'm not your wife anymore. What I am is

Devlin's and Danial's Oathed One. You can either be a part of that, or not."

Theo didn't reply.

"I'm sorry to be so harsh," I said quietly. "But those are the facts. I can't promise to be your one and only, Theo. You were always honest with me. I'm being honest with you."

"I'll work something out with Devlin," Theo said finally. "There has to be something else he wants more than you. He's a playboy, Sar, women are objects to him. Now that he's bedded you a few times already, he'll lose interest, if I can make the deal sweet enough—"

"He won't," I interrupted. "He wants—"

"Danial, I can talk to," Theo continued, talking over me. "He'll understand about the love spell's effects. And as for being separated, we'll call the lawyers and cancel it." He began kissing me.

"He won't, either—"

Theo silenced me with a kiss. "Shh," he said tenderly. "I have something to tell you that's way overdue." He paused, then said:

"The strength of the oak makes the tempest a mock,

The anchor holds firm in the hurricane's shock,

Our love is the anchor, the oak, and the rock.

I love you."

I stared at him, touched but also unnerved. His poem was so out of character for him that it brought thoughts of Devlin. "What?"

"It's from a poem, called Husband and Wife," Theo said a little shyly. "I'd planned to say that when I got down on my knees to propose, years ago. With me being taken and all that happened, I never said it." He clasped my hand in his and kissed it. "It means more saying it to you now after all we've gone through."

I fell apart and began weeping. "I love you so much—"

"Then it's probably a good idea if we stay married," he said, smiling down at me. "Now come here. We've wasted enough of this dream talking."

I kissed him hard, reaching down to grasp his stiff penis in my hand. He arched his back, groaning as he thrust up, then quickly sat my hips on his, pushing up into me.

Theo rocked me on him, groaning rhythmically, his hands sliding up my skin. Suddenly, he pulled me down on him, kissing my breasts, licking my taut nipples before taking them in his mouth to suckle eagerly. I moaned louder and louder, clasping his head in my hands, my climax building steadily.

Theo pushed back slightly without missing a beat. "Open your eyes," he grunted. "Look at me, Wife. Look down at me."

The need built, then burst. With a shout, my eyes opened, taking in Theo, his eyes midnight blue with desire. He roared, our bodies meshing in slippery sweat as we came together.

I lay grasping him, gasping. He was everything, all I wanted, all that there was.

He groaned, then kissed me again. With deft hands, he rolled over on me, our bodies still attached, and began again.

We made love over and over, almost frantically, coating ourselves in sweat and secretions. When my endurance gave out hours later, he laid me back on the bed and just kissed me. "I don't want to stop touching you, Sar."

I let out satisfied sigh. "Please don't, then."

A dark shadow fell over us suddenly. Theo stopped, his arms tightening around me. "It's nightfall," he said urgently. "The dream's ending. Quick, where are you? I'll get to you faster if I know."

I touched his cheek gently. "You are sleeping by my side, Theo, in our bed."

"God, that's a relief," he said happily, letting out a breath. "It drove me crazy those other times, waking up alone."

"Hold me tight," I said fearfully, "It's about to end."

As the dream faded, his arms around me did not. In the dim light, we gazed at each other in happiness. Then our eyes widened.

"What the hell?"

The room reeked of sexual excitement, as expected. But this time, it also reeked of sex. Theo and I were covered in sweat, my hair damp, his wet, the bed spotted with secretions from the both of us.

"We did in real life what we did together in the dream," Theo said, bewildered.

Apprehensive, I reached down between my legs, and felt the sticky wetness of semen.

We hadn't used any protection. I was off the pill. Oh, shit.

I ran to the bathroom, shut the door, and sat on the toilet.

"Sar?" Theo said, worried. "Sar!"

"I'm okay," I called back tearfully. "Just give me a minute."

*What should I do?* The easiest would be to call Camlyn for a morning-after pill. But if Devlin had gotten me pregnant by some incredible odds, that would abort the baby. I couldn't do that, not if there was any chance…

"What's the matter?" Theo said, more worried. The door began to open.

"Stay out there!" I screamed at him.

Theo came in the bathroom, then crossed to me. "Why are you upset?"

"Because we didn't use anything," I said tearfully. "Devlin's going to hit the roof if you've gotten me pregnant."

Theo hugged me, but didn't speak.

"I didn't know we'd actually have sex," I said, crying. "This never happened before."

"We were always separate before," Theo said softly. "Maybe this is what was always meant to happen."

I didn't answer, still crying.

Theo pulled off the top and bottom bed sheets, threw them into the bathroom hamper, and laid down some towels. "Come here, Sar. Crying isn't going to help what happened."

I wiped my eyes angrily. "Neither is getting back into bed with you again." I washed up, then left the room, shutting the door behind me. After letting the dogs out, I brought them into the basement with me, knowing they'd wake me if Theo tried to enter.

* * * *

The phone rang. Groggily, I looked at the clock. *Seven in the morning...*

At once, the events last night crashed down on me like lead weight. *God, what was I going to do?*

There was a knock at the door. "Sar, Danial's on the phone."

"Tell him I'll call him back," I called.

Theo opened the door, then handed me the phone. "He insists." He turned and left, stomping back up the stairs.

Theo was obviously upset, but I could only deal with one crisis at a time. "Hello?"

"How was Theo?" Danial teased. "As you remembered?"

I didn't answer.

"Sar? Are you there?"

"We talked about secrets," I said haltingly. "I told him everything—"

"Danial knew everything?" Theo griped angrily from the other extension. "You told him and not me? Jesus Christ, Sar, you're supposed to tell *me*, not *him*—!"

"I hear you're not finished talking, so I'll let you go," Danial said, laughing. "I won't expect to see you for a few days, either of you." He hung up.

I turned the phone off, just as Theo stomped back downstairs. Ghost and Darkness growled at him.

"I'm gone for a week and I'm forgotten," Theo said wryly, deep hurt in each word. "They don't growl at Devlin, do they?"

I didn't answer.

Theo walked past the growling dogs, then sat on the bed and took my hand. "Talk to me, Sar. Things are never going to be better than they are now

70

between us, unless you talk to me."

"There's nothing to say," I said with a shrug.

"Why did you tell Danial, and not tell me?"

"He can hear it in my voice," I replied. "He knows me better than anyone else, Theo, and he's a four hundred year old detective. There wasn't any way to hide it, though I tried."

Theo looked at me, storm cloud eyes serious. "From now on, Sar, you are to talk to me, before you tell anyone else your troubles, including Danial," he said firmly. "I'm your husband. No secrets between us, ever, not for any reason. I need to know your fears and feelings before you go around telling other men, even if you love them, too."

"I'm not your wife now," I said tiredly, "Even if I was then."

"Don't argue. Just agree that you'll do that for me, please."

"I agree," I said softly. "No more secrets."

"Good. Now come with me," he said, taking my hand. "We've hungry cats to feed."

At once, I thought of Phantom, wondering if Devlin was feeding him happily, and having no idea my actions might have shot all our plans all to hell. Tears again flooded my eyes.

Theo picked me up in his arms, then brought me upstairs. He'd remade the bed, and put me down on it. "You stay here, I'll feed the pets." He left.

I sat there for a moment, then turned on the shower. "Damn it, I should've done this last night." Quickly, I got into the cold water, and began to scrub myself clean. When I emerged, Theo was waiting for me in jeans.

"Couldn't wait to wash my scent off you," he said bitterly. "Could you?"

"I told you, I'm worried I'm pregnant—"

"You can always have an abortion," Theo said harshly. "If it's mine, that is. I'm sure you want Devlin's baby."

I stared at him, aghast, then my legs buckled. Theo moved fast, catching me before I hit the floor.

"You'd better lie down," he said worriedly. "Are you dizzy? I've never known you to faint before."

"I never have," I said weakly. "I'm just weak because I haven't eaten."

"Let me fix you some cereal," he said, pulling the comforter over me. "I'll be right back."

"Why are you being so nice?" I whispered. "You just accused me of...of—"

"I'm sorry," Theo said, pushing hair back from my face. "I get why you're upset. It's just that you know I wanted us to have one. Now that we're back together, I can't help hoping we can." He got up and left, returning quickly with a bowl of cereal on a tray. "Do you want some toast?"

"Are you cooking?" I asked wryly.

"I can make breakfast," Theo said defensively. "I'm out of practice, but I can make bacon, eggs, and toast. Pancakes, too, if I use a mix."

I began to eat, resisting the urge to cringe at the idea of boxed pancakes. "This is fine. I'm more tired than anything else."

"Me, too," Theo sighed, stretching out on the bed beside me. "I'm worn out."

"That's a new one," I teased, putting aside the tray.

He gave me a hungry look. "That doesn't mean I'm out of commission," he growled. Effortlessly, he pulled me into his arms, then began sliding his hands down my body.

"Stop," I said sharply. "We can't."

"What do you think might happen that already hasn't?" he asked, kissing my cheeks. "Or is it just that you don't want me in the real world anymore?"

I didn't answer.

Theo hugged me. "Please answer me, Sar. I can't fix whatever's wrong between us if you won't talk to me."

"There isn't any fixing it," I said hopelessly. "You know Devlin's got a year to make me pregnant. Like you said in the dream, he's wanted this for a while. He's going to be angry. If that wasn't enough, Samuel and the other Rulers will be, too."

"Sar, you know if we'd been awake, I'd have used protection," Theo said soothingly. "I've never refused to, even when I didn't want to. I'm sorry I put you in this position. I wouldn't have, if I'd had any choice."

"Titus said he was looking out for my interests," I said bitterly. "But he never warned me this could happen."

"Demons aren't the most trustworthy people, as a rule," Theo replied. "I'm still surprised he freed me."

"I just don't know what to do," I said wearily.

"That's because you're exhausted," Theo said, tucking the comforter around me. "Get some rest." He got up, and pulled on a shirt.

"Where are you going?"

"The dogs need a walk, and so do I." He walked out, closing the door gently behind him.

I sat there for many minutes, wanting to call Devlin and admit what had happened. But what if he became enraged, and sent Lash to kill Theo? What if he demanded I take a morning-after pill?

I'd never thought of abortion before, never been in a position to even contemplate having one. My beliefs—that 'til now had been vague at best—

were going to have to define themselves clearly by the end of today. Only one thing was clear: I couldn't tell Devlin or Danial what had happened until I made my decision.

\* \* \* \*

When I awoke, it was nearly noon. I was still alone. And ravenous.

I got dressed, then went looking for Theo. He was watching TV, with Ghost lying on one side of him and Darkness on the other.

"Good morning, Sleeping Beauty," he said, flashing me a smile.

"Hi," I said uneasily.

"We made up, as you can see," he said, scratching Darkness under her chin. She bared her teeth in a wide smile, her eyes closed.

"That's good," I said, washing my hands in the sink. "Are you hungry?"

"Are you cooking?" Theo asked eagerly.

"Feel like pizza? I could make some dough."

"I'd love that," Theo said, coming to stand behind me at the sink. "But are you sure you feel okay? You slept a long time."

I turned my head, giving him an odd look. "Just until noon."

"That was yesterday morning," Theo said, concerned. "It's Thursday afternoon."

I gaped at him. "It can't be."

He showed me the TV's digital guide. It was indeed Thursday afternoon.

I held onto the sink, my legs weak again. "God, what's happening to me?"

Theo hugged me. "You're fine, Sar. You just went through an ordeal these past weeks. You were sick—"

I pushed him away gently. "I was fine after Devlin healed me, better than fine. Now I feel weak again."

"You need to eat something," Theo said with authority. "Go ahead and make the pizza if you want to, but I'll make you a sandwich in the meantime."

I nodded. "Okay."

Theo was right. After devouring not one but two sandwiches, I felt much better. The savory smell of cooking pizza also added to my good mood.

Theo took my plate. "Can we talk now?"

I nodded.

"Sar, don't worry," Theo said confidently. "I'll talk to Devlin. I'll work something out." He took my hand. "I was worried when you went to Hayden. Was everything...you, um, had a good time?" He winced.

I rubbed my eyes. "He was moody, but it was fine."

"Are you telling me the truth?" he said, making me look him in the eyes. "Remember, no secrets."

"He hurt me, then healed me," I said flatly. "He scared me, then acted loving. Yet I didn't want to leave him, when it was time."

"That's an effect of his blood," Theo said.

"I know that," I said, irked again.

The stove buzzer went off. Glad to be interrupted, I got up and took the pizza out of the oven.

"We're not done talking," Theo said stubbornly. "Come back and sit down."

More irked, I went back to the couch and sat down.

"I've thought about what to do, and I think the best plan is to pretend we didn't have sex during the dream," Theo said. "I'll use protection from now on."

"And what if you got me pregnant?" I said angrily.

"Unless you want to get one of those abortion pills, you don't have any choice," Theo retorted. "Most likely with everything you went through, neither Devlin or I got you pregnant. It was one night, Sar. Could it have happened, sure, but we're not going to be able to tell for at least a few weeks if you're pregnant. It'll take longer than that to tell who the father is."

That was a relief to hear, as it was logical. "Say we do that. Then what?"

"You keep trying with him, and I'll use protection," Theo said bitterly. "We'll do that until I can find a way to get him to release you."

I got up, and began cutting the pizza. "You told me you wanted me to be honest. Well, I'm telling you Devlin is not ever going to release me, no matter what you do."

Theo sighed, but didn't reply.

We were just finishing the pizza when the phone rang.

"If that's Devlin, hand me the phone," Theo said in a steely tone.

I got up, and picked up the phone. "Hello?"

"Sar," Devlin purred. "How is it having Theo to yourself again?"

*What was I supposed to say that wouldn't anger either Theo or Devlin?* "I'm getting used to it," I said finally.

"I'm glad you're content with his prowess," Devlin said coolly. "I want to see you this Friday, as I told you previously. Get here at dusk tomorrow, or before."

"Give me the phone, Sar," Theo growled.

"I'll be there, Dev. Theo wants to talk to you," I said uneasily.

"About what?" Devlin said curiously. "There is nothing for us to talk about."

Theo picked up the other extension in the living room, and put it to his ear. "There is something to talk about. I want to cut a deal with you, Devlin."

74

"What kind of deal?"

"I know what you did to Sar," Theo growled, furious. "She told me everything. I'm grateful you saved her life, but your sexual relationship with her ends here. She is not coming to you Friday."

Devlin laughed luxuriantly, sending chills down my spine. "Who are you to tell me anything?" he purred. "I was loving women when your great-grandmother was not even born. I know what Sar likes and I'm going to give it to her on a regular basis, forever. We'll be copulating long after you are rotting in your grave—"

"You can give her enough of the virus in your bite, or by giving her your blood. I know you're Oathed. But that doesn't mean I'm letting you terrorize her. She says you hurt her the last time you had sex."

Devlin didn't answer. I felt instantly guilty for having told Theo what happened, but I couldn't apologize for the truth.

"I'm not saying that you can't have her blood. Danial can chaperone you, so you don't hurt her doing that. You don't need to—"

"It's true, I don't need to," Devlin said seductively. "But I want to, Theo. Moreover, I'm going to. Sar enjoyed our sex. If she told you otherwise, which I doubt, that's an effect of renewing your bond. Titus said she'd act oddly."

"Dev, you did scare me," I said gently. "You did hurt me, then heal me."

"I thought you understood that," Devlin said, taken aback. "I explained my actions."

"That didn't make them right," I said, uncomfortable. "But we can talk it over on Friday."

"Yes," Devlin agreed. "Of course, Love. I'm looking forward to seeing you."

"She isn't coming to you," Theo growled.

"Remember to stay off the pill," Devlin said to me, as if Theo hadn't spoken. "There is a good chance you could be pregnant, and I don't want you to miscarry." He turned menacing. "Theo, you had better be using protection with Sar or I'll geld you the next time I see you."

"Yes, I have been," Theo lied smoothly, his eyes on mine.

I looked back in shock. *When had he learned to lie that well?*

"But I'm not going to next time unless you promise not to hurt her," Theo growled.

"You will do it, or I'll send Lash for your head, end of discussion," Devlin snarled. "The same goes if you hinder her coming to me in any way, Cat."

Theo didn't respond; his eyes locked worriedly on mine.

"I don't hear you telling me your acquiescence," Devlin purred dangerously. "Lash is beside me, waiting for your answer."

"I'll do it," Theo growled. "For now."

"Good," Devlin said curtly. "Sar, I'll send someone for you Friday morning."

*Another ride with Lash. Ugh.* "You don't need to send anyone to bring me, Dev. I'll drive to you. I can leave about noon—"

"No, an escort is safer," Devlin replied. "I would send Titus to you, but he's busy fooling with that poison Danial let him have. Supposedly it's very potent."

He clearly wanted to use it on Theo. My expression turned to fear.

"Wear that silver colored sweater of yours for me," Devlin continued. "I liked it."

"All right," I whispered. "I will."

"Devlin," Theo said, desperate. "What would it take for you to leave Sar and I in peace? I know you don't care about money. But if you leave her alone, I'll do anything you want—"

"You'd work for me? Kill for me?" Devlin purred. "Anyone I asked you to?"

Theo looked at me for a long moment, his eyes emotional. "Yes."

"You do love her utterly," Devlin said with relish. "Because you know the type of kills I'd most enjoy having you make—"

Theo's patience snapped. "Just tell me who you want dead, damn you!"

"I have Lash for that!" Devlin snarled, enraged. "There is nothing, absolutely nothing you could offer me that would make me let her go!"

I recoiled back from their screaming voices. "Stop it!"

Devlin's rage turned to pleasure. "She is the only thing you have of value to me, Theo, the only thing. Much as I'd like to make you kill for me, it is nothing compared to being inside her, loving her as I drink from her—"

"You fucking bastard!" Theo spat back furiously. "I'm telling you, you aren't getting into our lives again!"

"I'll be getting into her this weekend, Theo, as deep as I want to," Devlin purred. "And there isn't a damn thing you can do to stop me."

Theo roared furiously into the phone, the volume deafening. "I'll kill you!"

"Sar," Devlin purred cruelly. "I think it's time Theo had a lesson. You remember how it was between us." He sighed in pleasure. "You said you loved hearing me come, that you wanted me more than you had ever wanted anyone. Let him hear from you how much you love me, how eager you are to be back in my arms again."

His voice enfolded me, bathing me in instant heat and wanting. "You know I do—" I whispered.

"But he needs to hear it, Love. I want him to hear it, to know that keeping us apart would hurt you as much as me. Say it for me, please."

Images flashed before my eyes of Devlin and I, of how much I'd wanted him, from the moment he'd come to me, of us making love, of him singing to me, or murmuring poetry, his golden eyes filled with desire. "I love you, Dev. And I will never stop wanting you, ever." I sank down onto the nearby couch, again unsteady.

"I hear it in your voice, Love," Devlin said lustily. "I am glad Titus's spell didn't affect your desire for me. Go, enjoy your kitten until we can be together again."

Theo growled hatefully. "I'll find some way to get her away from you, you son of a bitch, if it's the last thing I do."

Devlin gave a cruel and mocking laugh. "Don't you get it, Theo? Sar doesn't want to get away from me anymore. You are fighting a battle you can't win." His pleasure became a living, breathing thing. "The most delectable part, Theo, is that if you would have let Sar go to Danial in the fall, you would be sharing her with only him now. He probably would have agreed to an infrequent blood exchange, with a little sex thrown in here and there. But no, you couldn't stand the thought of she and him being together. You had to give her rules to follow, rules that almost killed her." He laughed triumphantly. "Look where your rules have gotten you, Theo: sharing the love of your life with not one, but two vampires!"

Theo was snarling in anger, his eyes yellow and slitted, his clawed hands scoring the phone. He was so livid he couldn't speak around his growing fangs.

"Dev, please stop," I said weakly. "Please."

"Only because you asked, Darling," Devlin purred. "Expect Lash on Friday afternoon, around noon." He hung up.

I returned the phone to its cradle. Theo slammed his back into its holder so hard I was surprised it didn't break.

I turned to him. "Can you live with this, with how our lives are going to have to be? I'll understand if you can't."

"I'm not leaving you," he said raggedly. "I'm not giving up on finding a way out of all this."

"I know what I said hurt you. But it's how I feel, Theo."

Theo walked over slowly, then sat heavily on the couch. "You've had his blood now, a lot of it," he said wearily. "It's not a surprise that you want him like you wanted Danial back in the fall."

I sat beside him. Oddly, my first desire was to comfort him. "What you said about him being a ladies' man was true; I saw the proof at his house. When he swore to me, he didn't swear exclusively." I paused, smarting at the memory. "He will probably break with me once he has his child. I don't know if he loves me, or if I just remind him strongly of a woman he loved years ago."

Theo nodded. "Annabelle. I know the story, and heard what he said about your blood being like hers."

I rubbed my eyes. "If more women were found with blood like mine, he probably wouldn't even be interested in me."

"No, he does care about you," Theo said, resigned. "He's done everything in his power to get you in thrall to him since the night he met you. It burned him that you wanted a life with me instead. I don't imagine he is a man who was ever jealous much."

Devlin had said something to that effect once. "You have to know something else, too: I wanted to leave you under the love spell, and not break it."

Theo gave me a look of incomprehension. "What? Why?"

"I thought that maybe with her you'd get the life you and I had talked about years ago. I wanted you to be happy, even if it wasn't with me."

"What?" he managed.

"I took you from your peaceful life in the West and dragged you back here into bloodletting, only to find out the life we wanted wasn't possible. I wanted you to have peace."

Theo reached out and hugged me. "Sar, what is a life like that worth without you to share it? I love you, only you. I want to be where you are, no matter where that is." He moved back slightly. "What I was doing out in Wyoming was temporary, not permanent. It would have only been a matter of time before someone came looking for me for revenge over someone I killed in the past or for the bounty that's on my head—"

"Danial mentioned that," I said, worried. "Is it because you're second now?"

"You might as well know now that there's more than one," he said tiredly. "There are at least two, besides this death threat now from Peterson. I'm planning on laying low and staying close to home for the next few months, around people I trust to watch my back." He took my hand in his. "I wanted a peaceful life for me and you, but I was dreaming, Sar. I can't quit, or just be a carpenter. I can't be anything other than what I am."

I hugged him. "I love who you are, the man you are. I don't want you to change."

His face broke into a smile. "So you still do love me."

"I always did," I said softly.

"Let's go for a walk together," he said, hugging me. "The dogs need it, and we could use the fresh air."

The dogs heard the "W" word immediately, and began barking and whining.

Theo and I got on our shoes and coats, then went outside, the dogs charging ahead of us through the snow as Theo slipped one of his guns into a side holster.

"Some of the snow's melted," I said, looking around. "It must have gotten warmer—"

There was a loud crash. Theo reacted, moving me smoothly behind him, his gun drawn.

I breathed a sigh of relief, and pointed. "No worries." A huge chunk of ice had fallen off the garage roof and hit the driveway, smashing into several pieces.

The rest of the walk was invigorating, but serene. We both threw snowballs for the dogs to catch, and Darkness rolled repeatedly in the snow, all her feet up in the air, until she was covered in it, white as Ghost.

"This feels like the calm before the storm," I said, apprehensive.

"It is," Theo said, slipping his arm around my shoulder. "Let's get back, it's getting dark."

We got back inside, stripped off our wet gear, and toweled off Ghost and Darkness. "I'm going to make some pasta," I said eagerly. "Sound good?"

"Sure," Theo replied. "While you do, I'm calling Dr. Camlyn to make you an appointment."

I turned to him. "For what? It's too early to know."

"It doesn't hurt to get an appointment on his books early."

I shot him an exasperated look. "I know you're eager for a baby. Why exactly is that, Theo? Children didn't matter to you only a few years ago."

"Because of Elle," he replied easily. "I want there to be a person that's part of you and me. I want us to make one together, and to raise him or her, to watch them get big. I used to look at her, and imagine that she was yours, Sar. That's why I gave her your name."

My heart softened. Maybe he wasn't the world's greatest father, but Theo had tried to do what was right by Elle. We'd almost missed out on a life together, and we'd found a second chance. *Should I deny him this, if I loved him? How many more chances was I going to get?*

I opened my mouth to tell him I'd have his baby, then closed it with a snap. That thought hadn't come from me, not the me I'd been this time last week.

"Sar?" Theo said, concerned. "What's wrong?"

"Go ahead and make the appointment," I said, turning back to the stove in disquiet. "I'll get the pasta boiling."

After dinner, we sat on the couch cuddling. "This is wonderful," I said contentedly. "I've missed spending time with you."

"I only wish you'd let us spend it watching something else," Theo griped. "This 'A-Team' is bullshit. They've made ten tactical errors in this episode alone. Also it's amazing how with all the gunfire and flipped cars, no one ever seems to die, or break their legs."

"It's family friendly," I said defensively.

The phone rang.

# Chapter Eight

"Don't answer it," Theo urged.

"It might be Elle." I got up, and went to the phone. "Hi, Danial."

"Sar," Danial said harshly. "Have Theo pick up the phone immediately."

Glad his tone wasn't for me, I handed the phone to Theo. "Danial for you."

Theo eyes went to slits. "Keep it, I'll get my own." He picked up the second extension. "I'm here," he said roughly. "What is it, Danial?"

"I just got off the phone with Devlin," Danial said icily. "You cannot deny him rights to Sar. You will have not only Perseus and Samuel after you and her, but the entire vampire community."

"I thought you of all people would understand that I don't want—"

"What you want is immaterial!" Danial snarled loudly, sounding just like Devlin. "This call is to inform you that I put up with your nonsense for years, and I won't any longer."

"What are you talking about?" Theo said, confused.

"You dictated what I could do with her and what I couldn't, how I could touch her, how much time she could spend with me alone—"

"In my position, you would have done the same," Theo growled.

"But no more," Danial went on as if he had not heard. "We are Oathed, Theo. I wanted to confirm her visit to me on Saturday. She and I spoke about it last weekend, when she was at Hayden. I want to make sure of the time she's arriving, so I can be here to welcome her."

The more he went on, the more upset I got. He was acting as Devlin had, more concerned with his rights to me than what I was comfortable with.

"—From my understanding, Devlin is expecting her on Friday, so there should be no problem—"

"There is a problem," Theo said coldly. "I'm her husband, and I say if she leaves or not. You and Devlin can't just call up whenever and demand she appear at your homes at a certain time. She's not a whore to come at your beck and call."

"Stop it," I said frantically. "I'd already agreed to go, Theo."

"You are not her husband anymore," Danial said, empathic yet firm. "You have no say in our arrangement. You're my friend, and I'm sorry to hurt you. But I love her, and I like spending time with her. Whether that time is in bed making love or not is entirely up to Sar. But you are not going to keep her from seeing me, not ever again."

Theo was silent.

"You must accept it," Danial said compassionately. "I know it's not what you wanted, but it's how things are. This situation is workable, if we do not constantly jostle one another for time, anyway."

"What are your terms?" Theo growled. "We've heard Devlin's already."

"Devlin has agreed to have Sar visit for just one day and night a week, as I have," Danial replied. "She'll remain at her house the other nights, or be wherever she wishes to go. It goes without saying you are always welcome here, Sar."

"Thank you," I said, feeling that some acknowledgement was necessary.

Theo was still silent.

"There is nowhere Devlin wouldn't find you, if you try to take her and run," Danial continued. "Don't enter into any foolish plan. Lash would track you down, kill you, and bring Sarelle back to Devlin."

Theo was still silent.

Danial went cold as ice. "Theo, if you try to turn Sar into a werecougar like yourself, it most likely wouldn't work—"

Theo started, his eyes sliding away from mine as he put his back to me. My eyes went wide in fear. That had been exactly what he had been thinking.

"—Even if you did manage to turn her, it wouldn't break our Oath. Devlin doesn't mind the taste of wereblood, though I'm sure Samuel would have you killed. But what should matter most to you is that Sar would hate you for doing that to her. If she wanted to be werecougar, she would have asked you by now to make her one, and she hasn't."

Theo didn't reply.

Danial sighed. "If you try to kill Dev, Lash will kill you for sure. Lash's older, he's more skilled, and he's faster than you are. Don't think because your status has changed to second in these past years that you are even close to his expertise. Remember the time he broke your neck—?"

"Danial, I can't do this," Theo whispered. "I can't be alone here all weekend, and think about her with you and him. I can't do that for the rest of my life—"

"How the hell do you think I feel right now?" Danial shouted loudly. "Knowing she's there with you, and dreamed with you again, and most likely loves you more than before?"

"Stop it," I said tearfully. "Please, stop it."

"I'm sorry for my outburst," Danial said instantly. "Please excuse me, Sweetheart. I didn't meant to upset you. If you wouldn't mind, hang up for now. I've got some things to talk over with Theo—"

"Say them," I said, weary but resolute. "I don't want to be left out of the decision process."

"Very well," Danial answered. "Theo, I leave you with this thought: it is better to have a little of something you love dearly than not to have it at all." He paused.

"What else?" Theo growled softly. "Say it."

"I have to inform you that I believe Devlin took Tasha, and gave her to Lash, as he wanted to. He wouldn't admit it, but she was gone this morning from the barracks. There was residue of demon teleportation."

"It may have been Titus," I whispered. "He wanted to kill her."

"Devlin's decisions command Titus's actions, Sar," Danial said carefully. "He gave the order. By now she is either dead, or wishing she was."

"Why would Lash want her?" I asked curiously. "I didn't understand that last night. He already has a...um, girlfriend."

No one answered me, something more frightening than talk of rape and torture.

"I'll call Devlin," Theo said gruffly. "Most likely, Lash found out who gave her the potion she used on me. I want to make sure it was Samuel."

"Fine, but don't antagonize Devlin further," Danial warned. "He'll kill you outright. It is only fear of angering Sar that stays his hand."

"I get it," Theo said gruffly. "I'll be nice."

"Sar, I talked to Elle, told her Theo is back with you. Though she's upset you took him back, I think she's happier, because she thinks things will go back to normal now." Danial paused. "She was upset that Devlin and you are together. I explained he had been a power to be reckoned with for many more years than I, that he had done terrible things, and had more respect from our peers than I did." Danial paused. "I'm not sure—"

"That's not important! Does she understand why I did what I did?" Theo asked loudly. "Did you tell her about the love potion?"

"She understands it wasn't your fault. She's angry at Tasha, not at you."

"Tell her I'm staying with Sar," Theo said, his eyes on me. "Tell her we are staying married. Ask her if she'd like to come here and spend this weekend with me."

"I think that would be good for everyone," Danial said in approval. "Hold on, I'll ask her."

"What are you doing?" I asked him, surprised.

Theo covered the receiver. "Danial's right. I need to accept this is how things are, at least for now. It will be good for me, and for Elle. We should spend more time together anyway, she won't be a child much longer."

"You know she's already wearing lipstick?" Danial said.

"What?" Theo roared. "She's only nine at the most!"

"Calm down," I soothed, going over to him. At once, the two phones began to give us feedback, being too close together. "Damn it—"

"I'm going to let you go," Danial said. "I've got a client on hold. Theo, Elle said yes, so expect her tomorrow morning sometime. Bring her back with you on Monday morning, if that's good for you."

"Yes," Theo said. "Bye." He hung up, took a deep breath, and then called Hayden.

Lash answered. "Dev's not here, Sar. Try back later."

"It's Theo, Lash."

"What do you want, Jerk?" Lash hissed.

"I need to talk to Devlin," Theo growled. "Put me—"

Lash hung up on him without another word. Theo roared in fury.

Irritated, I took the phone from him before he threw it, and dialed Devlin's cell. He answered on the first ring. "What is it, Sar?"

"Danial said you took Tasha. I need to know if you did, and if she's dead."

He was quiet for a moment, certainly thinking of a way to answer and still make himself look good. "I'll give you to Lash, so he can tell you—"

"No," I said firmly. "He can lie to me easily. You promised to tell me the truth. Now answer me."

"Yes, I took her," Devlin admitted. "She caused you a lot of misery. I also wanted to know exactly who gave her the potion she used on Theo. It doesn't matter if you hate me for it, because you still—"

"What you did was probably best, Dev," I interrupted. Out of the corner of my eye, I saw Theo pick up the other phone quietly. "What did she say?"

"She said that a man cloaked in grey came to her a week after Theo arrived. He told her what Theo was, though she didn't believe him. He gave her a number, and told her to call when she found out the truth. A month later, she saw Theo change into human form. She liked him on sight, but was young and shy. It took her a few weeks to muster up her courage to ask him if he wanted her. After a night with him, she knew she loved him. When she told him, he said he said had to leave as soon as he was healed enough, and it broke her heart. Who would have ever figured you for a heartbreaker, Theo?"

Theo growled softly.

"I knew you have to be at least decent in bed, or Sar wouldn't have wanted you back—"

"Leave the taunts aside, Dev," I said. "I know all this from Theo. Who gave her the spell?"

"I'm telling the story." Devlin cleared his throat, and started again. "Tasha called the man, and told him what had happened. He told her she needed to use a spell called Heart's Solace, that otherwise Theo would leave, and if he left, he would be killed by the people who had given him the injuries he'd arrived with."

"Clever," Theo said coldly. "She was naive enough to believe anything he said, as he knew she would be. She never questioned why he was willing to help her, or who he was, or that he showed up just when she was in most need of his help."

"She had another reason, too, Theo," Devlin said, his tone lilting. "As you found out later, she was to be married soon, to a man of her father's choosing. She hated him. She knew if she took a lover, and her betrothed found out she wasn't a virgin, he wouldn't want her."

"Is that what she said happened, after I left her?" Theo asked, embarrassed.

"She apparently told her fiancé, and he refused to marry her. It took her father a year to find another suitor for her, and by then, she had given up hope of you coming back. She thought you had gone back to Sar, which you had."

"We know all this," I said loudly, very annoyed. "Get to the point, Dev."

"How did she get another potion to put in the letter she wrote to me?" Theo asked, confused. "And why wait so long to send it?"

"That is the crux," Devlin said triumphantly. "The same man who'd appeared so mysteriously before appeared again this past November, saying there was one last chance. He gave her another potion, showed her what needed to be done, and gave her Danial's contact info, so she could contact you, Theo." He paused. "This time, the man didn't hide his appearance in a cloak."

"What did she describe the man looking like?" Theo asked.

"Old, thick white hair, short, hazel eyes, crackly voice, dressed in expensive clothes with an air of power. He used a cane with a dragon's head, made of crystal. Sound like anyone you know, Theo?"

Theo roared in fury, and crushed the phone in his hands, shattering it. He scowled, tossed the remains in the garbage, and stalked out of the room.

"Who was it?" I asked.

"By the description she gave, it had to be Cyrus, Samuel's magician," Devlin said.

Theo picked up the bedroom phone. "Samuel's watchdog, Cyrus," he growled. "I saw him at the gathering. He was standing behind Samuel during the face-off, Sar. He's the one who told Samuel that you and Devlin spoke the truth, that you were Oathed."

I remembered the aged voice that had answered Samuel's repeated question. "What are we going to do, Dev? I don't want any more spells cast on Theo or me."

"I have taken care of it, Sar," Devlin said smoothly. "I called Samuel an hour ago, told him I knew what had happened, and that if you miscarried our child because of his actions toward Theo, I'd consider it an act of war. He agreed to leave Theo alone, and sends his best wishes for your good health."

"How did you manage that?" Theo said bluntly. "You had to tell him we're back together, and he must have been pissed, to say the least."

"He does not mind if you bed her, just if you get her pregnant. You know me, Theo, just like he does. All I had to say was I had asked you into our bed."

God, had all those supplies in Devlin's bathroom been for men *and* women? I was afraid to ask. "Why is he being so agreeable, after all his dictates to me on New Year's Eve?"

"Mostly because of his newly acquired woman, Harriet," Devlin answered. "She is like you, Sar. Samuel and Perseus have given her a demon's blood, and are waiting for her blood to turn summer-like. As soon as it does, they are going to start trying with her for their own dhamphir."

*Ugh.* "Wasn't she with someone else? The man who, um, outed her that night?"

"Probably," Devlin replied. "But that doesn't matter; she is theirs now. She has Oathed to both of them, so you can be assured of their commitment to her."

"But she had no choice—"

"Better her than you, Sar," Devlin said sharply.

*Put that way...Hell, yes.* "Thanks for contacting him, and straightening this all out."

"Thank you," Theo echoed me.

"You are most welcome, Love," Devlin purred. "I want you to be calm, and it would not be good for our baby if you were worried or anxious—"

Theo growled again into the phone.

"Cougar, stop making noise, or get off the phone. I—"

"Devlin, I need to know. Is she dead?" I interrupted. "Tasha?"

"Yes," Devlin said bluntly. "After Lash extracted all the information he could from her, I drained her."

I was repulsed, then told myself to grow up. The only reason I felt any different about this versus what Theo had done to Manir was because Tasha was a woman. Manir had likely suffered much more than Tasha had.

"It's better this way," Devlin persisted. "You don't render your enemies harmless, you kill them, because there is always a motive for revenge otherwise."

"He's right," Theo said brokenly, wiping his face.

He was crying for Tasha. Maybe some residue of the spell on him was the culprit. Or maybe even magic love couldn't be erased completely.

"Oathed One?" Devlin said.

"I'm not angry, Dev," I said tiredly. "I killed Monica for less."

"Go rest, Love," Devlin replied tenderly. "Take it easy. Don't think about all the bad things that have happened. You are well again. Theo can keep you entertained until we meet again."

"Thank you," Theo said grudgingly. "Thank Titus for me as well."

"You are calmer, Theo," Devlin said thoughtfully. "Have you accepted how things are?"

"I hate it," Theo said angrily. "But I'm not suicidal. Lash won't find me in his way tomorrow."

"Good," Devlin said in approval. "I need to get back to business. Adieu."

Later that night, I lie in bed next to Theo, unable to sleep.

I didn't know if I should hope to be pregnant or not, and if yes, whose child to want more. Either way, I would have a new set of problems.

The best thing was to get more information. To do that, I'd have to bring my doctor into my confidence.

\* \* \* \*

The next morning, I called asking to speak to Dr. Camlyn. Stephen came on the phone immediately.

"I've heard about what happened at the Vampire Gathering, and also with Devlin," he said sadly. "I'm sorry that I didn't recognize what was happening to you." He paused. "You have every right to sue, or if you settle on a figure, I can have my lawyer—"

"As much as I'd love a windfall, you had no way to know," I interrupted. "I know you, Stephen. You've never have put me in danger knowingly."

"I'm glad you feel that way," he said, very relieved. "I'd been told you'd booked an appointment yesterday. I'd hoped it was a sign you weren't holding me liable. When Devlin called to announce that I'd be handling another dhamphir pregnancy soon, I—"

"That's what I made the appointment for. I need to know if I'm pregnant."

"There's no hurry, especially given the previous documented duration of insemination needed for a dhamphir pregnancy. Don't come in until you miss a period."

I floundered, then said, "I can't wait. I have to know."

"Sar, you've had a child successfully. Having another will be easier, despite the nature of the pregnancy. Now that we know what to expect with a dhamphir—"

"I may be pregnant with Theo's child."

"Devlin said you wouldn't be unprotected with anyone but him," Stephen said, confused. "Did the condom break?"

*God, thank you for that lifesaver.* "Yes. Two did, the second at the critical moment. We tossed the rest and started a new box. It must have been a defective package."

"You were on the pill for months," he mused. "You've only been off about a week. Was it only that time?"

"Yes. I thought maybe I should come to you and get a prescription for a morning after pill, but I was worried I might already be pregnant by Devlin." I paused. "We've only been together one night, but it was multiple times. Medically, what are my chances of being pregnant by him? I know that the spell he used was a different one, that you confirmed his fertility."

"Sar, considering what you've told me, in my experience, you are almost certainly not pregnant," Stephen said after a pause. "The spell Devlin used was a potent one, and he was 100% fertile just twenty-four hours after taking it. But pregnancy depends more on your body than his, like it always does with any male and female trying to conceive. The same goes for your accident with Theo."

"What do I do?"

Stephen sighed. "Do what I said. Call me if you miss a period, or if you have any other symptoms of pregnancy: nausea, cravings, or that Lust you had last time. It's too early to tell if you're pregnant." He paused. "I also have to advise you of a medical law that affects your situation. I understand you are Oathed again to both Danial and Devlin. By vampire law, as your doctor, I must inform them both of your health status after every visit with me, if they do not accompany you to the actual clinic. Both Danial and Devlin called to remind me of this law very early today. Since you didn't come in to ask me this question, I won't be notifying them of this." He paused. "If I were to treat you and not notify them, I could lose my license. Please, be careful."

He was saying that if I came to him for a prescription for the morning-after pill, he would have to report that to Devlin. "Thank you for telling me," I whispered. "I didn't know that."

"I'll write you out a prescription for prenatal vitamins, and put it in the mail for you today. If you aren't pregnant, it won't hurt you. If you are, with either kind of child, they'll help to keep you strong."

"Are there any restrictions?" I asked. "I can limit myself to one glass of wine."

"Don't have any rough sex with anyone," Stephen replied. "Don't drink more than a glass of wine at most. You already don't smoke. As for blood donation, keep it at a minimum. Devlin assures me he has knowledge about that. As much as I know his history, he brought you back to good health, so his advice has merit. Take it."

"Thanks," I said. "I will. Bye."

I put the phone back, and got a glass of wine, though it was only about three o'clock. *Thank God, Stephen had told me about that law...*

Theo came in and saw me drinking. "What happened?"

I relayed the conversation to him as I sipped my wine. "I needed a drink after that. Thank goodness I called and didn't go there to see him."

"That law's in place to help Oathed Ones, not hurt," Theo replied. "Danial used it not long ago against a vampire in Buffalo who drained his Oathed One, then claimed it was an accident because he didn't know she was anemic—"

"Be that as it may, the law complicates things," I interrupted.

"If you somehow are pregnant, either way, we'll have to tell Devlin," Theo said firmly. "There isn't anything complicated about it."

"That's easy to say," I replied, upset. "It's going to be a lot harder to do."

\* \* \* \*

I opened my eyes and yawned. Then I looked at Theo beside me, and everything came flooding back.

I'd see Devlin tonight, maybe sooner if Lash really came to pick me up at noon instead of five. God, I wanted him. It felt like weeks since I'd last kissed him, or heard his beautiful voice sing to me. Maybe he was in his bed, wanting me like I wanted him. I should go to him now, drive there this morning. If he wasn't there, I could wait for him. As he opened the bedroom door, I could be there in his bed, naked and beckoning wantonly...

A hand brushed me lightly as Theo turned over beside me, snoring softly.

Shame flooded me. What kind of life was I offering him? This wasn't fair to anyone, but it was most unfair to him. He deserved to be happy.

"I'm sorry," I whispered, smoothing his hair back from his brow. "I'm sorry."

"Don't be," he said, opening his storm cloud eyes. "Don't be sorry for anything. We've got each other, and that's all that matters."

"I have to leave tonight," I said, touching his chest tentatively. "Make love with me?"

He brought me into his arms, and began kissing me. First, the kisses were soft, and gentle, then rough and passionate. Breaking away, he rummaged in the nightstand drawer, quickly put on a condom, then rolled on top of me. With an eager moan, he slipped inside, already moving fast. I moved with him enthusiastically, writhing beneath him, crying out repeatedly. The sensation was undeniable, and it washed over us both as one, our screams blending together in raucous harmony as we spent ourselves.

Theo stopped jerking, then moved back from me, peeling off the condom. He threw it away, then spooned me. "That was wonderful," he said, sated. "I worried you were afraid to be with me, or something."

"I don't know what I was worried about," I said vaguely, snuggling into him. "At this moment, it's not important."

"No, it's not," he said lovingly, hugging me next to him.

* * * *

After a large breakfast of at least a thousand calories each, Theo and I arrived in the great room at Danial's house. No one was around.

I walked to Danial's door and knocked. He didn't answer.

Theo called out "Danial?"

"We're in here," Elle called out.

Theo and I went into her room. Danial, Elle and Theoron were lying on her bed watching the end of 'The Last Unicorn'.

"Mommy!" Theoron shrieked.

I picked him up, marveling at his size. He'd looked close to two years old before, and now he looked easily five years old. "You're big," I managed.

He looked at me and smiled. "I'm growing fast now, Mom. Tears says that I'll be as tall as Elle in a month."

His verbal communication was flawless. I was stunned speechless.

Seeing my upset, Danial came over to me. "Terian said that Theoron is going to grow faster now, Sar. He may well be an adult in December."

*Remain calm, or you'll scare the kids.* I eased myself quickly down onto the bed. "Why is that, Danial?"

"Can we see a movie today?" Elle asked suddenly. "Please?"

"I want to see one, too!" Theoron shouted. Instantly, his eyes bled to red, and his fangs descended.

"Theoron, control yourself," Danial said gently.

Theoron looked at his father, and took a deep breath, his eyes going back to their dark green as his fangs receded. "I want to go," Theoron said firmly. "I never get to go anywhere."

"You can't go with them," Danial said gently. "Not today."

"Danial," Theo said. "Why don't we all see that movie together? Elle and I can meet you and Sar and Theoron tomorrow night. If Terian comes, we'll have plenty of guards."

Danial looked at Theo in surprise. "That would be great," he answered. "I want to start taking him outside the grounds now that he's older."

"I'm hungry!" Elle said loudly and meaningfully.

I turned to her. "Go get your bag, and don't be rude. We're leaving shortly."

Elle scrambled to get her bag, then ran out the door, Theo following.

"I'll see you Saturday," Danial said. He drew me to him, kissing me lingeringly. "Have a good time today and tonight."

"Had to add that last bit, didn't you?" I smiled up at him.

"Dad," Theoron said, tugging at Danial's sleeve. "I'm hungry, too. When are the women getting here?"

I looked at Danial curiously. "Donors?"

He nodded. "I have two coming this afternoon. Theo is learning how to take blood while inflicting as little pain as possible. He's made much progress in the last week."

"I'd known this was going to happen, I just didn't think it would be so soon." I patted Theoron's head. "I'm glad you're doing so well. Just don't grow up too fast."

"It was the real blood right from a vein at The Gathering that caused his growth to accelerate," Danial said. "That mixture of dried blood Stephen gave us sustained Theoron, but it seems in retrospect, we should have given him fresh blood from the start. It is something I've passed onto Devlin. He's said he plans to use only that with your child."

I looked down at Theoron and tousled his hair again. "I am glad you were little for a while," I said wistfully.

"He's safer the older he gets," Danial said. "Remember, Sar, Theoron will likely have an increased lifespan. He'll still be ours, he'll just be bigger."

"I'm going to be really big," Theoron said proudly.

"You'll always be my baby," I said lovingly.

Theoron gave me a grimace. "I'm not a baby anymore," he said, his green eyes flashing.

Danial laughed. "His eyes are so much like yours, Sar, so spirited."

"Are you coming or not, Mom?" Elle yelled.

"Come on, you," Danial teased, grabbing up Theoron as he shrieked loudly in joy. "Let's go wish them off."

* * * *

We hadn't finished our meal at the restaurant when Elle started in.

"Theo, are you going to leave Mom again?"

Theo froze, glancing over at Elle, then me. I looked back at him expectantly.

"No," he said, swallowing hard. "I'm never leaving your mom again, Elle. I was wrong to do it the first time."

"Promise?" Elle persisted.

He put his arm around her shoulders. "I promised her, and I promise you, too."

"Good!" she said loudly. "Can I have another sleepover?"

"That means a lot of planning," I said firmly, glancing at Theo. "I'm not sure how busy this spring is going to be. The next few weeks is right out, Elle."

Elle gave me her best wheedling face. "Dad said I'd have to ask you and Theo."

"Maybe in a month," I said, considering. "What do you think, Theo?"

He looked back at me and nodded. "I'm in. Finish your pancakes."

"Great!" Elle said excitedly. She dug into her food, finishing before either of us. "Can I play the stuffed toy machine?"

I handed her some money. "Sure. But for five dollars, I expect more than one toy."

"You got it," she said boastfully, pocketing the money and walking away.

The waitress brought our check over. "Your daughter a beauty," she said to Theo and me with an appreciative smile. "She's going to break some hearts when she gets older."

Theo's eyes met mine as we both said, "Thank you."

"Being the only child can be lonely sometimes," the waitress said meaningfully.

"We want to have at least one more," Theo said, grabbing my hand. "Wish us luck."

The waitress smiled at us. "Good luck to you."

My stomach lurched. "I'm going to the ladies' room," I said quickly, then added a smile so he wouldn't think I was upset with him. "Keep an eye on Elle."

I hurried to the ladies' room, my nausea increasing. *What was wrong?*

Bile rose in my throat, and I choked it back. I breathed deeply over and over, forcing myself to think about absolutely nothing. Slowly the feeling passed.

When I was sure I wasn't going to be sick, I went and washed my hands and looked at myself in the mirror.

It was too soon for morning sickness. It was just the greasy food.

Quickly I left the bathroom, my face in the mirror not believing what I was saying any more than I did.

# Chapter Nine

"Devlin, I may be pregnant with Theo's child."

Cavity looked back at me from my bed, nonplused.

I let out a breath. "Damn it."

I'd been trying in front of the mirror in my bedroom for the better part of the afternoon to come up with some way to break that news to Devlin. So far, I still sounded lame.

Theo called out from the other room, "Lash is here!"

I sighed, grabbed my bag from the bed, and went out the bedroom door.

Lash was standing near the door. Elle was standing a little behind Theo, peering at him from behind her father's back in the stance of a much younger child who was afraid.

I wasn't surprised. Lash had that effect on most everyone, including me. There was an air of violence around him, no matter how nondescript he looked dressed in his simple black shirt and jeans. He stood there now almost defiantly, his arms folded across his chest, his jet-black hair wild-looking, the scar across his left side of his face and eye baring his long fangs in a lopsided smile that dared Theo to make a move.

His flat eyes flicked up to mine. "Ready?"

Lash was the only were I'd ever met who retained his animal eyes in human form. I'd concluded he'd done it deliberately somehow, to increase his fear factor. His snake eyes were always unsettling, not just for their alien quality, but the sheer cold flatness for them.

"You want to stare at me, you can do it in the truck as I drive," he hissed, his smile twisting his face further. "Get moving, My Lady."

I went over and hugged Theo and Elle. "Have a good time."

"Call me tomorrow evening, when you get to Danial's," Theo said firmly. "I'll see you later that night, for the movie."

"Remember, don't watch anything too scary with Elle. Try to—"

"Shh," Theo said firmly. "Just hug me and go. There isn't anything to say."

He was right. "I'll see you before you know it," I said, brushing the hair out of his eyes. I leaned in for a last kiss, then headed to the door without looking back. "Bye."

I walked out the door into falling snow, Lash following.

Try to be pleasant. "Nice truck," I said, getting into his Avalanche. "Devlin told me it was yours, not Danial's."

"It's dirty," Lash hissed coldly. "Goddamn black shows dirt like a bastard."

Appalled at his language, I didn't answer. The truck was indeed dirty from all the slush on the roads this morning. The weather forecast was calling for another six to ten inches by nightfall. I buckled myself in, glad that I wasn't the one driving

Lash started the truck, quickly backing up smoothly, turning around, and heading down the driveway. He was silent as he drove, not speaking. This was normal, as far as I knew. He'd acted standoffish every time I'd been around him, except for the night he'd tasted my blood. Even then, he hadn't been very friendly. That was fine by me, though. I'd planned to ask Devlin about teleporting to Hayden from now on, so I could skip these fun drives with Lash.

In any case, his silence gave me time to prepare my revelatory speech. I'd decided to tell Devlin about what happened with Theo and me during our shared dream. Danial would likely deduce the truth from me before I left him on Sunday. Before he made me break the news or told Devlin, it was better to break it myself. I'd spent the last six months keeping secrets. I wasn't going to keep any more.

\* \* \* \*

As we drove in through Hayden's gates and up the long driveway, I looked over again at Lash. In the entire drive, he hadn't put on any music, or tried to talk to me at all. Not talking for a while was normal between strangers. Utter silence for a solid hour was not only unnatural, but oppressive.

"Someone plowed," I murmured. "I hope it wasn't just for me."

"It wasn't," Lash hissed, parking in the garage. "Get out."

I got out, walking in front of him a few strides, then suddenly wheeled around to face him. Instead of startling him, he merely stepped back gracefully. His forked tongue flickered out, tasting the air.

"I want you to search me," I stammered out.

Lash lifted one black eyebrow, but his expression didn't change. "Search you how? And for what?"

95

"However you usually would search someone. You clearly don't trust me or like me. I can't do anything about the latter, but I can do something about the former."

"Stand facing the wall, your hands touching it," Lash hissed. "Then spread your legs," he added lecherously, putting emphasis on the last words. Uneasy, I did as he asked, ruing my offer and bracing for a grope or two. He patted me down thoroughly, but didn't touch me anywhere that wasn't necessary.

Lash stepped back as I turned around, then held his hand out to me. "Bag."

I handed him my duffel bag. He looked through it carefully, then he handed it back. There hadn't been much inside; just a change of clothes, that sweater Devlin liked, and my prenatal vitamins.

"You want to look in my purse?" I asked.

"No. Come with me," Lash said. We went into the kitchen, then through the living room to the base of the stairs. He took my bag, setting it on the stairs with my purse.

"Where is everybody?" I asked. "Is everyone on guard duty?"

"The bears and I weren't all down here for a damn horror movie," he said, smiling at me widely. "Devlin said he was going to make you scream, and we all wanted to hear that. Word around was you love to scream—"

"I hope you weren't disappointed," I said harshly, giving him a cold look.

"Not at all," Lash said, smiling wider. "You made him scream in a way we'd not heard before. You got a round of applause."

My mouth dropped open, my face flushing. Lash laughed, opened a door beneath the second story stairs, and began descending.

Devlin had told me Titus's workshop was down here in the basement. I expected a dank and dark dungeon, but this workshop was much like Terian's. There were many bottles, all neatly stacked and labeled, and a huge shelf of books, some of them very old. Underneath was a large rack of scrolls, some of them yellowed, the edges crumbling.

"Sarelle," Titus said in a friendly deep bass, then held out his arms to hug me.

"Hi, Titus," I said warmly, quickly hugging him. He was almost too hot to touch; in a few moments of contact, I was sweating. "Are you blocking your, um, blackness? I don't feel it very much today."

"You need to test her for poisons," Lash interjected. "I'll wait."

"Go tell Devlin she'll be right up," Titus said, glancing at him in dismissal. "After all, Terian has told me of her this week, it's probably unnecessary, but I'll do a thorough check. It'll take a few minutes."

Lash nodded, then slid his flat eyes to me. "Sure, you volunteered to be searched. That doesn't make me trust you, especially since your Cat's desperate enough to try anything." He turned from me without another word, and walked away, ascending the stairs. The basement door shut hard

I looked at Titus, uncomfortable. "Do I need to get undressed?"

"No." Titus held open his hand, then said some words under his breath. His hand glowed white, and my skin all over my body began to tingle. Looking at my hands, my skin itself seemed to be glowing from within.

"Answer, Sar, is there anything that you harbor that would harm Devlin?"

My answer was supposed to be no. *Cringe.* "I'm not sure."

Titus dropped his hand, perplexed. "That wasn't an answer I expected."

I put my hands on my hips, facing him accusingly. "And I didn't expect to wake up and find that the sex I'd had with Theo in the dream had happened in real life."

Titus gave me a long look, then gave a great rumbling laugh. "Indeed, your bond with Theo was renewed."

"It's not fucking funny," I said viciously. "I've been upset over what to tell Devlin since I woke up. I wasn't going to tell him, but I'm worried he'll find out accidentally. I'm not good at keeping secrets from Danial, and I'm going to see him tomorrow—"

Titus enfolded me into his arms. "I didn't mean to upset you. I'm sorry. Now you're worried how Devlin's going to take the news that you're possibly pregnant by Theo."

"Yes."

He stepped back from me, and again raised his hand. "Do you intend any harm to Devlin?"

"No," I answered.

Titus lowered his hand and nodded. "Follow me."

I followed him upstairs all the way to Devlin's bedroom, the steps groaning under his weight. Titus knocked.

Devlin's rich voice, full of lust, called out "Send her in!"

We walked in, and Titus shut the door behind us. Devlin was sitting in his bed dressed in some black loose pants and a loose black shirt, reading reports of some kind.

"You look very casual," I said, thinking he looked drop dead gorgeous, especially with the golden stubble covering his lower jaw. "Working in bed?"

"I'll shave, Love," he purred, moving aside his papers. "I fed just before you came. I'll probably do that from now on. I neither want to frighten you, nor sacrifice your health." He glanced at Titus beside me. At once, his eyes narrowed, his friendly expression souring. "What did you find on her?"

"Nothing," Titus replied.

"Then why not just send her up to me?" he said suspiciously. "Why are you here, Titus?"

"I'm here to take any punishment you might visit on Sarelle," Titus rumbled. "Theo and she had sex in life as they dreamed. Sarelle is afraid she is pregnant by him, and she could be, Devlin—"

"God damn it!" Devlin screamed wrathfully, his eyes redder than I had ever seen them. "How could you have let this happen? I'll flay the skin off you for this!"

"Go ahead, Master," Titus dared. He folded his arms across his chest, and faced Devlin, completely unfazed. "I'm not afraid of your petty torments."

Devlin screamed again in anguish and rage, his frustrated howl deafening. I shrank back against the wall.

Devlin stared at me. He drew in a long slow breath, then let it out. "You'd like that, wouldn't you? If it was his and not mine?" he said bitterly, every word sharp enough to cut me. "You didn't want my child, you only agreed because you were made to—"

"That's right!" I shot back. "I didn't want any more children at all, neither yours nor his. This happened in a dream, Devlin. I didn't do this on purpose."

Devlin closed his eyes. "That doesn't matter. If you had a choice of whose baby to have, you'd choose him."

*No, I'd choose Danial.* "That's not true."

"You want to flay me now or later?" Titus said mockingly.

Devlin whipped around and glared at him. "You didn't know this could happen? You had no idea? I don't believe that, Titus!"

"The dream they shared doesn't have a lot of documentation on it," Titus answered. "There isn't anything written about having sex in the dream and having it in real life, too, while being unconscious."

"This ruins everything," Devlin grated out. "You've put us all at risk with your mistake."

Titus let loose some of his blackness, making me shiver. "They love each other, Devlin. You can still have a child with Sar later, her having one with Theo won't—"

"She has to have mine!" Devlin yelled. "Not his!"

"What the hell is going on in here?" Lash hissed loudly, opening the door. "Dev, I could hear you screaming from outside—"

"I don't give a damn!" Devlin said furiously. "It's all gone to hell!"

Lash looked at the three of us, then tilted his head just slightly. "The bitch is already knocked up with a kitten," he hissed. He crossed the room and put his hand on Devlin's shoulder. "You should know you can't trust women by now."

Devlin shrugged off Lash's hand. Unruffled, Lash put it back on his shoulder again. This time, Devlin left it there.

Lash looked up at me, flat eyes gleaming. "Say the word, and he's dead, Dev. Titus could teleport me in no time—"

"No," Devlin said hollowly. "He didn't plan this, and neither did she. It's not anyone's fault, expect maybe mine, for agreeing to let Titus break him free of that love spell he was under—"

"I would have done it regardless of your wishes," Titus rumbled. "You know that."

Devlin looked at me, but his gold eyes seemed not to see me. "I should've made sure they dreamed apart. That, or had you sterilize him." He rubbed his eyes.

"We should do that in any case," Lash hissed. "The world could do with less werecougars—"

I had to soothe Devlin before he gave into Lash. "Look, I don't know that Theo's the father, or if I'm even I'm pregnant at all."

They all looked at me.

"I freaked out because I was a little nauseous in the bathroom at the place Theo, Elle, and I ate today. Given my life lately, that's likely stress-related. "

"We need to know as soon as possible if it isn't," Devlin said quickly. He turned to Titus. "Can you do anything to tell me, one way or the other?"

"Not without an invasive test," Titus rumbled regretfully. "If she is pregnant, it might cause her to abort the baby." He paused. "There isn't a need for that anyway, Devlin. The fertility spell you administered to Sar almost ensures that by the time Theo and she dreamed together, she was already pregnant."

All the blood drained from my face. "What?"

Titus looked at me with a faint smile. "The spell Danial used to become fertile again was a much less potent spell. Terian's blood is only half demon and much weaker than mine. I'm an accomplished sorcerer." He smiled widely, baring his rows of sharp teeth. "I don't leave room for accidents."

"What fertility spell did you give me?" I whispered. "When?"

"It was in your wine," Titus replied. "And in Devlin's, also, to ensure conception. The sooner you got pregnant, the sooner I could stop making daily potions for Devlin and get back to my real work."

Devlin had used those ornate glasses from his mantle when we'd returned to his room…and I'd trusted Titus when I shouldn't have. "Neither of you said a word to me."

Devlin was also annoyed at Titus. "You let me think that it was possible he got her pregnant. Why?"

Titus gave a great rumbling laugh. "I'm a demon. You'd think after all these years in your service, you'd know how much I enjoy seeing you lose your composure."

I glared at them for a moment, then strode into the bathroom, slamming the door behind me. I locked the door, then wiped at my filling eyes.

Lash said something low in the other room, then laughed raucously. There was silence for a moment, then Devlin began talking in a low voice, his words muffled.

I stripped off my clothes. I'd wanted to try the Jacuzzi. This was an opportune time as any. Maybe it would help me decide what to do now.

I slipped into the steaming water, sinking my body in until the sweet hot heavenly sensation covered all of me except my head. I lay back against the jets, letting them massage my shoulder blades, and tried to think of absolutely nothing.

There was a knock at the door. "Sar? Can I come in?"

"Wait, door's locked—"

There was the sound of a key in the lock, then Devlin opened the door. "You think you're the first woman to try escaping into my bathroom?" he said with a wide smile. "I had a key made to open the door from outside, after the first time I had to break down the door."

"That's so charming of you," I replied scathingly. "And just what I wanted to know right at this moment."

Devlin closed the door behind him, then took off his clothes. Despite my anger, I watched him hungrily, the sight of his excellent physique stimulating. He turned to me suddenly. I averted my eyes, blushing.

Devlin eased into the water with a sigh of pleasure. "I like your desire for me," he murmured, putting his arms around my shoulders gently. "Watch me openly, Sar."

"You're only being sweet because you've gotten what you want," I said tiredly.

"Would it be so bad to be already pregnant?" he said, lifting my face with his hand gently so I had to look at him. "Ours will be a beautiful baby, Love. I will see to your every want and whim."

I gave him a half smile. "It's going to hurt Theo if it's yours and it'll hurt you if it's his. It's a no-win situation for me."

"Has your love for him returned?" Devlin asked, curious. "You don't act as though you're head over heels for him."

I moved closer to hug him, resting my head on his shoulder. "My feelings for you are no different, nor mine for Danial. Maybe that was also something Titus just said to upset you."

"Don't tell me what you think I want to hear," Devlin said sternly. "Tell me the truth: do you love Theo?"

I moved back, giving him a dark look. "I'm telling the truth. Yes, I love him, but my feelings for you haven't changed." *Despite some odd thoughts here and there, anyway.*

"Sorry, Love," he said gently. "Come back here, please. I want to hold you."

I went back into his arms. We stayed like that for a while, just embracing in the warm water, not speaking.

"We should get out," Devlin said, rising and offering me his hand. "Come, I'll make you a fire."

Devlin helped me out, wrapped me in a towel, then led me to the fireplace. As I dried off, he added a few more logs. Soon the burning wood was crackling merrily.

We sat down on the gold love seat, and he pulled over our shoulders a long white blanket of soft, fluffy yarn.

"What is this?" I said, feeling the fibers. "Wool? Angora?"

"You should know, being a country woman," Devlin said with a smile. "It's alpaca."

"Ah. It's wonderfully soft," I said, stroking the blanket.

Devlin looked down at me, his great golden eyes shining in the light from the fire. "Are you hungry?"

I was lost in his eyes, and didn't answer. He leaned in to kiss me, and I kissed him back, my arms going around him.

He kissed me chastely, then drew back, his expression both seductive and happy. "You're right, we are unchanged, Love. Still, I need to know: are you hungry?

I hugged him tightly. "Yes. But I'm happy to stay here if you are."

"We can, if you wish," he answered. "Among her talents, Serena is a short order cook. She can make you dinner." He kissed my hand. "Besides groceries, I've also laid in a supply of chocolate. Danial reminded me of your favorite foods this morning."

"Did he?" I said, laughing. "Be careful, Dev. He might have told you wrong items just to make you look bad."

"Why would you say that?" Devlin said, hurt. "Danial wants you to be happy, for me to treat you well. He would not deliberately sabotage us. He is enjoying our shared Oath, that things have worked out between us three."

Shame suffused my face. Danial would never do what I had just accused him of. I moved back from Devlin, upset. "I'm sorry I said that, Dev. I don't know why I did—"

"Maybe the reason is your condition," Devlin said soothingly, bringing me back into his arms. "Danial warned me to watch for any sign that you might not be yourself." He kissed me harder, then brought my hand down to rest on his stiffening penis. "I am so looking forward to your lust," he whispered. "I can't wait for you to demand that I take you. Just the thought of it—"

The Lust was a double-edged sword, prompting me to entice violence from my lover along with sex by whatever means necessary. If I was pregnant with his child, Devlin would find that out soon enough.

Devlin's lips moved to my neck, his fangs pricking lightly in his passion "—I've fantasized about you coming after me, tearing my clothes in your haste—"

I didn't need The Lust to give him his fantasy.

"Take me to your bed," I said gutturally, grabbing his hair in my hands and pulling it back roughly. "I want to ride you until you scream—"

Unbidden, the image of Lash below applauding suddenly came to mind. I faltered, but Devlin had already thrown the wrap aside and bolted to his feet. He leaned over to pick me up.

*Forget Lash; he's not important.* "You're going to scream for me again," I demanded quickly. "I want to hear you come."

"You will, Lover," he said seductively. "Come here."

I grabbed Devlin's throat. Startled, he went motionless.

"Tonight, I want it all," I ordered, my eyes flashing as I squeezed. "Prove to me you're the best, Lover, or face the consequences."

Devlin's lips parted, then he lunged for me. With fangs bared, he strode to the bed carrying me. Falling back on it, he maneuvered my hips over his, then drove up into me with so much force I let out a scream.

"Me first," he panted, his hands clamped on my thighs, holding me immobile as he slid in and out of me as fast as he could. He closed his eyes, his body straining beneath mine as his back arched.

"Deeper," I hissed at him, digging my fingers into his chest. "I said all of you!"

Devlin's eyes opened, their red-gold depths hot as flame. With the next thrust, he put himself inside as far as he could, letting out a sharp cry of fulfillment.

My cry echoed his, pain edging my pleasure. Devlin was panting hard, possessing me as if he might never get the chance again. I screamed with every fierce movement of his body in mine, my hands gripping his skin, slippery with sweat.

Devlin's body began to tense, his orgasm moments away. I concentrated, using my internal muscles to squeeze him, tightening my body around his.

Devlin let loose a savage cry, his eyes like twin suns, his body shaking. Then he screamed my name, convulsing under me in orgasm. "Saaaaarrrrrr!"

He jerked a few more times, then lay shaking, gasping for breath. I stroked his chest gently, loving his tremors beneath my fingers.

"I can never get enough of you, Dev," I said, kissing his brow. "Not ever."

Devlin raised his head, his eyes bright. "Good. My desire's always been strong, just like my libido." He kissed me. "I'll need you to fulfill both for a long time, Love."

His talk about not being exclusive sprang to mind. "Just me?"

Devlin rolled over onto me, putting his finger to my lips. "Stop," he said firmly. "We are going to be together for a long time. I love you. That means all of you, Sar: your confidence, your fearlessness, your tenderheartedness that you hide behind your tough exterior just as I hide mine—"

I smiled. "You know me better than I thought."

"—all the things that make you who you are. It's true that as the years pass we might not be together as much and I might take a lover besides you—"

I frowned at him to tell him he was off his intended path. He ignored my look.

"—but I won't love anyone else like this. I don't love easily, Sar. I never cheated on Anna, and I won't be with someone else without your permission."

"Good to know," I said uncomfortably. "Though if you want to just sever our bond then, we could—"

He pushed me back to the bed, dominant. "We are never breaking our Oath, ever, end of discussion. Understood?"

I nodded.

"Good. You must listen to me carefully now, Love," he said, somber. "I have something important to tell you."

103

# Chapter Ten

It was going to be very bad, by his tone. "What happened?"

Devlin let out a breath. "I had a call from Samuel this morning about Harriet."

"And?" I prompted.

"Samuel reported that Harriet's blood has turned "summer-like" already. He and Perseus took the same potion I took last week. They're actively trying."

While my sympathy went out to Harriet, as I wouldn't have wanted either Samuel or his nasty ally Perseus to be my bedfellow, I didn't see why this was so upsetting to Dev, given his views on a female's right to refuse. "Why are you upset? It's not because of her situation."

"Because I don't know what will happen," Devlin said, his eyes sliding away from mine in guilt.

"To her or to them?" I demanded. "What did you do?"

"What I had to in order to keep you safe," Devlin replied stridently.

"Which was?"

He sighed heavily. "I had Titus do a spell to change her blood to resemble yours."

My sudden save at the Gathering hadn't been a miracle, but instead a well-orchestrated diversion. "How?" I got out. "When?"

"Titus took a sample of your blood that night I marked you. When I first got to the Gathering, at the beginning of the evening, I watched to see who might be with a woman they had just met. Harriet was with some low level vampire. He'd just picked her up that night, hadn't even tasted her yet. In an opportune moment, I injected her with some of your blood, and a transformative spell that Titus had prepared."

"You tasted her after? She tasted like me?"

Devlin shook his head. "Luckily, no other vampire there, save Danial and I, had tasted you, or they would have realized that Harriet's blood didn't taste the same as yours."

*God, this was diabolical.* "Why'd that vampire let you taste his girl?"

"He knew who I was, what I'd been. He knew enough about me not to refuse me when I asked to taste her." Devlin hugged me. "She tasted like flowers, Sar, but not like summer." He nuzzled me. "Not like you."

And there was no way in hell she'd birth a dhamphir, even if she managed to get pregnant. Devlin had known that, and still doomed her. "If months go by and Harriet doesn't get pregnant, they are going to suspect something."

Devlin nodded. "Samuel and Perseus are both cunning and intelligent. If they dig deeper into her past they'll find out they were tricked, and that the culprit was me."

"How long do we have?" I ventured. "A year? Less?"

"We have a year at most," Devlin said, resigned. "It's well known that it took me a year with Anna, and you and Danial about six months. Titus also checked his histories for reported incidents of human pregnancies resulting from vampires. While some of the documentation is likely wrong, the average is still about seven months."

*Those other women through the years had all died.* "What's your plan?"

Devlin gently kissed my throat. "I don't see a way out, Sar. That was why I was so upset about you possibly being pregnant by Theo. We need you pregnant by me when or before they find out I tricked them."

"How's that going to help?" I said sarcastically.

"They won't act until you've had our child," Devlin answered. "That will give us that many more months to find another woman whose blood is really like yours. Even now, many vampires are scouring the globe, looking. It's a matter of time before more are found."

*When they had, they were going to wish they hadn't been.* My skin crawled. "Dev, I have a better solution."

"Tell me, please," he said curiously.

"I never wanted all this attention," I said, choosing my words carefully. "I was lonely when Danial met me, without many prospects but the surety of hard work until I died. Now I tend to look back on that with nostalgia."

"I do not understand, Love. Are you unhappy?"

"No, but everything's so complicated now. I'm too much in demand, with three men on my dance card, and more looming in the shadows, waiting for an opening. I can't live like this for much longer." I took his hand. "I'm happy to be here with you, but understand, I'm not a teenager looking for a party, or a flavor of the month. I'm a grown woman who's looking for a relationship."

"We are building one," Devlin replied, giving my hand a squeeze. "In any case, there is no going back for a 'do-over'. All the other Rulers know who you are now, and what you look like. You must accept your situation, Love."

Devlin's tone was soft, but under that softness was hard, cold steel.

"I do accept it," I said slowly. "But I want you to understand that after I have your child, I...um, I want to get my tubes tied."

Devlin looked at me in silence for a few heartbeats. "Are you asking me for permission?" he said finally. "Because of the Oath?"

"No," I said. "It's my body, so it's my choice. But like you said, we're in a relationship. It matters that you're on board with this decision." *And under those damn vampire laws, Camlyn may not give me one without notifying you first.*

"You're correct that you'd be safer," Devlin said. "I'm 'on board', as you called it. One child is enough for me. But where does that leave Theo? You've made a point about how he's hoping for—"

"Having Elle almost killed Tawny," I said guiltily. "Everyone was quick to assure me that I wouldn't have that kind of trouble having Theo's baby, but I don't care. No matter how much he wants another baby, he's not going to get one from me."

"Have you told him that?"

"I will," I said defensively. "But I can't very well say something like that when I might be having his, can I? I'm so angry and frustrated that I'm in this position."

"Shh, Love," Devlin soothed. "I agree with you that having a normal baby is a big drain on a woman's body. Having two extraordinary babies should be the limit for you, unless there is something Titus or Stephen could do to help. Let's ask him next time you go for a checkup to instruct us on the best path to take. Titus I'll speak to tomorrow." He hugged me. "I want a child badly, Love, but not at the cost of your health."

He'd said he was on board with my plan, but everything he'd said in the past indicated that was only after I'd given him a child of his own. I didn't reply.

"Don't worry too much about Harriet," Devlin continued. "According to Samuel she is embracing her new lifestyle of luxury. She was and remains an eager participant, her chief desire to go down in history as you have. For your sake, and mine, I hope her enthusiasm is enough. Otherwise, we're screwed."

"Won't she die if she gets pregnant? If she's not resistant to the virus, she can't carry the baby to term, right?"

"Without knowing what it is about your blood, I can't say for sure how changed she is. All I can attest to is she doesn't taste like you do. Titus said that he did the best he could, that her blood was as close to yours as he could make it. She may be changed enough—"

"Or you may have doomed her."

"Sarelle," Devlin said, his tone razor sharp. "I had to have a backup plan to divert them in case I couldn't get Samuel to back down. I knew if another woman like you appeared at the right moment, that I could back them off."

Harriet had come to the Gathering for a good time. Maybe she'd had a life she'd loved. Now she was little more than the broodmare Lash had alluded to, some of that breeding maybe against her will. Likely, no matter what happened, she would die in a lot of pain.

"Sar, it was you on the auction block," Devlin said, resolute. "I would have sacrificed a hundred other women to save you, if that's what it took—"

It was there in his voice that he meant it. Although I was grateful for his devotion, I was also terrified at the level of his commitment.

"I told you that night we pledged to one another that you had my all," he continued, terse. "You asked me for my protection, as well as my love. I swore to you I would do whatever it took, whatever was necessary. This was necessary."

That didn't change the fact that Harriet was collateral damage. Worse, she wasn't the first; Devlin had held Brian's wife Demi captive for months, to ensure Brian's total commitment to protecting me. Something told me she wouldn't be the last.

"Say something, My Oathed One." Devlin's tone was hard, nearing anger.

I hugged him. "I understand it's necessary," I said carefully. "I just wish it hadn't been." I took a breath. "I remember how scared I was that I'd never see Elle or Theoron again, or that Danial would get killed. But no matter what guilt I feel, above all I'm glad you protected me, Dev."

"I would do it again and more," Devlin said lovingly.

Uneasy, I didn't answer.

"Now you know why I wasn't around at the beginning of the night," Devlin said in my ear, kissing it lightly. "I wished we'd gotten time to dance."

"I thought you were fashionably late."

"I was there from the beginning of the party, watching everyone as they came in. I saw you come in with Danial. It took me a half hour to find and dose Harriet, then another two hours for the potion to take effect." Devlin scowled. "I told that idiot she was something very special. If only Isaac had taken Harriet right to Samuel as I thought he would, we'd have avoided all the drama."

"Why would he?" I asked. "Wouldn't it be natural for him to want to keep her for himself?"

"They weren't in love, not remotely. Besides, Isaac is young. He likely doesn't have enough power in his blood to withstand the spell he would need to use to quicken his body."

I gave him an odd look. "I thought demon blood was transformative."

Devlin bared his fangs in a smile. "You mean you've seen Danial use it for staying power. Yes, it has that effect on vampires, when taken in a very small dose and mixed with a few other key ingredients. But the amount needed to make a vampire fertile is close to a lethal dose. Isaac would have died if he'd attempted to do what I've achieved." His eyes held mine. "Even if he somehow survived the spell."

"What are you saying? You're alluding to something."

"Just that you were lucky the vampire that you found that dark and stormy night was Danial, and that he had me to watch his back," Devlin said. "Vampires with less power and position are subject to those above them. Even with our laws, it's seldom that a vampire with little power holds onto something long that a more powerful vampire wants. Just as I desired you, Samuel would have stopped at nothing to get Harriet for himself."

"Maybe," I said scornfully. "You yourself said I was unremarkable, if I remember—"

"I am never going to hear the end of that, am I, Sarelle?" Devlin said, rolling his eyes at me and smiling contritely.

"No, Love, you aren't," I said almost peaceably.

Devlin laughed, the rich sound rolling out of him to wash over me.

I turned serious. "Dev, I've not wanted to bring this up before. What happened with Anna? If our blood was the same, or very close, why did she die?"

"It won't happen with you, Love," Devlin said, old pain of her loss again etching each word. "It was my fault," he said miserably. "Titus made it clear to me that I had to wait for the potion to change me completely before trying with you. He was not with me two hundred years ago. The alchemist that made it for me then said there was no need to wait. I'd used the mixture Danial used with you, to minimize pain and expense." He wiped at his filling eyes. "Anna trusted me, and I killed her."

I kissed his tears away. "It wasn't your fault—"

"Don't make excuses for me," Devlin said stubbornly. "I almost killed you, too."

"No, you—"

"I was the one who told Danial that it was safe, that he didn't have to wait. If you hadn't stuck to your guns the second time—"

"Stop," I said, covering his mouth with my hand. "What's done is done. We're going to have a child together." I wiped away his tears. "Titus seems certain, and he should know. We're together, Dev, like you wanted. Don't dwell in the past. Be here with me, now."

Devlin regarded me for a moment, then he gave me a radiant smile. "You're right," he whispered, showering me with soft kisses. "We have a lot to be grateful for. And I have wasted enough of the night not showing you how much I have missed you. Come to me, Love."

\* \* \* \*

I sat bolt upright in the dark, sure I was going to be late for something. Then I saw Devlin sleeping next to me, and remembered where I was. I lay back down with a sigh. God, I must have been dreaming about my old life, worried about making it to work…

Devlin stirred next to me. "What is it, Love?" he said, kissing my shoulder. "I felt you sit up suddenly."

"Nothing," I said, stroking his arm reassuringly. "I just forgot what day it was."

"Did you think you were with Theo?" Devlin said with a smile, indenting the skin of my wrist with his upper fangs. "Were you lunging up to get to me as fast as possible, so I could—?"

"No!" I said loudly, hitting him with a nearby pillow. He hit me back with another, and then we were whacking each other with glee, laughing hard, until he got a good one in, and I fell backwards off the bed.

Devlin moved fast, stopping my fall. "You're not getting away so easily, Love. Danial can wait until five, like I had to yesterday."

"Dev, why don't you call him Dan?" I asked. "He calls you Dev."

"It's a sore point," Devlin explained. "Our father called him that, Sar, because he was pissed that Danial's mother named Danial after herself and not him. Her name was Danialle."

"Why did she?"

"She announced that she had that right, as his true father would not claim him."

*Grim, especially as that action had punished her son more than his father.* "What happened to her?"

"She died one winter of tuberculosis," Devlin replied distantly. "She left Danial alone to tend a poor scrap of land. Even then, he was stubborn, refusing help from my father, and taking the little I could offer grudgingly. After a few years of that, Danial left the village. When he returned years later at twenty-five, there was a hardness about him that there hadn't been before, as well as a miniscule fortune. He married his childhood sweetheart, Beaulah, and they had a child." Devlin let out a breath. "As I said, the soil was poor. Danial wasn't much of a farmer, even with his family's help. He was on the verge of losing his land when I got him that job as a guard."

"Thank you for telling me some of what he went through," I said emotionally, touching his arm. "He said he knew poverty firsthand. I knew it had to be bad, but I never guessed—"

"He never talked about any of this with you?" Devlin said, his brows knitting. "Ever?"

"Only that night we first walked together with Ghost and Darkness in my forest. Any time after when I asked him about his past, he politely refused. If I pressed harder, he would excuse himself, or change the subject. Now I understand why."

"He is right in one regard, Love: that unhappiness is in the past. Leave it there."

"Yes," I agreed, cuddling close to him. "We've all had enough heartache."

* * * *

Devlin roused himself when I awakened at noon, blinking at me with eyes half open. "Are you hungry?"

"Rest," I said, pushing him back down on the bed. "I need to get something to eat, but I can do that on my own. I'll come back to bed after, at least today."

Devlin gave me look. "What do you mean?"

*Might as well say it.* "Dev, you make a crack a few days ago about how I wasn't on your schedule yet. I think it's fair to tell you I don't intend to be. I'm not saying I won't sleep in or spend time with you in bed during the day, but I can't pull a night shift every weekend or however often I see you. I'll be tired if I do, which means cranky."

"You did for Danial, when you lived there," Devlin replied, his tone intent.

"I like being in the sun," I said tentatively, not wanting to hurt him. "I like to plant, and do things outside, especially as it'll be summer soon. Theo is on a day schedule, and so is Elle. Theoron will be too, as soon as he starts lessons."

"I understand," Devlin said, nodding. "I didn't think when I said that." He cleared his throat. "But you do bring me to a subject I'd wanted to broach to you."

"Yes?" I said expectantly.

"Serena," he replied. "She appreciated the thank you cookies you sent her, and has asked me if you might teach her to bake—"

I gave him an odd look. "That's flattering, but why?"

"You didn't let me finish. She'd also like to learn some of your other skills."

"So long as you don't want me to learn hers," I said pointedly.

"If there are skills you are lacking in bed, I shall teach them to you,"

Devlin said arrogantly. He smiled appreciatively. "Not that I've found you lacking, Love."

"Thanks," I said, narrowing my eyes. "Now what skills are we talking about?"

"She mentioned the baking, but more than that, I think what she really wants is a friend." He paused. "I'm asking because of that, not because I expect her to keep us all supplied with pastries."

"I don't mean to snap." I rubbed my eyes. "I just don't know."

"You sound unhappy," He replied, hugging me. "Are you? Tell me if you are."

I glanced over at him, then away. "I shouldn't be. I have it all, now."

"Including bitterness," he replied evenly.

"I'm sorry," I said again, embarrassed. "It's just that for most of the last year, I've been facing health crises. I haven't done much of anything but the bare minimum. Now that I'm feeling good again, I want to keep busy."

"That's why I thought it was good for you if you made friends with Serena."

"I want more than a friend to bake with here," I replied, frustrated. "When I'm at Danial's, I help with his business. I need a purpose here, too, Dev."

"You do have a purpose," Devlin said seductively. "Your presence here makes me very happy. The child you are having means more than anything to me."

"That isn't what I mean," I said as gently as I could. "I need goals and tasks of my own, besides just being your lover and the mother of your child."

"Ah," Devlin said, nodding. "You feel like I did, when I first was disposed as Ruler. You need something of your own, not just to exist as a moon to my sun."

"Yes."

"Then if you'll permit me, I'll give you several tasks, Love," Devlin said, smiling. "Teach Serena some of your skills; specifically, how to plant and how to bake. Anything that isn't diner fare is beyond her. Also, teach her some basic sewing, so she can mend some of the clothes that always seem to need mending—"

"Wait, I need a pen," I said, rummaging in the desk drawer beside the bed. I hastily scribbled a list. "Why do you want her to know these things, Dev? Why does she?"

"I think she is feeling like an object. She came to me a few nights ago, and said that she was happy to keep seeing to the werebears' needs, but she wanted to have a little more respect from them. I have already told the males to be kinder to her, but I know that isn't the problem. There is a natural brand placed on women who are prostitutes, right or wrong, that that is all they are. She wants to break out of that. What she needs is a purpose outside her current job, another set of skills that I can both use and pay her for."

It was true self-reliance encouraged self-esteem. "I can help her do that."

"When spring gets more underway, I'll arrange for the bears to till the soil for you and Serena. You can plant a garden here, as well as at your house. Flowers, as well as vegetables, please. Perhaps you can also give some ideas to Lash for the flower gardens around the house, so they can be redone. Some white flowers, or maybe red?"

"Sure—"

"I understand from Danial you enjoy painting, and have a knack for decoration. Much of Hayden could also use your help."

I nodded. "You said Leri trashed the place. I haven't seen anything so far that's less than spectacular."

Devlin grimaced. "The ballroom has a wall badly crumbling. My men are earning a lot of overtime working on that. In addition, there are at least ten guest rooms that need new walls, fresh paint, and new carpeting—"

The more he talked, the more the weight on my shoulders intensified. *Where would I start?*

"Also, we should get the room to the right of mine set up for a nursery—"

"Enough," I said, putting my hand over his mouth. "I'm feeling challenged enough now, thanks."

"Listen, Love, I don't expect or want you to do the harder jobs. I don't want you toiling on your hands and knees. What I do want is your opinion and direction in decorating. I especially want you to design the nursery."

"Who do I see for ordering supplies?" I said, dreading the answer I suspected was coming.

"Lash," Devlin said predictably. "You'll find him easy to work with, once you get to know him."

I didn't want to get to know him. "When does Serena usually…um, have free time? I don't want to interrupt anything knocking on her bedroom door."

"Today, she will probably wake up at dusk. She'll have some time then, at least until Vince gets off his shift at midnight."

How was that schedule set up, so Serena didn't get exhausted and none of the bears got frustrated? Devlin had to have at least twenty male bears working for him. That meant even if they were only getting laid once a week, Serena had to service, on average, three a night, every night. How in Hell did she do it?

"Doing the math, Sar?" Devlin laughed.

"Yes, and pitying her."

"Don't. She's well compensated. Also, she does not see all my men, only half."

Since we'd already gotten into the subject, I might as well satisfy my curiosity. "What do the rest do?"

"Some of them have live-in girlfriends or mates. They are the most stable men, the mated ones." He nuzzled me. "Like I am with you—"

"Brian said that you had no women here except Leri," I said pointedly.

"When he was here, that was true," Devlin explained. "Leri was always jealous, and she tended to harass any other women. After she disappeared, I hired men with women, if the women were mated to them. I told you that I lost a lot of men getting Ebediah and Sola. The replacements I hired were all mated, as it happened."

"Do they have children?"

"Not yet," Devlin said. "Most are young, only in their twenties. Also, I have a mated couple that are gay. They both work as guards, and are two of my best men."

I gave him a look, not sure what he was getting at.

"We are not a big happy family here," Devlin said seriously. "This is dangerous work with a high mortality rate. If having young is an urgent desire, then that employee is in the wrong line of work. You could compare it to trying to raise a family while living in a war zone."

That gave me shivers. "Should I be afraid?"

"No, just aware that I have reasons for my decisions. To answer your curiosity, Serena sees seven of my guards regularly, which is at least two a day, every day."

"That's all I need to know," I said quickly, flushing. I got up from the bed. "I'm going to eat, then make a list of supplies I need, if I can get Lash to show me the rooms."

"Go, Love," Devlin said, kissing me. "Get started. You can show me what you've done when I get up at dusk."

I kissed him back, got dressed, and headed downstairs, pen and paper in hand. First thing was the kitchen. I couldn't teach Serena to bake if there was no baking equipment. Then I'd need some ideas from Lash of how big the flower gardens Devlin had spoken about were. I could at least make a list of possible plants to use. Lastly, there was getting paint. Lash should know also some of Devlin's favorite colors. With ten rooms to do, there would be leeway for some creativity.

Devlin had indeed laid in food for me. In the kitchen, I found fresh fruit, yogurt, Fig Newtons, cereal, low-fat milk, and a huge gift basket full of Godiva chocolate. The name on the gift tag said, "For Sar, from Dev."

I ate a piece as I made a healthy breakfast, just to sample it. It was better to eat higher calorie foods early in the day, as it gave me a better chance to burn them off. The first piece was so good I ate another. *Yum.*

After I finished breakfast and my outline of a list, I went through the kitchen. Devlin had absolutely no bakeware, not even a muffin tin or a mixing bowl. There was a set of blue glass bowls, but they didn't really count, being too small for making anything besides maybe one loaf of cornbread. There were also no spices, except for salt and pepper. Other than what Devlin had laid in for me, the fridge contained plenty of burgers, assorted meat, bread, cheese, and a little salad. The freezer held only meat, and a few frozen pizzas.

I made a list of baking groceries to get, and left it on the fridge for Devlin. The bakeware I would pick out myself. I had certain brands I relied on, and didn't want to end us with plastic measuring spoons, or non-dishwasher safe loaf pans. Good tools made a world of difference. Serena's experience with me should encourage her to bake, not discourage her.

Glancing at the clock, I sighed in irritation. It was close to three o'clock. To be to Danial's on time, I would have to skip talking to Serena today and starting any projects.

I rubbed my eyes, reminding myself that I didn't have a deadline for any of this work I was doing. This was supposed to be fun, not work. Instead, I was treating it like all my projects: very excited, fanatically into it as it developed, and annoyed when something kept me from making progress. But baking and decorating wasn't what I was here for. My only real job now was getting pregnant. *Was I just desperate to throw myself into tasks to forget about what Devlin really had me here for?*

Angrily slamming the cabinet, I went in search of Lash. Through the kitchen door, I entered a short hallway, then a large living area with a huge TV. I opened the door off it, and ran into a woman in jeans carrying a laundry basket.

Her short black hair reminded me of Suri. I gave her a smile. "Hi."

"Hello, Sarelle," she said, smiling back. "I'm Valerie, Jazz's mate."

Should I call her Val? I didn't know who the hell Jazz was, except he was most likely a werebear. "Good to meet you."

"Good to meet you, too," she said with a touch of respect. "Are you on an errand for Dalcon?"

I wondered whom she was talking about for a moment, and then realized she meant Dev. "Yes. I'm looking for Lash—"

"I'll take you directly to him," she said, dropping the basket immediately. "Follow me."

I walked with her back into the kitchen, then through the dining room into another hallway, where the guest rooms were located. Someone had already patched up the holes in the walls. Titus and Leri must have been having a hell of a fight, to make holes that had to have four by four sections of drywall to patch them.

The guest room hallway dead-ended at an ornate wider hallway that had been the site of an even bigger battle. There was some fresh joint compound, wire mesh, and other tools on a palette. Two men, presumably werebears, were working on some of the ceiling that had come down, patching a hole about one foot by a half, with cracks in all directions.

I wanted to make a comment about how this lover's spat must have been something to see with all the damage, but stayed quiet. I didn't know Val well enough. She might be close friends with Titus. I wanted her to like me if she turned out to be nice.

She led me past them into what had to be the ballroom, the scene of the battle finale. There was fallen plaster everywhere; the gilt mirrors that had lined the sides of the room shattered, pieces of silver glass lying here and there. The hardwood floor looked to be the only thing that was unscathed.

"Why are you here?" The cold hissing voice echoed in the room.

I looked up. Lash was on the balcony, staring down at me, dressed in black as usual.

"Dev asked me to come and see you," I replied. "He said to talk to you about fixing up some of the rooms. I need supplies."

"Stay there, and don't move," Lash hissed, moving from view.

I waited for him for several minutes. Valerie waited with me, though her anxious body language clearly showed that she wanted to leave before Lash got here.

Several more minutes went by.

"He's clearly taking his time," I said to Valerie. "You can leave me here if you want."

Obviously relieved, she left at once, jogging back towards the door.

I walked closer to the far wall, inspecting it. Some sort of huge blast had hit this back wall and knocked a section of it away, exposing five splintered two by fours. Cracks radiated from the blast site. There was plaster missing in places all the way up to the ceiling forty feet above.

"What did he ask you to do?" Lash said from behind me. His tone was standoffish as usual. "What do you need?"

I turned to him, trying my best to act friendly. "He gave me a bunch of things to work on when I'm here. He said to come and see you for help."

"Help with what?" Lash hissed, annoyed. "Get to the point already. I'm busy, Sar."

I forced a smile. "I just need a little direction. Tell me his favorite colors, so I can pick up some paint. I know he likes shades of grey, black, and white, and probably silver and gold. But the guest rooms would look austere or garish using just those shades. I would like to use colors, preferably ones he doesn't hate."

Lash eyed me for a moment. "Green-blue, like your eyes," he hissed. "Or darker. Red, like fresh blood. Yellow-orange like flames. Maybe purple, if the color was deep enough. No pastels or light colors."

That all made sense. "And brown or blue?"

"No, he doesn't like earthy colors," Lash hissed. His face twisted in something like a smile. "He doesn't like the outdoors. I have to drag him camping with me."

"Devlin said the equipment Danial had the night I found him was yours."

His face lost the smile. "Yes, though I don't see why that matters to you."

"It just solved a mystery," I said quickly. "I wondered sometimes if Danial had purchased it for show, once I got to know him."

"That's why he borrowed it," Lash hissed. "Danny doesn't like getting dirty." He smiled again, this one lecherous. "But I do."

I averted my eyes, appalled. "Can you tell me about the gardens around the house?"

"What about them?"

"Could tell me where each of them are in relation to the house, maybe show me what you can the next time I come here? He wants me to plant flowers in the spring. I need to know what kind of shade/sun to plan for."

"Sure, but you can't check soil type," Lash replied. "The earth is frozen."

I was surprised he knew that soil was important. "With the modern fertilizers, that shouldn't be a problem. Besides, I'm going to plant easy to grow flowers, nothing fancy."

"Practical," Lash said in approval. "Anything else?"

"I need painting supplies, baking supplies, and decorating stuff. I'd prefer to pick them out myself in person. Do you have an account at a certain store that I should use? Does it matter where I get them?"

"Dev wants you to bake for us?" Lash said, surprised. "Why?"

"He wants me to teach Serena."

"Arrive early in the morning the next time you come to see Dev," Lash hissed, sounding annoyed. "I will go with you to get supplies."

*Ugh. Hope hard, Sar.* "Don't you have to guard Dev? I could go with Titus."

"Until he knows if you are pregnant, Dev wants me with you anytime you are not with him, his brother, or his brother's men. Titus is occupied, and the bears are uncouth."

*If they were uncouth, what did Lash see himself as?* "Okay."

"Sarelle?"

I turned to see Devlin coming toward us.

"What have you accomplished?" he asked, laying his arm possessively across my shoulders.

I filled him in on the last few hours, ending with Lash's offer to get supplies next week.

"You are too efficient, Love," he said, pleased. "But remember, you are not to exhaust yourself. That is for me to do—"

"Do you want me to take her to Danial?" Lash interrupted. "Otherwise, I should get back to work."

"No, Terian is already here for her. He's down in the basement with Titus, looking again at that werecougar poison."

"What's the big deal?" Lash hissed, as he walked away. "So it's poison."

"It's more than poison," Terian said coldly, appearing next to Lash.

Lash neither jumped nor moved, just turned slowly, his expression unimpressed.

"What do you mean?" I asked, worried.

"Poison usually kills quickly," Terian said meaningfully, his cherry wood eyes angry. "This would've been excruciating for a long while before killing."

"Samuel must have more," I replied. "Is there an antidote?"

"No," Terian said knowledgeably. "But one is alluded to in Titus's Book of Poisons."

It bothered me that Titus was so into the dark arts that he was a poisoner. He seemed so nice, but he'd tricked me with that fertility spell. What were his real motives? What did he intend for Terian, now that father and son had been reunited? Would Titus lead him deeper into evil?

"What does it say?" Lash hissed abruptly, startling me.

"It says that a mixture can stop the pain and reverse the poison," Terian replied coldly. "But you need vampire blood and faerie blood."

"Fairies?" I laughed. "You mean like elves or something?"

"They're people like you and I, Sar," Devlin corrected, hugging me. "They're like humans; they can just do magic more easily and have a longer lifespan. Tatiana has faerie blood in her, and Leri was a full faerie—"

At the mention of his mother's name, Terian's eyes went red. "Sarelle, we should go." He grabbed my hand. Hayden faded, replaced by the great room at Danial's house.

I yanked my hand out of his. "Terian," I said, irritated. "You didn't need to—"

"He said her name on purpose!" Terian said hotly. "He knows she tried to

117

kill me—!"

Annoyed, I teleported back. Instead of the ballroom, I found myself outside the gates of Hayden.

What the fuck? I was freezing! I tried to teleport inside and couldn't, not even to a spot inside the gate. Walking to the gate, I pushed the gate buzzer.

"Yes?" one of the bears answered.

"Send Titus out, please," I replied, my teeth chattering. "It's Sar."

In a few minutes, Titus appeared. He grabbed my hand, and then we were in his workshop. "Sorry, I should have told you," he said, wrapping a blanket around me. "Only I and Terian can teleport into Hayden, due to security reasons."

"Can you do something, so I can, too? You know I'm not going to hurt Devlin."

Titus regarded me. "Only at his request. The order came from Lash—"

"Do it," Devlin said, coming down the stairs, Lash in tow. "I trust her, Titus."

"I'll amend the barrier, to let her through," Titus said, nodding.

"Take care, Love," Devlin said, giving me a long soft kiss. "Come back next weekend on Friday, or before that if you want to. If I know you're here, I'll arrange to come back."

"Are you still busy with Ebediah's affairs? Are you going to bring the bears and wolves here?"

"Not anytime soon," Lash hissed. "We can't trust them. Anyway, most have been traded by Devlin for assets we can use."

Devlin nodded. "I released most of the bears and wolves to provincial rulers in Canada in exchange for a tithe, which let them out of their contractual obligations to me. They get to stay where they prefer to live, and I get some money out of it. One older she-wolf is coming here to live sometime in late summer—"

"I told you not to let her," Lash hissed, rolling his eyes. "None of the wolves, Dev."

"She's going to be useful, Lash," Devlin retorted. "She's willing to take care of the housework. Jazz is getting sick of Valerie doing it and the other mated women refused to, even with the extra pay—"

"That's it?" Lash hissed suspiciously. "She's going to do housework? I don't buy it."

"Yes," Devlin said. "If she gives me any trouble, you can eat her."

"Fair enough," Lash said, nodding.

My stomach roiled. Devlin had been serious. *Ugh.*

Devlin's cell began to ring. I hastened to take my bag from Devlin's hand, gave him a quick kiss, and teleported. I appeared before Danial. His back was to me, his phone to his ear. I gave him a hug, startling him.

"There you are," he said, pleased. "Terian said you went back for your bag."

"Mommy!" Theoron cried. He grabbed me around my waist.

"Are you ready to see the movie?" I said, running my hands through his dark hair.

"It's at six," Danial said anxiously. "We need to leave now to meet Elle and Theo."

We made it to the movie with about ten minutes to spare. Theo and Elle were waiting for us in the cinema lobby. Theo broke into a smile when he saw us.

"Daddy!" Elle said, hugging Danial around the waist.

A few people passing by gave us considering looks. No doubt they were wondering which man was my current husband and which was my ex. I felt a rush of pride knowing that both were mine, then a stab of guilt.

"I got Theoron some popcorn," Theo said, holding it out to him. "I tried some, and it's fine."

From the looks of the bag, he had tried half of it, but I wouldn't be the one to say it. I was hungry enough to eat a bag myself. "Go get seats," I said, smiling. "I need some popcorn myself."

"Get me some candy!" Elle cried. Theoron echoed her.

"Okay!" I yelled.

Ten minutes later, I was back with soda, popcorn and candy. Theo met me at the theater entrance.

"There you are. Danial was getting worried."

"Here, help," I said, handing him most of the food. "I don't want to miss the beginning."

"I'm okay," Theo said quickly, as we walked back to our seats. "Being with Elle is helping. I just wanted you to know that."

Unsure how to reply, I nodded, and took my seat, my carefree mood dampened.

\* \* \* \*

After saying goodnight to Theo and Elle, Danial, Theoron, and I walked back to the Expedition. There was no moon, and the parking lot lights were dim. Catching my unease, Danial squeezed my hand and reminded me he was armed.

"Some of that was the movie," I replied. "I don't like these modern movies with unhappy endings."

"The bad man won," Theoron said sadly. "That never happens in my books at home." He looked from Danial to me. "Why didn't the good guy win?"

Danial picked up Theoron, not breaking stride. "In real life, that sometimes happens," Danial said seriously. "That is why I do what I do, to try to make sure that people who do bad things don't get away with them."

"Will you get killed, like those people did in the movie?" Theo said, tears threatening in his eyes.

"No, my son," Danial said confidently. "I'm going to be with you for a long time. So is your mom."

After that, the serious atmosphere became almost oppressive, like a funeral. It was definitely time for a mood boost. "Danial, how about some ice cream?"

"Please!" Theoron shouted. "Please, Dad!"

A few moments later we were at a nearby Friendly's, standing in line looking at the list of flavors.

"Can I get a twist and a sundae?"

"Just pick one," I said, ruffling his hair. "We'll come again another time, Theoron."

"Okay," he said with complete seriousness. "But I want a big one!"

"This was a good idea you had, Sar," Danial whispered, slipping his arms around me. "I wanted him to enjoy tonight, and not be sad. We should have picked a better movie."

"I have other good ideas for later," I said seductively. "If you're interested."

Danial turned my head with his hand, and gave me a soft kiss. "I look forward to hearing them at length," he said, then kissed my cheek. "Unless you just want to demonstrate them."

I was debating giving him another kiss on his inviting lips when the attendant asked "What will it be, Ma'am?"

"Maple Walnut—"

"Sar?" an appalled and familiar voice said from behind us.

## Chapter Eleven

I turned to see my mother in line right in back of us, my stepfather beside her. Shit. I was hyperconscious of Danial at my side, Theoron holding me around the waist. My mother was staring at me hard, murder on her face.

"Hello, Chris," Danial said politely. "Hello, Tina. How nice to see you."

"Danial," my stepfather said politely as well, and held out his hand. Danial shook it.

"Sarelle, can I talk to you for a moment?" my mother forced out, as she dragged me to the outside of the restaurant where she immediately laid into me. "What in the hell are you doing here with him?" she yelled, furious. "You are married to Theo, and he's a good man—!"

"Mom—" I said, panicked, yet trying hard for calm. *Thank God there was no one out here to watch this.*

"I know you must have a damn good reason for being here with Danial. So tell it to me!" my mother said roughly. "Tell me it's not that you're bored, or lonely, or-—"

"Theo knows I'm here with Danial and Theoron—" I said quickly,

My mother shook her head. "No way!" she spat back. "Theo would never agree to let you go out with Danial, even just out for ice cream. I saw you kissing him!"

There was no way out of this except one: the truth. "See that child holding Danial's hand, Mom? That's my son."

Her mouth dropped open as her face drained of blood. "Your...you and Danial...?" she breathed, not seeming to be able to form the words.

"His name is Theoron," I said, putting my hand on her arm. "Danial insisted we name him for Theo. I had him when Theo was gone."

She looked back at me, her eyes narrowed. "He's too old to be your son. He has to be about four or five. Theo was just missing for two years. You've only known Danial for three—"

"He's aging faster than normal," I answered haggardly. "He is Danial's child, and he's...he's supernatural."

"What?" my mom said, incredulous. "Why are you saying these lies—?"

"Look at my face, and tell me I'm lying!" I said scathingly. "I've done my best to protect you from some of the strangeness of my life, but I'm tired of pretending, and frankly, you should get to know your grandchild. He probably won't be the only one you'll ever have who is like this. But he is the first. If you can accept him, you can accept any that I might have afterwards."

My mother's eyes went wider still. "What are you saying?" she whispered. "Are you pregnant?"

"I'm saying Theo is what's called a werecougar. He can change into a cougar. Elle is the same. Danial is a vampire. Theoron, our son, is half vampire, half human."

She wobbled. I went to her. Together, we sank down on the bench outside the restaurant. We said nothing for some moments.

Finally, I reached over and grasped her hand. "Yes, I might be pregnant. If I am, the baby might be born a lion cub, like Elle was."

My mother looked at me in absolute terror. But she wasn't screaming yet. This was going pretty well, all things considered.

"Is it safe?" she whispered. "Will you be okay? Have you talked to, well, whomever you went to when you had your....your son?"

She said the last word so hesitantly I knew that it broke her heart that she hadn't known about Theoron. "I'm seeing a good doctor, and yes, he is going to take good care of me," I said confidently.

Theoron came running up to me, and hugged me. "Why are you over here, Mom?" he said curiously. "Who is this lady?"

I looked down at Theoron. "This is your grandmother, Theoron. You can call her Grandma."

"This is who you went to see at Christmas?" he said.

My mother let out a gasp.

"Yes," I said, pulling him up to sit between us. "And it's past time you met her. Say hi."

"Hi, Grandma," Theo said shyly, then he gave her a smile.

My mother reached out hesitantly, and smoothed Theo's dark hair back from his face. "You have your mother's eyes," she said, choked up.

"Would that he had Sarelle's hair, as well," Danial said gently, walking up to us. "But my darker coloring won out, I'm afraid." There was pride in his tone, as there always was when he talked about our son.

My mother looked up at him, and then back at Theoron.

"Give your grandma a hug, son," Danial said softly. "She has waited far too long to hold you."

As Theoron hugged my mother, her eyes closed and she let out a long breath. She hugged him to her fiercely.

"Is it true what she said, that you are a....a—" my mother looked at Danial, but seemed unable to say the word.

Danial looked at me, and sighed. "It's true, yes, though I wish she had not told you. I wanted you to—"

My mother cut him off. "And Theo and Elle are...different, too?" she said, again unable to say the words.

Danial glowered at me. I looked defiantly right back at him. My stepfather said nothing, playing it cool. He'd likely ask my mother to repeat everything for him at least twice later.

"Yes, it's all true," Danial said finally. "But these are not Sar's secrets to tell you. Theo will be upset you know. Elle loves you. I think of Elle as my daughter, Tina. Please don't hurt her, even—"

"I am not going to hurt her," my mother said forcefully, recovering a little of her composure with anger. "I love Elle and Theo. It doesn't matter to me if they aren't...what I thought they were. They're still part of the family."

"Grandma?" Theo asked in his small voice.

She looked down at him, her eyes moist. "What is it?" she said, again smoothing his hair back.

"Can I come next Christmas when Mom and Elle do?" he said softly. There was pain in my chest hearing his hope, mixed with a little fear that the answer would be "no."

"Of course," my mother said, hugging him to her. "Of course you can come, um—" She looked at me.

I mouthed "Theo" to her.

"—Theo," she finished, giving him a smile.

He gave her a dazzling one back, so much of Danial in it I had to smile myself. My mother thought the same, because she looked up at Danial, and said, "You can come, too."

"You do not have to include me because of a sense of pity," Danial said emotionlessly.

My mother interrupted him. "You are the father of Sar's child, Danial. I don't understand how you could be what she said you were and...um, have done that, but you obviously did." Her face flushed, as she floundered. "You've taken good care of him for however long he's been, um—"

Danial let out a breath, then leaned over, touching Theoron gently on his shoulder. "Yes, Theoron lives with me. Your daughter went through a lot to give him to me, because she knew I wanted a child with her more than anything. Because he is like me, he needs to stay with me. Sar couldn't take care of him, though she wanted to badly. But he is growing fast now, and you should know by next winter he may well appear much older than he does now."

"How much?" my mom whispered.

"He may be an adult."

My mother said nothing, just hugged Theoron even tighter. But he was enjoying hugging her and didn't mind.

"I know it is a lot to take in," I said gently. "That is why I never told you, Mom."

"I do not have to come to your home, Tina," Danial said pointedly. "It means a lot that you would let my son come."

"Come, please," my mother said, touching Danial's hand with hers. "I always wondered what my daughter saw in you, from what I knew of you, from what you let us see. I didn't understand why she was with you or how she could trust you with Elle, after you hurt her that time—"

Danial flinched. She squeezed his shoulder.

"—but this….what you've done was hard, and you did it alone. I raised a child alone. I know how hard it is, especially when they are babies—"

"I had help, Tina," Danial said graciously. "I was not alone."

"A pair of hands is one thing, and it's another to know all the responsibility for a life you helped create rests on your shoulders," my mother shot back defiantly. "Every decision you make you hope to God is the right one, because the life you are trying so hard to protect and nurture is so fragile. You made sure he was taken care of, every minute of every day, and that means something to me, Danial. I misjudged you. I'm sorry for that."

Danial said nothing for some moments. When he did speak, he was emotional. "You are as surprising to me as your daughter was, when she first accepted what I was," Danial said, respect in his eyes. "I expected you to run screaming from me if you ever found out the truth."

"I'd like to think I'm calmer than that," my mother said, getting to her feet, still holding Theoron. "Besides, it's not like you are really biting my daughter—"

My mother stopped abruptly, taking in Danial, who was giving her a small secretive smile, blinking his eyes at her a lot. I flushed scarlet, from my toes to my hair.

"You…you really…um—" my mom floundered again.

This time, my stepfather saved the day. "Look, whatever is going on here, the night's not getting any younger. Let's get ice cream, and we can talk about this at home."

"Ice cream!" Theoron shouted.

\* \* \* \*

Over our creamy desserts, we ditched our serious discussion, instead talking of pleasantries, my stepfather working in how he would like to take Theoron fishing in the spring as he had taken Elle a few times last summer. "I don't suppose you can go?" he said, glancing at Danial out of the corner of his eye.

"If you go at night, I will go with you," Danial said, with an apologetic look. "But days are out, I'm afraid."

"That's fine," my stepfather said. "You can still have a scotch or two with me, right?"

Danial reluctantly nodded. "As long as it's just a taste."

"Mom, Chris, you need to know something," I said abruptly.

Everyone looked at me, including Danial.

"Danial told me what he was from the first. He never hid what he was from me. I chose to be with him, to have his child. It matters to me that you know that. He and I were together because I wanted to be with him, not because he seduced me or anything like that." I forced a smile. "Those stories in the media are just stories."

"We get it," my stepfather said gruffly. "We didn't think that anyway, but it's good hearing you say that."

From the tone of his voice, that was exactly what he had been thinking. Glad I'd spoken up, I got to my feet. "We should get home," I said firmly, looking pointedly at Danial. "Theoron needs to get to bed."

When we reached the parking lot, my mother dropped a bombshell. "Bring Theoron to our house next week. I want to see more of him, especially if he's going to not be a child much longer."

"Sarelle can bring him to you during the day—" Danial began.

"No, come at night," she interrupted. "I would like to talk to you both about Theoron."

"As you wish," Danial said heavily, obviously worried about what my mother meant to say or ask.

"You don't have to talk about anything you don't want to," my mother said quickly, seeing his expression. "I just want to make up for lost time." She turned to me, tears on her face. "It hurts me to know you wouldn't have said anything to me, if I and your stepfather hadn't been here tonight, and run into you at the restaurant. You'd have let me go on thinking that you had no children. How could you have a child and not tell me?"

"I was going to tell you this year," I said weakly, hugging her. "I was trying to find a way to do it, that didn't 'out' Danial or make you feel bad for not knowing."

"I understand why," she said heavily, hugging me back. "I haven't been welcoming to Danial since you started living with Theo. I was worried you might leave Theo and go back to him."

Danial's eyes sought mine, surprised.

"I was honest about Theo, mom. He knows I'm here with Danial."

"I believe you," my mother replied. "About everything, as fantastic as it sounds. It explains a lot, actually." She drew back from me, and turned to Danial. "Do I have to ask for a hug?" she prompted.

Danial hugged her hard, drawing a little gasp from her. "Only this once, My Lady. Only this once."

\* \* \* \*

Danial and I didn't speak for most of the trip home. Finally, I said, "I'm sorry, for telling them your secret. I had no right. I didn't mean—"

"It's fine," he replied. "Your parents handled it well, far better than I hoped they would. I'm grateful that they accept Theoron. I'm astonished that they would accept me."

"I told you my family is strange, Danial," I said, giving him a smile. "We accept a lot of things normal people probably wouldn't."

Danial reached over and held my hand "Something I'm glad for, Love."

\* \* \* \*

After we'd put Theoron to bed, Danial and I retired to his room, where he lit us a fire in the woodstove. "What do you want to do the rest of the night?" he said teasingly. "This was the extent of my planning."

"I'm sure we can find something," I said, drawing him down to the floor. He responded immediately to my touch, his hand reaching into my hair to pull my lips down on his. I kissed him gently, but he was already wanting more than gentle kissing. Eagerly, I lay back on the floor, letting him coax my body into readiness with his deft hands.

"You remember the first night we were like this?" I said, running my hands up his chest. "I was so nervous."

"So was I," he said huskily. "I wanted you, but I expected you to stop me. When you didn't, I was worried that you wanted me just because you were hoping for a fantasy to come true."

"I was," I said, tugging him down to kiss me. "And you made it come true, Danial. Being with you in that dream, then later in the flesh was incredible." I gave him a tender look. "But you were always more to me than just a fantasy," I continued, stroking his cheek. "You told me at Christmas that I changed you,

126

just by being myself. You've done the same to me, Love."

Danial gave me an amused look. "Really? How so?"

"That day I held Theoron for the first time, when you hugged us both, I felt complete. I wanted to stay with you then, but I knew it would screw up everything again. I didn't want to hurt you. It was the same later, in the fall, when we made love. I knew I shouldn't have done it, that it had nothing to do with fighting The Lust." I swallowed hard. "But I loved you, and I missed being with you like that—"

"Why are you telling me this, Sar?" Danial asked abruptly, drawing back. "What are you telling me you want from me, or asking me for, that you are bringing this up now?"

I wiped at my rapidly filling eyes. "Tell me how I go on," I said brokenly. "How can I love you all equally? I feel so guilty—"

"Sar—"

"I'm in love with all three of you, and it terrifies me."

"Don't let it," he said, moving to hug me. "We are going to be happy, Sar. Trust me."

"I do," I answered. "It's not that. It's that I'm scared Titus's warning will come true, that I'll lose myself in that bond I share with Theo." I hugged him tightly. "I don't want to lose us."

"You won't," Danial said firmly. "We are Oathed, Love. My death is the only thing that could break that."

*Or mine.* Chilled at the thought, I slipped my hands under his shirt. "Come here then and show me," I said huskily.

Danial smiled down at me, then covered my lips with his.

\* \* \* \*

After, we lay together. I caressed him tenderly, his body that I knew better than anyone else's. "It never gets old, being with you like this," he whispered.

"I love you."

"And I, you," he said, giving me a long gentle kiss. "I want us to go away together."

Shocked, I sat up and looked at him. "What? Where?"

"Just us, for a long weekend, maybe a week, if I can get Theo to agree," Danial said, his tone implying he wasn't sure how I was going to take it. "It's been years since we traveled together, Sar."

"We can't," I answered. "Dev and Theo won't go for it."

"We'll schedule around them," Danial said right back. "We never got a real honeymoon. Even that time we went to Switzerland, I was working. I was always working. The few times I wasn't, you were either pregnant or unavailable to me."

*Whose fault was that?* "Um, I'm pregnant now, remember?"

"Maybe," he said. "It's too soon to tell. In any case, you are no longer unavailable to me, something I'm poised to take advantage of."

"We'd have to bring guards," I said slowly. "We wouldn't be alone."

"We don't have to, actually," he said, giving me an uncharacteristic grin. "You can teleport, Sar. If we are in any danger, you can just warp us home."

"Warp?" I said, laughing. "I can't believe you said warp!"

His response was to tickle me. Soon I was shrieking, pleading for him to stop. He relented, and I lay gasping in his arms.

"Well, where did you want to go?" I said, glancing at him.

"Where had you dreamed of going, back when you first met me?" Danial answered. "Rome? Paris? Jamaica? Acapulco?"

I thought about it for a few moments. "I would want to go and stay in a little house somewhere," I said finally. "Maybe near water. Somewhere where we could walk together, and not worry about a lot of people, maybe see some wildlife. I don't really want to go to a big city, or be in crowds." I looked at him hard. "Could you go somewhere where there wasn't Internet service?" I said teasingly.

Danial grinned back. "My cell is satellite. I can go anywhere, except maybe underground. I'll tell Terian our plans, and check in with him daily. He can also come and get us, if there is any trouble—"

Danial went on detailing out his plan. By the breadth of it, he had planned this as soon as he'd known I'd taken another Oath to him.

"—Theo can stay here with Elle and Theoron," Danial continued. "It will be safer that way. Janice and Ivan can watch your dogs at your place; they are practically mated already—"

"Theo is going to be upset, no matter what," I interrupted. "He doesn't like me coming to you now."

"He is lucky I don't press my rights more," Danial said, his eyes pricked with red tints. "Truly, I should get you at least two days a week, more if we went by the actual law—"

*What about time to myself? Argh!* "Enough," I said sharply. "I don't need another lecture about all the rights you have over me. It just reminds me of all the rights I've lost."

"I did not mean it that way," Danial said, giving me a pained look. "If you don't wish to be with me, you have every right to refuse. I would never make you do something against your will."

*Yeah, you're the only one.* I didn't reply, upset.

"Do you not want to go?" he said, crestfallen.

This wasn't his fault. It wasn't anyone's, but it especially wasn't his. "I'd like to go," I said tiredly. "It sounds relaxing."

"Let me check into places," Danial mused. "There must be someplace that we can rent relatively close by, where we can be alone."

His eagerness was hard to resist, hard enough I found my lips curving into a smile. "I can't imagine you not working for days on end."

Danial's eyes slid away from mine at my words guiltily.

"Have you been working without me?" I accused. "You told me we were closed."

"There is always someone who needs calling, some loose end—" Danial began.

I cut him off. "You said that you were shutting down the business for all of January, Danial. You have another two weeks, at least!"

"Yes, I'm overbooked for February. March isn't much better. I've been trying to ease the workload by finishing more pressing cases, and the ones that only take a night's work to complete. Terian's been teleporting me, watching me when it's overseas—"

"Theo said nothing to me—"

"I haven't been taking him with me, I've been taking Brian." Danial's eyes caught mine meaningfully.

"You must know where his loyalties lie. Aren't you upset with him?"

"No, I suspected right from the first. Devlin never lets anyone go who has been with him long, because by then they know the lay of Hayden. Even if he'd only worked outside the house, Brian should have had a scar or two from ending his contract with Dev early. What matters is he fanatically watches out for you."

"Does he know you know?"

"No, but he suspects. He is afraid to broach the subject with me, afraid I'll fire him."

"Don't do that. He's a good man. I trust him."

"I don't plan to," Danial soothed. "Now get on your clothes, Darling. Chuck just drove up with Annabelle Lee and Poe."

Excited, I hurriedly dressed. "So we're riding first?"

"Yes," Danial nodded. "But, no, I haven't forgotten the pizza. It will be here soon." He offered me his hand. "Come."

Happily, I took let him lead me outside, eager to hear the first welcoming neigh of a horse on the night breeze.

* * * *

Terian teleported Danial and I home late the next afternoon. I went about the house, greeting the pets and picking up, hoping the glow of contentment over me wasn't too noticeable, especially as Danial had elected to touch base with Theo.

"Why can't it wait?" I asked again, letting out Ghost and Darkness. "This isn't the time for you to talk to Theo, Danial."

Danial petted Cavity, who'd homed in on his lap and was already curled up, purring happily. "Maybe not, but I'm going to anyway."

Theo walked in, Elle at his heels. "You're home," he said happily.

Elle went right for Danial. "Dad, Theo says I can come every weekend!" she said happily. "Is that right?"

"Yes," he said. "Maybe we'll go to the movies again next weekend, too."

"Great!" she exclaimed, and then ran into her bedroom, to return with her bag.

"Ready to go?" Terian said from behind me, startling me.

"Yes," Elle said. Taking his hand, they both disappeared.

"Why are you still here, Danial?" Theo said pointedly, folding his arms across his chest. "There's nothing that can't wait until tomorrow."

"I'm waiting for Devlin to get here," Danial replied. "I need to talk to you both."

Theo's eyes cut to me questioningly. I shrugged.

Devlin appeared with Terian, who let him go, and then disappeared again.

"Why am I here?" Devlin said, folding his arms, irritated at Danial. "What is so important?"

"I want Sar to go away with me for a few days in the next month or so," Danial said casually. "I wanted to talk to you both about it, before I made arrangements."

"You are not taking her, brother," Devlin growled, his eyes red.

Theo came up to stand beside Devlin, also incensed. "He's right," Theo said. "Anything could happen."

"Like what?" Danial said in exasperation. "We're going to go someplace not very far away from here. If the Lust hits, I'll handle it. I won't let her roam by herself, unattended—"

"Danial," Devlin sang meaningfully. "She's having my child—"

Danial glared back, his answering words brusque and forceful. "If there is any sign of anything wrong, I'll call Terian to teleport her out of there. And that's only if Sar can't just do it herself."

"I want to come, too," Devlin said jealously. "I—"

"You just had some time with her alone a few weeks ago," Danial retorted, his eyes red now. "It's something I want. We're going to do it, Dev."

Theo opened his mouth.

Danial shot him a look. "And you had a honeymoon with her, so keep it shut!"

"Not a quiet one!" Theo retorted. "You were always calling—!"

"Stop it!" I shouted. "Before I kick all of you out!"

Devlin sighed. "If you want to go, go ahead. I'm okay with it, Love."

"I haven't agreed yet," Theo growled. "I have a say in where she goes."

Devlin rolled his eyes. "What objection could you possibly have if she wants to go, and she's safe?"

"It's not safe," Terian said, appearing suddenly in our midst.

Theo grabbed for his gun, I let out a yell, Devlin started, and Danial was knocked off balance, as Terian was standing too close to him when he appeared. He half sat, half fell down on the couch.

"Don't ever fucking do that again!" Devlin said, glaring at Terian. "You hear me, half-breed?"

Terian sneered at him. "Or what?"

Danial got up fluidly, and went to stand in front of Terian. "Dev's right, Terian. Enough theatrics. Lately you've been full of yourself, and it's annoying everyone, including me. Knock it off."

Terian's look was cold, not respectful. For some reason, that scared me.

"He's right," Theo said, his tone still electric with adrenaline. "Stop scaring people, especially Sar. You want to scare someone, save it for our enemies."

"Fine," Terian said coolly. "I was just making a point."

"What point?" Devlin said.

"That anyone can teleport in here at any time," Terian said. "I need to do some sort of spell here, as Titus did at Hayden. I've done one at your house already, Danial."

"So do it," Danial said easily. "I want Sar protected."

"There's more," Terian said uneasily.

"What?" we all said.

"Leri is back in town," he answered.

# Chapter Twelve

"What do you mean, she's back?" Theo asked. "Have you seen her?"

"No, but Titus has. She came to him one night in a dream, asked him for his forgiveness. She's always been able to do that with him, he said, but she has to be somewhere in the surrounding towns. She can't do it from a distance. So she's here—"

"Fucking great!" Devlin spat. "Before I know it, they'll be back together again!"

I looked at him, astounded. "She tried to kill Terian. Titus wouldn't take her back."

Devlin shot me a bitter smile. "She's tried to kill him before, Sar. Three times. He took her back every damn time."

*Fucking great, indeed.* "That's terrible."

"He might at that," Terian said sadly. "It was in his words how much he misses her, despite what she did to me."

I couldn't think of anything constructive to say, so I said nothing. Theo had no such restraint. "He'd have to be fucking crazy to do that. Devlin, if you let Titus take her back, if she lives with you at Hayden, I'm not letting Sar come to you at your home. Leri threatened her as well as Terian. She probably wants revenge on Sar for doing that."

"I agree, Dev," I said.

"I agree, also," Danial said, his eyes on Devlin. "Sar is not going to your house to spend time if Leri comes to live there again."

"Agreed, for now," Devlin said, holding up his hands in a submissive gesture. "I don't want Leri living there again anyway. She wrecked a lot of the house, and I'm just starting work on some of the worst areas." He looked at me. "Sar is helping with some of it," he said proudly.

Theo gave me a curious look.

Danial nodded. "I thought she probably would. She likes to keep busy, and fixing things is one of her favorite hobbies."

"There is a lot she is working on for me. In fact, Theo, you may need to let her come to my house more often—"

"Dev," Theo growled. "I've been very understanding about all this. Don't push it."

Devlin narrowed his eyes, but said nothing.

"Back to the business at hand," Theo continued. "I'll agree to Sar going with Danial on his getaway if you both okay her going west with me and Elle sometime in the summer."

"Why?" Devlin said quickly, glancing from Theo to me and back again. "Where?"

"Sar's in-laws want to meet me," Theo said proudly. "And I want to show Elle where Sar found me, where we spent time after she came to me. We'd stay a week or so."

"I don't have a problem with that," Danial said, after a moment. "But it has to be only a week at most. Teleport."

Theo nodded. For some reason, that small movement caused my simmering rage to boil over.

"I'll agree," Devlin said slowly. "If you let me have her for a week to myself as well—"

"Anyone want to bother asking me what I want?" I screeched.

All eyes turned to me. Theo and Devlin looked surprised, but Danial looked almost as if he had been expecting this.

"It's my decision," I said bitingly "If I go or stay, and who I go with where."

No one said anything for at least a minute. Then Danial cleared his throat.

"Are you saying you don't want to go with me?" he asked neutrally. "Because last night you made me believe that you did."

I knew I'd hurt him. Stifling my guilt, I made myself go on. "I want to go with you," I said, giving him a soft look. "Check into places, and let me know." I turned to Theo. "Yes, we should go out west. I haven't seen my relatives in a long time, and Elle should come—"

I met Devlin's eyes, red and wrathful. "And you can calm down. We spent time alone just a few weeks ago. You're swamped with your duties anyway. Sometime next fall we can take a short trip, when things settle down."

Devlin's eyes changed slowly back to gold. "If you're consenting to each request, what was your outburst about?"

"That this fighting over me has to end. No more taunts and nastiness, Devlin. No more trying to find a way to free me from my Oath, Theo. And Danial, relax already; I said I'd come to you. Don't freak out if I'm a few minutes late, because it's going to happen occasionally."

They all looked at me as if they weren't sure who they were looking at.

"Look," I said, folding my arms across my chest. "This is really hard for me. I was raised to believe it should be one man, one woman. It's not that I don't love you, because I do. I just don't like this situation, if you can call it that. As things are right now, I just can't do it."

I had their full attention now. "What do you mean?" Theo said.

"I need you all to stop demanding so much of me, or remove yourselves from our ménage-a-quatre. I like sex, probably more even than the average woman, but I am worn out—"

"Sar—" Danial said tenderly, reaching for me.

I stepped away from him, and held up my hand. "Let me finish!" I said firmly.

He nodded, and drew his hand back.

"Is everyone okay with what I just said?" I asked pointedly.

"I'm okay with it," Devlin said. "But you and I need to talk more about this, the next time you come to me. We should come up with some clear plan, so I at least am not contributing to your distress."

*Was he saying he'd need another lover? I'd have to find out then.* "Fine."

Devlin gave me a chaste kiss, then turned to Terian. "Take me back."

Terian took his hand, and then they disappeared.

Danial slipped his arms around me. "I'm okay with you visiting once a week. You can do nothing more than sleep beside me when you need to. Not every time, please, but I don't want you to feel the way you are feeling now. And it goes without saying, if you are pregnant that I won't expect sex until sometime after the child is born, when you're ready."

"Thank you," I said gratefully.

"I'll see you tomorrow." Danial hugged me. "Take me home, Sar."

I teleported him home in an instant. When I moved to step away from him in the great room, he stopped me. "Wait! I wanted to be alone with you."

"Why?"

"Devlin may ask you to let him be with other women. He has always had more than one lover, Sar. I wanted to warn you, in case you didn't realize it."

I took a burn. "Not when he was with Anna. He said he was faithful to her—"

"She was his. They spent every night together. He never had to share her like this."

"Then he should give me up!" I said angrily. "He—"

"Sar, it is within his rights to take you to Hayden, and keep you there," Danial said harshly. "Don't push him, because he wants to do that. He is waiting for Theo or you to give him an excuse to do just that—"

*Always about vampire rights and vampire laws!* "Danial, he gave me his word that he wouldn't be with anyone else for a decade! I told him I understood if he wanted to be, and he said he loved only me, that he wanted only me!"

Danial hugged me close. "He may have felt that way at the time, but he thought, as I did, that Theo was leaving you. If he only shared you with me, he probably could do it. But his sexual appetites have always run to excess. He'd likely have asked anyway when you are in your last months of pregnancy—"

"What are you advising?" I said abruptly. "Be blunt."

"Share him, as he is sharing you. Let him take other lovers. He can't give you anything. There is no danger."

"That was never the reason I didn't want him to be with someone else," I managed.

"I know, Love," Danial said, hugging me. "But if you really love him, you need to let him have what he needs."

Sickened, I nodded. "I'll take it under advisement. Now, I'd better get back to Theo." I teleported back to my home, not waiting for his reply.

Theo was on the couch vegetating. He shut off the TV when I appeared. "He wanted to talk to you in private, too?" he said, pulling me down beside him. "About what?"

I made a face. "He said Devlin will want other lovers, and to give him what he wants."

"Will you?" Theo asked.

"Probably," I said, after a moment. "What choice do I have? I thought he would get tired of me, just not this soon."

"If only he would," Theo said, hugging me close. "I want him to get tired of you, Sar, so it's just the two of us again. Well, three, but I don't mind Danial anymore."

The thought of losing Devlin to another woman made me feel like my chest was on fire. It hurt to breathe.

"I didn't realize how I was making you feel," Theo said gently. "We don't have to be intimate every night. It's enough that you are here with me."

"Thank you, Theo," I said, hugging him halfheartedly.

That night, despite my distraction over Devlin, I was aware of a change in Theo. Not only did he heat up dinner, he also made us popcorn. Later, when we went to bed, he held me, but didn't push for more. As much as I was relieved, I wanted to know this was real, not just temporary good behavior.

"Are you sure this is going to be okay?" I asked him.

"Is what okay?" Theo said, pushing my hair out of my eyes.

"Is this enough?" I said pointedly. "More importantly, is it going to be?"

"You only ever needed to say something," Theo replied, shifting uneasily. "Besides, I'd planned to take it easier with you in any case."

I shot him a look of bewilderment. "What?"

"When Tasha and I were together—"

I rolled away from him immediately, but he grabbed me. "No, listen, please!"

I lay there silent, fuming.

"She didn't put my needs above her own, like you did. When she told me her body couldn't take what I would do to her, I didn't believe her. I thought I was being careful. Then she went to a doctor here to get on birth control, and he wanted her to report me for abuse."

"Normal sex is sometimes rough—"

"He said that it had to be rape because I had bruised her so badly." Theo cleared his throat. "Just like I hurt you, I'm sure."

I didn't speak, or look at him, knowing he'd see the answer in my eyes.

"Now that I know I hurt you doing it, I'll be careful. I don't get off on causing you pain."

That was another dig at Devlin, but I let it slide. "Fine," I said neutrally. "Let's go to sleep. I'm exhausted."

* * * *

The following Monday afternoon, while eating lunch out with the kids and Terian, I brought up Titus.

"How are things with your father?"

"Why do you ask?" Terian said, giving me a funny look.

"I care about you and I'm beginning to like him," I said bluntly. "But some of the spells he uses are black magic. I can't tell if I should trust him or not."

"He's not as nice as you think he is," Terian said cryptically.

*Was he being overly dramatic, or honest?* "Elaborate," I requested, taking a sip of my hot chocolate. Elle and Theoron both were still eating their super-size sundaes. *God, what I would give to be a child again and not worry about calories at all.*

"Titus knows a lot of magic, Sar. He's almost a thousand years old."

"Wow. I hadn't suspected that."

"He does know a lot of dark magic, but that's the more powerful magic. And yes, he's teaching me some of it."

"Should I ask about what you want it for," I said gently, "or would you rather I didn't?"

"Titus told me about that spell he used on that woman," Terian murmured. "You know the one I'm talking about, right?"

136

*Harriet.* "Do you think it worked?"

"It should've," Terian said, nodding. "Though your blood might not be the only factor."

"What else could be?" I supplied. "My natural resistance?"

"Maybe. Possibly that you were with Danial so long, both before and after he gained power. It had to help that your body was strong, from the life you led." Terian paused, then whispered, "Harriet and you are very different, Sar. She is younger by about ten years, and her body is very delicate and thin."

"Her youth might be an advantage." *Provided, of course, that she didn't miscarry.*

"You know Monica asked me about altering her blood," Terian continued. "She wanted me to get a sample of your blood, so she could try to change hers."

*Every time I heard that wench's name, I got pissed off all over again.* "She told me that before I killed her."

Elle abruptly stopped eating, shooting me a look of disquiet.

*Shit.* I said nothing, hoping she'd not ask questions.

"I refused to help her," Terian went on. "She cared about Danial, but I knew he didn't love her, and that you would never agree—"

Just like that, my blood pressure skyrocketed again. "Damn straight," I said vehemently.

Theoron and Elle both stared at me, shocked.

Well, if they knew I killed people, knowing I swore wasn't that bad, so long as they didn't do it, anyway. Regardless, lunch was over. "Come on, kids. Let's head home."

Theoron opened his mouth, his gleeful expression testament that he planned to echo me.

*Dissuade, then distract.* "Don't use that phrase I just said," I said quickly. "Mommy didn't mean to say it, and it's not polite." I stood up. "Grab your things. It's time to leave."

"Okay," Theoron and Elle said together, gathering up their wrappers and coats.

"Yes, we should get back," Terian said eagerly. "I've got a lot to do this afternoon."

He wasn't just enthusiastic; he was a rampant lion prancing. "Spill it, Terian."

"Not that it's your business, but I'm back with Sundown," he stated.

I stared at him. *Jesus Christ. Hadn't he learned the first time she was bad news?*

"She's moving in with me at Danial's," Terian continued. "When you meet her, try to be nice."

"I'm always nice," I answered, miffed. "Did she come to terms with what you are?"

"She says she wants to try," Terian said carefully. "She hasn't been serious about anyone since me, or so she said."

I felt a sinking feeling. Terian was hopeful and positive, but Sundown had ripped out his heart the last time they'd broken up, back when he asked her to marry him. She'd likely do it again.

I managed a smile. "Good luck. I hope that it works out."

"Me, too," Terian said. "Let's get going."

\* \* \* \*

The next day, Tuesday, I called Dr. Camlyn, and explained the fertility spell situation to him. "Does that make a difference in how early you can test me?"

"Yes. I can test you in a week and a half," Stephen replied. "Have you had any other symptoms?"

"No, I haven't been sick or anything."

"Come in a week from Friday." He paused meaningfully. "Evening or afternoon appointment?"

"Devlin will want to be there," I replied, irritated. "Can you make it a night appointment?"

"Of course." He paused again. "You realize that if it's Theo's—"

"I told him, Stephen."

"Come in about eight," Stephen said, very relieved. "I'll let Danial know."

I hung up, considering if it was wise to have both Devlin and Theo there. I couldn't exclude one, and include the other. I grimaced. The way I felt now, I'd rather exclude them all and find out by myself.

\* \* \* \*

Devlin called late Wednesday night. "How are you feeling, Love?"

I'd missed his voice, and him. "I'm fine."

"I got your email," he continued. "I'll meet you at the doctor's at the time you sent me. What I'm calling for is to ask you to teleport to Hayden later tonight for an hour or so."

"Yes," I said, shooting a look at Theo, who was listening in on the other line. "Say eleven?"

"Yes. See you then—"

"Wait! Did Titus fix the barrier?"

"Yes," Devlin answered. "But only to the kitchen. Don't try to go to any other room, or you'll end up outside the gates again."

"Okay. See you then."

"Good-bye, my love," Devlin said, and hung up.

"What was that about?" Theo asked.

"I'm not sure," I said slowly. "But I'll let you know as soon as I get home."

"I'll be in bed when you get back," Theo said. "Just crawl in beside me."

"Don't shoot me," I said sarcastically.

"You're hilarious," Theo said, rolling his eyes. "Now come over here and cuddle with me. South Park's on."

\* \* \* \*

When I teleported to Hayden's kitchen, I startled a woman who was doing the dishes. Her brunette hair was to her shoulders, her skin like coffee with cream. She was cute, but not beautiful. Some of that was her hazel eyes, which bore a hunted cast like a deer in mid-December, right before the end of hunting season.

"Hi, I'm Sarelle," I said, extending my hand. "You must be Serena?"

"Yes," she said, and smiled. At once, some of the wariness left her eyes.

*Was she was Spanish or Brazilian by birth? Something to ask when I knew her better.* "Dev talked to me, about teaching you some baking," I said without preamble. "I'll be back on Friday morning, if you want to do some then."

"Let me check my schedule," she said quickly. "But yes, I want very much to learn."

"Good," I said, giving her a smile. "I like—"

"Sarelle," Lash hissed from the doorway. "Devlin waits for you upstairs."

I'd just gotten here, and I would have to run into him. I shot him a fake smile, and went to the base of the stairs.

"Friday morning you are already busy, Darlin', remember?" Lash hissed from behind me. "Be here about eight or so. The bears will not be coming with us. If we have a lot of purchases, Titus can teleport them to Hayden."

*Shit, I had asked him to help me get the supplies.* "Fine, I'll be here."

Lash nodded. "I'll tell Serena the bakefest will have to wait." He turned, heading back to the kitchen.

Did he see Serena, *in addition* to that snake waitress? I was repulsed at the thought, then shamed because I was looking down on him for maybe doing something that I was definitely doing with even more people. Grumpily, I went to Devlin's bedroom door, and knocked hard. "Your lover has arrived."

"Come in, Sar," Devlin said seductively.

I went in. Devlin was as he had been before, sitting on his bed, reading paperwork scattered about him. "Your intro doesn't fit with this scene," I teased, coming to sit beside him.

"I know," Devlin said, rubbing his eyes. "I'll be right with you. I'm trying to decide what to do with these companies of Ebediah's. I have high offers for both, money I can well use. But I have to look at every angle first before committing, a tiring enterprise."

He wasn't tired; he was exhausted, by his voice. "Do you want some help?"

Devlin looked at me, incredulous. "You don't have time," he said finally.

"You need help. I can spend a couple hours easily each week, at least. Like you said, this is temporary."

Devlin gave me a dubious look. "You already help Danial with Solutions, Inc."

"I could come Tuesday and Thursday," I said. "I used to just go in Mondays and Fridays to help Danial—"

Devlin put down his paperwork and pulled me into his arms. "Come in Wednesdays," he murmured. "One day is enough, Sar. I don't work as Danial does. If it was not for Ebediah's affairs, I wouldn't be so busy now."

"You said you could use the money," I said hesitantly. "Are you strapped for cash?"

He kissed my neck softly. "No. I was rich from the moment I first became Ruler of the States," he whispered. "I amassed a fortune in the centuries that followed. Most of my income comes from investments like company stock and cash. It requires little thought." He moved his shoulders, wincing. "I don't usually work this hard or this much. The strain is getting to me."

"Come sit on the loveseat for me," I said, getting up from the bed. "I can fix that."

Once he was settled, I began kneading his shoulders. Devlin groaned under my hands as I massaged out all the knots in his shoulders. By the time I was done, he was relaxed back into the cushion, a happy smile of ease on his lips.

I sat down beside him, feeling like a spider who'd baited a fly. "Now, why did you want me to come tonight?"

Devlin tensed up immediately, then said bluntly, "I want your permission to go to a few women I know for sex."

Danial had braced me for these words, but the situation was still surreal. I didn't answer.

"It will not be here," he said gently. "I want only you in my bed. But I can't do with just seeing you once a week, Sar. I'm sorry, but I can't." He tilted my chin up to look at him. "What I do with them will be…other than what I share with you."

I looked blankly back at him. "Like?"

140

"Oral sex," Devlin said bluntly. "No regular intercourse. I'm a sadist, Sar, as you know. I'd prefer you not see that side of me now."

*I didn't want to see that side, ever.* "If you want that, it's okay with me."

"You aren't angry? You aren't jealous?" Devlin said, flabbergasted. "I was sure you would be angry, after what I told you that night that I'd only be with you."

This was too unreal for me to feel much of anything. "Will you promise not to have regular sex with them?"

"Yes," Devlin said gently. "I promise everything else is for you. Just you."

I looked at him, imagining him having sex with another woman, her touching him, stroking him, and him crying out his orgasm, because she had brought him pleasure with her body. Jealousy engulfed me. "Do you want me now?"

"You're jealous," he said, turning his head and looking at me with veiled eyes.

"Yes, I am," I said, kissing him on his throat, and biting softly. "Be with me."

Devlin embraced me in a passionate kiss, and I clutched him to me, my passion a vortex that drew me ever deeper into darkness.

\* \* \* \*

I lay completely sated in his arms two hours later, my mind happily drifting.

"Love, it's a new morning," Devlin whispered. "I must leave to finish my business, but you are welcome to stay if you wish."

Theo would be wondering where I was. Pricked by a sharp stab of guilt, I made myself move. "No, thanks. I need to go," I said, giving him a final kiss. "Be safe."

"You, too," he said lovingly. "Take care."

A few minutes later, I crawled in beside Theo. Immediately, he snuggled me close, then jerked back. Though he didn't speak, I knew he was irritated, and the cause was Devlin's scent on my skin. Upset and angry, I left our bed, and went to the downstairs basement. Though I was comfortable enough there, I slept little, my fitful sleep full of nightmares.

\* \* \* \*

On Thursday, Danial and I went through several possible vacation destinations, finally settling on Letchworth State Park.

"There are several rental properties inside the park, Sar. Which do you like best?" Danial asked.

"Whichever you prefer," I said. "It depends when you want to go."

"This month," he said at once. "February."

I'd envisioned summer flowers and warm nights, not snowdrifts and wool coats. "These places are heated, right?"

"Yes," Danial laughed. "There is also a four star restaurant inside the park that delivers, and the houses themselves all have a full kitchen, if you don't feel like going out."

*God, that sounded great.* "I'm in," I said, nodding. "Just tell me the week you make reservations for."

"I'll call tomorrow," Danial said, pleased.

\* \* \* \*

Friday dawned clear, but warm. As I dressed, I thought resentfully that Lash had no reason now not to meet me. There had been a thawing of the winter chill this past week, and some bare patches were beginning to appear in the yard. Darkness and Ghost particularly enjoyed the thaw, spending a good portion of our walks seeking out and tearing up old mouse nests, shaking the dry grass everywhere. Yet while I'd loved the warm weather, it meant that there would be no reprieve from Lash's abrasive company.

Hurrying fast, I teleported to Hayden just in time to be in the kitchen at eight a.m. sharp. Lash was waiting for me. At once, he nodded to me, then making a gesture with his head to follow, he went into the attached garage and got into one of the Hummers.

I got into the passenger side. "Where are we going first?" I murmured.

"Bakeware, then hardware. I need to arrange for more supplies to fix the ballroom." He turned to me suddenly, fixing me with his flat eyes. "Is there someplace special you need to go to get what you need?"

*He sounded less irritated than he had before. Maybe it had been the volume of my voice he'd been annoyed over, not the words I'd spoken. I could try lowering it and see.* "Any department store or super-store should have what I need," I answered softly. "I need basic things, nothing fancy."

Lash nodded, then raised the garage door, and backed out slowly.

\* \* \* \*

Despite Lash's silence, our excursion went well.

He had worn a long wool coat, so his weapons at his waist were covered. Though he was again all in black, because of the time of year and the wool, he looked more like a yuppie than an assassin. With lightly tinted sunglasses to hide his snake eyes, he drew no attention in the stores save for a few stares over his scar. Yet I knew what he was, and it was still unnerving being close to him, even if he looked normal to those around me.

We stopped for lunch near noon. Another surprise was Lash's refusal to join me in eating, electing only for a glass of water. I had never seen a wereanimal of any type refuse food of any kind. More curious, the water was the only drink he consumed. For the length of my meal, he just sat there in his seat and stared at me unrelentingly with his flat eyes, not uttering a word.

If I had been a woman with a nervous stomach, or high strung, I probably wouldn't have been able to eat with him doing nothing but watching me. But I had never had a problem eating. Further, I didn't care if he liked me much, especially as he'd repeatedly made it a point for me to know he didn't.

"Do you want dessert?" he hissed, when I was done with my entree. "You might as well use the excuse to indulge, even if you haven't caught yet."

My hackles went up. "No," I said coolly, checking my watch. "We should get moving. I'll use the restroom while you sit here and think of more intelligent retorts."

When I returned, Lash was paying the bill at the register. As we walked to the car, he took a flask from his pocket, and swallowed a long pull. As soon as we got in the Hummer, I said pointedly "Should I drive?"

Lash laughed bitterly. "It's blood, Sar, not alcohol."

*Ew.* I could understand a vampire drinking blood for nourishment, but a wereanimal? Now I understood why he had wanted to taste me. I nodded, and didn't comment.

The rest of the afternoon was spent at the hardware store, most of that at the paint station. I gathered many paint strips to show to Dev, as well as several good brushes, a few rollers, some tarps, and an extending pole. Not wanting to return with no actual paint, I finally chose a deep green, dark, almost like moss when it first emerges in the spring.

Lash came walking up as I placed it in the cart, and nodded in approval.

"Are you set?" I asked.

"Yes. I ordered lumber, wallboard, and joint compound to be delivered."

"Are you going to replace the mirrors?" I asked, curious.

"Dev's thinking about it," Lash said finally. "He never uses the ballroom. Well, he used it once, or so he says. He has not used it in decades, because of security. But he wants it looking nice, just in case, I guess."

*In case of what, an impromptu visit by fifty guests?* "Ah," I said, not wanting to antagonize him.

"Is this all you need?" Lash hissed tiredly. "If it is, let's go."

\* \* \* \*

As soon as we arrived back at Hayden, I parted ways with Lash and got started painting. Serena met up with me in the kitchen an hour later, as I was washing paint off my hands. With her help, I unpacked and washed all of the baking equipment.

"We're ready to go," I said, pleased. "Can you meet me here at noon tomorrow?"

"What will you be making?" Devlin said, coming into the kitchen and hugging me.

At once, I was struck that there was something off about him. With sadness, I realized it was his mellowness; his movements and tone were telltale signs of recent sexual release. I fought up my rising jealousy and anger, rationalizing that I hadn't liked what little I'd seen of his sadism. It was better this way for both of us.

"Sar?" he prompted.

"Pie first," I said, managing a smile. "Then other desserts, breads, then meatloaf and soups. If you have any particular dishes, now's the time to tell me."

"Whatever you wish to make is fine," Devlin said to me. He looked to Serena. "Vince is waiting for you, upstairs."

She nodded once, and left.

"How did it go?" Dev whispered in my ear. "Lash said you were meeting him at eight to get supplies."

"Come and see," I said, beaming. I led him to the wall I'd painted. "Do you like it?"

"Very much," Devlin said, pleased. "Will you choose other colors, or just this one?"

"Many." I showed him some of the other color samples. "Choose a few."

After some discussion and deliberation with me, Devlin picked out the ones he liked best, handing them to me, then tossing the others in a nearby garbage can.

I took them out, incensed. "You should recycle. The earth is finite—"

He gave me an amused look, then took my hand and led me into the garage, where he introduced me to his stacks of recycling bins. "I do. I just forgot, in my excitement."

I put the strips inside the nearest one marked paper. "Oh," I said, chagrined. "Sorry."

"Most vampires are eco-friendly," Devlin said, his eyebrows raised. "I'm going to live a long time. I want the earth to be as it is now; not desert, one huge city, or covered with water."

"It would be hard to find blood that wasn't marine life," I quipped.

"It would be hard to find women, and dry surfaces to have them on,"

Devlin retorted, laughing. "Especially one particular woman, in a planet-sized ocean—"

Lash entered the garage, his countenance looking rested and awake. "Are you ready to go to Davy's?" he hissed. "Cin's expecting me tonight."

"Titus gave it to you," Devlin stated.

"Yes," Lash hissed, and grinned. "Now let's go."

Lash had taken another dose of whatever it was that kept him going. That was why he looked so spry.

Devlin grinned. "Sar, get your coat."

\* \* \* \*

When we got to Davy's there wasn't much of a crowd yet. In fact, it was so early there was barely anyone else there. At once, Cin came over to take our order, but before she said anything, Lash picked her up and took her straight to the back. Without another handy option, I decided to ignore the reason and just be glad he was gone.

Gary came over and took our order. As I gave mine, I pondered why he didn't mind Cin and Lash doing what they were doing in the back. *Perhaps Devlin really owned this bar, or maybe Lash did?*

Devlin and I bantered back and forth, our conversation teasing and easy. We'd just finished our first glass of wine, and I, my chicken fingers, when Lash came sauntering back.

"Stay with her," Devlin said, standing. "I'll be a little while."

Lash nodded, but I gave Devlin a blank look. "What?"

Devlin gestured. "Look at the bar. Blond, second to last."

I looked out of the corner of my eye. Yes, there was a blonde there. She was eyeing Dev like he was the last burger on the plate in a roomful of empty buns.

Lash nodded. "Sure."

Devlin sauntered over to her and struck up a conversation. A few moments later he whispered something in her ear, then led her outside to the parking lot.

"Is he going to kill her?" I whispered as soft as I could.

"Probably not," Lash replied, then grinned. "He got his rocks off earlier, plus he's on good behavior here." He smiled wider. "Like usual, when you're around."

Flushing again, I finished my wine. Lash downed his, too, then poured us both the rest of it, which was about half a glass each. He looked at me. "Want me to toast?"

I grimaced. "If it's something besides good times with women."

His smile widened, then he hissed, "To you and Dev; that it be his child inside you, not that stupid werecat's."

*Motherfucker!* I was completely still in my fury. Lash clinked my glass with his, then drank most of it down. I drank a good deal of mine down, too, in my anger. I sat there and trembled with frustration, furious with him.

"Something I said, Sar?" Lash hissed slyly.

"Fuck you!" I hissed back at him. "I tried to be nice to you all day, you jerk—!"

"Shut up," Lash hissed easily. "I'm Dev's friend. I'd do anything for him, including watch your ass, as stultifying as I find you. But Theo's a thorn in his side and mine. I've kicked his ass repeatedly over the years, yet he's stupid enough that he always comes back for more. A male has to know his limits. He should accept when he's just not good enough."

There was a good deal of resentment in his easy words. I sipped my wine and didn't reply.

"For example," Lash went on. "If it had been me there with Dev that night he came for you, he'd have gotten you without losing men, or getting shot." He turned menacing. "Later on, he'd have done whatever he wanted with you, because I would have stopped anyone interfering." He gave me an evil smile. "But don't think too much on it, Sar. It'd be such a shame if you weren't sitting here with me now."

# Chapter Thirteen

I averted my eyes. I was going to hit him. God, give me the strength to control myself until Devlin got back.

Abruptly, the first strains of Bad Company's "Feel Like Making Love" came on the jukebox, as a scantily clad woman in jeans strutted her way to her man at the bar.

"I can smell your anger," Lash hissed, pleased. "At least something's going right tonight—"

My control snapped. I turned to Lash, sprawled in his chair beside me. "Listen you—"

As my eyes met his flat ones, The Lust washed through me.

"Listen to what?" Lash hissed tauntingly. "Why don't you try and threaten me? I haven't had a good laugh in ages."

He was the nastiest SOB here for sure, the most dangerous, the worst of the worst. He would hurt me if he could. I shivered, because I wanted him to.

I wanted him.

I lunged at him, knocking over both chairs. As we both fell, Lash moved supernaturally fast, getting out from underneath me so we landed side by side, still entangled.

Devlin yelled, "Sar!"

If Dev got to us, I'd never have Lash, not how I wanted him. Cin could be a problem, too. I closed my eyes, teleporting us instantly. We arrived in Devlin's bedroom, still lying on the floor. I was immediately relieved to not be outside the gates.

Lash shot to his feet immediately, yanking me up as well. "Damn it! I told him to tell you that you had to go to the kitchen first!" he hissed angrily. "Take us back to Devlin, now!"

"No," I snarled. "I want you here on this bed. His bed."

Lash narrowed his eyes, but said nothing.

"Come on," I purred seductively, strutting closer. "Don't you wonder what it would be like with me? Why Devlin would give up his other women, just to share me?"

A cell phone rang. Not taking his eyes from me, Lash took out his phone, and held it to his ear. "Dev, we're at Hayden. Get here as soon as you can. Something is wrong with Sar. I'll hold her until you get here."

"The hell you will!" I sneered, striding fast to the door. "You won't do it, I'll find someone else to do the job!" *There had to be at least one bear here somewhere...*

I threw open the door, heard a soft hiss, then was yanked backwards, the end of Lash's whip coiled about my waist. He got between me and the door, then closed it.

"So this is the infamous lust Devlin's been talking about so eagerly," Lash hissed, turning to face me. "I knew it wasn't going to be what he thought." He gave me a grin, then pulled me toward him. "But this is too good to be true."

He was relishing this. I didn't want him to be happy; I wanted him to be angry. "Are you ever going to shut up—?"

"Ask me to fuck you," Lash hissed dangerously, baring his snake fangs, his tongue flickering out. "Beg me."

Slight fear twitched inside me, then was consumed by need. I grabbed a hold of the whip at my waist, struggling to undo it. Lash held it taut, then began to slowly pull me toward him.

Anger consumed me. I leaned hard away, pretending to strain to get free, then quickly ran towards Lash, closing the distance between us and catching him off balance. I took the opening, reaching quickly for his pants zipper with a sultry smile. He fended me off, dropping his whip and his phone on the bedroom floor as he grabbed my hands. At once, he shoved me hard to the side. I sprawled on the floor, struggling to get the whip off me.

I had to get it off and get us both somewhere where no one would find us. Titus would be here with Devlin in moments.

I finally got the whip off me. Lash was crouching, reaching for his ringing phone, which had skittered under the edge of Dev's bed.

I knew someplace where there were no phones, somewhere Titus wouldn't be able to follow. I grabbed hold of Lash just before he reached it and teleported us again, this time much farther. We were suddenly in a moonlit house, the air cold around us. I shivered, my breath a white plume. The furniture around me was covered in sheets, dust thick on the countertop.

Lash's head darted around wildly. "Where the hell are we?" he hissed in shock.

I took his confusion as an opening. Running my hands up into his wild black hair, I kissed him hard, moving my mouth hungrily on his. I'd expected his hair to be oily, or maybe spiky with gel, but it was soft under my hands. His lips were hot, his long, thin fangs hard beneath them. *Was all of him like that?* I groaned at the thought, pressing myself against him eagerly.

He broke away from me. "Sar, where are we?" he demanded. "Take us back to Hayden—"

"Fuck me first," I hissed back at him, then kissed him again. "I'm asking you. I want you, Lash—"

He pried me off him, thrusting me away. "But I don't want you, Sar. I don't particularly like you, even—"

"I don't like you either," I said with a snarl. "I just want to feel you come in me, feel your fangs inside me again. Only this time, I want them all the way in, just like you."

He went still at my words, like I knew he would. I knew men, knew what they wanted to hear, knew what they wanted me to do to them. A moment's hesitation was all I needed.

I kissed him again, trying to convince him with my passion to give in. This time he didn't push me away. I reached down and felt for him. Ah, my words had had the effect I'd wanted: he was tight for me, the bulge in his jeans rock hard under my hand. I stroked him through his jeans, still kissing him.

Lash wouldn't open his mouth to me, but he moved under my touch, flexing gently. *If I could push him over the edge…*

"Fuck me," I whispered sexily. "Now."

"No," he hissed back, then pried me off him and went looking for a phone.

Relentless, I went after him, pulling my clothes off as fast as possible. The cold made my skin contract, goose bumps rising almost immediately on my arms and breasts.

I was so cold. I needed his warmth, needed him warm inside me. My lust had reached a fever pitch, my patience gone.

Lash was just picking up the bedroom receiver when I jerked the cord out of the wall. I lunged at him again. He caught me this time, turning to slam me up against the wall. I stumbled over the cord, jerking the phone off the nightstand with a crash. I let out a gasp, and Lash covered my mouth with his, his mouth opening as his forked tongue began licking me, reaching deeply. His tongue twined around mine loosely, and stroked gently. The sensation was completely new, utterly sensual, spiking my arousal. I let out an eager moan, and clutched him tighter. He turned then and threw me on the bed, scrambling on top of me, then pressed down with a hard thrust of his hips.

"You want what I've got for you?" he hissed suggestively. "Hold still."

I went motionless under him, encouraging him with eager cries. He moved my hands into one of his, still kissing me. I went limp with momentary relief in his grip, then began writhing as he reached down to take off his pants.

"Yes," I moaned, my breaths coming fast. "Please, Lash!"

Then I felt the phone cord about my wrists. In an instant, Lash had me tied by my wrists to the bed.

*He'd been reaching for the cord!* "Damn you!" I swore loudly.

Lash gave me a grin, baring his fangs. "Stay there," he hissed. Then he got up and strode out of the room.

Livid with rage, and being denied, I yanked with my arms as hard as I could. The cord tightened, his knots holding.

*Damn him! They'd never come loose now!*

I was bleeding where the phone cord had bitten into my wrist. Letting out a scream of rage, I bit into the cord with my right incisor, grinding hard. The plastic frayed under my teeth. I yanked as hard as I could, the cord snapped, and I fell off the bed to land on the floor in a heap. I scrambled to my feet with hands still bound and went after Lash.

He was talking on a cordless phone, leaning against the kitchen counter. "I told you, she won't tell me where we are, Dev. I think it's in Wyoming though, that's where the phone book is from, and the area code matched up. What do you want me to do—?"

As I stalked toward him, his eyes flicked up to watch me. He held my gaze as he continued to talk. My eyes fell on the base of the phone on the far wall near the stove, and I switched direction.

"Okay, I understand—"

I ripped that cord out of the wall, breaking the connection and giving him a triumphant smile. Lash let out an angry breath, then threw the phone down with enough force to shatter it into plastic shards. He stalked toward me, grabbed hold of me, and pushed me down onto the floor, laying his body on top of mine. I tried to kiss him, but he held me down with one hand, and took out his knife with the other.

"I told you to hold still."

I went still under him, my wide eyes on the blade in his hand, shining in the moonlight.

Lash took my bound hands in one of his. With quick motion, he cut the cords, setting my hands free, then lay the knife to the side within reach. I ran my hands back into his hair, and kissed him again, murmuring, "Please. Take me. Please."

Lash kissed me again, then unzipped his jeans, shoving them down. He pressed his hips to mine, his erection nudging me. I moaned again at his size. *God, he was not as long as Devlin was, but he felt just as broad...Ahh...*

150

He said nothing, just pulled back my head by the hair, baring my throat, slowly sliding his fangs into me, simultaneously bearing down with his hips to slide his erection in. His long fangs felt like needles, they sank in to me so deep. Lash slid himself in to the hilt, then began moving fast, grunting with effort, keeping his fangs completely in me.

His mouth began moving on me, his tongue licking as he swallowed. The bastard was drinking my blood. Anger rose up instantly, then it was obliterated by desire. I wanted him to take it, to take all of me, everything I was, everything I had! I writhed under him, moaning and making soft cries of pleasure. *God damn, he felt so good...thick and hot and so slippery within me...ahh...*

Lash suddenly withdrew his fangs. He kissed me again, his tongue again twining around mine. I tasted my blood in his kiss, the coppery taste making me shudder. Lash broke the kiss at once, then plunged his fangs back into my throat, biting deep. The feeling of him biting me so deeply as he moved in me so eagerly was enough to bring me screaming, my howl of pleasure deafening.

Lash pushed his upper body away from me in an instant, bracing himself on his arms, still driving himself into me fast and deep. As my orgasm ebbed, I thrust up, holding his lower body as tightly against me as I could, his contracting muscles coaxing the last waves of pleasure from me. He jerked a moment later, a hot rush of warmth filling me. He spasmed a few more times, his body tightening against mine, then relaxing slowly.

Lash jerked a little as he withdrew. Easing onto his back beside me, he lay breathing hard.

He'd made no sound. Even in my lust for him, I found his silence eerie. But as I slowly came back to myself and felt the wetness of his semen on my inner thighs, I curled up in a ball facing away from him, praying he not say a word.

I'd just had sex with a man I loathed. Possibly the one man in all the world I didn't want to be with like this. Perseus or Samuel would have been better to be with. Alphonse would have been better to be with. Anyone but Lash, who had just told me minutes before this how much he hated Theo and me.

The silence stretched. Lash didn't speak.

Tears ran from my eyes. I bit my lip hard, because I had to talk to him. I had to get us back, to face Devlin.

"We're in Casper, Wyoming," I said softly. "The house Theo was living in, where I found him."

Lash said nothing.

"I'm sorry," I whispered.

There was the sound of shifting cloth, then a knife being sheathed as he got to his feet. A second later, my clothes were dropped next to my back. "Get dressed. I'll go grab the cords." Footsteps strode away.

I hurriedly pulled on my clothes. When I was dressed, Lash came back, then held out my missing sock and underwear. I took them and stuffed them in my pocket, blinking back tears.

Lash took my hand in his gently. "Take us back, Sar."

I teleported us back to Devlin's bedroom. He was there standing near the fireplace, one hand grasping the mantle, his expression worried. I dropped Lash's hand and sat down on the loveseat, my eyes averted. Devlin didn't speak, but took my hand in his.

Lash stood, arms folded across his chest. "I had her as she asked me to. You were right; she went back to normal. She said we were at the place she found Theo. No one saw us. I covered up the evidence and wiped down everything we touched."

"Thank you for doing what she needed, and for protecting her from herself."

"You know this means she might well have your child inside her."

"I am hoping like hell," Devlin said wearily. "Because otherwise, she's changing again, and this time, I don't know what is happening, or what to do."

"You need me; I'll be in the shower." Lash turned and sauntered towards the door. "I just hope that stupid cat finds out this—"

"You might need to do this again for her, for us," Devlin interrupted. "Are you willing or not? I need to know right now."

Lash paused, his hand on the doorknob, then looked back. "Dev, you know that I prefer weresnakes," he said casually. "But I enjoyed having sex with her. If she needs that again, just one of you tell me. It's not a problem—"

A rising scream built within me rapidly.

"If this is The Lust Danial spoke of, she probably will," Devlin continued. "And I need you to protect her. That means protecting yourself."

Lash turned completely around and faced Devlin. He paused a second, his expression resentful, then nodded. "I'll get checked out," he hissed. "I'll go call Stephen now, and have Titus teleport me tonight—"

"I need you to do more than that," Devlin said with a sigh. "I'm sorry to ask you, but I have to, Lash. For her sake, for the baby's, I have to ask for your word."

"Fine; you have it. I'll tell her I can't be with her anymore, not like we are at Davy's," Lash hissed bitterly, turning back to the door and opening it. "And we won't be together in snake form at all."

"Thank you," Devlin said, as Lash left, slamming the door behind him.

"Are you all right?" Devlin asked, squeezing my hand.

"He didn't hurt me," I murmured, after a moment.

"I know he didn't," Devlin said, annoyed. "I asked how you were."

"I'm fucking hysterical!" I shouted raggedly. Then I burst out crying. Devlin hugged me, whispering soothing words, then led me into the bathroom.

"Take a shower," he said, turning on the water for me. "You'll feel better."

He'd said those same words to me that day in the hotel room, when I'd also had sex I hadn't wanted. Not sure if he'd meant me to recall that memory, I didn't reply, just got undressed and showered off. When I emerged, he was on the bed reading paperwork, waiting for me.

Even though Dev hadn't acted like what had happened mattered, I couldn't just launch into pleasantries blithely. I sat down next to him. "Look, I don't know what to say—"

Dev held a finger to my lips. "Don't say anything. Danial told me what might happen. I just thought if something did, it would be with me. But I'm not upset this happened, not with you or him."

*That's great.* "I'm really upset, Dev."

He put down his paperwork, and brought me into his arms. "Why? You knew having this symptom was a real possibility, as did I. We can handle this situation. Lash will remain at your side at all times I'm not with you—"

"That's impossible—"

"Not if you stay here with me, it's not," Devlin said easily. "You don't want to risk any more illicit sexual encounters, so that's the best idea—"

"No," I replied firmly. "I don't want this to happen again, ever."

"Lash is safe to be with," Devlin said firmly. "He won't hurt you, despite what you may think of him. He'll keep his word. When he gets back from the doctor's he'll tell us the truth, no matter what it is."

With revulsion, I remembered we'd not used any protection. "Are you saying I need to worry about—?"

"He's probably fine," Devlin said reassuringly. "Lash is sterile, as a side effect of the potion he takes. But Cin does have a bit of a reputation. Lash is not the only one who goes to her, and lets her act out her fantasies. It's better to be safe."

This was nauseating, not to mention terrifying. "I should call Dr. Camlyn. I need to know now—"

"Lash will tell us tonight," Devlin said. "He'll bring you some meds if you need them. Don't worry, really. He can't catch most human diseases, and you can't catch weresnake ones. We are just being cautious."

"I'm afraid," I said softly.

"So am I," Devlin whispered. "But not for you and I, Love. We can conquer this together." He squeezed me gently. "Would you like me to sing to you?"

"Yes," I said, relaxing back into him. "It will help me relax."

Minutes later, lulled by his sweet voice, I fell asleep.

\* \* \* \*

When I woke a few hours later, I was ravenous. In my despondency, I accepted Devlin's offer of letting Serena make me a sandwich.

The first bite of melted cheese and ham was Heaven. "This is good!" I told her.

"Thank you," she replied quietly.

I'd just popped the last bite into my mouth when Lash came into the kitchen. I averted my eyes, swallowing quickly.

Devlin looked at him, then to Serena. "Leave us."

She quietly dried her hands on the towel, and left the room. Though she could most likely hear us from the other room, I appreciated the gesture of privacy, anyway.

"What did he say?" Devlin said, pouring us all a glass of red wine.

Wine sounded great right about now. It didn't go with grilled cheese, but screw it. I drank some immediately, trying to settle my quaking nerves.

Lash came over to the table. "I'm sorry," he hissed at Devlin. He put a plastic bottle with single pill in it in front of me with a sharp click.

I couldn't do anything but look at that one pink pill, all by itself in the bottle. It was huge. Worst of all, my name was on the bottle with Camlyn's. Bile rose in my throat.

No one said anything. The silence stretched.

"Sar, go to the bathroom and take it," Devlin said gently. "It should start to take effect in a few hours. What you have is not bad, and the pill will cure it. It won't hurt our baby. But you'll have to restrict Theo for about a week—"

Tears flooded my eyes, as guilt did the same in my heart. I'd opened myself for this. I hadn't insisted on protection, even though I knew he'd just been with Cin, and I'd suspected she was none too discriminating. Sure, I'd been under the control of The Lust, but I should have been able to do something…

"Sar, go take it, please," Devlin said again.

I got up as calmly as I could, and went to the bathroom, shutting it behind me without a sound. Reading the label, I was glad to see alcohol was not forbidden, though it agreed with Devlin: no unprotected sex for at least a week afterward. There was no pamphlet with it to tell me what disease the drug treated. *Screw it, I was happy never to know.*

I swallowed the pill, then tucked the bottle in my pocket, knowing I'd have to mark the days on my calendar, so I didn't forget. I'd be damned if Theo had to pay for my mistake. But there was going to be Hell to pay, anyway. I had to tell him what I had done and who I'd done it with. Knowing he'd be furious just made me feel that much worse.

I washed my face and fixed my hair, hoping that Lash would leave before I went back. When I left the bathroom, he and Devlin were still in the kitchen talking. I paused, just out of sight. From what I was hearing, I didn't want to be in the room.

"—it's over?" Devlin finished, amazement and empathy in his tone.

"She said she didn't give it to me, and I told her that she was the only one!" Lash hissed loudly, furious. "I gave her the meds, and she said she didn't have anything. I told her that we were done unless she agreed to take them, and that I was protecting myself from now on, because I couldn't trust her. She said we were done. Fucking bitch."

I looked through the door crack, next to the hinges. Lash drank his wine in one swallow, then hurled his empty glass across the room to shatter against the wall.

I cringed. This was the man I'd just been intimate with today; the man who'd given me the first STD of my life.

"I'm sorry," Devlin said softly. "I know you liked her a lot."

"She was my favorite," Lash said mournfully. "And she was close by. Shit!"

"There are other female weresnakes around," Devlin said gently. "What about that girl from Harrisburg?"

"I can call Lyssa, maybe see if she'd come up from PA on a weekday."

"I'll ask Titus to teleport her for you," Devlin said gently. "It should only be for another two months or so. You may not need to help us out again. I'm grateful you're helping me and Sar, but I don't want to screw up your love life."

"It's okay, Dev," Lash said with a drawn out hiss. "If I hadn't been with Sar, I wouldn't have checked, and then I still wouldn't know. You know what happens if you don't treat—"

"Yes, I know," Devlin said grimly. "That's why I wanted you to go today. Still, I'm surprised your immune system didn't just repel this—"

"I'm still fighting the poison," Lash said in an empty voice. "Between that and my age, I'm not surprised."

*Poison? What poison?*

Devlin didn't reply. Worried his silence meant he knew I'd been listening, I walked in, sitting back down in my chair.

Lash looked up at me, then held my eyes. "I'm sorry, Sar," he hissed.

I took a few seconds to call myself a coward, then said, "It was my fault. You said no, and I—"

"Just accept my apology," Lash said coldly.

"I accept your apology," I whispered.

He made a fist, and brought it down on the table hard, making the remaining glasses clatter. "I'll be in my room," he hissed. "Don't need me for a while, Dev."

"That's fine," Dev said, nodding.

Lash got to his feet in a graceful motion, sliding his chair back, then strode off, disappearing through the door.

Tears flooded my eyes. Devlin grabbed a paper towel and wiped them away. "I'll call Danial," he said quickly. "You need some time away from all this. I'll see if he can't move up your plans. He can't catch what you have, just as I can't."

"He won't be able to go tomorrow, not with his business—"

"Money talks, Sar. Besides, he alone knows best how The Lust affects you. He'll make it happen."

*Maybe that was for the best.* "Okay."

"Do you want something else to eat?" Devlin said gently.

"No. But please tell Serena I'll try to get back here on Wednesday somehow so we can bake." I got to my feet. "I should just go ask Danial now myself."

Devlin nodded, surprised. "I will. Please watch yourself, Sar. You shouldn't be with Theo alone, not until you have told him about your condition." He kissed my forehead. "Don't worry. He loves you. He'll understand."

I sighed. *If only it were so easy.*

\* \* \* \*

"You what?" Theo roared. "How could you be with him like that? He's tried to kill me twice—!"

"Shut up, Theo," Danial said angrily. "This is not about you; it's about Sar. She had no control, so don't judge her. You weren't here when Sar was pregnant before. The problem could easily have been much worse if she'd been at Hayden with a group of Dev's bears."

Theo went white.

*Thanks for that comparison, Danial.* "The problem is worse," I said awkwardly, flushing. "I caught something from him." I started babbling, my words coming out as fast as I could get them out. "I can't be with you for a week, Theo. But maybe I can spend next week with Danial and we can go away like he wanted us to. He can't catch this—"

"I never wanted to go away with you just for a tryst anyway," Danial said quickly. "We don't have to have sex—"

Theo rolled his eyes. "Like that would happen."

Danial looked affronted, but said nothing.

"Are you…um, did you see Camlyn?" Theo asked.

"I've already taken the cure. I'll be fine—"

"Not if Lash does you again," Theo spat, jealously heavy in his words. "He'll re-infect you—"

"He's taken the cure as well," I said hesitantly. "But I'm hoping it never comes to that again—"

"Fuck that!" Theo shouted. "I'm supposed to trust him? I can't believe—"

"Theo, shut up!" Danial shouted at him. "This isn't about you and Lash! If you can't handle this, then get out of her life! I am sick and tired of your pissing and moaning!"

Theo glowered at Danial, who ignored him, instead turning to face me. "Come here."

I went into his arms.

"I agree with Theo," he said softly. "I don't trust Lash. But Devlin does, and I know how he feels about you, Sar. He wouldn't put you in danger, especially now." He kissed me gently on the forehead. "If you need to be with Lash again, do so. Devlin said when he called me that he has told Lash that he needs to be with you at all times, unless he himself was with you. Though after this, I doubt Devlin will be leaving you alone for more than a few minutes at a time at Hayden."

"Sounds like you already talked to Devlin while I was walking over here to meet with you and Sar," Theo said sharply. "So once again you know before I do. Are you going to go away with her?"

Danial looked at him with all of his old arrogance and possessiveness. "Devlin told me about it earlier today, while she was sleeping—"

"He didn't tell me he told you," I stammered, looking from Danial to Theo.

"Whatever," Theo broke in. "Danial was most likely on the phone in that same minute he hung up with Devlin, arranging things."

Danial's eyes narrowed. "Yes, I was," he said curtly. "Everything is arranged. Sar and I will leave tonight, in fact. You are to come here tonight to stay with Elle and Theoron. Brian and Demi will go to your house to watch it for you and Sar. We'll be driving to the park. I need you to take her home and pack. I'll be by around seven, or so."

"Thought so," Theo said sarcastically.

"Theo, as much as you're my best friend, as much as I love Elle and know she's happier knowing you, sometimes I think it would have been better for Sar if Terian had kept his word to you," Danial said mildly. "If you had not come back, and had stayed with Aspen, or Tasha. Sar doesn't need the guilt you give her. She has plenty of it all by herself. And I don't appreciate it either, nor your constant griping and belligerence."

Theo drew back at Danial's words, his eyes wide, his expression deeply hurt. "How can you say that to me?" Theo whispered. "I love you like a brother. After Sar and Elle, you are the closest thing I have to family."

Danial held me tighter against him. "I feel the same about you. These past ten years, we've been closer than I was to Devlin for the last four hundred. But Sar was mine before she was yours or Devlin's. I am guilty of nothing but loving her. It isn't wrong that I want to be intimate with her, or spend time with her, as she and I used to do before she loved you. And as for my rights in hearing about her condition before you did—she and I are Oathed now, or did you forget?"

Theo sagged, all the fire going out of him. "Look, I'm sorry, Danial," he said quietly. "I know it might not seem like it, but I am trying. It just seems that the more I try to be okay with sharing Sar's love, the more people I have to share it with."

"I don't love Lash!" I said harshly. "He's—!"

"I worry that you're going to decide you don't want to live with me anymore or be with me anymore," Theo continued. "I know I'm touchy sometimes, and my temper can be bad. Now that you've had Lash...." Theo trailed off, then swallowed hard.

"So what?" I said, not comprehending his stricken expression.

"He's were, like me," Theo said.

"He's not you," I said emphatically. "He made it pretty clear he dislikes me, and the feeling's mutual—"

"But you enjoyed it," Theo said pointedly. "You came, right?"

I flushed and didn't answer.

"That's not important," Danial said scathingly. He held my gaze for a moment, then looked back at Theo. "What is important is you coming to terms with her carrying another dhamphir—"

Danial's look had been curious and worried, and it was nothing to do with what he was saying to Theo. Danial knew as well as I did that I hadn't ever come, or even been close to climax during sexual relations when The Lust had affected me before. Yet I'd come for Lash, a man I didn't even like. *Why?*

"I have come to terms with it, Danial—"

Lash had also succumbed to physicality, but he was a man. Most men could separate sex from love easily. That he was such a man wasn't a surprise to me.

"—I'm sorry. I know how much you wanted it to be yours," Danial finished.

Theo let out a deep breath. "It doesn't matter," he said, resolute. "It will be Sar's child, and I'll love it just because it's hers." He looked down at me, his eyes emotional. "Just like you loved Elle, because she was mine."

* * * *

Once Theo and I were on the road heading home, he began talking. "You heard that Janice and Ivan are going to mate later this summer, right?"

My face broke into a smile. Ivan, one of the werefoxes, had lost his best friend and brother, Demetri, and his lover, Suri, last summer. I'd been aware he'd found some comfort with Janice, another werefox, in early winter but hadn't known it was serious. "I'm glad. I'd like to go."

"Come with me?" Theo asked quickly. "It will be at night, but Danial has already said he might not make it, if he has business."

*He'd brought it up to make sure I'd go with him, not Danial.* After all I was putting him through, it was the least I could do. "Sure," I said, laying my hand over his. "It's a date."

He squeezed my hand. "Nineva is coming, to visit Elle. It's going to be something, seeing him again."

That was a shock. Nineva was an African lion who had been held prisoner in Europe. Danial had sent two vampire trackers to rescue him, believing him to be Theo. They had brought Nineva back to Danial, and he had stayed for a while, recovering from bad wounds. He had been the first one to show Elle how to change when she'd been stuck in human form. "I knew Nineva still wrote to Elle, but not of this visit. When is he coming?"

"I think in June," Theo replied. "He said he would tell us the flight number and arrival date when everything was arranged."

"It will be good to see him," I said, squeezing Theo's hand. "We should have him over for dinner. Tell him he can stay with us, too, if he hasn't already arranged to stay with Danial."

Theo nodded. "Alright." He paused. "You heard Sundown is living with Terian?"

There was uneasiness in his voice. Maybe he was as worried as I was about that situation. "Yes, he told me. I'm worried she's going to hurt him again."

"She might," Theo replied, uncomfortable. "But that's not what I find unsettling."

"What is?" I asked, shooting him a curious glance.

"She looks like you," he said carefully, as if he was worried the news would scare me. "Her hair is shorter and straighter, but she has your green eyes. Your bodies and features are similar."

Terian had never told me that. "How similar?"

"Enough so when I first saw him kissing her in his lab, I told him I was going to kick his ass," Theo said ruefully. "Then she turned around, and I saw it wasn't you. I apologized for mistaking her for you, which only made Terian that much more uncomfortable."

I shrugged. "Lots of women are dark blond and my size. When I meet her, I'll have to see how much—"

"Titus arranged a meeting between Terian and Leri," Theo interrupted.

I almost got whiplash I turned so fast. "What?"

# Chapter Fourteen

"Titus, Leri, and Terian met. Leri asked Terian to forgive her for what she did," Theo explained.

"Did he?" I asked. "I wouldn't have, but Terian has always been more forgiving than me, despite his demon nature."

"He said that he told her that he forgave her for trying to kill him and for abandoning him, but that he would never forgive her for what she did to his brother. He said he would hate her the rest of his life for that and that he never wanted to see her again."

"Well, that went pretty well," I said sarcastically, shooting Theo a look. "Terian must be really a saint, not a half-demon."

"I thought so, too," Theo nodded. "Weirdly, I think Titus was disappointed. He wanted Terian to accept Leri and welcome her back like he has."

"Is he delusional?" I said incredulously. "Terian might be a nice guy, might believe the best in people, but he's come a long way from the naive man who tried to hold me hostage years ago."

"Titus loves Leri," Theo said flatly. "Men do strange things, when they're in love. Look what you've done to Devlin, for example—"

I almost said Titus was a demon, not a man, then told myself that was borderline racist. What I'd really be voicing was my worry that as a demon, he wasn't capable of love. "I haven't done anything to Dev, Theo," I said, shifting uneasily. "He's still the same sadistic and ruthless man he was when I met him. He just hides that part of himself from me now, because he wants me to believe he's changed."

"I didn't think you knew that," Theo said quietly. "I thought you believed he had changed."

"I forget sometimes, because he is trying so hard to make me believe he has." I sighed. "But every so often the glamour shifts, and I see that beneath it he's the same as he was. The only thing that has changed is his feelings towards me."

Theo didn't reply.

\* \* \* \*

When we arrived home, Theo parked his blue Chevy outside the garage. "I'm leaving in six hours," he said, as he got out I   stopped   midstride,   giving him   an   odd   look. *Why   did   he   think   I   cared   where   he   parked?   Hmm.* I immediately walked to the garage and flipped open the keypad.

"Stop!" Theo said, panicked. He quickly canceled the command, before the door could rise.

"What's in there?" I said, turning to face him. "You didn't buy live rabbits again, did you—?"

"No, but you have to keep it secret. Promise me," Theo said urgently.

"Sure," I answered, giving him a lopsided smile. "Spill it."

"You know that Danial had a cat a while back, right?"

"Yes," I said slowly. "He never said what happened to it." I'd assumed the worst: that it had been run over accidentally, or that one of the werefoxes had eaten it.

"It died of old age. He loved it a lot. He called it Blackavar, Blackie, for short."

"It was a black cat?" I asked. Danial had always liked Cavity best of all my cats. He was all black, too.

"Yes. Anyway, when I was bringing over more wood from the woodshed last night, I found a black cat in the woodshed. Though it clawed me up, I managed to get it inside the garage and get out without it escaping. It's really thin—"

"Why didn't you say so?" I said emphatically, practically gushing empathy. "Did you feed it? Give it water?"

"Yes and yes. I grabbed the heated bowl and bed from the basement. He ate two cans of food, a bag of treats, and some dry food, too. He was friendly afterwards, when he saw I wasn't going to hurt him."

I wasn't surprised Theo had found him in the woodshed. People often dumped cats near barns, thinking that there had to be farm animals inside, and no one would care if another cat showed up. But in my barn there were no animals to keep it warm, no water to drink, and no food. It was also locked up tight, to protect my equipment. The cat would have met a bad end if Theo hadn't gotten the wood. I might have missed the cat entirely, and likely would have been too slow to catch him if I had.

"I want to bring him to Danial, for a present," Theo continued. "I know

Danial will take good care of him. But I want him to be checked out by a vet first. The earliest appointment I could get was tomorrow at four."

"You're afraid he has something?"

Theo nodded. "He coughs. If he's sick, I want to know with what," he said grimly. "If he's only going to live a little while, I want Danial to know that up front."

Danial would certainly outlive the cat, even if it were young. He should know going into it if he might have twenty years with his new pet or only two months. "I won't say anything."

After I got the fire going again, and let the dogs out, I began packing while Theo checked on the cat.

After gathering some food in a box and a cooler and my vitamins from Camlyn, I went into the bedroom, wondering what else to pack.

Besides my fox head choker and earrings, the first thing that came to mind was the red dress, Danial's favorite thing for me to wear. But as that was in one of Danial's memory boxes, it wasn't an option. Besides, it was going to be cold, and we were staying in a park, supposedly in order to enjoy the outdoors, neither condition optimal for wearing a dress. A better bet would be jeans and lots of polar fleece.

With my one duffel full of warm clothes, I opened the other, debating lingerie. Danial was thinking of this as a sort of honeymoon, regardless of what he said. Blood wasn't all he would be after…

Instantly, my memory of being with Lash sprang into my mind in vivid detail. Nauseous, I went to my calendar and marked the days I'd have to be careful. By next Sunday night, I should be safe. Even so, I should see Dr. Camlyn, just to make sure. Maybe he could test me first, to make sure I was free of whatever disease this was.

My nausea increased. I'd never worried too much about STDs before. Sure, I'd gone to the doctor's regularly, but I'd never thought this could ever really happen to me. I'd been able to count my lovers on one hand before Lash. But those days were over, had been over the minute I'd let myself be with someone I hardly knew…

*Get a grip already.* I was smarter now, and going to stay smart. Maybe I couldn't control who I let have me when I felt The Lust. But I could be conscious of who I was with at all times, and make sure to never be alone with someone I wasn't sure would be safe for me to be with.

Theo came in. "The cat's fine; he's eating again. Want to go for a dog walk?"

I nodded. "Sure. If it keeps being this warm, it's going to be spring."

We took the dogs for a long walk, walking hand in hand in the snow, just enjoying the soft wind and the warmer weather. Then when we got back to the house, they both saw my bags and immediately began to be agitated, panting and giving me uneasy looks punctuated with whines.

"Sorry," I said affectionately, hugging them. "You can't go with me this time. The rental houses all have a no pets policy." I gave them some dog cookies, then gave my cats some treats as well. "But here, treats all around."

Cavity and Jessica inhaled the snacks in seconds, then meowed for more. As I watched them eat, I decided to bring some treats to Devlin's cat the next time I visited. Dev would appreciate it, even if Phantom was one of those rare cats who didn't like treats.

Theo came in with his duffel bag. "I'm set. Do you want me to heat up something for dinner?"

We had another hour before Danial got here, but Theo's hungry expression wasn't for food. "What did you have in mind?"

"Maybe ravioli?" he offered, going to the cupboard. "I'm not particular."

Instantly, The Lust washed over me. "I am," I said huskily, going after him and kissing him hard. "And I'm not after food, Cat."

He kissed me back, his arms crushing me to him, his tongue thrusting into my mouth. Then he tried to stop me. "Wait, we can't," he groaned, agonized. "Stop, Sar—"

"We can, Theo. Remember our honeymoon?" I said, kissing him on his neck. "Remember what I did for you?"

Theo pulled back from me, his eyes a dark midnight blue. He picked me up, and quickly carried me to our bedroom. A second later, he was kissing me, grinding into me, as I helped him to pull off his shirt and pants. He let out a gasp as his penis came free of his clothes, gently bobbing, already erect for me. I pushed him down on the bed, then went down on him.

He was too close for finesse, too close for gentleness. I just stroked him hard and fast. A moment later, he spasmed within me, letting out a roar of pleasure.

I slipped his softened penis out of my mouth and began stroking him gently with my fingers. In a moment, he firmed up again, and began to contract in my hands. I began to rub my body on him, to bite him gently, to run both my hands and lips over him. But I didn't take him inside me. Soon he was straining up towards me, impossibly hard, trembling in desperate need.

"Tell me what you want, Theo," I said silkily, working him with my hand. "Tell me how good I feel to you." I bit him again gently, licking him.

"Sar, please!" he said raggedly. "Please."

"Please what?" I whispered, then gently slipped my lips over the head of him. He let out a cry, and thrust up hard. I was ready for him, moving back quickly to avoid being impaled. "No. Not until you tell me," I hissed gently. "Not until you beg me—"

Theo took hold of my neck and head, his hands like a vise. I shivered to feel him hold me like that, knowing what he was going to do.

"Take me in you all the way," Theo growled, pure desire in each syllable. "And don't stop taking me, even when I come."

I didn't reply, just slipped my mouth over him and swallowed. He arched up, burying himself into my throat, his hands holding me as he thrust. I took him in over and over, moving on him, sucking him. *I wanted him, wanted him to scream for me, wanted him to give himself to me!*

Theo thrust himself in deeply, screaming, jerking as he came. I kept moving on him, sucking and squeezing, and he kept coming, crying out repeatedly. Finally, his cries subsided, and he began to shrink. As he did, The Lust left me. I relaxed to the bed, my muscles aching from being rigid for so long.

Theo pulled me gently up into his embrace. "Was it too much?" he said, vastly contented, yet also concerned.

My jaw muscles were a little sore, but I'd keep that to myself. "I'm fine, Theo."

"You never said things to me like that before," Theo growled softly. "You felt so good, Sar, the way you touched me. It was wonderful."

"The Lust had me," I admitted.

His eyes widened. "I thought you just wanted me badly," Theo said, clearly disappointed.

"I did." My face split in a large smile. "Though I was worried you might be too much for me."

"That's a new one," Theo said, turning to look at me curiously. "Explain."

"I know you recover fast after climax," I said tactfully. "You always have." I gave him another smile. "I'm glad you were satisfied with what I could give you."

"I'm were," Theo said, as if that explained everything.

I gave him a blank look. "And?"

"From what I understand from the foxes, most of us have fast recovery times." He took my hand and squeezed it. "I like that you're multi-orgasmic, that I can bring you again and again. But I don't need that every time. I can be completely satisfied with one, like Danial and Devlin are."

It had been two, not one, but I didn't say anything, too engrossed in thoughts of Devlin. He wasn't were, yet he'd managed to acquire that skill somehow. More importantly, if Theo could rein himself in, so could Devlin. He didn't have to have marathon sex. One orgasm could be enough, if he wanted it to be. *But would Devlin agree to that?* Something told me he would not. He liked the act itself, not only the end result…

"Why are you frowning?" Theo murmured.

"Because I have to get up," I lied quickly. "Danial will be here soon."

Less than a half hour later, Danial's headlights shone in the darkness as his Expedition drove down the driveway.

"Call me," Theo said quickly. "Every day, just to check in."

"Sure," I said, hugging him. "But don't get upset if it's late in the day."

He gave me a last deep kiss, and then turned away, heading into the other room.

"I love you," I whispered, knowing he would hear me. I hugged Ghost and Darkness good-bye, and then went out to Danial, my bag over my shoulder, the box and cooler stacked in my arms.

I put the box and bag in the backseat, then climbed in beside him. Danial flashed me a ready smile. "All set?" he said, giving me a soft look.

"Yes," I replied, buckling myself in. "Hand your navigator the maps."

He handed me a piece of paper. "The route's simple. It is four hours, maybe five, if we hit traffic or construction. We'll be there about midnight, probably."

*Plus there was still checking in to do, once we got there.* "Sounds good."

"Was Theo okay?" Danial asked after a few minutes.

*He regretted the comment about how it would have been better for me if I hadn't found Theo.* "He's fine. He knew you didn't mean it."

"I didn't," Danial replied. "I was just tired of his constant complaining."

"Can I ask you some things?" I ventured.

"What?" Danial said, glancing quickly at me.

"There are some things we should have talked about years ago. I know you don't like to talk about your past—"

"I don't like to remember the time before I met you," Danial said quickly. "I don't want to talk about it, Sar. I have never understood why you would want to hear about it, either."

I didn't reply. I'd heard this so often in the years I'd known him that I was used to it now. The silence stretched.

It was more than an hour later when I broke the silence. "We have issues that need to be resolved. Not talking about them doesn't make them go away. Please, instead of putting me off; just give me the answers I need, Danial."

"Go ahead," Danial said after a moment, his tone neutral.

"Understand, I'm not judging you, or looking for you to give a certain response," I said gently. "I just want to know the truth. Please tell me, even if you think it will hurt me—"

Danial pulled over to the side of the road and shut off the engine. Then he turned and faced me, his eyes gleaming red in the dashboard light. "Why are you saying these things to me? Why now? You know how much I wanted to finally be alone with you—"

"There was never a good time," I said bluntly, cutting him off, "even when I lived with you. You always gave me the same answer you did earlier tonight. I was okay to let it go then, because it wasn't worth fighting with you over. But I've had enough of secrets. A few of my questions are long overdue for answers, Danial, and only you possess them."

Danial sighed. "You are your mother's daughter," he said, shooting me a look. "Will any of what you'll ask cause me to swerve when I'm driving?"

"Only one. It has to do with your past."

"Then ask it now, while we're stationary," Danial said curtly.

"Why did you name your son from your first marriage David? Devlin's father, your father, he wanted you to be called David, but your mother refused. If you hated him so, why name your son after him?"

Danial sighed, and looked away from me. "Because we were dirt poor. When you work hard for weeks and months, and have nothing to show for it, you grasp at straws. I knew if I named him David my father would be pleased. I hoped that he would take care of my son and my wife, as he had my mother and me, if something happened to me. I worried about them the way I worry about you, Sar. The life expectancy of a guard was short. Old age was forties and fifties in those times. I expected to die before I saw David grow into a man."

I went to take his hand, but he held it out of reach. "No, Sar," he said coldly. "Keep asking your questions. I know you aren't finished."

"Why be a guard, if you thought you might be killed?"

"I cared more about my family than myself. Devlin must have told you about the drought we faced, when he told you about our youth."

I nodded, even though he wasn't looking at me. "Was Theoron your mother's brother?"

"Yes," Danial said curtly. "He was the only one who was kind to me, of my mother's whole family. They all knew whose bastard I was."

I didn't reply.

"Are you done?" Danial said angrily.

"Yes," I said reluctantly.

He turned to me. "Why would you need to know that?" he said, his eyes searching mine. "What have you gained by having me dredge this up for you?"

"I wanted to understand why you didn't want to name our child David. I knew you picked Theoron in part for Theo, but I knew how much you loved your firstborn son. I almost suggested the name David to you then, but I wasn't sure how you would take it. After Devlin told me what he did about your past, I was shocked. I didn't understand why you had done what you did, and I wanted to."

Danial's look softened. He put his hand over mine. "I'm sorry," he said quietly. "I have many bad memories, Sar. Don't think badly of me, for wanting to forget them and just think of you, Elle, and Theoron."

"I won't ask you again about your mortal days. I give you my word."

Danial restarted the Expedition. "By your very tone, you have more to ask. Ask."

"Did you have to pay off Tony or his boss Thane when you and Dev killed Angelica?"

"No," Danial answered curtly. "But I know you don't care if I had to pay them off. When you ask your questions, Sar, explain what you are confused about, so we don't spend all night talking around the real question. What do you really want to know?"

*It was harsh, but it would save time.* "I want to know if the mob is angry with you for what you did back then. I need to know if they might be after any of us. Devlin is still doing jobs for them, so maybe it's all in the past. Theo said there were bounties on his head, and you said a month ago that there was one on yours. Is it the mob?"

"No," Danial said. "Tony and Thane know what I am; Dev, too. Angelica was no relation to them, and she had no family. I told them point blank what I did to her and why. They agreed she had it coming for betraying me the way she did. She didn't have pain as you had when we bit you. It was quick for her, a matter of minutes. Also, the mob doesn't care what Devlin does, so long as he gets their jobs done quickly and cleanly. They would not have raised any fuss over a murdered girl."

I looked up at him, then away.

"She's buried out in my forest, in the graveyard. I gave her no marker, but I go there sometimes to remember her. I buried her with her choker, if you are going to ask that next."

His words held sadness. "I wasn't," I said softly. "But she would have liked that."

I'd hated Angelica, but she was dead. Danial had killed her because of me. The least I could do was forgive her, these years later.

"Monica is next to her," Danial said quietly. "She also has no headstone."

Neither of us spoke for some minutes.

"I had a choker made for her, at her request," Danial continued finally. "She gave me her Oath one night, and I accepted. She was jealous of you. I compounded the problem by calling her by your name one night when we were intimate. I thought if she also had one to wear, maybe she wouldn't be so envious."

"She said that. That night I shot her, she told me that. But I didn't know you were Oathed." I tried to add I was sorry, but couldn't bring myself to lie.

"We were," Danial replied. "She wanted to be in my bed, to be my only lover. I gave her my promise that she would be. I knew she loved me, though I didn't love her."

I face him skeptically. "It's okay if you loved her, Danial. I know about what she was going to do for you, that she wanted to have a child for you. I know she asked Terian to get some of my blood so she could try to change hers, so she would be able to—"

Danial swerved, narrowly missing an RV. I grabbed onto the seat, holding on for dear life, letting out a scream. He finally got the SUV under control, and pulled it again to the side of the road.

"How the hell could you just announce that, damn it!"

"I'm sorry," I said meekly. "I thought you knew, that she'd talked about it with you or at least that you had an inkling of what she was planning—" I trailed off. Danial was slumped over the steering wheel, shaking as he cried.

"I'm very sorry," I said quietly. "I thought you knew." I reached out to touch him, and then thought better of it. Instead, I settled back into my seat and let him grieve. Danial cried only briefly, but stayed there resting his head on his arms in silence for another half hour.

"I'm glad you told me," he said brokenly. "I hated her so much after what she did to you and the children. I wondered how I'd been so stupid to think she really cared for me. But she had to love me if she wanted to do that for me, even if her actions in the name of that love were deplorable." Danial took the tissue I offered him, and wiped his eyes. "Are you sure it's safe for me to drive now?"

"Actually, I'll drive. You could use a break."

Danial got out and switched places with me without a word, his motions weary.

We drove for a few moments in silence, him reclining in his seat, his eyes glancing at me every so often. "Are you done with your questions?" he finally asked.

"Yes," I said quickly.

"No, you're not," Danial sighed. "Just ask Sar. We've come this far. Finish."

"If you made a vampire, would you have the kind of power over it that Dev had over Garrett? For all that you wanted the power, I've never heard you mention using it, not once."

169

"In theory I would, yes. But I've only made one vampire, and I couldn't control her, so maybe not."

He was referring to the woman he'd made a vampire by mistake. "Why did you want the power then?"

"For the wrong reasons," Danial continued distantly. "I wanted it chiefly because Devlin had it. I thought I deserved to have it, too. That was a mistake of epic proportions, Sar. I sometimes wish I'd stuck to Solutions, Inc." He grabbed my hand. "But I need my status now to help me protect you and our children." He abruptly let go, taking his hand back. "I sometimes feel in over my head, like I did at the Gathering with you on New Year's Eve. I hate that, feeling like an amateur, playing at filling my brother's shoes."

"You were never less than regal, when you faced the other Rulers and refused to let them take me," I said proudly, reaching for his hand and taking it. "We were outflanked and outnumbered. Things were about as bad as they could get, but you never wavered." I squeezed his hand.

"I couldn't have done any less, Love," Danial said warmly, pleased. "You were mine to protect, just as you are now."

"Will you ever have to make a vampire, like a test of sorts?"

"Yes," Danial said, looking away, resigned. "Though it's a self-imposed one."

I was jealous at once, irrationally. "Has one of your donors asked to be turned?"

"No. I don't turn my donors. In fact, I let them believe that I still don't have that power. It's easiest for all."

"Then who?" I asked curiously.

"Mary's daughter, Jennie," Danial replied, nodding. "She's got stage four cancer. She's most likely going to die. Mary asked me if I would try to turn her. In return, Jennie would agree to take over for Mary when she retires in a year."

Mary had been Danial's housekeeper for decades. She was a pleasant woman in her sixties, very efficient and kind. "She mentioned retiring once. I'd wondered what was going to happen when she did. I didn't know she had a daughter. She never mentioned one."

"They are trying chemotherapy and a few other experimental treatments as a last resort. Jennie doesn't know what I am. She's only met me once or twice. Mary kept my secret all these years. It's obvious she would prefer that her daughter not be what I am, but she doesn't want her to die."

"I'm sorry. If there is something I can do to help, please let me know."

"I will. Now, is there anything else, Sar?"

"Did you have to fight someone to gain control of New York years ago?"

"I thought you knew that," Danial said, his mouth curving into a faint smile. "I disposed Garrett about eleven years ago now. That was the cause of the fight during that first Hallow's party of mine you attended. He just finally went too far in his insolence."

Danial had killed Garrett soon after we'd met, when Garrett had challenged him at his annual party instead of showing respect, as the other vampire guests had. "You alluded to it, as I remember, but I wasn't sure what happened."

"I was much older and stronger. I beat him easily, so I didn't kill him when he yielded, as is the usual custom. He chafed under my rule ever after that. I was remiss in my duty, in that I should have executed him right after he refused to bow to me the first time."

"Your duty?" I said, confused, my eyes shifting to him.

"I'm responsible for the vampires in my territory," Danial said patiently. "I am supposed to keep them under control. They have to respect me, in order for me to do that. If anyone steps out of line, I have to discipline them harshly. You must have heard Devlin speak of this before?"

"Yes. Has anyone else given you trouble?"

"No. For the most part, everyone is pretty well behaved. It's the newer ones that usually make trouble, and there aren't many younger vampires in New York. The youngest is at least fifty years old. I haven't had to discipline anyone except Manir."

I shivered, remembering. Manir had attacked Danial's home twice looking for Theoron, trying to take him for his own. Theo had killed him last summer, but his name still made me uneasy. "Who rules New York now? When you took Devlin's power, someone had to fill your shoes."

"You remember Akira, from the Hallows parties? He rules New York now, with Chi at his side. He's doing a good job so far."

"Yes." Akira and Chi had been Japanese Samurai at the first Hallows party I'd attended, though I couldn't remember seeing them since then.

"We are almost there, Sarelle. Please tell me you are done asking questions."

"Is there anything you can do about the bounties on Theo's head, and do you know who put them there?"

"There are three now," Danial corrected. "The Peterson one is done with—"

"Can you do anything?" I said anxiously. "I'm worried."

"I've already done what I could," Danial assured. "There has never been a time Theo has not been in danger, even before he worked for me."

I gripped his hand tightly. "Who are they? You said it's not the mob."

"Samuel, for one. He tried to call it off, but the assassin he hired was

171

already paid. But that will probably work itself out without trouble." He paused. "Tasha's father has also put out a hit on Theo. He knows by now that something happened to his daughter, and that Theo was the one she left with. He has offered a million dollars to the man or men who kills Theo, and brings him proof." He paused again. "But that is not the worst."

"What could be worse?"

"Robert," Danial said with finality. "He works for Zane. He's what you might call the third most well-known assassin, after Lash and Theo."

"Third ranked?"

Danial nodded. "But that's not enough for him. He would like to be the best, yet he doesn't dare go after Lash. Second place is what he's after."

"Why is he scared of Lash and not Theo?" I said, irritated on Theo's behalf. "Theo's scary, or he can be, when he's angry."

"By now the word has spread that Theo is married, that he's settled down and thinking of raising a family. Robert thinks this is the best time to strike."

"How do you know?" I asked, looking at him wildly. "Has he tried—?"

"Watch the road!" Danial shouted, grabbing the wheel.

I pulled over and cut the engine. *God, it was midnight already. Shit, we were never going to get there at this rate.* "Has he tried?"

"Yes," Danial answered. "Robert tried to shoot him back in November during an overnight trip. Theo dodged the bullet, then shot him in the arm. Theo went to finish the job, but Robert escaped, because someone reported the gunfire and the police showed up. We had to get away, before we had to answer any questions, as it was nearly dawn."

*Theo hadn't told me. We'd been dealing with a lot then, maybe he hadn't wanted to worry me.* "I didn't know any of this."

"He'll be okay, Sar," Danial said soothingly. "He can take care of himself."

I nodded, but I wasn't so sure. Theo and I would have a talk when I got home.

Finally, like a miracle, the park sign was before us. I pulled into the entrance to the park, which was surprisingly little more than a dirt road. "This is rough. Isn't this supposed to be a big place? Hundreds of acres?"

Danial checked the map, as I drove slowly.

"It's a lot more wild than I thought it would be," I continued, looking around.

"Yes," Danial said tentatively. "Because you are on the wrong side of the river. You took the wrong entrance."

"No, I didn't," I said haughtily, and continued to drive. A few moments later, the dirt road became a worn track of mud accessible only by all-terrain vehicles. Very irritated, I carefully turned around. Danial was smartly silent.

I drove back the way we came. After crossing a bridge over the river a few moments later, the main entrance to the park appeared, huge gates that looked like brick or stone in the headlights. I gaped at them appreciatively. This was a little more like what I'd been expecting.

The park office at the gate was closed, so I drove on through slowly, careful of the twisting road and the massive stonework walls near the road. In a few minutes, we came to a large parking lot and several buildings. "The Glen Iris Inn is next to a fountain," Danial said, pointing. "Park here. The front desk will have our keys."

"Thank you for answering my questions," I said politely, as we got out. "I know you didn't want to talk about—"

"Enough." Danial pulled me to him tenderly, then kissed me fervently.

I kissed him back tentatively, then passionately. He was right. We had just this week. While we were here, it was best to make the most of it. When I got home, I'd make some plans with the knowledge I'd just gained.

Danial pulled back from me. "I have something to ask of you, Love." He handed me a dark green velvet box.

*More earrings?* I opened it. In the light from the fake gas lamp above shone a pair of wedding rings.

"Marry me, Sarelle," Danial asked softly.

# Chapter Fifteen

"Danial, I'm already married," I stammered. "I can't."

"For this week," Danial implored, his eyes looking into mine hopefully. "Wear it just for this week, when you're mine and mine alone. Please?"

*Did it matter?* I was going to be removing Devlin's choker from my neck while we were here, and wearing Danial's instead. That promise hadn't meant any less to me than the one I'd sworn to Theo. *In fact, it had meant more.* I slipped off my rings from Theo, and put them into my purse's inner pocket. Then I took out the wedding band from the box, and studied it. It was beautiful, one of a kind, but then Danial was never satisfied with the ordinary. It was comprised of many colors, swirled together, like paint almost. "Are those different metals?"

"Yes. It's made as swords are made, hammered and folded. Each one is unique."

There was an inscription inside that looked like it was in another language. "What does it say?"

"It says 'Forever'," Danial said softly. "As does mine."

I slipped it on, then the diamond he had given me from my left hand. Taking the box from me, Danial removed his fox head ring, then put it on his other hand. I had never seen him take it off, not in all the time I'd known him, not for anything. Carefully, he put the wedding band on his ring finger. Then he reached out and took my left hand in his

"Come, Love," he said happily. "We should go inside before you get too cold out here."

We walked past the frozen fountain, lit up with lights, then past the wrap-around porch to the front door. I followed Danial inside to the front desk. He rang the bell.

"Yes?" a matronly woman said, getting up from her chair.

"Hi," Danial said charmingly. "I'm Danial Racklan. This is my wife,

Sarelle—"

I flushed suddenly. The elderly woman looked at me curiously.

"We're here on our honeymoon," Danial said smoothly. "We've made reservations for your stone house, and we're very tired. We'd like the keys, please."

The woman nodded, and looked through her papers. "No," she said, after a moment. "Your reservations are for our cottage."

Danial was annoyed at once. "Are you sure?" he said, laying on the charm. "I'm sure it was for the stone house, the largest one. I paid a large deposit, earlier today."

"I'm sorry," the woman said pleasantly. "You were the one who called, and asked that we move up your reservations. You could have had the house the week after next, but the cottage was the best we could do on short notice."

I was tired, cranky, and in no mood to go back and forth at this time of night. "It's fine," I said, squeezing Danial's hand. I flashed the woman a smile. "Just point us in the right direction."

She handed Danial some keys, and gave us a map of the park. "Call the front desk if you have any questions."

We walked out, Danial grumbling. A few moments later, we parked before a full size three-bedroom house. Danial carried in our bags, and I followed with the food. Dropping it on the floor, I began to look around. "This is nice—"

Danial came back in, shutting the door after him. As he did, I saw what he was trying hard to conceal beneath his coat. "You brought your laptop," I said, rolling my eyes. "Some honeymoon."

"Just in case," Danial said, placating. "I might need to check—"

"Please," I said, smiling, holding up my hands. "After all this time, I'm not even surprised. All I want is some food."

As he set up his computer upstairs in the spare bedroom, I went into the kitchen and unpacked, making myself a bagel. As I was finishing wolfing it down, he came in. "Did you check the fridge?"

"No. Why?"

He opened it. "At least they got this right," he said happily.

Inside were two gift baskets all wrapped up in plastic, and also a single red rose. One huge basket of was of apples, grapes, cinnamon bread, bananas, and crackers. The other was of chocolate, and various flavors of cocoa.

Danial handed me the rose. "For you, Love. I didn't intend you to have to bring any supplies on this excursion."

"You are to die for," I said lovingly, then gave him a long kiss. Danial picked me up in his arms, and began carrying me upstairs.

"Danial, what about my bags?" I teased.

He lay me down in the bedroom and shut the window blinds. "They can wait."

I turned on the light, wanting to see him. Slowly we embraced, kissing tenderly, touching each other with gentle caresses. Finally, he drew back from me. "It's nice to be with you and not worry we're going to be interrupted. To know I have you all to myself, not for hours, but for days."

"I'm yours," I said lovingly, leaning back provocatively.

To my surprise, Danial got up, and moved to leave.

I sat up. "Where are you going?"

"To get your bag," he said, looking at me seductively. "It's way past your bedtime, Sar."

* * * *

When Danial brought the bags upstairs, he set one of his aside. "This is full of blackout curtains. We'll put these up tomorrow."

"I'm glad you thought to bring them," I said, relieved.

"It wouldn't be much of a honeymoon if I couldn't be where you are," Danial teased. "I have something else for you, too," he added, handing me a gift bag.

Inside was a silk sheath, black with iridescent glitter. As I moved my hands, it shimmered in the lamp light.

"Wear it for me?" Danial asked. "Tonight?"

I nodded. "Be right back."

In the bathroom downstairs, I put on the nightgown. Removing Devlin's choker to my ankle, I put on my fox head earrings, and fastened Danial's symbol about my neck. After swallowing a few of my vitamins to bolster my blood, I went back upstairs.

Danial was waiting for me in bed naked under the covers, his arms behind his head. I twirled for him, making the fabric shimmer, earning an appreciative look.

"Come here, Sweetheart."

I crawled in beside him. He brought me to him quickly, his kisses intense and possessing. Danial ran his hands over me for many minutes, rubbing and squeezing my body he kissed me. Slowly he stripped the sheath off me, then dexterously moved me into position beneath him. With a careful thrust, he pushed himself inside me gently.

"Tell me if it hurts and I'll stop," he whispered.

I froze under him. Danial had never said anything like this to me before. I knew why he was saying it now. I let out a sob.

Danial withdrew from me quickly, taking me in his arms. "Shh, Sar."

176

Immediately, I began crying.

"Sweetheart, don't cry. It's all right. You'll be fine. If you don't want to have sex, that's fine. It's enough we're alone here together—"

By this time I was howling, grasping him desperately, and Danial stopped talking, and just held onto me.

I got myself under control a few minutes later. Embarrassed, I gazed up at him with unshed tears still heavy in my eyes. "I'm sorry—"

"Don't be," he assured me. "I'm not upset. Just lie here with me and relax. I just want to be here with you. Just let me hold you."

I hugged him. He stroked my hair for a long time before I lost myself in sleep.

* * * *

The next morning I awoke, groggy. Remembering where I was, I turned over to Danial and kissed him. "It's morning," I said, yawning. "We should hang up the curtains. I'm starving."

Danial nodded. His gaze traveled to our bedroom window first. It was maybe two feet by two feet, little more than a porthole, almost near the ceiling. There were blinds covering it. "This window should be fine," Danial said, making a dismissive gesture. "It's high and small. Let's do the others." He grabbed the roll of curtains.

Around the house, most windows had blinds if not drapes also. They were keeping out the sunlight, but several had sunlight getting in around the edges. Danial stood out of range while I hung the blackout panels over them one window at a time. When I was done, the majority of the house was sunlight-proofed, filled with darkness. The kitchen was a problem, though. There were no blinds, and the curtains were small frilly valances. I took them down, then hung up the full length blackout curtains. The flimsy rods held, but just barely.

"The curtains are a lot heavier than the valances. The rods might give way. You'd better stay out of the kitchen by day," I warned, taking them down.

Danial nodded. "We'll eat separately anyway for this meal."

*What?* "How? Are you getting teleported home to meet a donor?" I hoped one wasn't coming here, or he wasn't going to disappear for a few hours later tonight. If he spent most nights seducing other women to feed from, this wasn't going to be so romantic.

"I arranged for some long distance feeding," Danial said, giving me an offhand smile.

I nodded, knowing what he was referring to. There was a spell known to vampires that could be used to send a woman dreams that were shared, in some sense like the dream I'd shared with Theo, but with one big difference. Through her dreaming of him, Danial could feed off her life force. A small taste would be enough to sustain him for the week we would be here. "That's a relief."

"Go eat," Danial said, kissing me. "I'll do the same. We'll meet up a little later."

"How does this work?" I asked, curious.

"The woman who's going to dream of me works the night shift. She'll be asleep by now, at least, she told me she would be. And she wants to dream of me, so I'm sure she's waiting for me by now."

"Do you have to concentrate or drink something?" I asked, as he was going up the stairs.

"No, I can feel her, if she's sleeping, and wearing what I asked her to wear," Danial said from upstairs. "I only have to sleep and I'll enter her dreams. I can leave anytime, which will break the connection and wake her. But I need you not to come upstairs until you hear me get out of bed again."

"I take it she likes to sleep with you in the dream," I said, stating it as calmly as I could.

"Yes," Danial said from upstairs. "And I'll most likely make noise, in my sleep. It is not something I thought you should witness."

Uncomfortable, I nodded. "Sure. Just come down when you're done."

Danial went upstairs. Uneasy, I opened both baskets, and gorged on fruit, cinnamon toast, and cocoa. The food was excellent, but even a second helping of everything didn't quell my upset. I finished that off and had some chocolate, but Danial still had not come down.

I tried to rationalize what he was doing. The woman was giving him her life force. It had only been an hour. He should be making it worth her while. I had two other partners, and he was faithful just to me. This was fair, and it made sense.

I was still jealous, anyway. *Ugh.*

Angry with myself, I decided to look around while I waited. Locating a stereo, I found a soft rock station. I was just singing along to an old Aerosmith song when I realized I had never called Theo like I'd promised.

I got my cell phone from my purse—which luckily I'd left downstairs over a chair last night. Theo picked up on the first ring.

"Sar, I'm glad you called. I was getting worried."

"We just got up a little while ago. We didn't get here until after midnight, and then it took us a while to unpack, and make sure the house was as safe as we could make it against sunlight."

"Don't worry about it," Theo said, more mellow now. "I just wanted to tell you things are fine. Elle says to have a good time. She wanted to know why she didn't get to go with you." He paused, then his words came out in a rush.

"Danial hadn't told her you were probably pregnant, Sar. I let it slip—"

*Good job, Theo.* "It's okay," I said, trying to keep irritation out of my response. "She was going to have to know anyway if I was. If I'm not, I will be soon enough."

"What do you mean?" he demanded, jealous.

Irritation rose up in me. "I have to keep trying with Dev. We have to document it, so—"

"Sar, you're sounding like Devlin!" Theo exclaimed. "I thought you didn't want his child—"

"I don't have a choice!" I replied, agitated now. "I'd rather have his child than some other vampire's. You remember what Samuel said at the gathering."

Theo went quiet.

"We've been over this," I added harshly. "This is how it's going to be. We don't need to rehash it every other day, Theo."

Theo sighed in defeat. "I hope it is his, then. The sooner you have a child for him, the sooner he can stop trying with you to make one, and get out of our lives."

Theo was hoping that Devlin would forget me once he had what he wanted from me. But I'd heard Dev say too many times over the past weeks that he intended to be with me for a long time. There wasn't going to be any reprieve. And I wasn't sure I wanted one, anyway.

Theo took my silence for anger. "Sar, I just meant I—"

"We'll find out on Friday, Theo. We'll find out then and go from there."

"Be safe, and don't go out without Danial, unless you're armed."

"Will do," I said quickly. "Watch your back. I love you."

"I love you, too," Theo said warmly. "Goodbye."

I hung up, grumpy. Danial had still not come down.

Devlin hadn't asked me to call, but I had time. *Why not?* I dialed his cell phone.

He picked up on the third ring. "Sar?" he said, curious. "Is everything all right there?"

"Yes," I said, smiling at his innocent tone. "I just wanted to check in."

"Danial must be feeding," Devlin said knowingly, after a moment. "Or you wouldn't be calling me."

"Yes," I admitted. "But I wanted to ask you something anyway—"

"Are you still coming to me Wednesday?" he asked quickly. "Serena is looking forward to it."

He was worried I'd called to tell him I wasn't coming. The pressure I was feeling mounted. "I'll be there about eight. I would like you to send Lash here to guard Danial while I'm with you on Wednesday. Is that possible?"

Devlin paused. I knew he was thinking that I just wanted Lash to be absent from Hayden when I was there. He was right.

"Dev, this is a normal wooden house. The lock isn't great. We sun-proofed the house, but Danial will be here by himself. I'm worried about leaving him alone here during the day with no guards. He could be burned."

"I'll send Titus," Devlin said, after a moment. "He can get Danial out of there no matter what. Lash has no teleportation powers, which is what is most needed."

I thought about protesting, but I knew it wouldn't do any good. "Thanks."

"Wait, didn't he get the stone house?" Devlin said slowly. "Why are you in a wooden house?"

"Because of me," I said dejectedly. "Because we had to move the trip up by two weeks—"

"Stop," Devlin said sternly. "Danial jumped at the chance to be with you. Just enjoy yourselves, all right?"

I didn't reply, upset.

"I'll send a man to watch the house during the day, okay? Don't worry."

"Thank you," I said softly.

"Take care, Sweet Sar," Devlin said seductively. "Don't wear yourself out. Remember, that's my job. In fact, do you want me to teleport up for a quick—"

I told him good-bye and hung up, still hearing him laughing.

Danial came down the stairs. He was radiant, his skin shining, his eyes gleaming darkly. "How was breakfast?" he said, hugging me close. "Was the food good?"

"Wonderful," I said honestly. "Yours?"

"Just what I needed," he said, smiling just a little. "Ready to shower?"

"Over ready," I said, as I let him lead me into the bathroom.

We managed to get clean, though we were spoiled from using Danial's shower. I froze while waiting for him out of the spray. By the time we were done, I was chilled, despite the warm temperature of the bathroom.

Danial helped me dry off, then took me upstairs. He laid me on the bed, and rubbed me down with body lotion, kneading my muscles as he caressed my skin. I luxuriated in his deft touch. By the time he was done, I was more than warm; I was relaxed, sated, and logy with happiness.

Danial wrapped me up in my black velvet robe, then cleared his throat. "I have to talk about this," he said gently. "Please don't get upset."

I tensed up again instantly, waiting grimly.

"What you have may cause you pain when I enter you. If it does, just tell me to stop, and I will."

"Okay," I said tonelessly.

180

"Sar, by Thursday you'll probably be cured," Danial reassured. "We'll have that night, even if we can't make love until then."

*That didn't make it any better.* "Okay."

"Just lie here with me," he said, lying down. "Know I love you, and that I'm here for you. Come here."

I snuggled against him. After a while, I fell back asleep.

I awoke again about three p.m., ravenous. As I disentangled myself from Danial, he woke up.

"I have to get up and eat," I explained. "I'm starving."

"Don't eat too much," he said, slipping his hands over my hips. "I want us to go out for dinner in a few hours."

"Should I make reservations?"

"Already done," Danial answered. "We have some for around seven for each night we're here."

"You always think of everything," I said gleefully.

"I try," he said immodestly.

I cracked up laughing. "Do you want to come downstairs with me?"

He shook his head. "I need to check in with Theo, then check voice mail."

Rolling my eyes, I headed downstairs. In the space of a few minutes, I devoured fruit, soup, toast, and an entire small box of chocolate. There were only six pieces in it, but by the time I'd eaten it, I was shocked at my binging. I had to be pregnant. There was no other excuse for how hungry I was.

I settled down on the couch for just a moment to rest. Danial woke me up when he came down two hours later. "Sar, are you okay?" he asked, concerned.

"I've got to be pregnant," I said sleepily. "I'm eating everything in sight."

"Eat as much as you want," Danial said lovingly. "I'll order in more food, if you go through what we have here."

"Thanks," I said ruefully. "But I think we should have enough. It's Monday night, and we'll only be here until—"

Danial looked very guilty.

"What is it?" I said, folding my arms across my chest.

"I need to have a conference call on Wednesday," Danial said delicately. "Just a short one in the morning."

As much as Danial's devotion to his business sometimes aggravated me, this time it just made things easier. "That's okay. I need to go and see Devlin that day, anyway."

"What?" Danial said crossly. "Why? He said nothing—"

"I said I would help him with paperwork for a few hours. And I want to bake some bread with Serena. Devlin asked me to try to be a friend to her."

"Be careful, Sar," Danial cautioned. "She's part coyote."

"I never would have figured you for a racist," I said casually. "She also has fox blood."

Danial blanched at the "r" word, then he nodded once. "Point taken," he said, letting out a breath. "Just don't advertise the fact to Cia, okay?"

I nodded. Cia was one of Danial's werefoxes who also happened to be a good friend of mine. Her parents had been killed by a bounty hunter for their pelts. They had been given up to the bounty hunter by a werecoyote. It seemed wrong to blame a whole breed for one individual's mistake, but if it'd been my parents that had been killed, I might feel differently. At the least, I couldn't tell her it was wrong for her to be distrustful. It was better not to advertise the fact Serena and I were friends.

"Will you be back by dusk that day," Danial asked, "so we can have dinner?"

"Yes, of course. Titus is coming here to guard you while I'm gone."

"You arranged this with Devlin?"

"We were both worried about you being here alone."

"You're right. I have to remember I'm not at home. Terian is not here or Theo." Danial's smile became a grin. "Let's go out. I could use a walk."

We dressed quickly in polar fleece and wool, and put on heavy coats. Outside it was snowing, the kind of wet snow that sticks to everything and makes it white. We were covered in it by the time we had gone a few hundred feet. Everything was beautiful though. The trees were huge and majestic. The night was cloudy, with just a few distant stars sparkling in the sky.

"See Orion?" Danial said, pointing up.

I looked for Orion's belt. Sure enough, there were the three stars in a row. I nodded.

"There is Lyra."

I saw the swayed rectangle and its one leg, straight overhead. "Yes."

"Cassiopeia," Danial said, pointing again.

I found the "W" over to the side. "There's the Big Dipper," I said with a gesture.

"Ursa Major." Danial nodded, then pointed out several more constellations. We walked along the road, looking at the bright stars, pointing out more gatherings of stars to each other. Elle loved astronomy, and had often gone stargazing at night with Danial, who in turn had fostered that love in her and in me. Many evenings, Danial and I had lain in his bed and looked up at the night sky painted in glow-in-the-dark-paint on his ceiling. He had whispered the different constellations to me, as they glowed above us. But it was magical to be here with him under the dark sky, experiencing them in a new place alone together.

We walked for a long time along the road, finally ending at one of the scenic spots along the gorge. Tired, I sat down on one of the stone tables that dotted the landscape. "Who made all these?" I said, running my gloved hand over the smooth surface.

"The C.C.C.," Danial said with authority. "Civilian Conservation Corps. During the Great Depression, this was one of Roosevelt's projects. He employed a lot of people with the C.C.C., especially here, laying stonework for bridges and walls, and building all these tables and shelters."

"They're exquisite," I said, looking at the workmanship.

"I've always liked stone work, sculpting," Danial said with emotion, running his hand along the table. "I wish I had Theo's talent for it. You know he was the one who made that bench in my mud room and the carvings, right?"

"Yes. He has a lot of talent, as Elle does. But you sell yourself short, Danial. I remember that pumpkin you carved last Halloween. You are talented."

Danial said nothing, but I could tell he was pleased I had remembered. "We should head back," he said, taking my hand. "We'll be late for dinner."

We walked back to the house slowly, enjoying the quiet night. Arriving at the cottage just in time to change clothes, we hopped into the SUV and drove down to dinner. Surprisingly, the restaurant was crowded, and the hostess advised us it would be a few moments to get our table ready. Instead of waiting in the throng, Danial and I slipped back outside to look at the falls lighted under the dark cloudless sky.

"Danial, have you ever been here before?" I asked. "You know a lot about it."

"I visited Letchworth when I drove up from Colorado to see Devlin, years ago," Danial said. "I stayed here for a week as a sort of vacation, and walked the trails. It was peaceful. But I never seemed to find the time to come back, until now." He breathed a sigh of satisfaction. "It hasn't changed much since then, I'm relieved to say. So much has."

"I'm glad to share it with you," I said, clasping his hand.

"Come. Our table must be ready by now."

\* \* \* \*

Dinner was spectacular. I had a cheese appetizer, then filet mignon with potatoes, and some chocolate cake for dessert. Danial shared my glass of wine with me, but only had a swallow or two. He enjoyed feeding me though, and no one noticed that he ate nothing. By the time we headed back to our house, I was stuffed.

Danial and I listened to some music for a while on the couch. Part of me wanted to initiate sex, but I was afraid, too worried about possible pain. It wasn't until we went upstairs many hours later that I found the courage to speak.

Taking off my clothes, I climbed into bed beside him. "Touch me. I want to try."

Danial kissed me softly. Soon he was running his hands over me, stroking my skin, squeezing me gently. He slipped his fingers inside me, then shifted in surprise as I wasn't pliant or ready. In all our time together, that had never happened before. I'd never been scared the way I was now, that what we wanted to share together might hurt.

Danial kissed me leisurely, slowly deepening the kiss until I let go of my fear. I slowly gave in under his gentle caresses, moving against him insistently, moaning softly. Sometime later when he slipped his fingers inside me again, I was slippery for him. He made a soft eager sound, then got into position. He gently pushed inside, holding still every few inches, until I prodded him on with my hands. Soon, he was sheathed inside me. With a soft moan, he began to move very carefully, withdrawing and entering slowly. I was afraid at first, sure it was going to hurt or that The Lust was going to rear its head. But nothing bad happened. There was only pleasure at his touch.

"Are you okay?" Danial whispered. "How's this feel, Love?"

"Wonderful," I murmured, kissing him deeply. "I want you, Danial."

He kissed me almost desperately, instantly more forceful, bearing down with his hips to get in as deep as he could. I clasped his hips to mine, loving the feeling of his body contracting over mine, over and over.

*Like Lash, that night he had bitten me so deeply…*

In seconds, The Lust took control. I grabbed Danial's hair, made a fist, then yanked it back hard. Danial winced, then looked down at me in worry. "Sar?"

"None of your sweet love," I hissed.

He knew immediately what had happened. "What do you want?" he said gutturally. "What do you need?"

"You," I said, thrusting up hard against him, so he let out a gasp. "Your fangs, your hardness in me as far as they'll go. Drink me down like water as you take me."

Without a word, Danial began to push himself savagely into me. He reared back, baring his fangs, then sank them in deeply. I cried out loudly, clasping him close as he sighed, drinking deep. I shook under him in pleasure. *I was so close, so close!* The pleasure went on and on, never cresting, only building higher and higher. Danial began to shake.

He would come in a few more seconds. *I needed him to bring me! I couldn't bear it, if he stopped now, leaving me so close!* "Bite me again!" I said desperately. "Again!"

Danial paused, then growled and sank his fangs into the other side of my neck. I came at once, screaming his name, convulsing under him. He held me tightly, his mouth locked on my neck as he thrust deeply into me one last time, shuddering as he expended himself.

As my orgasm ebbed, Danial began healing the bites he had given me. Relieved the pain was easing, I lay still under him, breathing as hard as he was.

He embraced me loosely. "You never came for me before like this when The Lust had you. Never."

"I know. Something's different."

"When you were with Lash, the result was the same? Did he also take your blood?"

He was asking because he was worried, not out of jealousy. Still uneasy, I admitted, "Yes, to both questions. But maybe if you have drunk my blood, back when I was first pregnant, I would have come then, too—"

"God damn it!" Danial swore, his tone recriminating. "I'm not supposed to drink your blood when you're pregnant. Damn it!"

"I have been taking the vitamins," I said, trying to soothe him. "You didn't take much."

"All the same," Danial said. "I won't drink your blood again. But I'm very happy you enjoyed it." He paused. "I thought the drug would take effect by now. You had only just been exposed—"

"Can we not talk about that?" I said, putting my finger to his lips. "I'm glad too, but I don't want to remember any of that, not here. Not now."

Danial nodded. "Of course. Get some sleep."

\* \* \* \*

Tuesday passed in a blur. I slept for most of the day after breakfast, again two helpings worth.

Theo reported via phone that Danial's new cat was fine, and it was now at his home. "It had a bad upper respiratory infection, but he's better already from the shot the vet gave him."

"I'm proud of you," I said warmly. "You saved its life." As I went upstairs afterwards, I was pleased. Living with me was rubbing off on him.

Danial slept all day, cradling me as he liked to when I joined him. I watched him sleep for a little while, liking to see him so relaxed and happy. He'd been unhappy most of his life. He deserved to be as happy as I could make him.

We awoke at dusk, and again went for a walk, though this time it was in the other direction. We walked down close to the river, heard the rapids rushing unseen in the darkness, admiring the beautiful stonework of the many small bridges and fences. I was dismayed to see many of the fences were crumbling. Some stairs steps had eroded and broken, making them treacherous, and a more than a few stones were missing from the topmost edges of the many walls. "What happened?" I asked. "Why is the old stonework not being repaired? It looked like things are falling apart and aren't being maintained."

Danial turned back to look at the lower falls, the spotlights shining through the heavy mist rising around us from the cascading water. "Time," he answered. "There is no one who is willing to do what needs to be done here to fix things, in these times of greed, not for what the parks could afford to pay."

"But it's so beautiful," I said dejectedly. "To just let it fall to ruin—"

Danial put his arms around me. "Everything changes," he said softly, resting his head on mine. "The curse of all things is that they age and die, be they works of man of living beings. But I will stay the same, Sar. And you will age more gracefully, too."

There was dampness on my face from the mist, but also from his tears. The roar of the waterfall was loud, but his next words crystal clear.

"You don't know what it means to me to know I don't have to lose you. That now after all the lonely years, I don't have to be content with just a few decades, or a half-century. We'll be together always, just like we are tonight."

His relief and love enfolded each word, their sheer power not only making me blissfully happy, but also a little afraid. "How did you adapt, Danial? I'm used to the world the way it is. I'm afraid to see it transform, after how much I've seen it change just in my lifetime. I worry I won't be able to keep going when everything I'm used to fades."

"I'll be here with you. So will Dev," Danial said, holding me tight. "Theoron will also be with us, and Dev's child, and Terian—"

"But Theo is mortal. So are Elle and my parents and all of the weres we know. It's not a problem now. We're all relatively young. But what about when he's fifty or sixty? When these people I love begin to die and I still look the same?"

"Are you worried you won't love him when he's old?" Danial said chidingly.

"I'll always love him. But Dev said I would live to see him die. That hurts so much, Danial."

"Now you know how I felt when you were mortal," Danial replied. "Enjoy the time you have with him. That is all that you can do, Sar. There is no other option."

"There is a potion Lash takes," I said quickly. "Could we possibly get Theo to take it? Lash said he was over a hundred—"

Distaste filled his eyes, loathing his tone. "That potion he takes is not a good thing. Lash has life when by all rights he should be dead. He pays a heavy price for that life. The side effects of that potion are said to be many. Come, we'll be late for dinner."

\* \* \* \*

The next morning I awoke a little after dawn, starving. Grumpily, I grabbed a red oversize fleece shirt of Danial's, and slipped it on. Where had last night's spectacular dinner gone? I'd been stuffed when we'd walked back up the steep hill to the cottage.

Danial stirred. "Where are you going?"

"To get some breakfast." I kissed his cheek. "I'll be back soon."

I went downstairs softly singing "Lady in Red" to find Lash waiting at the kitchen table.

# Chapter Sixteen

I blinked. Lash was still sprawled at the table, sitting there quietly reading a book.

*Lash read books?* "What are you doing here?" I blurted out, my voice so loud in the room I immediately flushed.

Lash slowly looked up from his book, moving his head sinuously, his flat eyes fastening on me. Those eyes traveled unhurried from my feet to my face. I got redder and redder, thinking about how I didn't have anything on underneath, how I had to smell of sex. *Please, God, let The Lust not show itself until he was gone...*

"It is ten a.m., Sar. Devlin was worried when you didn't show up at eight," Lash hissed finally. "He had Titus bring me here, when he teleported in for the day. Rather than interrupt your playdate with Danial, I thought it best to wait downstairs."

"For two hours? You've been down here waiting for two hours?" I squeaked.

"Yes," Lash hissed. "Are you ready to go? Serena is waiting for you."

*Get a grip already, Sar. So what if we'd had sex...* instantly I got a visual memory and looked away from his flat eyes, flushing again.

Lash smiled a little, just enough to twist his scarred face. "Take your time. I'm at a good part." His tongue flicked out, then vibrated. "I want to relish it."

*I'll bet.* "I need to go tell Danial I'm leaving and get dressed." *How could I back out of here without seeming to back out?*

"Danial," Lash said, nodding once.

"Lash," Danial said coolly, as he came up behind me. "Go upstairs and get dressed, Love. I'll wait here."

"You should be more careful," Lash said softly to Danial. "You didn't hear me slide myself in hours ago. The door you thought you locked was not locked at all, not to me. And I want you to know, Danial, if you leave me an opening I can wriggle into, I'll get in again just like I did before."

My heart was beating out of my chest, because he wasn't talking about this house at all. He was talking about me.

Danial's arms tightened around me as he bared his fangs. "You had better be careful of your words, Snake," he said coldly. "Now you've given your message, go back to Hayden and tell Devlin that Sar will be along in about a half hour. I want to talk with her in private before she goes."

Lash nodded, his eyes moving from Danial to me, then back to Danial. He got to his feet. "I'll tell him," he said calmly. "Remember my warning." He looked to me. "I'll be seeing you at Hayden, Sar," he hissed, a strong undercurrent of meaning in his words. He went to the door, grabbing his wool jacket from the coat rack with an easy motion. The door shut behind him soundlessly.

Danial locked the door behind him, and then hugged me tightly. "Do you want to shower?" he asked. "I don't want you to go out with wet hair."

I didn't count teleporting as "going out", but if I was going to be around Lash, I wanted Danial's scent on me as much as my choker. "No, I'll do that when I get back before dinner."

I got dressed quickly, and then kissed Danial good-bye. "Be careful, okay?"

"Always. Come back by dusk," Danial said, giving me a soft look. "I'll be done by then."

I went to leave, but he stopped me. "Forget what he said, Sar," Danial said soothingly. "He's never liked me, and he liked me a lot less after I took Dev's power away from him. He wanted to hurt me, and he knows how I feel about you. That was all there was to it."

I nodded. "I'll see you tonight." Before I lost my nerve, I teleported, ending up in Hayden's kitchen. Serena was there waiting.

The sight of her immediately put me at ease. "Are you ready?" I said, giving her a smile. "I'm sorry I'm so late."

"Don't mention it, Sar. I know how it goes," she said smiling. "Sometimes they go all night."

*Whoa, complete TMI.* To cover my lack of reply, I quickly got out one of the cookbooks I had bought when I'd been out with Lash, and paged through it to the baking section. "How does banana bread and apple pie sound for today?"

"Great," she said. "I told Vince last night about your teaching me to cook. He asked if we would be making pie. He keeps in touch with Brian, and Brian has told him what a good cook you are."

I didn't want to make anything for Vince. I still thought of him and Kev as marginal jerks for attacking my house that night. But to be fair, I'd forgiven

Devlin, the ringmaster behind that attack. Vince and Kev had just been following his orders. Serena would be the one making him pie. I was just the one teaching her how to do it.

I showed her how to mash the bananas, and crush up the nuts in the new blender. We made a double batch, with her completing the second one. Soon, the smell of baking bread permeated the kitchen.

"We have about an hour," I said, washing my hands. "Let's work on the pie. It won't take long."

I showed her how to work the food processor, and how to prepare the filling. "Pie crust is easy, provided you have a good pastry cutter and a good rolling pin." I showed her how to make the dough, but as before, I let her do all the work.

Serena was quieter that Cia or Janice had ever been when we'd cooked together. While some of it might be her personality, I chalked it up to her not knowing me that well. I could understand that. I was a little shy myself.

"Is that it?" she said worriedly. "It doesn't look right."

"You flute the edges with your fingers," I said, demonstrating the technique. "Or use a fork. The prettiest thing to do is use cookie cutters."

"But we aren't making cookies," she said, her brow knitting.

"You can use them to form the pie dough into shapes. Here is a leaf one, or a heart one, if you prefer." I offered them to her. Serena blushed, then took the leaf one.

I showed her how to lay the leaves on the edge to make a border, and then I brushed the pie with cinnamon and sugar. "It's done," I said with approval. "When the bread comes out, let the stove heat up to a higher temperature for the pie, and then put it in for the set time. The timer is right here."

"Thanks," Serena said, giving me a smile. "I appreciate you doing this for me. I wasn't sure you would want to."

"Why not?" I asked. "Because you're part coyote?"

She looked utterly shocked.

*Shit! Maybe I wasn't supposed to know that?* "Sorry, if I—"

"No, because of what I do here," she said almost inaudibly. "The other women avoid me."

*Bitches.* I'd known I wasn't going to like Valerie as soon as I saw her blue eyes, that same shade Monica's had been. Good thing I hadn't told her she could call me Sar. Sarelle was good enough for her.

Serena was still quiet and crestfallen.

"What you do is important," I said carefully. "I don't judge you for it. I have more than one lover. Sometimes it happens."

"You aren't paid to do it," she whispered. "You do it because you love them."

I had no answer to that. Instead, I busied myself instead cleaning up some of the mess we had on the counters, loading the dishwasher. Serena worked next to me in silence for a while.

"This was a new recipe for me," I said finally. "I'd have to try it, the next time I make a pie for Theo—"

"Is it true that you were with Lash?" she said suddenly.

I froze. "Why do you ask?"

"I'm sorry," she stammered. "I—"

"Before I answer, who is within hearing distance?" I said, turning around to face her. I didn't want anyone else to hear me confirm that, much less any details.

"No one," she said, closing her eyes and listening. "I don't hear anyone moving."

"Yes, I was," I said, still working. "What is it you want to know?"

"I'm sorry—"

"You must want to know something particular or you wouldn't be asking," I said bluntly. "Just ask your question. Unless it's crass, I'll answer it."

"I understand that the nature of your pregnancy compelled you to seek out a lover," she said carefully. "I want to know if you were afraid."

*Afterwards, when I came to my senses.* "Yes and no," I said awkwardly.

"I'm afraid of him," she said, shivering. "I'm afraid to be alone with him."

If she had a reason, I didn't want to know it. "Some men are…um…"

She shook her head. "No. He's never hurt me in the months I've been in Dalcon's employ."

*Did that mean he'd hurt her before that?* "I think he likes people to be afraid of him. Dev and he are much the same. They thrive on fear, on making others cower before them."

Serena nodded agreement. "Having been with him, are you afraid of him now?"

I shook my head. "I'm not afraid he'll hurt me. I'm afraid I'll want him again, though."

"Was he bad?" Serena said curiously.

Her earnestness caught me off guard, breaking the tension like a snapped rubber band. I began laughing hysterically, almost crying. Serena looked at me quizzically for a moment, then joined in.

It was good to laugh. If I could laugh, things weren't that bad. "Sorry," I managed. "It's just good to share this with another woman." I met her eyes. "I couldn't tell anyone, you know?"

Serena nodded.

"No," I answered, wiping my eyes. "He was good, very good actually. He did what I needed him to do. It was over pretty quickly."

"Are you sorry?" she asked.

I turned to her. "Yes. I took vows that I take seriously. When I'm like this, I just don't care about anything so long as I'm sated. Most of all, I'm scared it'll happen again. I don't like not being in control."

"I understand," she said. "I won't ask again about it, Sar."

"It's okay." I managed a smile. "I want to be your friend. We'll get to be friends faster, if we share some truths like these with one another. Tell me a secret, Serena."

"All right," Serena replied. "I wanted you to teach me skills mostly because I was lonely. I miss having a woman to talk to."

"Why do the jerks here give you grief?" I asked.

Serena knew whom I meant. "The usual," she said, sighing. "They're afraid I'll bed their mates, should they turn up at my door asking." She made a face. "As if I wanted more lovers."

"I understand that, girlfriend," I said, grinning. We both burst out laughing.

The oven beeped. Serena carefully took out the banana bread and set it to cool on a wire rack.

I changed the oven temperature. "You're set. When the light goes off, put the pie in and set the timer. When it goes off, let the pie cool on the rack. The bread will be done by then."

Her face fell.

I put my hand on her shoulder. "I'll be back after I see Dev. He needs some help."

"Ah," she said, with a knowing smile. "I'll see you later then."

"Not that kind of help. Paperwork," I elaborated as I walked away, flushing.

I went upstairs, and knocked on Devlin's bedroom door. "Room Service."

"Come in," he said, aroused.

I went in. Dev was lying on his side. "Want to come, under the covers with me?" he proposed, giving me a sly look.

"Always playing with words," I said, kissing him on the forehead. "I'm here for business, Dev, not for pleasure. Or did you just send Lash out of jealousy?"

Devlin sighed, and rolled over on his back. "Lash said Danial kicked him out of your rental house. He said something to Danial, didn't he?"

"Yeah. He insinuated that he would be having me again, if he got the chance."

"That's just the truth," Devlin said, shrugging. "I thought it was something bad. Never mind."

I rolled my eyes. "Whatever."

Devlin shoved off his covers, and got up, walking nude to his closet. I watched him, rapt. He was everything a woman could want in a man, in a lover. The irritating thing was he knew it. He put on a little show for me, turning his body so I could see him fully as he dressed.

"Stop teasing!" I said, trying not to smile. "You're going to make me reconsider."

"Too late," Devlin said with a lofty look. "I'm dressed now. You missed your chance."

His ego had reached epic proportions. Yet if I hurt his pride, he might get angry. His self-esteem was easily bruised, despite how gorgeous he was. "My bad."

"Come with me." He led me out of his bedroom, down the stairs, and into the basement. He went through Titus's workshop to a door in the cellar wall.

"Dev, where are we going?" My voice sounded shrill in the darkness.

"Scared?" Devlin purred, then ran his fingers down my arm.

"Show me what you brought me here to help you with or I'm leaving now," I said angrily. "Enough already with the games."

Devlin took my hand and led me through the door into a passageway. The walls were stone, and there were many doors along both sides. "Is this your dungeon?" I whispered, being careful to stay in the center of the room, away from the doors.

"No," Devlin laughed, almost roaring in his mirth. "This is storage. Look for yourself."

I stepped closer to one of the doors. He was right. There was furniture and some boxes, everything covered in protective plastic, and a layer of dust and cobwebs.

"The dungeon is through the other door, off Titus's lab," Devlin said gently. "There is no one there now, anyway. But stay out of there, Sar. It is no place for you."

*Fucking A. Like I would* want *to go there.* "Sure. Lead on."

I followed him down the third door on the right. He gave the handle a twist. Despite the gothic look of the hallway, the room itself was carpeted and painted white. There were filing cabinets along one wall, and along the other, there were many stacks of boxes. "What is all this?" I asked.

"Financial records," Devlin said. "Deeds. Birth Certificates. Employee Records. Receipts."

"For how many years?" I said.

"All of them," Devlin said, his eyes going over the boxes.

*Holy shit. This would take years to sort through.* "Are the filing cabinets full?"

"No, they're empty. I had them delivered yesterday, when you said you would help. I have never wanted to do this, and never trusted anyone else to know my business as completely as you will when you are done sorting through this mess."

"Do you have a shredder? There has got to be some stuff you don't need here."

"I need the deeds, the birth certificates, and employee records going back thirty years. Save all of Lash's. His records will go back much longer. Tax stuff should be in an accountant's portfolio for each year since income tax began. I need only the last ten years for that as well."

"I'm surprised you don't get nailed for all the illegal profits you make," I said sarcastically.

"I overpay my taxes, by quite a bit," Devlin said loftily. "So long as Uncle Sam gets his due, I'm left to my own devices."

I looked around me. *Where to start?* "Are they in any kind of order?"

"No," Devlin said sheepishly. "I never did anything except label them by decade or year."

*Well, I'd asked for it.* "I'll get started," I said, kissing his cheek. "It'll take a while, but I'll get it done."

"I'm going back to bed," Devlin said, eyeing me like the kiss had reminded him who I was. "Work until three, then come up to me."

It wasn't an order, but it had been more than an invitation. "I'll be there."

"I'll send Lash down on my way upstairs," Devlin said. "He won't bother you."

Again, he wasn't asking. I nodded.

After he left, I began to go through the box from the past three years. Using the manila folders, paper clips, highlighters, fine tipped markers, plastic tabs and hanging folders provided by Devlin, I began to organize the files. Lash came in just as I finished putting the last of the tax packets into the filing cabinet. He sat down in a chair he'd brought and began to read a book called *The Tibetan Book of the Dead.*

Whether he was ignoring me out of nastiness or just being professional wasn't apparent. Either way, I was glad of it. It made things easier.

\* \* \* \*

By one p.m., I had to break the silence. "I'm headed upstairs for lunch."

Lash looked up, his expression considering. I expected him to make some snide comment, like he was ready to be eaten or something. Instead, he just nodded his head.

"I'll go up with you," he hissed.

He followed me up to the kitchen. Serena's pie lay cooling on the rack. I left her a hasty note saying it had come out nicely and that I'd see her this weekend as I waited for him to leave. Lash remained there, hovering.

I didn't want to eat with him. Still, he'd been decent enough this morning. It was worth some discomfort not to offend him. "I'm going to make a sandwich, and have some chips," I said, rooting around in the fridge. "Do you want me to make you one?"

"No, but thank you for the offer," Lash hissed. "I will be in the dining room. I need to eat and you will not want to watch." As he came to the fridge, I moved aside for him. He got out a piece of raw beef and took it into the other room.

At least he'd been polite. That was something. I made my sandwich, ate it, then made another one. There was also a good bit of chocolate left, so I had a few pieces, savoring the sweet taste.

As I washed my dirty dishes, Lash returned with his empty plate. Loading it in the dishwasher, he faced me. "Are you going up to Dev?" Lash asked, leaning against the counter.

I checked my watch. I had a good forty-five minutes. "No. Back to the cellar," I replied, giving him a tentative smile.

He nodded, and led the way back down. Titus was still not in his workshop, but it made sense he was likely sleeping, as Lash was now working days. They had to trade off shifts so someone was always guarding Devlin.

As I worked, I debated trying to talk to Lash. I was tempted to ask what his book was about, as it sounded dark, maybe a horror novel. I'd read one once called *The Book of the Dead* that had been pretty decent. *But what if Lash's wasn't fiction? Better not to ask.*

At five to three, I closed the drawer I was working on, and turned to Lash. "I'm going to have a bunch of papers that can be shredded or burned. Can I leave them here in a pile, or should I carry them upstairs?"

"Leave them here," Lash hissed. "Titus can incinerate them, when he comes in tonight."

"I'm heading up to Dev." I wanted to add, "Thanks for guarding me," but didn't.

Lash stood up, and blocked my way.

I felt a shiver of fear, but held my ground. "What?"

"Give me your cell phone," Lash hissed. "The one Danial gave you to use."

My shiver became a small stream of fear as I got it out of my purse, and handed it to him. He pushed a few buttons, and then handed it back to me, his cold snake eyes looking into mine.

"I was programming in my cell number," Lash hissed. "I won't always be able to guard you as closely as I did today, say when you are painting, or if I'm supervising the work in the ballroom. But I'll never be very far away. Now you can call me, should you need me."

I knew what he wanted me to call him for. I flushed beet red.

Lash went on as if I was my normal pale self. "I don't leave on my phone usually, or carry it with me when I'm here at Hayden. Dev has asked me to when you are here. Call if you need me, and stay wherever you are. I'll come to you."

I turned redder, but nodded.

"Go to him," Lash hissed softly. "He has missed you."

I went past him quickly, and ran up the two flights of stairs to Devlin's room.

"Come in, Sar," Devlin purred.

I opened the door. Devlin was lying on his side under the covers, as he had been before. "Come and join me," he commanded.

Relieved at his nearness, I eagerly got undressed, and climbed in beside him.

"Hold me?" he asked, suddenly hesitant.

I squeezed him tightly in my arms. He sighed contentedly. "Did you get it all sorted out?" he asked lightly, teasing.

In annoyance, I bit him softly on his neck, working his skin between my teeth with a growl. Instantly, he let out a cry, and began kissing me urgently, trying to maneuver my body under his.

"Stop it!" I said loudly, pushing him back. "I'm not ready!"

Devlin went still, then he moved off me. "Sorry," he said, kissing my neck. "I thought you wanted sex, and wanted it now. But you don't, do you?"

I gave a mental sigh. "I always want you, Dev. But take your time; we've got hours."

"But I want to have you more than once," Devlin said peevishly. "We have only two hours—"

*Time to get things out in the open.* "Why can't once be enough? That night we Oathed—"

"You want me to sate myself quickly, so you can run back to Danial!" Devlin said, his harsh voice like thunder. "You are not going back to him, Sar, not until I've had my fill of you, no matter how long that takes—

I shuddered under him. He felt it, and it made him angrier. "Does the thought of me loving you make you shudder now?" he said in a deadly calm. "There are other things I could do to you, Sar, to make you shudder for me. But they would not be half so much fun for you—"

At once, The Lust curled up out of me, an almost raging force. I looked him full in the face, meeting his angry golden eyes. "Make me shudder for you, Dev. Make me scream! Do your worst to me! But first take me hard, fast, and as only you can."

Devlin went absolutely still above me in disbelief, his eyes wide with shock.

"Now you hesitate? Coward!" I hissed. "Where are your arrogant words now, you prick?"

"You want me to hurt you," Devlin said, almost gasping. "You…you—"

"Do it, Dev, or I'll call Lash," I said, smirking. "He'll do what I need if you can't."

Dev snarled, his eyes red as blood, glowing with rage. He shoved his length into me forcefully. I let out a cry of pain and he silenced me with his tongue, kissing me roughly. He moved hard and fast, driving deeply into me, still snarling.

Only one thing was missing. "Bite me!" I screamed.

Devlin sank his fangs into my right breast to the hilt. I screamed, thrashing under him. He held me down, thrusting hard and fast, contracting his jaws over and over. Then he pulled his teeth out and looked up at me, his great golden eyes hot with lust, my blood on his face. "You wanted this!" he hissed. "You're going to take everything I give you, until I'm done!"

*Yes!* Steeped in utter satisfaction, I thrashed below him, moaning. He quickened his pace, hammering himself into me forcefully, then began to jerk.

*No! Not yet! I was so close!* "Bite me!" I screamed again.

Devlin sank his fangs into my other breast. I came screaming, shrieking, flailing under him as he screamed my name so loud I expected the ceiling might cave in on us. He collapsed on me, convulsing hard, still shouting loudly, the both of us jerking as the orgasm ebbed.

Two seconds later, the pain hit me like a slap in the face. I let out an agonized scream. Devlin recoiled, looked at me in fear and worry.

"Argh!" I screamed, crying. "It hurts! It hurts so much, Dev—!"

Devlin moved supernaturally fast, holding his mouth to my wounds, giving me his blood to heal the bites he had given me. He put pressure on the shallower one as he healed the first one he had given me which hurt far more. Then, he healed the other. The wounds healed fast. I breathed a sigh of relief, when the pain subsided. Devlin began to clean me off with his lips and tongue, licking up the blood that had spilled out of the deep wounds. Though I was repelled by Devlin's obvious enjoyment, I didn't stop him. Why let the blood go to waste?

Within minutes, he had gotten most of it. He got up and brought me back a wet washcloth from the bathroom. I wiped the rest of the blood off my body, then handed it back. "Thanks."

He nodded, then took the washcloth back to the bathroom.

To my distaste, there were blood specks all over the sheets and his upper body. In a few places, there were more than just specks. *Yuck and OIY, as well.* "I've ruined your sheets."

"Forget that!" Devlin said, utterly gratified. He slid back into bed. "Who cares about sheets? I'll buy new ones. That was fucking amazing, Sar!" He nuzzled me gently. "That was better than I could ever have hoped it would be. Your eyes were so dark, so demanding, so—"

"Angry," I said tiredly. "The Lust is always looking for danger, anger, force. When you threatened me, you brought it out."

"This is so wonderful," Devlin whispered, practically shaking with pleasure. "Now I know how to bring it out of you, I can do it every time I'm with you. I won't have to worry that you might need to be with Lash."

I wasn't surprised; he was a sadist, he enjoyed inflicting pain. Still, I was repulsed to hear the absolute delight in his words. He had liked hurting me. He had loved far more that I had asked him to.

"Don't worry about blood on the sheets—"

"There's more than blood to consider," I said bitterly. "I'll say things that—"

"I can handle what you said," Devlin said quickly. "This was a kind of role-playing, with me being what you needed. Forgive me, if I scared you. I didn't mean any of what I said; I just was trying to satisfy—"

"You did mean it," I said more bitterly, disentangling myself from him. "You say you don't want me to be scared, but that's not true. You use my fear to control me."

Devlin was silent, watching me speculatively.

"If you really believed I loved you, you wouldn't need that. You would know I cared about you. You wouldn't threaten me the moment I asked you for space or told you I was too exhausted for hours of lovemaking." I turned from him and fell into an exhausted sleep.

\* \* \* \*

"Sar, you need to wake up," Devlin whispered gently. "It's five o'clock. Danial expects you."

I'd need to shower first to remove the remains of blood and the smell of our lovemaking... *Screw it.* There hadn't been any love in what we'd done, not on either side. Swallowing my upset over that, I moved to get out of bed.

Devlin wouldn't let me. "Look at me," he said softly. "Please."

Devlin was not often the polite brother. I looked over at him in surprise. "What?"

"Sarelle, I'm sorry." Devlin's voice was small and sounded very young. His golden eyes were unsure as they looked into mine as if they might find strength there. "You're right. I will try harder to be better to you. You deserve not to be scared any more, after all I have put you through since you've known me." He paused. "The truth is, I am afraid."

"Of what?" I asked. "You know I love you. I don't say those words idly, Dev."

He relaxed his grip. "I'm afraid I'm going to lose your love. I'm not a good man like Danial or Theo. I never even pretended to be until you needed me to be."

"I told you before; you can be anything you want to be—"

"No, I can't," Devlin said with finality, looking away. "I need to be what I am to keep you safe from the other Rulers. Being that way is easy, because I've been like that so long. It's far harder to be gentle, patient, or understanding. Those things still feel unnatural. It's difficult to change after training yourself to be one way for years."

"That is true for everyone. Loving someone, really loving them, is hard work."

"When Danial fell for you so fast, I laughed and called him a fool," Devlin said bitterly. "When you left him again after having Theoron, I called him a fool again, and told him he should bring you back by force. I couldn't understand why he wouldn't."

"He promised me he would let me go."

"I couldn't understand that," Devlin said, perplexed. "I still don't. He wanted you, and he had the power to keep you. How could he not use it?"

"He loved me and wanted me to be happy."

"If it had been me, I would not have let you go," Devlin replied. "I love you too much, Sar, to ever let you get away from me."

"I know. That's because you don't love me as he does. You love me as he did the first time, when his need to possess me outstripped everything else."

"I can't help the way I feel. I know it drove you from him," Devlin said reluctantly. "I'm afraid it will drive you from me, too."

"I may not like it," I said honestly. "But I gave you my word, Dev. Whatever I might feel, I'm yours."

"So you aren't upset about what happened earlier today?"

"I'm old enough to understand the difference between consent and force, and so are you. I know you won't hurt me on purpose, despite your shouting and blustering when you're angry."

"Tell me again you love me," Devlin said, desperate. "Please."

"I love you," I said, hugging him tightly. "And I love your eyes, your beautiful golden eyes. I'm not leaving you or Danial. Not ever."

"Ah, Sar," Devlin sighed. "I love you enough to let you run, but far too much to let you fly."

"And I love your glances meeting mine, across forever or a room. Your touch, Dev, is strong enough for me to hang my aspirations on."

Devlin shot me a dazzling smile. "I didn't know you were familiar with McKuen," he said, kissing me gently.

I gave him one back. "I've been brushing up on various poets, the better to amuse you." I threw back the covers. "Now I really ought to go shower."

Devlin followed me to the bathroom, where he examined the bites he had given me as the shower warmed up.

"Are you worried? Aren't they healed? They don't hurt."

"They were really deep," Devlin said, lust threaded through his words. "I wanted to make sure before I let you get in the shower. But you're right; they're healed."

\* \* \* \*

When I emerged, he was dressed and waiting. "I'll see you on Friday night for the appointment at Stephen's office," Devlin said, giving me a kiss. "Come, I'll walk you down."

"Do you want me to help you change the sheets?" I asked.

"No," Devlin said longingly. "I'll do it later."

*Would he change the sheets at all? Maybe he liked it. Eww.*

I followed him down to the kitchen. The pie and bread were gone.

"I love you," Devlin whispered, hugging me again. "Tell Danial I said hi."

I gave him a sarcastic look and teleported, arriving in the great room near Danial. He was sitting on the couch, his laptop in front of him.

"I should've known you'd be working," I said.

"You smell faintly of blood," he said, worried. "Your blood. Are you okay?"

"Dev brought The Lust. He bit me deeply, but they're healed now."

Danial hugged me, relieved. "He went on and on about how much he was looking forward to seeing you under it. I hope you let him experience the full scope of it."

"He liked it," I answered, trying to keep the distaste out of my voice, and not succeeding. "A lot—"

"Still, he can satisfy it for you," Danial said seriously. "I'll do whatever you need me to, of course, but I prefer not to hurt you, even though I can heal you after." He took my hand. "Come. We just have time for a walk before dinner."

* * * *

For a long time that night, we just laid together on the bed, touching gently as we talked.

"Did you call Elle today?" I asked.

"Everything is fine at home," Danial reassured. "Elle has started some advanced dancing lessons. Theo took her today. I could tell by his voice he was enjoying the attention."

Theo made it a point now to dress in tight T-shirts whenever he picked Elle up from her dance class. The other mothers, as well as the instructor, fawned over him, wanting to hear his latest stories of "working security detail." He'd probably worn his tightest jeans, too.

"Elle has talked about piano lessons also," Danial continued. "Would you mind if Devlin gave them to her?"

"He plays piano? I didn't know."

"Didn't you see his grand piano at his house?"

"No," I said. "Maybe it's in storage."

"Probably," Danial said thoughtfully. "It used to be in the ballroom, and that's being worked on. He wouldn't have risked it being damaged."

"No, I don't mind her learning from him. For all his capability of being a pain in the ass, he was a good teacher when he gave me voice lessons."

Danial laughed, then said seriously, "Elle also wants to have another sleep over. She said June. Is that doable for you?"

"That should be fine. I'll be six months along by then."

"You're sure you're pregnant? We haven't seen the doctor yet."

"The Lust has been raised four times in less than a week," I said flatly.

"Are you sure it's The Lust?"

"I have no symptoms of weakness, and my health is perfect, thanks to you and Dev. So it's got to be that. I'm pregnant with a dhamphir."

"I'm so excited, Sar," Danial said tenderly. "Theoron will have a half brother or sister, like I had in Devlin. They won't be separated, like he and I were, because of different social standing. They'll be true siblings."

That was a silver lining in all this. My heart lifted. "Yes," I responded, pleased. "Yes, they will."

\* \* \* \*

Thursday passed quickly. We both knew it was our last day together, and we spent every moment of it in each other's company. The weather had taken a turn for the worse, so we stayed inside, making love and sleeping. I also managed to finish off the baskets of fruit and chocolate. That night, I wore the red dress Danial so loved to dinner.

"I meant to ask you to bring it—" I began over dinner.

"I found it when I was moving the boxes one day last fall. It still smelled like you."

"I wanted you to have it," I said, putting my hand over his. "I didn't want to wear it for anyone else, ever."

"I'm going to have Tatiana copy it," Danial murmured lovingly. "The original I'll save, but the replica I'll keep with your other clothes, for you to wear when you and I go out."

"Good," I said, happily.

There was something sad about that last night, even in our beautiful surroundings enjoying the excellent food. I felt as Danial smiled at me across the table that he was already missing me, thinking of tomorrow night, when he would be alone, and I would be with Theo. It was in his eyes.

Later, after we had gone to bed, I initiated lovemaking again, trying to tell him that I loved him, not to be sad, because it didn't matter if we weren't together like this every day, he was still in my heart.

\* \* \* \*

Friday dawned bright and early. It was then I remembered Devlin's words about meeting me at Camlyn's.

I turned to Danial, and woke him. "Should I pack? I have to be back in time for my appointment."

Danial blinked. "What appointment?"

# Chapter Seventeen

*Wonderful.* I'd told Theo and Dev, then forgotten to tell Danial. "I have a doctor appointment tonight at eight. We can teleport, though. There's no rush."

Danial got up. "Get dressed, Love. We need to talk to Titus. Devlin set him to watch the house. See if he can drive back the car, if I teleport with you. If he can't we'll have to try to drive back. I think if we leave here right at dusk, we can make it. Worst-case scenario, you can teleport there without me, if you have to."

I pulled on some clothes. "I'll go out to the SUV and get the maps. Titus will see me come out, if he's out there."

Danial nodded, still dressing.

I was rooting around in the SUV for maps when I felt a wave of evil blackness engulf me. "Hi Titus," I said, not looking up. "How's it going?"

"You should be more careful," Titus said in his deep rumbling voice, looking in the opposite SUV window. "It could have been any demon, Sar, not just me. We all feel this way, you know."

"I knew it was you." I looked up, smiling. "Dev said that he set you to watching the house by day."

Titus walked around the SUV, dressed in only a T-shirt, and jeans. With the heat he generated, he probably never wore more than that. "I'm leaving at dusk, tonight," he said, his red eyes serious. "I've got a lot to do. Though I don't mind the cold, I've completely caught up on my reading. Guard duty is so stultifying."

Titus thought he was too much of an intellectual to spend hours watching a house. Maybe he was. He did know a lot of magic. Guard duty probably really was stultifying…My amusement lessened sharply, remembering Lash had used that same word to describe me.

"Will you and Danial be okay?" Titus rumbled. "I would rather be bored than to leave you in a dangerous position."

Even standing a few feet away, his heat was still warming me. *Ahh.* "No, actually, that's what I came out here to ask you. I need to head back for an appointment. Can you drive the SUV back, and our things if I teleport myself and him home?"

"Sure," he replied. "When are you leaving? I'll stay until you leave."

"Take off," I said, giving him a quick hug. "We're leaving at dusk tonight. We should be fine until then. I'll be awake the whole time we'll be here, and I'll teleport us away, if anything happens."

"You're sure?" Titus said hesitantly. "I don't want anything to happen to you."

I noticed he didn't include Danial in that. *Where did his loyalty really lie?* Devlin had not included him on his short list of persons he trusted. Maybe there was a reason for that.

"Why do you work for Dev?" I asked. "You don't seem to like him much. Do you have to?"

"Yes," Titus said curtly.

*Had Devlin summoned him out of Hell so he had no choice but to do what Devlin told him?* The thought of the real Hell complete with the devil and brimstone and fire gave me chills. "Why?"

"I work for him because he's a good employer," Titus rumbled, giving me a strange look. "I could either work for myself, selling my magical knowledge or my strength, or work for someone like him using the same talents. It's easy working for Devlin, especially as he's a Ruler. He's not a bad boss, and he gives me what I need, which is a big plus."

I gave him a quizzical look. "What's that mean?"

"Terian told you he ate flesh and blood sometimes?" Titus prompted.

Suddenly I didn't want to understand, because I could guess where this was headed. "Yes."

"I'm a demon, Sar," Titus said, his eyes burning into me, his smile a little sad. "I can't eat real food. That is all I can eat. What I need to eat."

I got it loud and clear, yet I couldn't seem to get the words out. "You...you eat—"

"Sometimes," Titus said in a low voice. "I prefer not to. I prefer to eat only animals. But sometimes I have to, to be healthy and stay as powerful as I am."

I was very, very glad I hadn't eaten breakfast. I'd have gotten sick for sure.

"They are never alive," Titus rumbled gently.

The ramifications of that hit me like a fist. I swayed, holding onto the SUV door. I couldn't bring myself to say it was okay that he ate people, even if they were bad. That they weren't alive when he ate them only made it marginally better. I understood now why Devlin had taken Garrett's body with him that

204

night he had taken Neoline.

My stomach rolled. *God. He'd taken Tasha to feed to Titus, too...* I held onto the door with both hands.

"It isn't something I relish," Titus said, averting his gaze, upset. "I don't have a choice about it, Sar. I would have rather been born an angel or a human, in retrospect."

I fastened on that, anything else to get off this topic. "There are angels? Real ones?"

"I think so," Titus replied. "I'm not sure. Books refer to them sometimes. But I've never seen any, and I've seen a lot in the centuries I've lived."

I was not going to ask him if the Devil was real. I was too afraid of the answer. Titus kept talking, his rumbling voice like stone grating on stone. "In any case, I have what I need to survive and Devlin pays well. I'm loyal to him for that, despite some of the reprehensible things he does sometimes." Titus paused. His next words were softer, content. "I'm as comfortable as I'm going to be in this world, anyway."

"Are you getting back with Leri?" I asked flatly.

"I love her, Sar," Titus said defensively, meeting my eyes with his red ones. "I'm sorry for what she did to you and Terian, but I love her and I want to be with her."

Like father, like son, I thought but didn't say. "How's that going to work? Devlin won't let her stay at Hayden."

"She's staying in the village below it, for now. We are taking it slow. I want to be able to trust her. I don't yet. And I care about my son; I don't want to alienate him after I've missed so much time with him already."

"I understand that, but I don't want to see her, Titus. She fucked up Terian badly with what she did to him. I'm not going to forgive her for that."

"Understood," Titus said, nodding. "I won't be bringing her to Hayden anyway, so you should never meet her. Now I should go, and report back to Devlin you are leaving at dusk." He left, fading out of sight in an instant.

*Was he irritated I wasn't jumping on the Leri Bandwagon?* Grumpy at that thought, I went back in with the maps.

Danial came over to me immediately. "What were you two talking about? You looked upset."

I relayed the conversation to him. "Devlin draining Tasha was just. Knowing she got eaten after makes me feel guilty."

"You had to know he ate flesh and blood," Danial said with disbelief. "He's a demon. That's what they do."

I was an idiot. I'd thought of Titus as a nice demon, who only ate pork chops and steak when I'd known what he was capable of. "I didn't think of it, really."

The phone rang.

"Please answer it," Danial said, taking the maps. "I'll look over these. Perhaps we do have time to drive home."

*Why would I want to drive home when I could teleport?* I picked up the phone. "Hello?"

"Sar," Theo said, relieved. "I'm headed out for the day. I wanted to touch base before I left."

"Will you be in time to meet me at the doctor's? I can't remember if I told you about the appointment—"

"You did. But I'm not coming. I don't want to be there."

"Why?" I said, trying not to sound hurt. "It might be—"

"It's not," he said flatly. "You have The Lust, Sar. I can't stand there and watch him look at me with glee knowing how much I wanted it to be mine."

"All right," I said softly. "I understand."

"I'll be waiting for you at Danial's house. Come there after your appointment, and I'll drive you home."

"Okay," I said. "Bye."

I stared down at the receiver, the dial tone loud in my ears. Hate and resentment rose up in me; for Theo in his bitterness, for the situation I was in, for the vampires who controlled my life now…

Danial took the phone from me and hung it up on the wall. "You look angry."

I rubbed my eyes, my anger dissipating. "I'm just tired of all this."

"Then come," Danial said, taking my hand. "We still have today. Come share it with me, while it lasts."

"Yes," I said compliantly, following him upstairs.

\* \* \* \*

Danial and I left the house as soon as the sun had set. Stephen greeted us at the door, his blue eyes kind, his weathered face crinkled in a smile. "Come in," he said pleasantly. "Devlin's already here."

He was standing over near the exam room door. Lash was with him. Nice. "Please wait out here," I said pointedly, walking past them.

After taking a sample of my blood, Dr. Camlyn asked me to undress, then went to leave.

I nodded. "What's the blood sample for?"

"Devlin told me he bit you, and there was a lot of blood," Stephen said, annoyed. "I told him not to do it again, but I need to make sure that you are okay."

"I've been taking the vitamins, both kinds."

He nodded. "That will help, but I may need to give you some of that blood replenishing formula."

*Fabulous.* That stuff tasted like used car oil. "I'm fine, really."

"We'll look and see. Please undress."

I did as he asked, then lay on the table in my paper gown. When the door opened a moment later, I turned, expecting it to be Stephen. Instead, it was Devlin and Danial.

"Stephen said we could come in," Danial said hesitantly. "We both want to be here with you when you find out."

"You had better switch your rings," Devlin said with amusement. "Theo's sure to notice."

"Thanks," I said, flushing, and moved my rings around so the band and diamond Theo had given me was again on my ring finger and Danial's rings were on my right hand.

"I had to remind him to switch his as well," Devlin said with more amusement. "You two are just like a pair of teenagers."

I rolled my eyes, laughing. But as the minutes passed my easygoing nature slipped. Soon I was grumbling silently, thinking about how I was sick of being naked on tables and men wanting things from me.

Stephen came in. "Sarelle, as it did before, your blood shows that you should have turned a long time ago, but—"

"She is not turning," Devlin said in restrained fury. "I have turned enough women to know, Camlyn."

Stephen glanced at him, then back at me. "Devlin seems to know what he is talking about. You are healthy, almost overly healthy. All your vitals look good. I don't think you'll need any additional vitamins either; at least I won't prescribe any at this time. I do need to check to see if you're pregnant. If you aren't, I can at least confirm that your scars are or are not healed enough so you can try to be."

"Couldn't you say something else, Stephen?" I said irritably, lying back down.

"What would you like me to say?" Stephen said pleasantly, sitting down by my feet.

"Checking my reproductive system, maybe? Seeing if I'm ready to have children? Anything that doesn't mention scars."

"Is she always this way?" Devlin asked Danial.

"When she's here like this, yes," Danial said, giving him a quick raise of the eyebrows.

"I saw that," I said, glaring at them both. "Why don't you both wait outside?"

"Not a chance, Love," Devlin purred, moving over to stand over me. "I want to know if the deed is done, or if I get the pleasure of trying anew tonight."

Theo was expecting to take me home after this. If I went to Hayden instead…I tensed up immediately.

"Relax, Sar," Stephen said. "Breathe deeply."

I let out a breath irritably, then a few more.

"I'm done," Stephen said, moving back from me.

He'd barely touched me. Yet I had to be pregnant; I had The Lust…

"What is wrong?" Danial asked anxiously. "You exude worry, Stephen."

"Sar is pregnant," Stephen said. "I am guessing about three to four weeks, but it could be less."

All three of us gaped at Stephen.

"The baby is developing fast, a little too fast. I want you to come in every other week until you are about six months, and then every week after that. If the baby gets too big, we'll do a C-section, Sar. Don't worry—"

"This is wonderful," Devlin said, grinning from ear to ear. He stepped over to me quickly. "This is the happiest day of my life, Sar—"

"It's not yours, Dalcon," Stephen said.

We all froze.

"Sar's blood has a little were DNA in it," Stephen continued. "It never had any before. It has to be from the baby, because the baby is were—"

"No," Devlin gasped.

"It can't be! Sar has The Lust!" Danial exclaimed. "She has all the symptoms—!"

"Sar's part vampire now," Stephen retorted. "She may have The Lust no matter what kind of child she is carrying, be it mortal, vampire or were."

For a half second silence reigned. Then Danial burst out laughing. Devlin turned to him in a split second and slammed him against the wall, holding him by the throat. Danial struggled, but continued to laugh, almost choking on it as it poured out of him.

"Damn you!" Devlin shrieked. "You orchestrated this somehow! How did you—?"

"I did nothing," Danial choked out. "I'm ecstatic that for once your well-laid plans are for naught. That Theo, who has loved Sar far longer than you have, will get the child he has been wanting with her for years. He has only years, Dev. Sar can bear you a child after she has this one for him—"

"They are not for naught," Devlin said, his tone cold. "Sar is mine. She'll bear my children or none at all."

Danial fought loose, shoving Devlin out of the way, then got between us, glaring defiantly at his brother. "How dare you say that?"

"You'll not abort my child!" I yelled at Dev, incredulous. "How could you even think it?"

"Hush," Danial said forcefully. "No one is going to. Dev is just letting his ass overload his mouth."

Devlin glared at him, then folded his arms across his chest.

"You have to let this take its course, Dalcon," Stephen cautioned. "Sar should not have achieved a pregnancy this soon after all of her health troubles these past six months."

"What are you saying?" I asked.

Stephen's eyes held regret. "That it's possible you'll miscarry, even likely—"

I blinked back tears. "I can't go through that again—"

Danial held me tightly, stroking my hair, trying to soothe me. "What can we do? There must be something. I don't want her to go through that again."

"Neither do I," Devlin said irritably, after a moment. "She could die like Annabelle did. Her health is our top priority."

"You need to limit sharing the virus with her," Stephen replied. "Keep giving her blood as she needs it, but not a lot. I don't know if the virus will affect the baby—"

"You just said the baby will be were," Danial said, glancing at Stephen. "Vampire virus and were virus do not affect one another. Bloodletting shouldn't affect the child—"

"Don't take her blood if you can help it," Stephen interrupted. "If you must bite, fine, but—"

"She is not anemic," Devlin shot back. "You just said she was healthy, overly so—"

"You want to take the chance you'll hurt her or her child?" Stephen said angrily.

"No," Danial said, glaring at Devlin. "Of course we don't." Devlin echoed him a moment later, glaring back.

Stephen turned to me. "I'll write you another prescription for some prenatal vitamins, Sar. These ones are specifically for weres. Other than that, come back in a month for a checkup, and call me with any problems." He gave me a smile, then left..

Danial handed me my clothes. "Do you want a ride home?"

"I can't believe this happened," Devlin said, anguished.

"What will it mean for us?" I asked as I dressed.

"Nothing, in terms of you coming to me," Devlin said pointedly.

My hackles went up at his possessive tone. "I mean what about Samuel and the rest?"

"I'll find some way to deal with them," Devlin said. He gave me a quick kiss on the cheek. "I'll call you later, Love. Remember, I expect you this weekend, and on Wednesdays as well." He strode out.

"Do you want that ride?" Danial asked.

*What I really needed was some time to myself.* "No. Can you send him home early, though? I need some time to think about all this."

"Of course," Danial said. He hugged me. "Remember, you don't have to face this all on your own."

I gave him a blank look, buttoning my overshirt.

"We are Oathed to each other," Danial said, concerned. "Dev and I will figure out a way for you to have this baby, don't worry—"

*I have to get out of here, now.* I kissed him quickly, then teleported home, the walls of Exam Room One dissolving into the brightly colored walls of my home. Ghost and Darkness began whining and barking happily, and I led them over to the couch. I sat there stroking them, too overwhelmed even to speak.

I was having a baby and it was Theo's. Devlin's well-laid plans were in tatters, as Danial had said; the Rulers would certainly demand me back, as soon as they knew. But what was the worst was I wasn't sure I wanted this baby at all.

I rubbed my eyes, feeling despicable. *What the hell was I going to do?*

Ghost jostled my arm with his big white nose, whining eagerly.

"Well, the first thing to do is to take you for a walk," I said, wiping at my eyes. "Thank God for dogs."

I put on my coat, and took the two dogs outside into the gently falling snow. There was not much on the ground, enough so I could walk without too much trouble to the gate at the end of the field and beyond. As the dogs ran and played, I went through my options, none of them looking any better.

I believed in a woman's right to choose, especially in the case of rape or sex coerced under an influence that impeded a woman's right to say no. Despite the odd nature of my circumstances, my case was squarely within those parameters. I'd never have had sex with Theo willingly...

*Wouldn't you,* an inner voice asked. *You've loved him for years, no matter what sexy vampire was calling you theirs. You were always his, really...*

"Stop it," I said aloud. "That isn't true."

*Of course it is,* the inner voice persisted. *You're soul mates; Terian said so. Titus said something similar. What else could allow you to get pregnant from one night after all you went through during Christmas and New Year's?*

"Maybe," I murmured, then turned to home. "Maybe I'm just going batty from all the supernatural shit."

I had just gotten back through the gate when Theo came running up, gun drawn. "What in the hell are you doing out here!" he yelled. "I've been worried sick."

"The dogs needed a walk," I said defensively. "I'm pregnant, not crippled."

He grabbed my arm, then began to march me back to the house. "At least it's done," he said roughly, running his free hand through his hair. "Once you have the baby, you won't have to go to him anymore. We'll be free of him. I'll do whatever I have to in order to keep him away from you—"

"That's not going to happen," I said arrogantly, an odd glee rising up from within me. "Devlin isn't done with me."

"He will be," Theo growled. "He'll have his baby, and—"

My glee grew into sudden happiness, then pure joy. "Theo, you aren't listening." I stopped walking and kissed him, then pulled back for effect. "My baby's going to have a tail."

His eyes widened, then he abruptly went down on his knees before me in the snow. Ghost and Darkness ran over to him, barking worriedly.

"I'm okay guys," he managed, then got to his feet. He hugged me very delicately, as if I might break. "You're sure?"

"Stephen confirmed it. There's werecougar DNA in my blood."

Theo let out a loud whoop of joy, and then picked me up and began walking fast.

"What are you doing?" I said, laughing as I half-heartedly struggled to get free.

"Taking you inside where it's warm," he said with a grin. "We have celebrating to do."

\* \* \* \*

About a half-hour later, I teleported Elle and Theoron to my house, so we could tell them together.

"What's going on, Mom?" Elle said, once she sat down. "You're very happy, but serious."

"Your mom is going to give you another brother or sister," Theo said, his joy radiating out of him, suffusing every word. "He or she will be werecougar like you are, Elle."

"Really, Mom?" Elle asked eagerly. Theoron looked dubious.

"Yes, really," I said happily, hugging her.

Theoron climbed up on the couch and hugged me, too. "I hope it's a boy. Boys are better."

"I'd rather have a sister," Elle said, sticking her tongue out at him. "I want someone to dance and sing with me the way you and I do, Mom!"

"There's not a choice," I said, laughing. "Sorry, I can't choose."

"When can we find out if it's a boy or a girl?" Theo asked quickly.

"Another month and a half," I answered. "There's a test Stephen can do on my blood. If it's a boy, there will be "Y" chromosome DNA in my blood—"

"Does Grandma know?" Elle interjected.

"No," Theo said, giving me a smile. "Let's go tell her, Mom."

I opened my mouth.

"Yes, we'll bring Danial," Theo said, putting his hands up. "I know the standing rule that Theoron goes nowhere socially without him." He took my hand. "Besides, it's time we came together as a family, anyway. No more secrets."

As he squeezed my hand in his, I wanted to say that Devlin should also be there, that to leave him out of this was like keeping a secret. He had a place here in the family, too. But I didn't speak up, not wanting to spoil Theo's happiness.

\* \* \* \*

Danial was obviously nervous as we approached my parents' home, Theo and the children trailing us. He glossed it over as he always did, shaking Chris's hand politely.

"Good to see you, Danial."

"Theo," my mom said, ignoring Danial. "Go right in to the kitchen. There's a fresh pumpkin pie waiting for you and—"

"If you'll serve him and the children some pieces, Tina," Danial said kindly but pointedly, "We have exciting news we would like to share."

As my mother was bringing in the pie to serve us, Theo reached his limit. "Sarelle's pregnant!" he said happily to my mother. "I'm going to be a father again—"

My mom stopped walking and swayed, dropping the pie she was carrying. Danial reacted with lightning speed, grabbing it and her before either hit the floor. He put the pie carefully on the table with one hand as he eased her into her chair with the other. "Sit down here, Tina," he said gently. "I'll serve the pie."

"Congratulations," my stepfather said, beaming. "I'll get the thirty-year Port Ellen. Be right back."

My mother cast worried eyes my way. "Not that I'm not happy for you both, but... How safe is this?"

"Sar's fine," Theo said soothingly, taking one of her hands in his. "She's going to a good doctor, the one who she went to when she had Theoron. We'll keep you posted on how the baby is developing, and let you know as soon as there's a due date."

"It's going to be...like you?" she whispered.

"Yes," Theo said, putting his hand on her shoulder. "Just like Elle—"

A wave of fear hit me. Tawny had died because Elle had gotten too big too fast. *What if that happened to me—?*

Danial put his hand on my shoulder. "Stephen will take care of you," he said tenderly. "Don't worry, Sar."

*He was right. There was nothing to worry about. Theo would take care of me.*

\* \* \* \*

"Did you leave Danial the cat?" I asked, as Theo and I lay cuddling on the couch.

"Yes, in a large cage with a bow in Danial's bedroom. He's got food and water, but it won't be long before he's discovered. I let Elle in on the cat."

That was good. Danial would be missing me tonight like I was missing him.

"I was given an invite for us to Ivan and Janice's mating," Theo said. "It's in mid-June, on a Saturday."

"Put down four people," I replied. "You, me, Elle, and Theoron. That way Danial won't have to worry about skipping out on a meeting if he has one that night. He can just meet us there whenever he's able."

"Sure." Theo paused. "I have to ask; was Devlin mad when you found out it was mine?"

"Yes, livid. But he said it didn't matter. Danial told him he could essentially wait his turn."

"So long as he accepts it. That's the best I hoped for." He paused again. "I'm a little afraid. I've wanted this for so long, and now I finally have it."

"I'm not going anywhere, if that's what you're worried about," I said, kissing him. "I'm going to need your help, the bigger I get."

"I'll be here," Theo said, kissing me. "Just tell me what you need."

"Nothing right now," I said softly, kissing him. "I have everything that I need right here."

"I'm glad you're happy," he murmured lovingly. "I was worried you wouldn't be."

I gave him an odd look. "Why do you say that? Of course I'm happy."

"It doesn't matter now," Theo said soothingly. "I love you, you love me, and that's all that matters."

\* \* \* \*

That night, I awoke in a sweat. Theo lay beside me, still sleeping soundly.

I looked around for what had awoken me, but saw nothing amiss. The dogs were sleeping peacefully, and there were no noises from the cats sleeping in front of the fire.

Maybe that was it; the fire was out. It was cool in here. As I got up to go out to the woodstove, I brushed back my hair, and felt it snag hard, radiating pain through my scalp.

Carefully, I felt around. My hair was caught somehow in my choker. Carefully, I reached back and unfastened it, untangling my hair from the gold links. To my surprise, it was Danial's fox head, not Devlin's bear. I'd forgotten to switch them after coming back from the trip.

I went to my box, and opened it, putting Danial's choker inside. As I did, I noticed a few sheets of paper folded in the bottom near Devlin's poetry. Closing the box, I replaced it, then brought Devlin's choker with the papers into the other room.

The fire was not out, just low. I added wood, then sat in a nearby chair to wait for the flames to catch it. As I did, I read the papers.

I'd written them, but I didn't recognize myself. This Sar was besotted with Devlin, crazy in love, completely in thrall to him. She hated Theo for leaving her, and blamed him for everything. Some of the accusations and graphic details were terrible. *If Theo should ever find this, he would be so hurt...*

I opened the woodstove, and quickly cast the pages into the now roaring flames. I turned down the damper, watching the fire consume the written ravings.

They had been ravings; ravings of a madwoman. I wasn't that woman anymore; I was back to my old self.

The pages were soon ash. I looked down at the choker in my hand, the bear's eyes gleaming green. I had an instant desire to throw it in too, but then it passed.

Devlin had saved me, not Theo. I not only was Oathed to him, I owed him. The least I could do was honor the promise I had made.

I clasped the choker around my neck, feeling the ends sliding together. Then I turned out the light, and went back to bed.

## About the Author

Tara Fox Hall's writing credits include nonfiction, horror, suspense, action-adventure, erotica, and contemporary and historical paranormal romance. She is the author of the paranormal action-adventure *Lash* series and the vampire romantic suspense *Promise Me* series. Tara divides her free time unequally between writing novels and short stories, chainsawing firewood, caring for stray animals, sewing cat and dog beds for donation to animal shelters, and target practice.

## Other works by the author with Melange Books, LLC

*Return To Me*
*Surrender to Me*
*The Origin of Fear in* Spellbound 2011 Anthology
*Night Music in* Midnight Thirsts II Anthology
*Partners in* Midnight Thirsts II Anthology
*Kink in* Wicked Christmas Wishes Anthology
*The Oath in* Wicked Christmas Wishes Anthology
*Bedtime Shadows Anthology*
*Make Me Behave Anthology*
*Latham's Landing, An Anthology*

### The Promise Me Series
*Promise Me, Book 1*
*Broken Promise, Book 2*
*Taken in the Night, Book 3*
*Taken for his Own, Book 4*
*Promise Me Anthology, Book 4.5*
*Immortal Confessions, Book 5*
*Her Secret, Book 6*
*Point of No Return, Book 7*

### Coming Soon

*Lost Paradise, Book 8* of the Promise Me Series